Praise for Delores Fossen

"The perfect blend of sexy cowboys, humor and romance will rein you in from the first line."
—*New York Times* bestselling author B.J. Daniels

"From the shocking opening paragraph on, Fossen's tale just keeps getting better."
—*RT Book Reviews* on *Sawyer*, 4½ stars, Top Pick

"*Rustling Up Trouble* is action packed, but it's the relationship and emotional drama (and the sexy hero) that will reel readers in."
—*RT Book Reviews*, 4½ stars

"While not lacking in action or intrigue, it's the romance of two unlikely people that soars."
—*RT Book Reviews* on *Maverick Sheriff*, 4 stars

Also available from Delores Fossen

The McCord Brothers

Texas on My Mind
Blame It on the Cowboy

To see the complete list of titles available
from Delores Fossen, please visit
deloresfossen.com.

USA TODAY BESTSELLING AUTHOR

DELORES
FOSSEN

⤙ THE McCORDS ⤚
RILEY & LUCKY

MILLS & BOON

THE MCCORDS: RILEY & LUCKY © 2024 by Harlequin Books S.A.

TEXAS ON MY MIND
© 2016 by Delores Fossen
Australian Copyright 2016
New Zealand Copyright 2016

First Published 2016
Second Australian Paperback Edition 2024
ISBN 978 1 038 90858 2

LONE STAR NIGHTS
© 2016 by Delores Fossen
Australian Copyright 2016
New Zealand Copyright 2016

First Published 2016
Second Australian Paperback Edition 2024
ISBN 978 1 038 90858 2

Published by
Mills & Boon
An imprint of Harlequin Enterprises (Australia) Pty Limited
(ABN 47 001 180 918), a subsidiary of HarperCollins
Publishers Australia Pty Limited (ABN 36 009 913 517)
Level 19, 201 Elizabeth Street
SYDNEY NSW 2000
AUSTRALIA

MIX
Paper | Supporting
responsible forestry
FSC® C001695

® and ™ (apart from those relating to FSC®) are trademarks of Harlequin
Enterprises (Australia) Pty Limited or its corporate affiliates. Trademarks indicated
with ® are registered in Australia, New Zealand and in other countries.
Contact admin_legal@Harlequin.ca for details.

Printed and bound in Australia by McPherson's Printing Group

CONTENTS

Texas On My Mind

CHAPTER ONE

THERE WERE TWO women in Captain Riley McCord's bed. Women wearing cutoff shorts, skinny tops and flip-flops.

Riley blinked a couple of times to make sure they weren't by-products of his pain meds and bone-deep exhaustion. *Nope.* They were real enough because he could hear them breathing.

See them breathing, too.

The lamp on the nightstand was on, the milky-yellow light spilling over them. Their tops holding in those C-cups were doing plenty of moving with each breath they took.

He caught a glimpse of a nipple.

If he'd still been a teenager, Riley might have considered having two women in his bed a dream come true. Especially in this room. He'd grown up in this house, had had plenty of fantasies in that very bed. But he was thirty-one now, and with his shoulder throbbing like an abscessed tooth, taking on two women didn't fall into fantasy territory. More like suicide.

Besides, man-rule number two applied here: don't do anything half-assed. Anything he attempted right now would be significantly less than half and would make an ass out of him.

Who the hell were they?

And why were they there in his house, in his bed?

The place was supposed to be empty since he'd called ahead

and given the cook and housekeeper the week off. The sisters, Della and Stella, had pretty much run the house since Riley's folks had been killed in a car wreck thirteen years ago. Clearing out the pair hadn't been easy, but he'd used his captain's I'm-giving-the-orders-here voice.

For once it had worked.

His kid sister was away at college. His older brother Lucky was God knew where. Lucky's twin, Logan, was on a business trip and wouldn't be back for at least another week. Even when Logan returned, he'd be spending far more time running the family's cattle brokerage company than actually in the house. That lure of emptiness was the only reason Riley had decided to come here for some peace and quiet.

And so that nobody would see him wincing and grunting in pain.

Riley glanced around to try to figure out who the women were and why they were there. When he checked the family room, he saw a clue by the fireplace. A banner. Well, sort of. He flicked on the lights to get a better look. It was a ten-foot strip of white crepe paper.

Welcome Home, Riley, Our Hero, was written on it.

The black ink had bled, and the tape on one side had given way, and now it dangled and coiled like a soy-sauced ramen noodle.

There were bowls of chips, salsa and other food on the coffee table next to a picture of him in his uniform. Someone had tossed flag confetti all around the snacks, and some of the red, white and blue sparkles had landed on the floor and sofa. In the salsa, too.

Apparently, this was supposed to be the makings of a homecoming party for him.

Whoever had done this probably hadn't counted on his flight from the base in Germany being delayed nine hours. Riley hadn't counted on it, either. Now, it was three in the morning, and he darn sure didn't want to celebrate.

Or have women in his bed.

And he hoped it didn't lower his testosterone a couple of notches to have an unmanly thought like that.

Riley put his duffel bag on the floor. Not quietly, but the women didn't stir even an eyelash. He considered just waking them, but heck, that would require talking to them, and the only thing he wanted right now was another hit of pain meds and a place to collapse.

He went to the bedroom next to his. A guest room. No covers or pillows, which would mean a hunt to find some. That sent him to Lucky's room on the other side of the hall. Covers, yes, but there was another woman asleep facedown with her sleeve-tattooed arm dangling off the side. There was also a saddle on the foot of the bed. Thankfully, Riley's mind was too clouded to even want to consider why it was there.

Getting desperate now and feeling a little like Goldilocks in search of a "just right" place to crash, he went to Logan's suite, the only other bedroom downstairs. Definitely covers there. He didn't waste the energy to turn on the light to have a closer look; since this was Logan's space, it would no doubt be clean enough to pass a military inspection.

No saddles or women, thank God, and he wouldn't have to climb the stairs that he wasn't sure he could climb anyway.

Riley popped a couple of pain meds and dropped down on the bed, his eyes already closing before his head landed against something soft and crumbly. He considered investigating it. *Briefly* considered it. But when it didn't bite, shoot or scald him, he passed on the notion of an investigation.

Whatever was soft and crumbly would just have to wait.

RILEY JACKKNIFED IN Logan's bed, the pain knocking the breath right out of him. Without any kind of warning, the nightmare that he'd been having had morphed into a full-fledged flashback.

Sometimes he could catch the flashback just as it was bubbling to the surface, and he could stomp it back down with his mental steel-toed combat boots. Sometimes humming "Jingle Bells" helped.

Not this time, though.

The flashback had him by the throat before Riley could even get out a single note of that stupid song he hated. Why had his brain chosen that little Christmas ditty to blur out the images anyway?

The smell came first. Always the fucking smell. The dust and debris whipped up by the chopper. The Pave Hawk blades slicing through the dirt-colored smoke. But not drowning out the sounds.

He wasn't sure how sounds like that could make it through the thump of the blades, the shouts, screams and the chaos. But they did. The sounds always did.

Someone was calling for help in a dialect Riley barely understood. But you didn't need to know the words to hear the fear.

Or smell it.

The images came with a vengeance. Like a chopped-up snake crawling and coiling together to form a neat picture of hell. A handful of buildings on fire, others ripped apart from the explosion. Blood on the bleached-out sand. The screams for help. The kids.

Why the hell were there kids?

Riley had been trained to rescue military and civilians after the fight, after all hell had broken loose. Had been conditioned to deal with fires, blood, IEDs, gunfire, and being dropped into the middle of it so he could do his job and save lives.

But nobody had ever been able to tell him how to deal with the kids.

PTSD. Such a tidy little label. A dialect that civilians understood, or thought they did anyway. But it was just another label for shit. Shit that Riley didn't want in his head.

He grabbed his pain meds from the pocket of his uniform and shoved one, then another into his parched mouth. Soon, very soon, he could start stomping the images back into that little shoe box he'd built in his head.

Soon.

He closed his eyes, the words finally coming that he needed to hear.

"Jingle bells, jingle bells..."

He really did need to come up with a more manly sounding song to kick some flashback ass.

CHAPTER TWO

"HI DA TOOKIE," someone whispered.

Riley was sure he was still dreaming. At least, he was sure of it until someone poked him on the cheek.

Hell. What now?

"Hi da tookie," the voice repeated. Again in a whisper.

Obviously this was some kind of code or foreign language, but Riley's head was too foggy to process it. He groaned—and, yeah, it was a groan of pain—and forced his eyelids open so he could try to figure out what the heck was going on.

Eyeballs stared back at him.

Eyeballs that were really close. Like, just an inch from his.

That jolted him fully awake, and Riley automatically reached for his weapon. Which wasn't there, of course. He wasn't on assignment in hostile territory. He was in his own family's home. And the eyes so close to his didn't belong to the enemy.

They belonged to a kid.

A kid with brown eyes and dark brown hair. Maybe two or three years old, and he had a smear of something on his cheek.

"Hi da tookie," the kid said again. He didn't wait for Riley to respond, however. He jammed something beneath the pillow.

A cookie, aka tookie.

And it had an identical smell to the one Riley had just been dreaming about. Except it was no dream. Riley realized that when he lifted his head and the crumbs fell onto the collar of his uniform. *Hell's Texas bells.* He'd slept on a chocolate-chip cookie. But why the devil was it there in Logan's bed?

Like the women in his own bed and the gibberish-talking kid, an answer for that might have to wait a second or two because Riley had a more pressing question.

"Who are you?" he asked the kid.

"E-tan," the boy readily answered.

That didn't explain much, and Riley wasn't sure how much a kid that age could explain anyway.

"Tookie," the boy repeated. He took one of the crumbs from Riley's collar and ate it.

All right, so maybe that did explain why he'd slept on a cookie-laced pillow. This kid was responsible. But who was responsible for the kid? He didn't get a chance to find out because the little boy took off running out of the room.

Riley got up. More groaning. Some grimacing, too. The damage to his shoulder and knee weren't permanent, but at the moment it sure as hell felt like it.

The docs at the base in Ramstein, Germany, had told him he needed at least three more weeks to recover from the surgery to repair the damage done by the shrapnel when it'd slashed into his right shoulder and chest. After that, he'd start some physical therapy for both the shoulder and his wrenched knee. And after that, there would be a medical board to decide if he could continue being the only thing he'd ever wanted to be.

An AF CRO. Short for Air Force Combat Rescue Officer.

It twisted his gut to think that it could all be taken away. That whole "life turning on a dime" sucked donkey dicks, and he could go from being part of an elite special ops force to someone he was darn sure he didn't want to be.

That was a violation of man-rule number one: don't be ordinary.

Frustrated with that thought, with the pain and with the whole world in general, Riley headed into the adjoining bathroom. When he came out, the kid was still nowhere in sight.

Brushing away some more cookie crumbs from his uniform, Riley went into the family room to look around. No sign of E-tan there. Someone had cleaned up the party remains, so Riley headed to his own bedroom. *Good gravy.* The two women were still there, still asleep. Riley was about to wake them, to tell them about the cookie-hiding toddler, but then he caught a whiff of something else.

Coffee. The miracle drug.

And he heard someone moving around in the kitchen. Since Della and her sister, Stella, had sworn on John Wayne's soul and their mama's Bible that they would follow Riley's orders and stay far away from the place, there shouldn't be any sounds or smells coming from anywhere in the house. Still, if this was a break-in, at least the burglar had made coffee. He might just give up everything of value to get a single cup.

Once Riley hobbled his way to the kitchen, he saw that E-tan had already crawled into a chair at the table. Like the rest of the house, the kitchen was sprawling, and even though they had two other dining rooms, Riley had eaten a lot of his meals in this room. In fact, he'd sat in that very chair where the kid was sitting now.

Riley immediately located the cookie source. There was a plate of about a dozen or so of them on the kitchen table. He spotted the source of the moving-around sounds, too.

Another woman.

A blonde this time. Her hair was cut short and choppy and fell against her neck.

This one was very much awake. She was at the stove, her back to him, and she was stirring something in a skillet. Her body swayed a little with each stir, and despite the F-5 tornado in his head, Riley noticed. Hard not to notice since she was wearing denim shorts that hugged a very nice ass.

An ass that was strangely familiar.

She turned slightly to the side when she reached for the salt-shaker, and Riley got a look at her face. Familiar all right.

Claire.

A real blast from the past. Calling Claire Davidson a childhood friend was a little like saying the ocean had a bit of water in it. Once they'd been as thick as thieves, but he'd pretty much lost touch with her after he graduated from college.

Riley took a moment to savor the moment. There was always something about Claire that reminded him of home. Of the things he'd left behind. Not that she'd been his to leave, but it always felt a little like that whenever he thought of her. Now he didn't have to conjure up a memory. She was right there in front of him.

Wearing those nice-fitting shorts.

Riley went to her, slipped his arm around her waist to give her a friendly hug.

And Claire screamed as if he'd just gutted her with a machete.

Along with slapping him upside the head with an egg-coated spatula.

She made some garbled sounds. Hit him again. This time on his already throbbing shoulder. She took aim at him once more, but her common sense must have kicked in, and she looked at his face.

"Riley, my God, you scared the life out of me!"

"Really? I hadn't noticed." He didn't mean to sound grouchy, but hell in a handbasket, that spatula had hit the wrong spot.

Claire's face flushed red. Then she smiled. And despite his eyes watering in pain, he had no trouble seeing it. That smile always lit up the room, and it gave him a sucker punch of attraction. But as Riley had done since about the time he'd first sprouted chest hair, he stepped back. For the past fifteen years or so, Claire had been hands-off.

Not that she'd ever actually been hands-on.

Evidently she didn't have the same rules about the hands-off part. She put her arms around him, pulled him really, really close to her for a hug. He wasn't able to bite back a grunt of pain so the hug was short and sweet.

"I'm so sorry." Claire grabbed a tea towel, began to wipe the egg off his face. "I heard about your injury, of course."

Judging from the noodle banner, so had everyone in town. "I'll be fine. I just need a few weeks to recover."

At best, that was wishful thinking. At worst, an out-and-out lie. It was a sad day when a man lied to himself, but right now Riley needed anything that would get him through this.

Lies and oxycodone.

She stared at him, made a sound as if she hadn't fully bought his answer. Her smile faded. "Should I ask how much you're hurting right now?"

This was easy. "No."

Claire nodded, maybe even looked relieved. *Good.* Because if she was uncomfortable talking about it, then maybe it wouldn't come up again.

"About an hour ago someone dropped off an Angus bull that Logan bought," she said as if this were a normal conversation. It wasn't, but he guessed this was her way of chit-chatting about anything but his injury. "It must have been worth a fortune the way they were treating it. The men wore white gloves when they touched it. Don't worry. One of the guys took care of the paperwork and such."

By *guys*, she probably meant one of Logan's assistants from the office in town. Or maybe a ranch hand who tended the horses and cattle that came and went through the stables and grounds on the property. Other than a couple of riding horses for their personal use, none of the livestock stayed too long, just enough for Logan to make whatever amount of money he intended to make off the deal. As a broker, Logan usually dealt in bulk purchases.

Since Riley hadn't been home in nearly six months, he wasn't sure exactly who was on his brother's payroll for McCord Cattle Brokers or for managing the livestock on the grounds. *His* payroll, too.

Technically.

But while the house would always be Riley's home, it was Logan's heart and soul in the family business. Logan had been as happy to stay put, and buy and sell cattle as Riley had been to head out for more exciting pastures.

He looked out the back bay window at the sprawl of green grass, streaked with white fences and dotted with a dozen barns, corrals, the hands' quarters and outbuildings. Everything looked exactly the same as it always had down to the yellow Lab sleeping under one of the shade trees. Both a blessing and a curse as far as Riley was concerned.

"How'd you get from the San Antonio airport?" she asked.

"Taxi."

That earned him a raised eyebrow because Claire likely filled in the blanks. Riley hadn't called anyone to come and get him because he didn't want to see anyone. And he hadn't rented a car because he was in too much pain to drive. It'd been worth every penny of the hundred-dollar cab fare to get a driver who hadn't asked him a single question.

"Logan called the house phone earlier to check and make sure you got in all right," Claire went on after lowering that eyebrow. "He said he didn't want to call your cell and risk waking you. Oh, and no one's been able to get in touch with Lucky yet."

That was all right. He didn't want to deal with Lucky. Or Logan for that matter. They were his big brothers, and he loved them—most days anyway—but Riley wanted to go the less-is-better route with his recovery. Actually, he wanted the none-is-best route.

"Why are you here?" he asked Claire, and since it was probably all related, he added two other questions. "Why are there women in my bed?" No sense asking about the one in Lucky's because that was often the case. "And who is he?"

Riley tipped his head to the kid, who was now out of the

chair and eating the bits of scrambled egg that'd fallen off the spatula and onto the floor.

"Ethan, no. That's yucky," Claire scolded, sticking out her tongue and making a face.

She scooped up the little boy, wiping that smear off his cheek. It was chocolate. And in the same motion she eased him back into the chair. A chair with a makeshift booster seat of old phone books.

"Don't wiggle around, or you'll fall," Claire told the kid. "I'll get you some eggs when they've cooled a little. The women in your bed are Wilbert Starkley's twin granddaughters," she added to Riley without missing a beat. "The one in Lucky's room is their sister."

After she moved the skillet from the burner to the back of the stove, Claire got busy cleaning up the egg mess on the floor. Cleaning off Riley, too.

"Wilbert Starkley's granddaughters?" Riley repeated. Wilbert owned the town's grocery store and was someone Riley had known his whole life, which was pretty much the norm for Spring Hill. "No way are those his granddaughters. They're just kids. The two in my bed are grown women."

With boobs that jiggled when they breathed.

Claire smiled as if she knew exactly what he was thinking. "Not kids. They're nineteen and home from college for the summer. Their sister is twenty-one and works for their dad. Wilbert dropped them off last night, and they fell asleep waiting for you to get in."

He listened, still didn't hear them stirring around. "Are they deaf? Or drugged? They slept through your bloodcurdling scream."

"I guess they're just deep sleepers. Anyway, when they heard you were coming home to recover and that Della and Stella were on vacation, they wanted to help."

Claire lifted her eyebrow again on the vacation part of that explanation. With reason. Della and Stella didn't normally take vacations and never at the same time. One of them was always around to take care of the place and the McCord clan.

"I *wanted* Della and Stella on vacation. I'm the one who told them to go. And how are those other women supposed to help?" Riley located the biggest cup he could find and filled it to the brim with coffee. Judging from the size of the headache he was going to have to cure, he'd need at least six more cups.

"They want to help by doing things for you so that you can get all the rest you need. That's why I'm here. To fix you breakfast."

It wasn't as if Riley didn't appreciate Claire's efforts. He did. However, it didn't help his confusion that was growing with every new bit of this conversation. "But why are you here? As in *here* in Spring Hill? Did you move back?"

Claire nodded. "I came back about six months ago when Gran got sick. I still have my apartment in San Antonio, though. I'm still working as a wedding photographer, too. But I'm staying on awhile longer here to clean out Gran's house so I can get it ready to sell."

Yeah, that. He had no trouble hearing the grief in her voice. "I was sorry to hear she passed away."

Claire didn't even try to dismiss his sympathy. Probably because she couldn't. She'd been close to her grandmother, and it didn't matter that the woman was old and had lived a full if not somewhat eccentric life. Claire obviously hadn't been ready to let her go.

Still multitasking, Claire took out two plates from the cabinet, scooped some of the eggs onto both of them and set the plates on the table. Apparently one of them was for him because Claire motioned for Riley to sit. The other plate was for the kid.

"And who's the kid?" Riley pressed.

"That's Ethan, my son. He's two years old." She smiled, this time one that only a mother could manage. Ethan gave her a toothy grin right back.

Riley's attention went straight to her left hand. No ring.

Claire followed his gaze. "I'm not married."

"Oh." And because Riley didn't know what else to say, he went with another "oh."

Man, he was way out of the gossip loop. His sister, Anna, had told him about Claire's grandmother dying two months ago but not about Claire being a mom. Better yet, Anna hadn't said a word about who had made Claire a mom.

Probably Daniel Larson.

Except Ethan didn't look a thing like Daniel. Ethan had dark brown hair more like the color of Riley's own. Daniel could have passed for a Swedish male model with his blond hair and pale blue eyes. Maybe that meant Claire had met someone else. Someone who looked like him.

But Riley rethought that.

Of course it was Daniel. The kid just got his looks from some past ancestor with that coloring. Because Claire was with Daniel. Daniel had captured her heart and just about every other part of her their sophomore year in high school, and Claire had chosen him.

Over Riley.

It hadn't been a particularly hard decision for her, either. And Riley knew that because she'd left her binder behind in chemistry class, and he had seen her list of why she should pick one over the other. Fifteen years later, Riley could remember that list in perfect detail.

Beneath Daniel's name, Claire had written, "Cute, reliable, good listener, likes cats, no plans to move off and join the military." Beneath Riley's name, she'd written only one word.

"Hot."

Hot had stroked his ego for a minute or two, but he definitely hadn't stacked up against the cute, cat-loving Daniel. And while Daniel and Riley had once been close friends, it'd been nearly four years since Riley had seen him. That was plenty enough time to make a two-year-old.

Now Claire was a mother.

He supposed that was the norm seeing she was thirty-one, the same age as he was. People did that. They made babies. Stayed in one place for more than a year. Didn't get shot at as a general rule. They had lives that Riley had always made sure to avoid.

Claire dodged Riley's stare, looking at the plate of cookies instead. Then she huffed, put her hands on her hips. "Ethan, you took another one of those cookies, didn't you? Where'd you hide it this time?"

"Logan's bed," Riley answered when Ethan didn't say anything.

But, man, Riley wished he hadn't ratted him out. The kid looked at him with wide-eyed bewilderment and betrayal. Ethan's bottom lip even quivered. Riley felt as if he had violated a major man-pact.

"So, that's what's in your hair." Claire plucked some crumbs from Riley's head. "I'm sorry. Ethan knows he's not allowed to have sweets without asking. He took at least two cookies last night when we were over here before you got home. He ate one, hid the other and now he's taken another one." She pointed her index finger at him. "No computer games for you today, young man."

The kid's look of betrayal intensified significantly.

"Sorry, buddy," Riley said.

Claire put some toast on the table, poured Riley a glass of OJ from the fridge, topped off his coffee. She clearly hadn't forgotten the waitressing skills she'd learned from her afternoon job at the Fork and Spoon Café in high school.

"Eat up, Ethan," she told her boy. "We've got to get going soon. The next shift should be here any minute."

Riley looked at her midbite. "Shift?"

Claire nodded, started washing the skillet she'd used to cook the eggs. "Misty Reagan and Trisha Weller. They're coming to help you get dressed and then will fix your lunch."

Both women were familiar to him. *Intimately* familiar. He'd had sex with only two girls in high school.

And it was those two.

"Misty's divorced, no kids," Claire went on. "That brings the total to nine divorced couples in town now in case you're keeping count."

He wasn't, but divorce was a rare occurrence in Spring Hill—less than 1 percent of the marriages had failed. It was the cool springwater, some said. Most folks just fell in love, got hitched and stayed that way. Riley thought it didn't have as much to do with the water as it did with lack of options. Little pond. Not many fish.

"Trisha never married. Oh, except for that time she married you, of course." Another smile tugged at Claire's mouth. This one didn't so much light up the room as yank his chain.

"Trisha and I were six years old," Riley said in his defense. "And she had brownies."

That perked up Ethan. "Boun-knees." Obviously, the kid had a serious sweet tooth, something else he had in common with Riley.

"Well, I guess a home-baked dessert is a good reason for marriage," Claire remarked.

It sure seemed that way at the time. "It was Trisha's version of put a ring on it. No marriage, no brownies."

"And you did put a ring on it." Claire dried the skillet, put it away and dropped the spatula in the dishwasher after she rinsed it. "I seem to remember something gold with a red stone in it."

"Fake, and it fell apart after a few hours. Just like our fake marriage."

That eyebrow of hers went to work again. "I think she'd like to make that marriage the real deal."

Riley frowned. "Trisha said that?"

"Not with words, but she's a lawyer in Austin and cleared her schedule for the next two weeks just so she could be here. I'd say she really, really wants to be here *with you*."

Well, hell. Riley liked Trisha enough, but he hadn't wanted anyone hanging around, including a woman who was looking for more than a plastic ring from a vending machine.

"Call them," Riley insisted. "Tell them not to come, that I don't need or want any help. I really just need to get some rest—that's all. That's why I told Della and Stella to take the week off."

The words had hardly left his mouth when Riley heard the sound of car engines. Ethan raced to the window in the living room with Riley and Claire trailing along right behind him. Sure enough two cars had pulled into the circular driveway that fronted the house.

Wearing a short blue skirt and snug top, Misty got out first from a bright yellow Mustang, and she snagged two shopping bags off the passenger's seat. She'd been a cheerleader in high school and still had some zip to her steps. Was still a looker, too, with her dark brown hair that she'd pulled up in a ponytail.

She might be trouble.

After all, she'd lost her virginity to Riley when she was seventeen after they'd dated for about four months. That tended to create a bond for women. Maybe Misty would be looking to *bond* again.

Then there was Trisha.

Riley had lost his virginity to her. And there'd been that wedding in first grade, possibly creating another problem with that whole bonding thing.

When Trisha stepped out of a silver BMW, she immediately looked up, her gaze snagging his in the window. She smiled. No chain yanking or "light up the room" smile, either. All Riley saw were lips and teeth, two things Trisha had used quite well on the night of his de-virgining.

"Oh, look," Claire said. "Trisha brought you a plate of brownies."

Yeah, she had.

And other things were familiar about Trisha, too. Like those curves that had stirred every man's zipper in town. Now all those curves were hugged up in a devil-red dress. She still looked hungry, as if she were ready to gobble up something. And judging from the smile she gave Riley, she wanted him to be the gobblee.

Another time, another place, Riley might have considered a good gobbling. Or at least some innocent flirting. But there was that part about people seeing him in pain. Plus, there was always the threat of a flashback. No way did he want anyone around to witness that little treat.

"Come on, Ethan," Claire said, scooping him up. "It's time for us to go."

"So soon?" Riley wanted to ask her to stay, but that would just sound wussy. His testosterone had already dropped enough for one day.

"So soon," Claire verified. She waggled her fingers in a good-bye wave and headed for the door. "Enjoy those brownies."

She probably would have just waltzed out, but Claire stopped in her tracks when their gazes met. She didn't ask what was going on in his head, and the chain-yanking expression was gone.

Hell.

He hadn't wanted her to see what was behind his eyes. Hadn't wanted anyone to see it. But Riley was as certain as he was of his boot size that Claire knew.

"Finish your breakfast," Claire instructed. Her voice was a little unsteady now. "I'll deal with them. I can't guarantee they won't come back, but you'll have a few hours at least. Is that enough time?"

Riley lied with a nod.

He used actual words for his next lie. "You don't have to worry about me, Claire. Soon I'll be as good as new."

CHAPTER THREE

"PAY DOUGH!" ETHAN squealed when Claire held up the picture of the painting.

Claire checked to make sure she was showing him the right one. Yes, it was van Gogh's *Starry Night*, but there was no Play-Doh on it.

"That's really close, sweetie, and the artist's name does sort of rhyme with Play-Doh," Claire encouraged.

"Pay dough!" he repeated, speeding up the words a little.

She tried not to look disappointed. The directions on the "Making Your Toddler a Little Genius" packet had said to make this activity fun. Or rather *FUN!!!!* Claire only hoped that the creators of this product had raised at least one semigenius child and that they hadn't just tossed some crap activities together to milk her out of her $89.95, plus shipping.

"Try again," she prompted, waving the picture at Ethan to get his already wandering attention. "You got this right yesterday." And, according to the rules, she wasn't supposed to move on to the next picture until he'd gotten this one right three days in a row. They'd been working on it for two weeks now with no end in sight.

Ethan studied the picture and grinned. "Money!"

Claire was certain she didn't contain her disappointment that time. "No. Not *Monet*." That'd been last month's lesson.

She snagged one of his toy vehicles. A van. And she held it up with the painting while trying to make a running/going motion with her index and middle fingers. Her nails nearly tore a hole in one of the star blobs. Evidently, $89.95 wasn't enough to buy higher-quality paper, and her example was obviously too abstract.

"Ri-wee!" Ethan squealed with more excitement than money or Play-Doh.

Frowning, Claire put aside the picture and the van. "No, not Riley." Or rather Ri-wee. "Why don't we work on this later? You can go ahead and play."

You would have thought she'd just announced he could have an entire toy store and unlimited chocolate-chip cookies for life. Ethan scooted across the floor and went back to his cars. The auto crashes started immediately.

"Ri-wee!" he repeated like some kind of tribal shout with each new collision.

Even though he didn't have the pronunciation down pat, Claire knew her son was only repeating what he'd heard her mumble for the past two days—Riley. For some reason, Riley's name kept popping into her head and then continued to randomly pop out of her mouth.

And there was no good reason for it.

A few bad reasons, though.

Riley was an attractive man. Still hot. No denying that. He was also very much hands-off since he wouldn't be around for long, as usual. Maybe her brain would figure that out soon enough and stop sending these ridiculous impulses to the rest of her body.

Claire stayed on the floor next to Ethan but grabbed her laptop from the sofa. Since she had struck out in creating a baby genius, she might as well get some work done, and she downloaded the last photo she needed to edit. When she finished, it would almost be bittersweet because it was also the last of her work in the queue.

More photo shoots would follow. They always did. But it was best if she didn't have any free time on her hands right now.

Of course, she could fill that free time, easily, by sorting through more of her gran's things. However, that was more bitter than sweet, and it was also the main reason she kept procrastinating. And overeating. She'd put on six pounds since the sorting had started. Soon, she'd either have to pay for therapy or Weight Watchers.

Her phone buzzed, and Claire saw Livvy Larimer's name on the screen. Her best friend and co-owner of their business, Dearly Beloved.

"Well?" Livvy started.

No greeting. Which meant she expected Claire to dish up something exciting. And the dishing up that Livvy wanted was about Riley. Best just to give her a summary and hope it didn't lead to too many other questions.

"Riley finally made it home day before yesterday after his flight was delayed. I fixed him breakfast, and I came back to Gran's to get some work done on the Herrington-Anderson engagement photos." An engagement that Livvy knew all about because she was the wedding planner for the event.

"That's it?" Livvy asked.

Here come the questions. But Claire made Livvy work for the answers. "What else were you expecting?"

"Fudging details. Specifically, fudging you did with Riley."

Fudging was the compromise they'd worked out instead of using the *F* word, one of Livvy's many favorites. They also used *sugar* for *shit* and *bubble gum* for *blow job*, something that came up surprisingly often in her conversations with Livvy.

They were still working on one for *asshole*.

Ethan's little ears picked up on anything Claire didn't want him to hear while selectively shutting out van Gogh, and since

Livvy cursed like a meth dealer in an R-rated movie, they'd resorted to acceptable substitutions.

"No fudging," Claire explained. She was finally able to keep a straight face when she said it. "I only fixed Riley breakfast and ran interference from some unwanted visitors."

Livvy made a *yeah-right* sound. "And you've fawned over him for the past decade."

"Fawned over? What the heck does that even mean? Is that a new compromise word?"

"Yes, it means you dream of fudging and bubblegumming Riley."

Claire huffed. "Does any woman actually dream of bubblegumming a man? I don't. It's more of something that just sort of evolves during foreplay."

"Foreplay," Ethan said with perfect clarity. Great, they needed a compromise word for that now.

"Sugar yeah, you dreamed of fudging him," Livvy went on. "You pointed out his pictures in your high school yearbook. You've talked about him. And then there's Ethan—"

"Riley and I were friends in high school. *Friends*," Claire emphasized.

"You can fawn over friends. And fudge them, too. I've seen pictures of Riley, and he'd make a great fudge."

"Riley has never fudged me." Claire paused. "He's hurt, Livvy."

That reminder flicked away the annoyance she was feeling about Livvy's interrogation. But Claire replaced the flicked-away emotion with one she'd been trying to keep out of her head.

Worry.

"Is it bad?" Livvy asked.

"Maybe." *Probably*, Claire silently amended.

"God, I just can't imagine doing what he does. Ever googled *Combat Rescue Officer* and looked at some of those pictures?"

Once. It had been enough.

Livvy made a shuddering sound. "And to think, he's been doing that job for a long time."

Nine years. Since he graduated from college and joined the Air Force. Riley had been on six deployments, and even though Claire didn't know the exact locations, she was betting there'd been plenty of other times when he could have been wounded or killed.

Ethan grumbled something, clearly not pleased about his car-bashing game. Claire glanced over to make sure all was well. It wasn't. One of the cars had broken. Again. Thank heavens it wasn't one of his favorites so his reaction was mild. The Terrible Twos wasn't just a cliché when it came to her baby boy. He often aimed high to live up to that particular label.

She needed to find a toddler genius kit to help her with that.

"You think Riley's got PTSD or something?" Livvy went on.

This was even less comfortable than the fudge question. "If he does, I'm sure there's help for that at the base in San Antonio. From what he told his sister, he'll be starting physical therapy there soon."

The military would patch him up, both physically and mentally if needed, and Riley would go right back out there on deployment again. To someplace dangerous. Because that's what he did. What he'd always wanted since middle school.

"You haven't asked me about the hot date," Livvy said a moment later.

"Date-date, or are we talking fruit now?" And Claire was serious. Livvy had a thing for trying new foods and men. Lots of men. She had been married three times and was always on the lookout for ex number four. Thankfully, she didn't live in Spring Hill or she would have single-handedly skewed their divorce stats.

"Date-date. You know, the guy I met from the dating site. I told you, didn't I?"

"I don't think so." She'd been living vicariously—sexually anyway—through Livvy since having Ethan. "How'd it go?"

"Sugar hot," Livvy declared. "His name is Alejandro just like the Lady Gaga song. He's an albino drummer in a heavy metal band." She giggled like a schoolgirl. "I predict lots of fudging in my future."

Since Livvy seemed excited about his name/career/pigment/fudging combo, Claire was happy for her. Or rather cautiously optimistic. "Is he nice?"

"Of course. I wouldn't go out with a grouchy asshole again. Sorry, we'll work on that word. Anyway, other than his pink-eye, he's perfect."

"Uh, I don't know a lot about albinos, but I think pink eyes are normal for them."

"Not pink *eyes*," Livvy quickly corrected. "Pink*eye*. He's using drops for it, though, so it should clear up soon. You really should use this dating site, Claire. It's the best one yet."

She'd rather have pinkeye. "I'm on hiatus from dating. Until I get Ethan potty trained." Of course, there was no correlation. None. But thankfully it was an argument that always worked with Livvy.

"So, making any progress getting the house ready to sell?" Livvy asked.

Claire wanted to say a hallelujah for the change of topic. "Some. Gran wasn't a hoarder exactly, but she didn't throw away much. I'll keep at it until a new job comes in."

"Already got two. Wedding announcement photos. I'll email you the dates and details."

There were clearly more procrastination possibilities on the horizon. It was probably depression over Gran's death, but Claire felt stuck in Neutral.

"Oh, and Daniel called the office, looking for you," Livvy added. "Said his fudging phone died after a software update, and he lost all his sugar, including your phone number."

The timing was odd. What with Riley's arrival back in Spring Hill. Like her, Daniel no longer lived there, but that didn't mean a gossip or two hadn't called him in San Antonio with news of Riley's homecoming.

Rather than come out and ask that, Claire took the round-about route. "Did Daniel want anything specific?"

"Well, I'm guessing he wanted *you*. I gave him your number, so I figure you'll get a call from him soon."

"Good." And Claire would be happy to hear from Daniel. Almost. "Gotta go," she said when Ethan yawned and stomped on one of the cars. "I'll send you these engagement pictures as soon as I'm done."

The moment she ended the call, Claire hit the save button on her files and picked up Ethan. He started to fuss right away. In part because he knew nap time was coming. Also in part because he needed a nap.

She changed his diaper. Not an easy feat now that the grumpy boy had emerged. Still, she loved grumpy boy just as much as the other boys that materialized throughout the day. Ethan had her heart. And the little sugar knew it.

"No getting up," she warned him when she put him in his crib.

He was quickly outgrowing it. Outgrowing naps, too. And it wouldn't be long before he really would be ready for potty training.

Her baby was growing up so fast.

Not that she would miss the whole diapering thing and having him test his aiming skills by trying to pee in her eye. She'd convinced herself that it was a labor of love. But it was also time when she had Ethan close and he wasn't running away from her.

Plus, she'd lose that excuse she kept giving to Livvy about not dating.

Since Ethan might or might not obey that no-getting-up part and since he might try to climb out of the crib again, Claire knew she'd need to spend at least fifteen minutes with him while he fell asleep. No use wasting that time, so she went into the hall to bring one of the cardboard boxes into the makeshift nursery with her. She had plenty of boxes to choose from. At least thirty that she'd already dragged down from the attic or found in the back of her gran's closet.

There'd been spiders involved.

Something that made her shiver just thinking about it.

The various cousins had already gone through the house and taken items of furniture and such that they'd wanted. Which wasn't nearly enough to clear out the place. Every room, every corner was still crammed with bits and pieces that reminded Claire of the woman who'd raised her. The woman she'd loved.

Damn it.

The tears came. They always did whenever she thought of Gran.

God, she missed her.

Opening the box wouldn't help, either, but going through whatever was inside was the next step to getting the house ready to go to on the market. Claire wasn't exactly strapped for cash. Yet. But her savings had dwindled considerably what with all the time she'd taken off to be with Ethan.

She didn't regret that time off, not for a second, but she didn't have the comfortable financial pad that she needed. Since Gran had left her the house free and clear, anything Claire got from the sale would be hers to keep.

She put the box on the floor, glanced over at Ethan. Still not asleep, but his eyelids were getting droopy.

The tape holding the box was so old that it gave way with a gentle tug, and Claire opened the flap. Checked for spiders.

Nothing scurried out at her.

So she began the sorting. She'd set aside another area at the end of the hall to deal with the contents of each box. One pile for stuff to keep. Another for items to be donated. A final one for trash.

She'd yet to put anything in the trash pile.

Not a good sign.

Of course, it was probably wishful thinking on her part that a charity group would want copies of old magazines and newspapers, panties with shot elastic and mismatched socks. This box was pretty much the same. Magazines from the 1980s. More newspapers. A Gerber baby food jar filled with buttons. Another had sequins. There were some Mardi Gras beads, though Claire couldn't recall Gran ever mentioning a trip to New Orleans.

And then Claire saw the old photo of Riley's parents—Betsy and Sherman.

More bittersweetness.

Claire had been in the car with them the night they'd died. Still had both the physical and emotional scars from it. It'd been pouring rain, and they'd given her a ride from the high school basketball game where the Spring Hill Mavericks had won by eleven points. Daniel was away visiting his sick aunt and had missed the game. Riley had stayed behind to be with Misty. Anna was home studying. Logan was on a date. And Lucky was at a rodeo.

She remembered all those little details. Every last one of them. The knock-knock joke that Mr. McCord had told just before the crash. Mrs. McCord's laughter at the lame punch line. The Alan Jackson song playing on the radio. The way her band uniform was scratching against her skin. But Claire couldn't remember the accident itself.

Sometimes she would recall a blur of motion from the red car that'd plowed into them. But Claire was thankful that it stayed just a blur.

She put the picture aside—definitely a keeper—and moved on to the next items in the box. Desk calendars. At least a dozen of them stacked together. They were freebies that an insurance company had sent Gran, but there was a handwritten note on the first one she looked at. January 5.

Enroll Claire in school.

She checked the year, not that she didn't already know. Claire had been five years old. And two days earlier her mother had left her at Gran's house. Dumped her, really, not even taking the time to say goodbye. If her mother had known it would be a real goodbye, that in a year she'd be dead, maybe she would have said a proper farewell.

At least that's what Claire liked to tell herself.

The ache came. The one that crushed her heart and had her eyes burning with tears that she refused to cry. Never had, never would shed a tear over her worthless excuse for a mother. Claire pushed it all aside. Not her bridge, not her water. Not anymore. And she wouldn't repeat the mistakes her mother had made. She'd be the best mom ever to her son.

She flipped through the calendar and saw another note. "Bennie" with a heart drawn around it and the time 7:00 p.m. No doubt a date. Claire had vague memories of the man. He'd worked for Riley's family and had been seeing Gran around the time Claire moved in.

Claire did the math. Her grandmother had been in her late forties then, a youngish widow, and had no trouble attracting men. Apparently, she didn't have trouble unattracting them, either, because six weeks later, Bennie's name had a huge *X* through it, their date obviously off.

Beneath the *X*, Gran had scrawled, "Pigs do fly if you kick them hard enough in the ass."

Ouch.

Claire moved on to the next calendar. There were more notes about doctor's appointments, parent-teacher meetings and more dates with men who'd initially gotten their names enclosed with hearts. Then, had been *X*'ed out.

She hadn't remembered her grandmother having an appointment book, and the woman didn't use a computer, so this must have been her way of keeping track. A good thing, too, since there were a lot of date-dates to keep track of. Claire read each one, savoring the little tidbits Gran had left behind.

Get cash to pay McCord boys.

That was an entry for the September when Claire had been ten. There were two more for the same month. Events Claire remembered because she'd been close to the same age as the McCord boys and had begged to help Riley and Logan move the woodpile and do some other yard chores. However, Gran had insisted it wasn't work for a girl and that she would pay Riley and Logan despite their having volunteered.

More entries. All of them brought back smiles and childhood memories. Until she landed on October 14 of that same year.

Give Claire the letter.

Claire frowned. *What letter?* It'd been a long time, twenty-one years, but she was pretty sure she would have remembered Gran giving her a letter. And who was it from?

Hoping she would find it, Claire had a closer look in the box. Not the careful, piece-by-piece way she'd been taking out the other things. She dumped the contents on the floor and riffled through them.

Nothing.

But there was a book. Judging from the battered blue hardback cover, it was old. She opened it, flipped through it, hoping the letter was tucked inside. But no letter. However, it wasn't just an ordinary book.

It was a journal.

Her mother's journal.

Her mother had scrolled her own name complete with hearts and flowers on the inside cover. Then Claire's attention landed on two other words centered in the first page. Her mother had drawn a rectangle around it.

Fucking kid.

Claire slammed it shut and couldn't toss it fast enough back into the box. She definitely hadn't wanted to see that. She wanted to erase it from her head.

She didn't want to cry.

Where the heck was that letter? It'd get her mind off those two words that were now burning like fire in her gut. She stood to get another box but didn't make it but a few steps when her phone buzzed.

Riley.

And this time, the name didn't just pop into her head. It actually popped onto her phone screen. She checked on Ethan. Asleep, finally, so she eased the nursery door shut and went into the living room to take the call.

She also took a minute to steady her nerves. No way did she want Riley to hear she was shaken up by two words written by a woman who'd abandoned her.

"Claire?" Riley greeted her.

Just the sound of his voice calmed her. It excited her in a different way, too, but for now, she'd take it. Claire needed something that wasn't dark and heart crushing.

She scowled when she felt the little flutter in her stomach at the mere sound of his voice. "Eat any good brownies lately?" she asked.

"Very funny. You might have run off Misty and Trisha, but you still left me here with three women barely old enough to be classified as women. And Trisha and Misty didn't stay away. They returned and didn't leave until the swing shift arrived." He cursed, and he didn't use any of the compromise words. "At least I haven't been involved with any of them."

Not that batch. These were women from the historical society. Nobody under sixty in the bunch. Of course, it was possible one or two of them had the hots for Riley. He seemed to bring that out in women of all ages.

"They won't be coming back," Riley continued. "Neither will the twins, their sister or the midmorning shift."

"Really? Trisha will be so disappointed." But for reasons Claire didn't want to explore, she actually felt good about disappointing Trisha. Probably because Trisha had used her 36-Ds to seduce Riley in high school.

Seriously, who had boobs that big in the tenth grade?

"Not sure *disappointed* is the right word for it," Riley went on, "but she seemed upset that I didn't want her here. Like I said, it's nothing personal. I just need some peace and quiet."

"But not peace and quiet right now? Or are you calling to tell me I'm off breakfast duty tomorrow?"

He huffed. "The peace and quiet doesn't apply to you right now. And, yeah, you're off breakfast duty."

Good grief. That stung. What she should feel was relief. Being around Riley wasn't good for her. He was a forbidden-fruit kind of thing, and she didn't need any more choices of fruit, fudge or bubblegum in her life.

"All right. If you're sure," she said. "If you change your mind, though, just give me a call." Claire was about to say goodbye, but she thought of that note. "By any chance, when we were about ten years old, did Gran ever say anything to you about giving me a letter?"

"Letter?" Claire couldn't be sure, but she thought maybe he hesitated. "What kind of letter?"

"Don't know. It was something she'd marked on her calendar, and I thought maybe you remembered it since you did some yard work for her around that same time."

Of course, it sounded stupid now that she'd said it aloud. At ten years old, Riley would have been less interested in some letter than in finishing the duties that Logan had no doubt volunteered him to do.

"Sorry, I can't help you." Riley paused. Mumbled something she didn't catch. Paused again. "But maybe you can help me. Is it my imagination or do some of those women who came over think I'm Ethan's father?"

Claire was so glad he wasn't there to see her expression. She was certain she'd gone a little pale. "Uh, do they?"

"Yeah. I heard some whispers about Ethan having my smile. As if anyone's seen my smile since I got back. Has anyone come out and asked you if I'm his father?"

Several dozen times. "Once or twice," she settled for saying. "I denied it, but I don't think they believed me."

"Even when you told them we've never had sex?"

"Well, I didn't really tell them that. I sort of hoped they would infer it when I said you're not his father."

"They're not inferring it right. They think the kid's mine because he looks like me."

"Does he?" No way in hell on a good day would Claire confirm or deny that, and she could practically hear the next question that was about to come out of Riley's mouth.

Since I know I'm not Ethan's father, who is?

Claire decided to put an end to it before it started. "Get some rest, Riley. I'll call you soon." And before Riley could utter another word, or ask another question, she hung up.

CHAPTER FOUR

RILEY WAS SURE someone was watching him. Since this was downtown Spring Hill and not hostile territory, he wasn't overly alarmed, but he could sense that someone had him under surveillance.

He glanced around Main Street at the line of shops and buildings, including the Fork and Spoon Café, the bank and the pharmacy where Riley had just picked up a refill of his oxycodone. The biggest building, however, was the two-story Victorian inn that Logan had converted into headquarters for the family business. Logan had added a new sign in the past six months. *McCord Cattle Brokers* was emblazed on a copper-and-brass background.

Classy.

But then Riley hadn't expected anything less from Logan. His brother was a ball-busting Renaissance man in a four-hundred-dollar cowboy hat.

Since it was close to dinnertime, Riley hadn't expected to see so many people milling around Main Street. None was especially looking at him, though he did get a friendly wave from Bert Starkley who was in the doorway of the café he owned.

He got a not-so-friendly look, however, from Misty. The woman was coming out of the bank, but when Misty laid eyes on him, she whirled around and went back in. Clearly he'd ruffled some feathers by refusing her help, but he preferred that to some of the TLC that was being offered.

Hell, Trisha had wanted to run his bath for him, and he didn't think it was his imagination that she would have joined him in the sudsy oasis if he'd been agreeable. She'd also eyed that saddle on Lucky's bed. Riley wasn't in any shape for suds, saddles or Trisha.

"Want a cold glass of sweet tea?" Bert called out to Riley. "It's on the house for our local military hero."

"Thanks. If the offer's still good tomorrow, I'll take you up on it then," Riley answered.

Maybe.

Riley made sure to smile. Hoped it didn't look as forced and creepy as it felt, but it was something he was working on.

He still wasn't in a socializing kind of mood, but he had needed a flat surface to walk so he could get in some exercise. Only every other step hurt now. Well, all of them hurt, but only one out of two made him see gigantic stars. Riley figured that was a good sign. What wasn't a good sign was that he still needed lots of pain meds to get through every minute of every hour.

And then there were the flashbacks.

Since the bad one two nights ago, he'd kept them from trying to claw their way to the surface. "Jingle Bells" and a good mental boot stomping had worked. Temporarily. But he needed another weapon in his arsenal. Sex, maybe. Lately, he'd been thinking a lot about sex.

And Claire.

Too bad he'd been thinking about them at the same time.

When he got the niggling feeling again that he was being followed, Riley glanced quickly behind him and spotted the twins. Not exactly being stealth-like because he heard them giggling before they darted into their grandfather's store. He hoped they'd stay there. He didn't want to see any glimmer of a nipple.

"Just admiring the view," one of them called out. And giggled again.

The view being his butt. Now, normally he would have been flattered by something like that, but if Wilbert found out that his backside was the object of his young granddaughters' attention, then Riley would have one more riled citizen on his hands. He'd get that sweet tea all right—dumped on his head.

Riley picked up the pace in case the twins came in pursuit, and he ducked down the side street just as his phone rang. It was his sister, Anna, the one person he did want to have a talk with, and that's why he'd already left her two messages. If she hadn't been all the way over in Florida where she was attending college near her military fiancé, Riley would have gone after her for a face-to-face chat.

"Don't you know I have certain skills that make it dangerous to piss me off?" Riley said when he answered.

"And how did I piss you off?" Anna didn't pause, didn't miss a beat, which meant she'd no doubt been expecting his surly protest.

"When I got home, I found two women in my bed."

"Okay. And I guess you want to thank me for that?" she teased.

"No. They're young women. Too young. And you sent a team of women to my house to babysit me."

"I heard about you giving Della and Stella time off. I knew Logan would be busy because he's, well, Logan, and Lucky is, well, Lucky. I couldn't be there with you, so I made a few calls to let people know you'd be at the house. *Alone*. While recovering from an injury that could have killed you."

Oh, man. Anna's voice trembled on that last handful of words, and Riley felt the tremble tug right at his gut. "I'm okay."

"Yes, because you got lucky. Don't bullshit me. That shrapnel was just an inch from your heart."

"Shrapnel I got because I was trying to rescue a kid from

a very bad situation." And that's all he could and would say about it.

Jingle bells... Jingle bells...

Anna didn't argue. Wouldn't. But she wouldn't just accept this, either, because she was his kid sister, and it was in her job description to worry about him and nag him. "Look, I'm not asking you to give up what you do. You love it. You're good at it. And it's you. I'm just asking for you to accept their help so you can recover."

"I did accept help. *Some.* Those women stocked the fridge, brought over even more food. And Claire fixed me breakfast." Which reminded him of something else he wanted to ask. "Claire's got a kid. Why didn't you tell me about that?"

"Because I thought it was something you'd eventually want to tell *me.* Ethan's your son, right?"

Riley found himself cursing again. "Jesus H. No, he's not. Why does everyone think that?"

Anna made a sound of mock contemplation. "Hmm. Maybe because it's true?"

"It's not. I've never had sex with Claire. She's Daniel's girl."

"Yes," Anna stretched that out a few syllables. "In high school, she was. I just figured you two had hooked up since then."

"I can't move in on a best friend's girl even when the girl becomes an ex. That's man-rule number three—never take anything that's not yours."

"Even when the relationship happened in high school?" No teasing tone this time. Just lots and lots of skepticism.

"Even then. It's a *forever and ever amen* thing."

"Sheez. Who makes up these stupid rules?" she asked.

"Men. *Real* men. Including me. Besides, Daniel might not be her ex. I'm thinking they're back together and that he's the kid's father."

"Did you ask Claire about that?"

Well, he hadn't gotten a chance because she'd hung up on him. "It's none of my business."

More of those hmm-ing sounds. "But you're curious or you wouldn't have just asked me to gossip about it."

"Man-rule again. It's not gossip if the dirt comes from a sibling. Especially a sibling who owes her brother because said sibling unleashed a horde of horny females on him."

"I'm not speculating about Claire, her sexual partners or her exes. But I'm scratching my head over that so-called rule and code. Men are idiots," she concluded.

Perhaps in a woman's mind, but it still made sense to Riley. Rules kept him grounded and marked his territory. Marked others' territories, too. "You're engaged to a man. One who no doubt has some codes and rules since he wears a uniform just like me. How's Heath by the way?"

Even though he couldn't see her face, he figured that got her to smile. "He's enjoying me."

Riley winced. "I don't want to know that. You're my kid sister, and as far as I'm concerned, you're an eternal virgin."

"Thank God you're wrong about that. Heath's enjoying me a lot. Oh, and his new instructor job. Surprised?"

Yeah, about the new job. But then maybe not. Since Heath Moore and Anna had gotten engaged, Heath had settled down some. That restless streak in him wasn't so restless, and last Riley had spoken to Heath, he was talking about the possibility of them having a wedding as soon as Anna finished law school.

Riley wasn't sure how a Combat Rescue Officer went from heart-stopping, life-on-the-line missions to being a fiancé with a desk job, but it had worked for Heath. Riley was thankful for it, too, since the happiness of both his sister, and future nieces and nephews was at stake.

"Tell Heath hello for me," Riley said, ending the call, and he was still in the process of putting his phone away when he practically ran into the woman who was coming out of the side entrance of the What's Old Is New antiques shop.

Trisha.

No brownies with her today. Nor was that a gobbling smile. Trisha gave him a cool glance instead. Still riled, apparently.

"Going to Claire's?" she asked, also cool-ish.

"Huh?" Riley looked up, to see exactly where he was, and, yep, he was only about a half block from Claire's place.

It wasn't intentional. It was just the way the town was laid out. All roads here didn't lead to Rome but rather to Claire's grandmother's old house.

"I've heard rumors," Trisha said before he could say anything else. "I heard Claire isn't really going to sell her grandmother's house, that she's too attached to it."

All right. So not a rumor about his alleged fatherhood. And Riley had heard that same rumor about the house, as well, from the swing shift crew before he'd dismissed them.

"Understandable, I suppose," Trisha went on, examining her nails. Then his crotch. "Claire loved her grandmother and was happy living there with her. I mean, after her mother dumped her and all."

Yes, *and all* was a good way to sum up the emotional shit Claire had likely gone through. Not that she'd ever shared that with him. Claire wasn't the shit-sharing type.

"I'm not sure how Daniel will feel about Claire staying here, though," Trisha added. "He'd probably rather see her back at her place in San Antonio since it's so close to where he lives."

It seemed like a good time for Riley to answer with "Oh." It was a noncommittal answer, didn't really encourage gossip, but hearing anything about Daniel did pique his interest.

Trisha fluttered her perfectly manicured fingers toward the small shop across the street. Over the years, it'd been a bakery, a florist and a bookstore. All had come and gone, but there was no sign on the front now.

"That's Daniel's office," she supplied. "He only uses it a couple of times a month when he's showing property in the area, but he's been using it a lot more since Claire returned."

"So, they're back together." Riley hadn't actually planned on saying that aloud, but he sort of had to say something when Trisha stopped talking.

"I'm not sure what's going on between them. What does Claire say about it?"

"Not much." Not to him anyway.

"What about you? Are you seeing anyone?" she asked. Another glance at his crotch.

Normally he wouldn't have minded glances like that, but Riley nodded since those glances and her question seemed like the start of an invitation he didn't want to get and wasn't in any shape to accept.

"Yes, I'm seeing someone. Her name is Jodi." It was an on-again, off-again relationship.

Mostly off.

Heck, who was he kidding?

It wasn't *on* with Jodi even when they were together. She was a friend he had sex with. A no-strings-attached kind of friend, which suited them both just fine. Not that he was totally opposed to strings and rings, but in his experience most women didn't want to get into a long relationship with a man whose job description included deployments into direct combat.

"Jodi's a photographer," Riley added just because he felt he should be adding something.

"A photographer, like Claire?" Trisha made a weird little sound that made this seem like a big coincidence.

Or no coincidence at all.

Nope, they weren't going there. Plenty of people knew he'd been hung up on Claire, but that didn't mean he chose facsimiles of her to take to bed.

"Jodi does combat photos for a couple of big magazines and newspapers." The opposite of Claire, who shot wedding and engagement pictures. In fact, the only thing Jodi and Claire had in common was the general overall label of photographer. And the blond hair.

Yeah, the green eyes, too. But other than that, they were nothing alike.

Trisha blinked. "Oh."

That had a liar-liar-pants-on-fire ring to it. One that Riley didn't like much. Of course, there wasn't much about this conversation he did like. "I thought you'd be back in Austin by now," he threw out there.

"Not yet. I decided to take some time off to catch up with friends and make sure you're doing as well as you claim. Besides, I can do most of my work from here anyway." She moved an inch closer. "Riley, you know if you ever need my help or whatever, all you have to do is ask?"

He did know. He also knew what that *whatever* entailed, too. "Thanks, but I'm fine."

Liar-liar-pants-on-fire came in the form of a frown this time. "The offer stands." The frown was still on her mouth when she checked her phone. "I should be going. Enjoy your visit with Claire."

Since Trisha didn't move and since she appeared to be waiting for him to head in Claire's direction, that's what Riley did after they exchanged cheek kisses, goodbyes and one final crotch glance.

Great day. Next time he needed to walk in the pastures. Or buy a treadmill. A ten-minute conversation with Trisha, and he'd spilled more than he should. He'd asked about Claire, and he was betting it wouldn't take that long to hit the gossip mill. Riley was convinced that telepathy was involved, considering the staggering speed with which news got around Spring Hill.

And that was the reason he wasn't going to stop by Claire's.

If anyone saw him, and they would, it'd get back to Daniel, who'd think Riley was horning in on his woman and son.

Riley picked up the pace, intending to limp his way past Claire's house, but when he was still within fifty feet, he heard a sound that had him slowing down so he could see what was going on.

Someone was crying.

The kid.

And not just ordinary crying—he was wailing as if he'd been hurt or something. That got Riley moving faster, and he hurried through the gate and into the front yard. Ethan was sitting on the porch of the old Craftsman-style house, and Claire had stooped down in front of him and was trying to console him.

"Is he hurt?" Riley shouted. He stomped down the flashback. *Not now.* "Jingle Bells" had to get the mojo working and fast.

Claire snapped toward him, clearly not expecting the sound of his voice or his presence in her yard. She didn't scream this time, but Riley could tell he'd given her another jolt.

Well, she'd given him a bit of one, too. Sadly, just the sight of her could do that to him. Maybe she was the cure for flashbacks.

"No. Ethan's not hurt," Claire answered. "He broke his favorite car, that's all."

Sheez Louise, that was a lot of loud crying for a car, especially since there were about fifty others on the porch. But Riley soon saw why this particular one had caused tears. It was a vintage red Corvette. Even as a toy, it had plenty of sentimental value, and Ethan seemed to get that even though he was just a kid.

With a part sigh, part huff coming from her mouth, Claire stooped even lower so she could give Ethan a kiss on the cheek. No shorts for her today. Instead, she was wearing a denim skirt and a top. Barefoot. And with the way she was stooping, he could see her pink panties.

Trisha wasn't the only one whose gaze wandered in the wrong direction.

Riley reacted all right. He felt that stirring behind his zipper. Felt his testosterone soar past normal levels.

He glanced around, mainly because he needed to get his attention off her underwear, and he pretended to look at the house. It was in serious need of a paint job, and the white picket fence needed repairs, but the place had always had good bones. However, something was missing.

"No cats?" Riley asked. There'd been at least a half dozen around when her grandmother was alive.

"Gran gave them away when she got sick."

Too bad because Claire had always loved them, and apparently it'd been one of the tipping points for her choosing Daniel.

"Ix it, peas," Ethan said, holding out the car to Riley.

It took Riley a moment to work out the translation: fix it, please. The car was in three pieces, and Riley took them with all the reverence that a vintage car like that deserved.

"You don't need to trouble yourself," Claire insisted. "Just sit down and relax. You look exhausted."

Judging from the cardboard box and its contents scattered on the porch, she had been going through her grandmother's things, and she pushed some of the items aside to make room for Riley.

"I can get Ethan another car like that the next time I go to the store," she added.

But the fat tears rolling down Ethan's cheeks let Riley know the kid didn't want a new one. Riley eased down onto the porch next to him and tried to remember how he'd repaired his own toy cars after he'd given them a good bashing. After all, what else was a kid to do with toy cars other than create a perpetual stream of wrecks, increasing the gore of those wrecks with each new play session?

"Got any superglue?" Riley asked her.

Claire nodded, moved as if to go inside, but then stopped. "Really, you don't have to do this."

Riley couldn't be positive, but he thought maybe this had something to do with his walking-wounded status. Something that automatically put his teeth on edge. "Just get the glue."

Hard for his teeth to stay on edge though when she ran inside, leaving him alone with the kid. Ethan looked up at him. "Ix it?"

"I'll sure try." Riley glanced around at the other cars, but he soon spotted what had likely caused the damage. Several big-assed action figures. He wasn't certain who or what they were supposed to be, but they looked like a mix of the Grim Reaper, Cyclops and Mick Jagger. With big-assed lips and wings.

"Here you go," Claire said when she came racing back out.

Riley took the glue and tipped his head to the action figures. "Your idea?" Because they darn sure didn't seem like something Claire would buy.

"No. Livvy, my business partner, is responsible. She took Ethan to the toy store for his second birthday and told him he could pick out anything he wanted. He wanted those. They're supposed to be some kind of protectors of the universe."

Riley nodded. "Good choice."

Ethan grinned. The man-pact was back on, and the kid seemed to have forgiven him or at least forgotten about the hidden cookie caper.

"Why are you out here anyway?" Claire asked.

"Walking is part of my physical therapy." Riley squirted the first dollop of glue to get the rear axle back in place. "I just saw Trisha by the antiques shop. She said Daniel's got an office here in town."

Riley wasn't going to win any awards for being subtle, but he figured it wouldn't take more than a minute or two for the car repairs, and then he wouldn't have any reason to stay. Any good reason anyway.

"Yes, he does," Claire answered.

Clearly not chatty today. Riley went in a slightly different direction. "I guess Daniel did that so he could see you. And Ethan."

She didn't huff, but that's exactly what she looked as if she wanted to do. "You know how you don't want to talk about your injury or the pain? Well, I don't want to talk about Daniel. Deal?"

Since she was as testy as he was, it was best to let it drop. Besides, it really wasn't his business, only idle curiosity as to why the kid looked more like Riley than any real kid of his probably would.

Best to move on to a different conversation thread. "How's the box sorting going?"

The sigh that left her mouth was one of frustration. So, testy, nontalkative and frustrated. Oh, yeah, this was a good visit, but at least the car repairs were going well.

"I'm still looking for the letter Gran mentioned on the calendar. I have no idea what was in it or even if it was from her."

Riley glanced at the stack of letters that'd been tied together with white ribbon. "It's not one of those?"

Another sigh. Man, he was picking at scabs today. "No. Those are from various men," Claire said, her forehead bunching up. "Gran was obviously, um, popular. It's strange to learn she had so many things going on in her life that I never knew about."

Apparently that was a pattern Claire was continuing to follow when it came to her son's paternity. Riley frowned. He really needed to get his mind on something else. Heck, the memory of her pink panties flash was better than this.

"I brought down more boxes from the attic, and I've got at least twenty others to go through," she went on. "Maybe I'll find the letter in one of them."

"Maybe she decided not to give it to you," Riley suggested. "Or she could have lost it."

He'd dropped in that last idea only because the first one sounded kind of sinister, as if the letter might be so god-awful that her grandmother had decided Claire shouldn't see it after all.

"I think it might have been from my mother." Claire didn't look at him. She suddenly got very interested in picking at the nonexistent lint on her skirt. "Or my father."

From her mother, yes, he could understand that. The woman had ditched Claire and then had died a while later. Not in a clean, it's-your-time kind of way, either. She'd gotten drunk, thrown up and had choked to death on her own vomit. But Claire's father was a different matter.

"Do you even know who your father is?" Riley asked.

She shook her head. Didn't add anything else. Apparently, any talk involving fatherhood was off the table. In this case, that wasn't a bad thing.

From what Riley had heard, her father had never been in her life and had left her mother before Claire was even born. That made the man lower than pig shit, and as a kid Riley had often thought about what it would be like to punch the idiot for doing that.

His own parents had disappeared from his life when he was a teenager, but that's because they'd been killed by a drunk driver—an accident that Claire knew about all too well since she'd been in the vehicle.

And was the sole survivor.

Being in the backseat had saved her from dying in the head-on collision. The drunk driver had died on impact. His parents, shortly thereafter.

It had hardly been his parents' choice to leave. And despite the fact he'd been planning to go out of state for college, Riley hadn't left, either. He'd stayed at home with Logan to help raise his then fourteen-year-old sister and Lucky. Though Lucky had been Logan's age, only younger by a few minutes, he had still required some raising.

Along with occasional bail money.

Heck, Lucky still required occasional bail money.

Riley had wanted nothing more than to get out of town fast and find his destiny, but instead he'd gone to college in nearby San Antonio to be closer to Anna until she turned eighteen and headed off to her own college choice. Logan had taken it a step further and even dropped out of the University of Texas to be home. It was just something family would do for family.

Unlike Claire's scummy parents.

Riley added the last bit of glue to put the car's hood back in place and blew on it so it would dry. It didn't take long, and he examined his repair job before he handed it to Ethan. However,

Ethan reached for it first and missed, and his hard little hand bashed right into Riley's shoulder.

Riley bit back the thousand really bad curse words that bubbled up in this throat. The pain exploded in his head, and it was a good thing he was sitting, or it would have brought him to his knees.

"Sor-wee," Ethan blurted out.

Riley wanted to lie and say it was okay. No sense making the kid feel bad for an accident, but he was having trouble gathering enough breath to speak. However, he did manage to utter a "shit."

"Sugar," Claire corrected. She scrambled toward him, and before Riley could stop her, she started unbuttoning his shirt. "Here, let me take a look."

"Are you qualified to do that?" he grumbled.

"Sure. I've been *looking* all my life."

Riley appreciated the smartass-ness, but he knew it wouldn't last. And it didn't. When Claire eased back the bandage on his shoulder, the color drained from her face. Every last rosy drop. He didn't have to see the raw, angry gash to know that she was about to lose her lunch.

"God, Riley," she said on a rise of breath. A breath that landed right against his neck.

Apparently, there was a semicure for blistering pain after all, and it was Claire's breathing. Of course, it helped that her mouth was now plenty close to his. Close enough to kiss...if he'd been in any state to kiss her, that was.

He wasn't.

Did that make the desire go away? *Nope.* Which meant this situation with Claire could turn out to be trouble.

"Sugar," she said. And then she added other words. *Fudge* and *divinity.* Substitutions for the kid's sake probably. "I didn't know you were hurt this bad."

Even though every movement throbbed like hell, Riley jerked

his shirt back together and even managed to do some of the buttons. "We agreed not to talk about this, remember?"

"Yes." Claire cleared her throat. "I'm not sure I can hear it anyway. It hurts too much to think about it."

And he couldn't take that look on her face. Pity. Something he divinity sure didn't want.

"I'm all right," he told Ethan. Riley forced a smile that possibly looked even creepier than his earlier one since the muscles in his face were stretched tight. "My shoulder just needed some fixing like your car, but it's better now."

No way did the kid believe that. No way could Riley take the time to convince him, either. Not with the pain still shooting through him. Plus, he felt a flashback coming on, and he didn't want to have one of those in front of the kid.

Not in front of anybody.

He fished through his pocket, grabbed the new bottle of meds and downed a couple of them, somehow managing to get to his feet in the process. "Better go. These knock me out pretty fast."

Still pale, still looking at him as if he were the most pitiful creature on earth, Claire stood. "You want me to drive you home? It's nearly a half mile, and that's too far for you to walk—"

"No, thanks." Riley was already off the porch and into the yard when he heard the footsteps hurrying after him. Not Claire. But Ethan.

"Sor-wee," Ethan repeated and he held up one of the winged action figures. He took Riley's hand and put the toy in it. "For you."

Well, that was far more touching than Riley had ever thought it would be. The kid had a good heart. "It's okay. I'll be fine. You don't have to give me your toy."

But Riley was talking to himself because Ethan gave him a little wave and raced back toward the porch.

Riley felt a tug of a different kind. Something akin to the

same feelings he'd had with his kid sister when he'd helped raise her. A stupid tug in this case because Ethan wasn't his to raise.

Even if everyone in town thought he was.

Yeah, the whole situation with Claire was definitely trouble. So much so that even "Jingle Bells" might not work on this one.

CHAPTER FIVE

CLAIRE WISHED SHE could go back in time and stop her grandmother from purchasing a single roll of wallpaper. Or better yet, use that going-back-in-time superpower to stop wallpaper from ever being invented.

She held the steamer over the wallpaper, following the instructions to a tee. She waited, then scraped. Like the three million other steam, wait and scrape sequences, she didn't get a lot for her efforts. A postage-stamp-size piece of the paper came off. Only to reveal another layer of wallpaper beneath that one.

There was enough of it to create a quarantine facility to contain an outbreak of Ebola.

That's the way it had been for the bathroom and the kitchen. Layer after layer and layer. It was entirely possible there weren't even any walls left, that the entire house was held together with varying colors of floral wallpaper—each layer seemingly more butt ugly and more steam resistant than the last one.

Steam, keep steaming, scrape.

She got off another piece and tried to hold on to the reminder that one day this would all look as if it weren't stuck in the seventies. One day she'd be able to finish off the walls and the floors, and clear out the boxes so that she could see a sign she wanted to see.

For Sale.

Steam, keep steaming, scrape.

But on the scrape segment of this particular square inch of space, Claire heard something that had her climbing off the step ladder. It wasn't Ethan, either, because she could see him. He was sitting nearby creating a toy-car postapocalyptic scene on the floor.

Claire stepped around Ethan and looked out the screen portion of the front door. She'd left the actual front door open to catch the semicool breeze.

Uh-oh.

This was an unholy alliance if ever Claire had seen one.

Livvy, Daniel and Trisha.

All three of them had just exited their vehicles and were strolling toward the front porch. Claire was sure there was a joke in there somewhere: a blond Realtor, a brunette lawyer and a redheaded wedding planner all walk into a house...

But she couldn't quite come up with a punch line that would ease the sudden knot in her stomach.

Claire had known Livvy was on her way because Livvy had called to say she'd be there sometime that afternoon. But the other two certainly hadn't given her a heads-up. Too bad or she would have been somewhere else. *Anywhere* else.

If Claire had still been in third grade, such wimpiness would have earned her the chicken-dookie label, but it was a label she would proudly bear if she could have just delayed this meeting with Daniel.

Thankfully, Livvy had brought wine with her.

Claire put her steamer and scraper aside, opened the screen door and steeled herself for this visit.

Livvy went ahead of the other two, teetering up the limestone walk on sparkly silver heels so thin she could have picked her teeth with them. They matched her sparkly silver pants and top stretched around her latest boob job. Like with her husbands, Livvy liked to trade up in bra sizes every couple of years.

Claire wasn't sure exactly what Livvy's natural hair color was. That, too, had changed frequently over the past eight years since they'd bought Dearly Beloved together. Today it was *I Love Lucy* red with threads of acid green and was piled on top of her head like a volcanic eruption.

Somehow, Livvy made it all work.

"Vee!" Ethan squealed, and he rushed out to greet Livvy. She scooped him up, spun him around and made piggy snorting sounds while she kissed his neck.

Ethan laughed like a loon, and Claire lapsed into a smile despite that abdominal knot. Yes, Livvy always made it work not just with her son and hair but also with everything else. Livvy created magic.

"I've got something for my favorite boy," Livvy announced. She set him back down on the porch and plucked a silver toy car from her cleavage.

Another squeal from Ethan. Another laugh. God, he was such an easy kid to please. Despite the car stash he already had on the porch and in the house, he obviously thought this one was special.

"And this is for you, Claire. I stopped at the grocery store for this." Livvy held up a bottle of wine, the sweet, cheap stuff they both favored. She gathered Claire into her arms, smacked a kiss on her cheek and added in a whisper, "These two saw me in town, and I wasn't able to shake them."

Of course, Livvy didn't actually whisper it softly enough for Daniel and Trisha not to hear her. Which was probably Livvy's intent all along. She played a little passive-aggressive with people she didn't like.

"Claire," Trisha said, obviously taking Livvy's cue and hugged Claire, too. She looked as if she were about to head off to a photo shoot for Chanel number whatever. Smelled like it, too. "We came to check on you. To make sure you weren't wallowing in your grief."

"No wallowing," Claire assured her, sounding as genuine in her response as Trisha had been with the comment.

No genuineness whatsoever.

Daniel stayed back, waiting his turn, and when Trisha stepped away, he moved in for his own hug. "Good to see you, baby," he said in a real whisper, and he went in for a kiss. Not a cheek smacker like Livvy, but the real thing.

Claire felt her muscles go stiff. Felt that knot in her stomach tighten. *Nerves*, she assured herself. *Not repulsion.*

Daniel stepped back, taking in everything with a sweeping glance. Her shorts and top. Bare feet. Ethan's car menagerie. The boxes she'd been sorting through. The bits of wallpaper stuck to her hair and face.

"I thought you'd be further along in clearing out this stuff," he commented.

Daniel started a lot of sentences with those three words, including the contraction—*I thought you'd*. Anything that came after that would almost certainly be a drawled dressing-down that he would then punctuate with a smile.

Right on cue, he smiled.

Livvy wasn't the only one who liked to play the passive-aggressive game.

"I'm making progress," she assured him though it didn't look like it at the moment.

This latest round of boxes was mostly paper—more calendars, magazines and old bills. Claire had put some rocks and terracotta pots with dead plants on top of the various piles to keep the wind from blowing anything away.

"Did you find the letter?" Livvy asked. She had plopped herself down on the porch with Ethan and the cars and didn't seem to notice the way her question snagged Trisha's and Daniel's attention.

"What letter?" the pair asked in unison.

Claire had to shrug. "It was just something Gran mentioned on a calendar. But she never gave me a letter." She waited to see if either of them knew anything about it, but Trisha had moved on to checking her phone and Daniel was more interested in observing her half-up, half-down ponytail.

"I thought you'd have called me by now," he said. The smile came just as the *now* was slipping from his mouth.

The mess on her porch actually came in handy. "I've been busy."

He made a sound that could have meant anything and picked up the folder beneath the pot holding a dead spider plant.

"How's Ethan doing with the Little Genius kits?" Since Daniel had been the one to recommend them, he clearly had an interest in them.

Claire made a so-so motion with her hand.

"Maybe I can give it a try. Sometimes boys respond better to a man's voice."

She would have liked to challenge that, but Daniel did do a lot of reading about child development. More than she did.

Daniel took the picture on top, van Gogh's *Starry Night*, and he held it up. "Ethan?" Of course, he had to repeat it because Ethan was bashing his new car into the old ones. By the time he'd said Ethan's name four times, Daniel's voice was more of a bark.

"Remember the *FUN!* part of this," Claire mumbled to herself.

Ethan finally realized he was being summoned and looked at the picture. "Money!" he yelled.

"He means Monet," Claire translated.

"No." Daniel drew that out a few syllables, probably not nearly as frustrated with Ethan as he was with not proving the point about that whole male-voice thing. "Try again."

"Riley!" Ethan shouted. And no Ri-wee, either. This was very, very clear.

Trisha and Daniel turned to her so fast that Claire heard necks pop. "Riley's been working with him on these?" Daniel's question sounded a lot like a jealous accusation.

Which it probably was.

"Of course not," Claire answered. "Riley's recovering from his injury. He doesn't have time to play with Ethan."

Daniel looked at her as if he expected her nose to start growing. But it wasn't a lie. It'd been three days since Riley's visit, and he certainly hadn't played with Ethan then. Riley had fixed Ethan's car and then left looking as if he was about to collapse from the pain.

"Give me that." Livvy craned her long, lithe body up enough to snatch the picture from Daniel. She didn't even have to say Ethan's name to get his attention. "Okay, see this." She held up the toy van.

Claire nearly confessed that she'd already tried that, but she decided to watch and see how this played out.

Livvy tugged off one of her shoes, wiggled her toes and put the van right next to all that wiggling.

"Van Gogh!" Ethan squealed.

Claire laughed.

But Daniel huffed. "How does that help him, giving him a clue like that?"

"Seriously? It helped because he got it right." Livvy put her shoe back on, plucked another car from her cleavage—a candy-apple-red Mustang—and gave it to Ethan. "Here's your prize for guessing right." That brought on more squeals of delight, more giggling.

More huffing from Daniel.

And a bitchy look from Trisha. "What else do you have in there?" Trisha tipped her head to Livvy's boobs.

"A picnic basket." Livvy stood and patted Trisha's arm, and Claire could almost feel the condescension coming. Livvy looked at Trisha's breasts, which were impressively sized but looked more like fried eggs when compared with Livvy's. "Maybe you can try growth cream on them or something. Then you'll have a place for a Lunchable or maybe just some Goldfish crackers."

Time for some interference since Trisha was no doubt gearing up her bitchy-response generator. Claire looped her arm around Livvy's waist. "Livvy and I will get some iced tea."

Trisha must have taken that as a call to arms because she followed them, leaving Daniel and Ethan on the porch.

"Are you falling for Riley again?" Trisha asked the moment they were out of Daniel's earshot.

Claire kept moving toward the kitchen. "That's an are-you-still-beating-your-wife question. Because you're assuming I've fallen for Riley before."

Claire had, but that wouldn't help her win this argument, and if she started losing too much ground, Livvy would step in and try to win the argument for her. It could turn into a catfight. Not an actual one, but there'd be some name-calling and shouting. Something that Claire didn't want Ethan to hear.

"Riley won't be as good with Ethan as Daniel," Trisha added as if it were gospel.

And, of course, if Riley was indeed with Ethan and her, then he wouldn't be with Trisha. That's really what this was all about, but Trisha skittered out of there before Claire could remind her of that. Trisha probably hurried so she could tell Daniel he needed to watch his back, that he had some competition.

Livvy unscrewed the wine bottle, dumped a generous portion into a glass measuring cup that she took from the drying rack in the sink. "You want a side of backbone to go with that slice of milquetoast?"

Claire didn't have to ask for clarification. Livvy was talking about Daniel's and Claire's reactions, or Claire's lack of reaction, to each other.

"I can't imagine you ever having sex with that guy," Livvy added.

Claire skipped a glass and drank right out of the bottle. "Daniel's really good-looking."

"So is that painting by van Gogh. Doesn't mean it'd be great in bed." Livvy downed half a glass of the wine in one long swig. "Was he ever a *great*?"

"Of course." Claire had more wine. Figured she'd regret what she was about to say but said it anyway. "If I grade it on a curve."

Livvy leaned in and lowered her voice to a real whisper. "Never grade a fuck on a curve, Claire. Never."

And with that screensaver-worthy advice, Livvy gave a satisfied nod.

Probably because Livvy knew she was right. Still, there were other things more important than sex. Like being with a man who hadn't had a hole blown in his shoulder. A man who would go back for another hole-blowing as soon as he could.

Gosh, that was a dismal thought. One that ate away at that safety net she'd spent too long building around herself.

Since it seemed as if Livvy was about to dole out more advice, Claire went on the offensive. "How are things with the albino? Did his pinkeye clear up?"

Livvy had more wine before she answered. "It didn't work out. He said my tits were hard as rocks."

"They are." Claire went to the fridge, took out the pitcher of iced tea, a juice box for Ethan and some glasses. "Hugging you comes with risks. I think you inverted one of my nipples once."

"Ha-ha. I'm not arguing with you, but he said my tits bruise his chest when I'm on top."

That wasn't an image Claire wanted in her head. Too late. It was already there. "So, you're not going to see him again?"

"Nope. I have another date next week. I'll call you afterwards and tell you all about it. Come on. Give them their tea so they'll get the hell out of here and we can have a good visit."

Livvy helped her with the glasses, and they made their way back to the porch. Trisha and Daniel were having a whispered conversation, but they broke away as if they'd just been caught picking their noses.

"Is there a problem?" Claire asked.

Daniel cleared his throat. "I thought you'd want me to correct Ethan. I told him not to keep crashing the cars." He paused, gently put his hand on her shoulder. "Because it might bring up old memories for you."

Maybe it was the rush of sugary wine to her head, but it took Claire a moment to make the connection. He was talking about the accident that'd killed Riley's parents. "Uh, I know the difference between a toy car crash and a real one."

And thankfully Ethan seemed to get that, too, because he kept playing his crashing game, which pretty much shot that theory about boys listening better to men.

Maybe that's what put Daniel in such a sour mood, but Claire was betting it had to do with the gossip floating around about Riley's visit to her place. And the other five-hundred-pound elephant on the porch—gossip about why Ethan looked so much like the man whose name her son loved to squeal. Whatever it was, it caused Daniel to slip his hand in Claire's and maneuver her to the other end of the porch. Away from the metaphorical elephant. Away from Livvy and Trisha, too.

Of course, since Livvy and Trisha weren't actually talking to each other, and the porch was only about ten feet wide, this likely wasn't going to be a private conversation.

Or one that she especially wanted to have.

"Look, Daniel, Riley will be going back soon, so there's really no need for us to discuss him." There. She'd gotten that order of backbone after all, and it felt good.

"I don't want to talk about Riley. I know you're not interested in him and haven't been since high school."

Oh, if only that were true.

Claire didn't mention that, though.

"Besides," Daniel went on, "if he was Ethan's father, he would have manned up and told me that he'd stabbed me in the back by sleeping with you. Riley's got a lot of faults, but lying isn't one of them."

And he stood there, clearly waiting. Claire didn't have to guess what he was waiting for. This was the part where he wanted her to tell him who Ethan's father was. One way or another, it came up every single time they were together. After a dozen or so interrogations in which she hadn't confessed, Daniel had let her know that he forgave her for being with another man. Since, after all, they'd been in an off phase at the time it'd happened.

Claire didn't confess today, either.

She wouldn't.

Because a confession would only lead to a second confession and an admission that Daniel was not going to want to hear.

"I thought you'd have made up your mind about us before now," Daniel went on. Of course, he smiled, but it was brief and strained. "I mean, you know how I feel about you and know I'd love Ethan as my own. I'm good for you. I know what you need."

God. Not another proposal, and she didn't have time to stop it. Daniel took a box from his pocket and dropped it into her hand.

A box just the right size for an engagement ring. And the right color, too, since it was Tiffany blue. She didn't have to look at it to know that it would be big and budget breaking.

"Don't say anything right now." Daniel made sure she didn't by kissing her again.

"Fudge," Livvy mumbled.

Trisha squealed.

Claire wanted to throw up. That knot in her stomach was now making its way to her throat, and it didn't ease up even when Daniel broke the kiss and stepped back.

"I thought you'd have made up your mind by now," Daniel repeated, "but since you haven't, I'm giving you one week."

Daniel waved to Trisha and Ethan and delivered the rest of his proposal from over his shoulder as he walked away. "Or else."

CHAPTER SIX

GET THE HELL **out now!**

The words roared through Riley's head, but he couldn't listen to that warning even if he knew gut deep that it was more than just a warning. The only thing that mattered right now was time.

He had one minute left, and those seconds were ticking off.

Riley couldn't see shit. The wall of sand had rolled in, swallowing him up and had erased everything within view at the rescue site.

Everything but the sounds.

He could hear the thump of the Pave Hawk's blades behind him. Could hear the cry for help just ahead.

His extractions.

An airman and a kid, injured from an IED. Riley knew why the airman had been there. He'd been doing his job, but Riley didn't want to guess about the kid. Didn't want to think about the kid, either.

Focus.

A quick in and out.

Forty-five seconds left.

Riley trudged forward. Fast but cautious steps toward those sounds. His crew was around him, nearby, and every now and then he caught a glimpse of one of them from the corner of his eye before the sand curtained them again.

His heartbeat was drumming in his ears. His pulse too fast like those seconds that were ticking away. He'd done rescues like this nearly a hundred times but never with that warning punching him in the gut.

Get the hell out now!

"I got a visual," one of the crew said. Not a shout but loud enough for Riley and the others to hear. "McCord, your one o'clock."

Riley automatically adjusted, moving slightly to the right, and he spotted the extractions. Both down. Both injured. He knew after just a glimpse that the airman wouldn't make it, not with the blood spurting from his femoral like that. The kid was fifty-fifty.

Sixty-forty if Riley went in even faster and got him back to the Pave Hawk in under thirty seconds.

So that's what he did.

Riley pushed forward, his boots bogging down in the sand, and made it to the kid. He scooped him up, knowing someone would be right behind him to take the airman. Riley focused on the kid. He would save him and get the rest of his crew and the airman back on the Pave Hawk.

But that didn't happen.

The sounds stopped. Everything stopped. Like that split second of watching and waiting for a pin to drop onto a tile floor.

This was no pin, though.

The pressure exploded in his head. And the pain came, cutting off the air to his lungs. Strangling him. Riley couldn't move, couldn't run, but he could feel the blood, all warm and thick. His blood.

Get the hell out now!

"Riley?"

The sound of someone calling out his name gave him a jolt. Riley's eyes flew open, but since the nightmare was still with him, it took him a moment to realize this wasn't one of his extractions.

It was Claire.

And she was leaning over him, her mouth so close to his that he nearly kissed her. She was a welcome sight, all right. A lot more welcome than the flashbacks. But she was sporting a very concerned look on her face.

"You were dreaming," she said.

Yeah, that was a good word for it. Better than the brain-fuck label that Riley had slapped on it. Because it hadn't been just a dream. All of that, and more, had happened in the blink of an eye.

Since Claire's mouth and therefore that kiss was still within striking range, he waited until she backed away a little before Riley sat up in the porch swing. He only grunted once. Only felt the blinding pain twice.

She looked amazing. Since this was Claire, looking amazing was a given. Her face was a little shiny with sweat. Her top, a little clingy—also from the sweat. But she didn't smell like sweat. She smelled like roses. Except he soon realized that smell wasn't coming from her. She really did have some roses in her hand.

"I wouldn't have woken you up," Claire added, "but you were talking and thrashing around. I was afraid you'd hurt yourself. Do you need your pain meds?"

He did, and needed them badly, but Riley shook his head. "I'm off the oxy, and the new stuff makes me drowsy."

Which explained why he'd fallen asleep in his uniform in the porch swing. It was spring, but in Texas that meant it was already hotter than hell. Of course, that pretty much described three and a half of their four seasons.

Riley put his feet on the porch but didn't risk standing just yet. The porch was swirling beneath him. However, there was maybe something he could do to get that look of pity off Claire's face.

"I nearly kissed you," he admitted.

As expected, the pity vanished, and she looked about as

shocked as if he really had kissed her. "When? Wait, that wasn't part of the dream, was it?"

Uh, no. "I nearly kissed you just now when you were leaning over me."

Since he had never kissed her, this would have been the time when most women would have asked why he'd nearly done that. Or at least continued on the subject a bit until she got some more info. Claire didn't. She dropped back another step.

"What happened to the kid?" she asked. She hooked her fingers around the neck strap that was holding a camera. "The kid in the nightmare you were having?"

Ah, hell. How much had he said? Apparently, too damn much. Since that was the last thing he wanted to discuss with her, with anyone, Riley went on the offensive.

"I heard about Daniel's proposal. Including the *or else.*" He wouldn't give her his opinion about that.

She nodded. "Trisha blabbed." That was it. Her complete response on the matter before Claire suddenly got very interested in looking at her fingernails.

"Do you think we can find a subject that we both will actually discuss?" he asked. "If not, this is going to be a very short visit." And while he was at it, Riley added something else that was sure to get her mind off what he had said or hadn't said while napping. "Why are you visiting anyway? Did you bring me flowers?"

His tone alone should have put her off since it wasn't very welcoming, but Claire didn't huff or look insulted. She sank down on the seat next to him. "I'm just taking a break from stripping wallpaper and sorting boxes. And, no, the roses are for your mother's grave. They're the first batch from Gran's garden, and I thought your mom would like them."

That put an instant lump in his throat. He wasn't usually so lump prone when it came to the mention of his mother, but those flashbacks had left him raw, as if some of his skin had been stripped away. It made it too easy for the feelings to get in.

"Mom would like them," Riley settled for saying.

Claire nodded, smiled, put the flowers on the railing. "I'll swing by the cemetery on the way home, but Ethan wanted to play with Crazy Dog first. I brought my camera so I could get some pictures. He's growing up so fast that I'm trying to hang on to the minutes by making sure I get at least one new picture of him every week."

Since Riley hadn't heard a peep from Ethan, he looked at the yellow Lab's usual resting spot, and as predicted Crazy Dog was there, sleeping, and Ethan was tugging on his ears, trying to get the dog to move.

Good luck with that.

"Crazy Dog's not so crazy anymore," Riley remarked. And he hadn't been for the past six years or so.

But before that, he'd been worthy of the name that Lucky had given him. Well, actually the name had been Bat-Shit Crazy Dog, but that hadn't gone over well with Della and Stella. Neither had Ol' Yeller—Riley's suggestion. Logan hadn't offered any name options, but he had been the one to call a dog obedience instructor.

For the most part, Crazy Dog slept under that particular tree during the day, though there was a doggy door for the house so he could come and go as he pleased. The only time he went inside was to eat and do more sleeping. The vet had assured them that the dog wasn't sick; all the tests had been done to rule that out. Apparently, Crazy Dog was more Lazy Dog now.

"You're wearing your uniform," Claire commented.

Riley hadn't forgotten he had it on, of course, but he glanced down at it. "I was at the base getting physical therapy and a checkup first thing this morning. I'm healing," he added so that she wouldn't ask.

Nor would he explain that wearing the uniform to the appointment hadn't been necessary. Riley just felt better when he had it on. Not like the ordinary Riley with the head-exploding pain. In the uniform he was Captain McCord, CRO. People saluted him, called him sir and there was the awe factor of being special ops.

Since his comments about the dog and his physical therapy hadn't generated any safe conversation, Riley went back to an unsafe subject. "What are you going to do about Daniel's proposal?"

Her lips tightened as if she might tell him it was none of his business, but it was a sigh rather than a huff that left her mouth—which he was still thinking about kissing.

"I don't know." She leaned back in the swing, sighed again.

All right, so maybe she had come here to talk this over. It made more sense than Ethan playing with Crazy Dog since there was zero playing going on.

"What would you do?" she asked.

"I wouldn't marry him, but then I'm straight." He flashed her a smile that had her rolling her eyes. Riley waited until the eye roll was done before he continued. And here was the six-million-dollar question. "Do you love him?"

"Some." She screwed up her face and shook her head. "I know, I know. Livvy said I shouldn't grade love…or sex on a curve."

Livvy was obviously a font of wisdom. "You shouldn't." And, no, that didn't have anything to do with Daniel himself. Or Claire. "Why would you have to grade sex on a curve anyway?"

"Clearly, you've never had mediocre sex. But then you're a guy. Lucky told me once that for guys, no sex is actually bad. Some times are just better than others."

Riley was sure he screwed up his face, too. "When the hell did my brother tell you that?"

"Oh, I guess I was about nineteen or so and home from college. We ran into each other at Calhoun's Pub." She dismissed it with the flip of her hand.

Riley sure as heck didn't dismiss it, and the next time he saw his brother, he'd rip off Lucky's ears—maybe his dick, too.

Sheez. Was nothing sacred with Lucky? Because his brother

had obviously been hitting on Claire if he'd broached the subject of sex with her. Of course, Lucky hit on every woman within breathing range, but even Lucky should have had enough brain cells to know that Claire was off-limits.

And Riley really didn't want to think about why Lucky would know that. He just would.

Claire thankfully missed his little mental implosion because she groaned, scrubbed her hand over her face. "What am I going to do, Riley? There are only three days left on Daniel's *or else* deadline."

Shoot, he might rip off Daniel's dick, too. "I should probably stay quiet on the subject, but why would you let him give you an ultimatum like that, especially when you only love him *some*?"

Claire's attention drifted to Ethan who was now using Crazy Dog's back as a track for two toy cars.

Oh.

Claire's drifted attention gave Riley a reminder that he'd been trying to forget. That Daniel was almost certainly Ethan's father.

Well, shit.

That explained Daniel's ultimatum. If Ethan was Riley's kid, he would have wanted to raise him, too. He was an all right kid. Creative, too, since he used the folds on Crazy Dog's neck to hide one of the cars, and Ethan was doing it gently enough so that Riley knew the boy cared.

"I've been with Daniel a long time," she finally said. "It feels a little like an investment, you know?"

Riley didn't have a clue, and that only riled him even more, but he nodded anyway.

"Sometimes, I just think…" She paused. "Well, sometimes I wonder if my slogan is just a pile of sugar."

All right, he really, really didn't have a clue. "Huh?"

"I say sugar instead of shit because I don't want Ethan to curse," she clarified in a whisper. "And I meant my sugary slogan—Making Fantasies Come True. That's the slogan Livvy and I picked for our business, but…"

"Daniel's not doing it for you, fantasy-wise?" Oh, he so should have given that some thought before it came out of his mouth. Too bad the new pain meds hadn't made him comatose instead of just dizzy and drowsy.

A teeny-tiny smile crossed her lips and then vanished. "Do you really want to talk about me and Daniel having sex?"

Yeah, right after he slid down a mile-long stretch of razor blades. Riley hoped his silence, and possibly his wincing, let her know that it was not something on the discussion table.

"Are you sleeping better?" she asked.

Not exactly a safe subject, but they were running out of topics here. "Some."

And that led him to something else he'd been thinking about lately. He tipped his head to the flowers she'd brought. "How did you deal with the memories of what happened to my mom and dad?"

Claire gave him a long look. "I don't have a lot of memories. It's more like little bits and pieces, you know?"

This time, he did know, but bits and pieces could still come together for an ugly picture.

"And the bits and pieces aren't all of the accident itself. Your father told a joke," Claire went on. "Your mother laughed. Then the crash happened."

He knew all of that. It'd been a knock-knock joke.

His dad: Knock knock.

His mom: Who's there?

Dad: Boo

Mom: Boo who?

Dad: Ah, don't cry, honey.

Riley hadn't been there, but Claire had filled him in over the years. Those last moments of their lives were as clear in his head as if he had witnessed every second of it. *Heck*. He wished he had. Then he could have had the chance to say goodbye.

He looked at her, hoping that her eyes weren't burning like his. Because if Claire lost it, Riley would have to pull her into his arms. It wasn't a good time for that to happen. Not with all this nervous energy zinging between them.

But no tears. She smiled when she glanced at the roses.

"You have nightmares about it?" he asked her.

She drew in a long breath. "Not very often. Why are you asking? Are you having a lot of nightmares? Is that what was happening when I woke you?" Thankfully, she didn't wait for him to answer. Or for him to flub around with an explanation. "Because what helped me was a picture of you."

Riley had to go back through that to make sure he'd heard her right. "Me?"

She nodded. "You just seemed to be holding things together a lot better than I was. So when I'd have bad dreams and sad thoughts, I'd look at your picture in the yearbook—the one with you in your football uniform—and I'd remind myself that if you could do it, then so could I."

He definitely hadn't been holding it together. But Logan had. He'd swooped in and taken care of all the funeral arrangements, the business stuff. Even Anna. Riley had put on a front, but it was just that—a front. It'd been good practice, though, for the front he was putting on now.

"I still look at your picture sometimes," she went on. "Because every now and then the dreams come back."

"And looking at my picture actually helps?" Riley wished he hadn't sounded so astonished, but he was.

"Sure. Well, for the nightmares but not for thunderstorms. You don't work for me in thunderstorms."

Yeah, Claire had a thing about storms, spiders and zombie movies. But Riley hadn't had a clue she'd even attempted to use his picture or anything about him to help her get through it.

"Riley!" Ethan called out. The kid had obviously noticed he was awake and sounded excited to see him. Riley was mildly surprised that he was excited to see Ethan, too.

Ethan had given up on his Crazy Dog playdate, and he barreled up the steps toward them. But he didn't just come onto the porch. He crawled into the porch swing, wriggling his pint-size body in between Claire and him. He had a toy car in each hand. Several were crammed in his pockets, and the ones in his left pocket dug into the outside of Riley's thigh. Since that was his sore leg, the pain nudged Riley a bit, but he didn't move. Riley wanted to hang on to this closeness for a little while.

"Angel," Ethan said, and he pointed to the Combat Rescue Officer badge on Riley's uniform. The kid climbed into Riley's lap to get a better look at it.

"No." Claire immediately reached for her son, probably because she thought it would hurt Riley.

And it did. More than just a nudge this time, but Riley stopped her from whisking him up. Instead, Riley fished out his phone and maneuvered Claire closer so that her head was right against Ethan's.

"Smile. It's a picture for Anna," he said, snapping the shot. "She wanted to see how big Ethan's getting."

That was such a huge lie that Riley thought it might spur even Crazy Dog to action. Claire gave him that look, the one that let him know that she knew he was lying, but the look also told him that she really wasn't sure she wanted to know what was simmering beneath the lie.

Good.

Because Riley turned the phone and snapped a picture of just her. She was caught with her mouth slightly puckered, as if she was waiting for that kiss he'd been considering.

Hell. He just might have a cure for those flashbacks after all.

CHAPTER SEVEN

THE MIGRAINE WAS chasing Logan McCord, and it was winning.

The blind spots were already there. The little swirly bright dots, too. He figured he had less than a half hour before he would have to pretend he was so exhausted that he needed a morning nap.

At least Della and Stella wouldn't be around to try to mother him because they wouldn't be back until tomorrow from their forced vacation. Riley wouldn't be there, either, since he was at physical therapy. Lucky was still off doing things that Logan didn't want to think about.

But the reporter and photographer were a different story.

The reporter, Andrea-something, came up the steps behind him, her heels sounding like a persistent woodpecker. She was persistent about getting this story, too, and if Logan hadn't wanted this article to promote his new business venture, he would have sent her and those heels clacking.

The photographer, whose name Logan didn't bother to catch, lagged along behind her while he adjusted his camera. Occasionally, the photographer scratched his balls, too. Logan wasn't opposed to ball scratching, but even that sound was amplified so it seemed as if the guy was scratching a hundred chalkboards.

"We'll just need a few more pictures," Andrea said in between the clacking-heel sounds.

She was a reporter for one of the San Antonio newspapers, and even though she'd already interviewed Logan at the office, she had insisted on snapping a few pictures here at the ranch.

"One picture," Logan said. He used the tone that he knew would set her teeth on edge. He knew all the tricks for doing that because people with their teeth on edge didn't stay in his face pestering him.

Trying to make as little noise as possible so he could buy himself some time with the migraine, Logan opened the front door.

And the first thing he saw was the naked woman.

"Ta-da!" she said, and then a split second later she shrieked louder than a horde of banshees with bullhorns.

Trisha.

Even with the blind spots and aura speckles, Logan could make out her face. Though he had to admit her face wasn't the first thing that'd caught his attention. It was her huge breasts and the tiny patch of shiny red fabric that he supposed was meant to be panties. An eye patch would have more fabric than that little thing.

Trisha shrieked again, and she scurried to the sofa to grab a dress that she held up in front of her like a shield. A piss-poor shield because it didn't cover her left boob or that panty swatch.

The photographer snapped a few pictures of her.

Logan shot him a look to let him know that he was going to delete each one he'd just taken. A hard look wasn't that difficult to manage since Trisha's shrieks had caused the migraine to close in on him.

"Logan, what are you doing here?" Trisha asked.

"That was the question I planned to ask you."

"I was waiting for Riley," she said as if that explained everything.

And maybe it did.

Logan hadn't heard any rumors about Riley and Trisha getting back together, but maybe his little brother had found a new way to relieve pain.

Logan closed the door, leaving the reporter and the ball-scratcher on the porch. "Riley's at PT in San Antonio," he told Trisha.

"I know." She huffed, blew at a strand of her hair that'd fallen onto her cheek. "I called one of the ranch hands, and he said Riley should be back by now. I, uh, wanted to surprise him. Please, Logan," she repeated. "You can't tell anyone about this."

He wouldn't, but the photographer would. Probably the reporter, too. By noon it would be all over town, possibly posted on the internet, and the gossips would add that Logan had stepped behind closed doors with her. That meant Logan needed to call his girlfriend, Helene Langford, and let her know what had happened. Since Helene and he had been together for years, she would believe he hadn't cheated on her with Trisha, but he didn't want Helene blindsided by the bullshit.

Trisha started to wiggle into the dress. It was a testament to how much pain he was in that he hoped she would hurry.

"What are you doing here anyway?" Trisha asked. "You were supposed to be on a two-week business trip and shouldn't be back for three more days."

"I wrapped up things early—" He would have continued his own questions if Trisha hadn't interrupted.

"But you rarely stay here anymore. I didn't figure you'd be coming home."

So the gossips had picked up on that, too. And it wasn't just gossip. Logan had indeed converted the third floor of his office building to a loft apartment, and with the hours he worked, it was easier just to sleep there. Besides, it wasn't as if he had family here now that Anna had moved off to Florida.

But Logan had no intentions of getting into that with Trisha.

"Where's your car?" he asked, hoping he didn't have to drive her anywhere.

She hitched her thumb toward the back. "I parked behind the house. I was going for an element of surprise."

"Element accomplished."

Logan went to the door to tell the reporter and photographer to take a hike, but it wasn't only them on the other side. It was Riley, too. And he practically punched Logan in the gut because he was reaching for the doorknob.

"Go," Logan growled to the news crew. He glared at the photographer. "And if those photos or anything else about this situation show up anywhere, you'll deal with me."

Logan didn't wait for their reaction. The blind spots were getting even spottier. From the looks of it, Riley wasn't faring much better in the pain department.

Riley stepped in right before Logan shut the door, and his brother volleyed glances between Trisha and him. It didn't help that the front of Trisha's dress was still hiked up, and he could see that sad excuse for panties.

"Trisha wanted to surprise you," Logan summarized. Some people probably would have just let this all play out, but he wanted to hurry things along. "I'll take a nap while you two have fun."

"Thank you," Trisha said at the exact moment Riley said, "I can't. I need to talk to you, Logan," Riley added.

Shit on a stick. That didn't seem like an end to a conversation but rather the beginning of one Logan didn't want to have.

Riley turned to Trisha. "I haven't seen Logan in months. We need to get some family things settled."

Translation: Riley didn't want what Trisha was offering behind those red panties.

"Plus, I'm in pain. It was a rough session of PT today." Riley rotated his shoulder and winced. Probably not fake, either, like that family-things comment.

Riley never wanted to discuss family things.

"I'll call you," Riley told Trisha when she didn't budge.

Maybe the last bit of her dignity kicked in because the woman finally scurried to gather the rest of her things. Of course, she had on woodpecker heels, too, and they hammered against the hardwood floor. Trisha turned, heading toward the back of the house, but then she stopped.

"I just thought…" she said to Riley. "Well, I just thought I could cheer you up. I mean, I thought you might be feeling a little blue what with Claire marrying Daniel and all."

Translation: pity sex.

And judging from the way Riley's expression soured, he might just be in need of pity something. That wasn't the expression of a man who'd just learned a *friend* was getting married. No. But then, Riley had always had a thing for Claire.

"Call me," Trisha reminded Riley. She dropped a kiss on his cheek. Paused. As if waiting for Riley to do something more than make it a cheek kiss. When he didn't, Trisha finally left.

"Sorry about that," Riley mumbled. He was wearing his uniform, and with the exception of that weary, pained expression, he looked every bit the part of a military superstar. Which from all accounts, he was.

Logan considered repeating that part about needing a nap, but instead he found himself sinking down on the chair across from Riley. "Want to talk about it?"

Riley dropped the back of his head against the sofa and let out a long breath. "Which part—Trisha or the PT?"

"Both. Or neither," Logan amended. "Or you can talk— *briefly*—about Claire and Daniel."

Riley lifted his head and made eye contact with him, and for a moment Logan thought Riley would question that *briefly* part. To the best of his knowledge, Riley didn't know about the migraines, and Logan wanted to keep it that way. Besides, his little brother no doubt had him beat a thousandfold in the pain department.

"Claire hasn't decided if she's marrying Daniel, but he did propose again, and he gave her a week to decide. There's only one day left on his deadline. Trisha wants a repeat of what we did in high school. The PT's going nowhere."

Logan dismissed the first two topics, went with the last one. "How much time do you have left on your medical leave?"

"A month, maybe less." He aimed his eyes at the ceiling, avoiding eye contact. "If I can't pass a physical, I might be given a medical discharge."

Riley said it in the same tone as someone would admit they were dying from cancer or some other horrible disease. But he wasn't dying. He just wouldn't be able to lead the life he wanted more than being near family.

"Are you still having flashbacks?" Logan asked.

That got his eyes away from the ceiling, and Logan earned a glare for his question. "Who said I was having them in the first place? Hell. Claire told you?"

"No. One of the ranch hands heard you when you were sleeping on the back porch, but if Claire knows, at least you're talking to someone about it."

"I'm not talking to her about it. Not talking to you about it, either."

Logan decided it was a good time to listen. Besides, it was easier to deal with the spots if he didn't have the sound of his own voice echoing in his head.

"I can't get kicked out of the Air Force," Riley snarled. He motioned toward his uniform. "This isn't just what I do. It's who I am. I help people. I rescue them. I save them from dying. Most of the time," he added.

Logan nodded. This wasn't anything new. "Man-rule number two—don't be ordinary."

"It's man-rule number one," Riley snapped.

Right. The headache must have fuzzed his memory up a little. As often as Logan had heard those rules, he should have remembered. "I don't need to know the number of the rule to know what it means, Riley. You left home because you wanted something more than this place could offer."

Logan's strong suit wasn't being warm and fuzzy, and clearly he missed the boat this time, too.

"You stayed because you chose to stay," Riley reminded him.

Ah, hell. That was not the thing to say right now. It wasn't the first time it'd come up, and sometimes Logan just walked away from it.

Not today, though.

"I stayed to make sure the business that Dad started didn't go under," he reminded Riley. "I'm the one who made it what it is today. The one who went to parent–teacher meetings for Anna—"

"You stepped up to do that."

"Yeah. But Lucky and you could have stepped up, too. You didn't, and neither did he. When you say you don't want to be here because it's ordinary, just remember you're calling my life and everything that I've worked for ordinary, too."

Logan stood and said the rest of what he wanted to say while he was walking away. "I need that nap now."

The migraine, and this conversation, had caught up with him and was already kicking him in the nuts.

CLAIRE OPENED HER back door to take out the trash, and that's when she saw it. A creature was just sitting there on the steps. It was in the shape of a ball, with gray fur sticking out in every direction.

And it had one eye.

She shrieked, scrambled away from it, banging her hip against the kitchen counter, but all the commotion didn't stop it from coming closer. It just ambled in the house as if she'd given it an invitation.

"Whoa," Ethan said. He scooted down from his booster seat where he was eating his lunch. "Cat." Or rather "tat."

Claire had already picked up the broom to try to shoo it out, but she gave it another look. Maybe it was a cat. It squalled, a sound that a cat might make, so maybe Ethan was right.

"Don't get too close, Ethan," she warned her son. If she could catch it, she'd take it into the vet to make sure he or she was okay and wasn't the survivor of some radiation experiments.

But Ethan didn't listen. He immediately offered the critter a bite of his PB&J sandwich. There was some sniffing involved on both the cat's and Ethan's parts before the animal took a bite. Clearly, it was starving if it would go after that.

With the broom still in her hand and while keeping an eye on their visitor, Claire poured some milk in a saucer, sloshing it all over her and the floor before she managed to put it in front of the animal. It took a lap but went back for another taste of the PB&J.

"Whoa," Ethan said again, giggling.

Well, Whoa was certainly a good name for it, but she hoped this wasn't an omen. A bad one. Of course, she'd been looking for omens and signs all day since the deadline for Daniel's marriage proposal was only hours away.

"Don't get too attached," she told Ethan. "We can't keep it."

Claire used the PB&J and the saucer of milk to lure the cat back out onto the porch, and shut the screen door before it could get back in. Ethan sat down on the floor to watch, and she saw something in his eyes that she instantly recognized.

Love.

Apparently, pet fever ran in the family, and while this was no cute fur ball, Ethan didn't seem to mind. Too bad she couldn't explain that it was a stray and this might be the one and only time they saw him.

She gathered up the stuff to make Ethan another sandwich, but she heard the *NSYNC ringtone, and it sent her heart banging against her chest. *Sheez.* She braced herself for the conversation she was going to need to have with Daniel, but she saw a name on the screen that she hadn't expected to see.

Logan.

She tried to hit the button so fast that she nearly dropped her phone. "Is everything okay?" she asked.

What she really wanted to know—was Riley okay? Logan

must not have picked up on that subtext, but judging from the sound he made, he was a little taken aback by her frantic tone.

"I've got a big favor to ask you," he said. "I have to take another business trip, and I need you to check on Riley for me."

No frantic tone for him. It was cool and terse, which pretty much described the man himself. Of course, like the rest of the McCord men, he was hot and gorgeous. Alarmingly handsome. So hot that Claire wasn't immune to getting a little tongue-tied around him. She suspected that Logan used those good looks to coerce women, like her, into doing favors, like this, for him.

"But you just got back from a business trip yesterday," she said, stalling so she could come up with a good answer.

"Yeah, but something came up, and I need to leave right now. Will you do it? Will you make sure Riley's okay?" he pressed. "Now?"

"Uh, you're sure he wants me to check on him? It's all over town that he's not happy about women visiting him."

"It's all over town about Trisha," he corrected. "And you're right. He's not happy about that, but I want you to see to him anyway. He had a nightmare last night. Loud enough to wake me, and when I went in to see if he was okay, he was looking at a picture on his phone. A picture of you. He said it steadied his nerves."

So, he hadn't sent the photo to Anna after all. Claire had known something was up with that.

"Did it? Steady Riley's nerves, I mean?" she asked.

"I'm not sure. He wasn't fully awake, and he said something about it maybe not working in thunderstorms."

She smiled. Then undid that smile. "Look, Logan. I'm in a weird place right now—"

"Because of Daniel's proposal. Your *or else* answer is due today. And, yes, that's all over town, too. But Daniel shouldn't mind if you visit a friend."

Wanna bet? Daniel was the green-eyed monster when it came to Riley. And for no good reason. Riley had kept his hands off her during the entire time he'd been back in Spring Hill. The entire time before that, too.

"You'll do this for me, right?" Logan asked.

Oh, well. At least Logan hadn't tried to play the daddy card—he hadn't insinuated that since Riley might or might not be Ethan's father that the paternity obligated her in some way to check on him.

And give him a picture to scare off nightmares.

"Yes, I'll check on him." She was in the middle of saying goodbye when Logan rattled off a thanks and hung up.

Claire stared at the phone a moment, wondering if she should call him back and say no. Or at least attempt to. Riley was a temptation she didn't need right now. However, her ringtone went off again before she could finish the debate she was having with herself. And this time it wasn't Logan.

It was Daniel.

She got another slam of her heart and made a quick check of the time. Even though she still had a couple of hours left on Daniel's proposal-ultimatum, this was a pee-or-get-off-the-pot kind of moment.

*NSYNC just kept on singing "This I Promise You."

The *pee* was a natural thing, she reminded herself. Marriage to a longtime partner was what women her age did all the time. And getting off the pot could mean there were zero chances of getting a shot at making those fantasies come true.

More *NSYNC. More debate. Until the singing finally stopped, and the call went to voice mail. She'd have to give Daniel an answer, of course.

First, though, she needed to prove to herself that Riley wasn't a reason for her to get off the pot.

CHAPTER EIGHT

SHE WAS ONLY doing what Logan had asked. At least that's what Claire kept telling herself on the walk over to the McCord Ranch. Riley had apparently had another nightmare, one so serious that it'd troubled Logan. And serious enough for him to ask her to check on him.

What Logan hadn't asked her to do was kiss Riley.

But that's exactly what she intended to do.

Kiss him. Right on the mouth.

Claire kept going over how her response to Daniel's proposal would play out. If she said yes, she might regret it down the road. And the reason for that regret was something that was hard for her to admit.

She might not have gotten Riley out of her system.

The best way to determine that was to kiss him. If she felt something, then she'd tell Daniel no, that she couldn't marry him when she might have feelings for another man. Of course, that other man might not have feelings for her, and even if Riley did, it didn't mean they would ever have a future together. Still, she needed to test this. For her own sake.

She huffed. *All right*. Maybe she just wanted to kiss him, and it didn't have diddly piddly to do with the proposal. She just wanted to know if there was something more to feel than only the lukewarm heat she did with Daniel.

God, she hoped so.

Ten minutes into the walk, and Claire was sorry she hadn't driven over instead. The April sun was bearing down on her, and by the time she made it to the ranch, she was hot and itchy. That didn't go away when she spotted Riley.

Her mouth went dry.

She hadn't expected to see him out of the house or off the porch, but there he was—in a corral with two other men and some horses. He wasn't wearing his uniform today but was instead dressed in jeans and a button-up, and the sun was hitting him just right to spotlight that face. That hair.

Yes, he was still hot.

And, yes, she was going to kiss him.

"Horses," Ethan squealed.

Riley looked up, smiled when he saw them and started toward them. He looked like his usual self. No limp, no signs of pain. Not until he got closer, that was.

He opened the corral gate, his grip on the metal latch turning his fingers white. Now that she could see him better, he looked ready to pitch face-first onto the ground. Claire tried not to seem so obvious, but she hurried to him, slipped her arm around his waist.

"Thanks," he whispered. Riley glanced back at the ranch hands, thanked them.

Ah. She got it then. Riley didn't want them to know he was in pain. Of course, he didn't like anyone knowing that, but it would probably break one of his man-rules if he showed any signs of weakness to the hands.

"Horses!" Ethan squealed again.

Riley nodded, eked out a smile. "Cutting horses. Logan's new project," he added to Claire. "He arranged to have them delivered today, and he needed me to sign for them. Logan's sneaky like that. He leaves for a trip, knowing I'll have to get involved."

Yes, Logan was sneaky. After all, here she was.

"Let me guess," Riley continued. "Logan asked you to check on me."

"He did," she readily admitted. "But I came here to…"

Heck, she just went for it. Claire came up on her toes to plant one on his mouth. At that exact moment, though, the stars aligned against her. Riley grimaced, turned his head, and her lips landed on his cheek instead.

He froze. Turned. Looked down at her. "Was that meant to be a real kiss or was it an accident?" he asked.

Good question. Claire nearly wimped out, but hey, this was her test, her rules. "Real," she admitted.

Riley kept staring at her. And staring. Specifically, he looked at her mouth, and the muscles in his jaw stirred like crazy. Then, his gaze drifted to Ethan—who was also staring at them.

"Tell you what," Riley said, his voice all low and doused with eighty-three gallons of testosterone. "We'll make it real but not in front of the kid. And after you've turned down Daniel's proposal."

"Man-rule?" she grumbled under what little breath she had left. Being near all that testosterone had tightened her throat and chest along with making her nether regions do some whining and begging.

"Man-rule number three," Riley confirmed. "Don't take anything that's not mine."

So, there it was. Her entire debate rolled up into one ball. Or rather two—the testosterone thing was really stuck in her head. She could toss away a fifteen-year relationship that came with a marriage proposal, or she could kiss Riley. Even though that kiss might not lead to anything.

Claire was still leaning toward the kiss.

She didn't spell that out to Riley, though. Didn't have to. His sly little smile told her that he knew what she knew—that the kiss was probably going to happen even if it meant it could be the start of a good heart crushing for her.

"Questions?" he asked.

Yes, but it was best to change the subject. To one that would make Riley as uncomfortable as the kissing topic had made her.

"I heard about Trisha's visit." She got them moving toward the porch. "Were her panties really as small as the gossips are saying?"

Claire whispered *panties* just in case Ethan was paying attention. But he wasn't. He spotted Crazy Dog asleep in his usual shady place and started running toward him.

"They were that small," Riley admitted. "By the way, I saw your pink panties. On the porch the other day when I was at your place."

Now it was her turn to freeze.

"I just thought you should know," he added.

"Uh, why?" Had he been thinking about her panties?

He shrugged with his good shoulder. "It's just something I remembered when the subject of panties came up." Riley looked at her, and the moment seemed to freeze, too.

Oh, those eyes. That mouth.

She wondered if she could call Daniel right now and nix the proposal, but that would seem sort of desperate. As if she couldn't wait to get her mouth on Riley.

Thankfully, she got another reminder of why that kiss couldn't happen now. Ethan squealed and clapped when Crazy Dog lifted his ears. It only lasted a few seconds, but the signs of life clearly pleased her son and caused Riley to chuckle.

"So, is motherhood everything you thought it would be?" he asked. He was hobbling a bit now as he made his way over toward Ethan and Crazy Dog.

"Almost."

He made a sound of pain, which he tried to muffle; then he followed it with a grunt of confusion. And, yes, she could tell the difference. "Almost?" he repeated.

Another hard question. "Well, you know how it is the first time you had sex? It hurt and was great all at the same time.

That's how motherhood is." Too bad she hadn't come up with a different analogy.

"I don't remember the hurt part."

Because he was a guy, he wouldn't. And since his first time— according to the gossips anyway—had been with Trisha, Claire hated the analogy even more. "I mean, when Ethan gets hurt, I hurt probably more than he does. His smile turns me to goo. But then he can frustrate me."

"Like with the cookie thievery and the Baby Genius packets. Gossip," he added when she looked surprised with his packet knowledge. "Why would you make him do those anyway?"

He stopped beneath the shade tree, several feet from Ethan.

"Don't you remember?" she prompted. "I was barely a B student in school. I want more for Ethan, and the Baby Genius kits aren't just supposed to help with IQ. They're supposed to help with discipline, potty training and such."

Riley's left eyebrow lifted. Skepticism. Something she couldn't argue with because she was skeptical, too.

"I'm working on the discipline," she continued. Unfortunately, she got a reminder of one of the big discipline concerns. Ethan stomped on a clump of grass for no reason. Then he hurried to another clump to stomp it, too. "Like that."

"Huh?"

"He likes to stomp on things," she clarified.

"Well, that's an easy fix, and you don't need a Baby Genius kit for it. Give him something suitable to stomp on. Like bubble wrap or some ants. Lucky used to pee on things. Anything. My dad gave him a peeing tree, and that all stopped."

Pee. That word sort of killed the mood.

Sort of.

Riley pointed out the tree that was only about ten feet from them. It was by far the smallest live oak in the yard, and she wondered if all that pee had somehow stunted its growth.

"Lucky potty trained me the same way," Riley added.

She thought of Lucky. Logan's equally hot twin brother with

the reputation for the quickest zipper in town. It didn't go with
the peeing image. "Lucky potty trained you?"

"There was some pressure involved. He was two years older
than me, four at the time, and he apparently didn't like tripping
over my little potty seat in the bathroom that we shared." He
looked at her. Looked at her mouth. "Maybe you should think
about making that call to Daniel?"

"Now?" she asked, sounding way too dreamy and schoolgirl-
ish. Actually, she sounded aroused. And was.

"Now," he verified. "Then we can test that kiss."

She nodded and reached for her phone but then stopped when
she heard the splashing sound. Except it wasn't a splash exactly.
It was Ethan, and he had hiked down his elastic waist jeans and
diaper and was peeing on the pee tree. He looked back at them,
grinning, and finished his first out-of-diaper toileting experience by hosing down the lawn.

Ethan giggled. Claire did, too. And somehow in all their
laughter and jumping around, she ended up in Riley's arms.
The giggling and jumping immediately stopped. Claire thought
maybe her heart had, too.

Yes, her answer to Daniel would definitely be no.

"Am I interrupting anything?" someone called out.

Claire looked in the back door and spotted a woman coming
onto the porch. She was tall, blonde and was wearing a sand-
colored outfit. But she didn't stay on the porch. With a wide
smile on her face and her attention fixed on Riley, she hurried
down the steps and made a beeline toward them.

"You know her?" Claire asked. She intended to whisper it,
but she obviously failed because the woman heard her.

"Of course Riley knows me," she answered.

Judging from the way he grunted, he did indeed know her.
And Claire got more proof of that.

The blonde made her way to Riley, practically elbowing
Claire out of the way, and hooked her arm around Riley's neck.

"I'm his girlfriend," the woman purred.

Girlfriend? Claire coughed, not a normal-sounding one, either. It sounded, well, guilty or something. Probably because it was. After all, she'd just been lusting after this woman's boyfriend.

Of course, Claire had heard the gossip about Riley being involved with someone, but since the gossip had come from Trisha, Claire had blown it off—figuring that it was something Riley had told Trisha to show he wasn't interested.

The woman smiled, all her attention on Riley. The pee on the tree held more interest for her than Claire did.

And the smiling, purring woman took things one step further. She pulled Riley to her for a kiss that should have been Claire's. At least it would have been if Claire had gotten a chance to make that call to Daniel.

Sheez.

It was French. Who the heck French-kissed in front of a toddler? Apparently this woman and Riley, that's who.

"Uh, I should be going," Claire said, trying to tear her gaze away from them.

Thankfully, Riley did some tearing, too. He took his mouth from the woman's, wiped his lips with the back of his hand. He also made some of those *uh* sounds of his own.

"Claire, this is—"

"Jodi Kingston," the woman interrupted. "Like I said, I'm Riley's girlfriend." She thrust out her hand for Claire to shake. Claire did. Then she winced at Jodi's lumberjack grip.

Show-off.

All right, that was too catty for someone she didn't even know because after all, Riley hadn't put a stop to that French kiss. He'd let it go on and on and on.

"And you are?" the woman asked. She slid her arm around Riley again.

"Claire Davidson." She didn't add a label like old friend. Old flame. Or the woman who'd nearly kissed your boyfriend. "And that's my son, Ethan."

Of course, Ethan had turned, facing them, and was doing a full monty since he hadn't mastered the art of pulling back up his diaper and jeans. Claire hurried over to fix that.

"Surprised to see me?" Jodi asked Riley.

Claire hadn't planned to eavesdrop, but Jodi didn't exactly whisper the question.

"Definitely surprised," Riley answered. Unlike Jodi, he was volleying his attention between Claire and her. "I thought you were in Kandahar."

"I was. I finished up early. Hitched a ride on a C-130 to get to Ramstein. Then bummed another ride with some Turkish guy on a motorcycle. He got me to the airport, and I caught the first plane out of there so I could come see you."

Riley nodded. Nodded again. "Jodi's a civilian combat photographer for a couple of the big newsmagazines," Riley explained to Claire. "We run into each other sometimes in the field."

Jodi laughed as if that were some sexy inside joke. Riley didn't crack a smile, though, probably because he felt uncomfortable. He hadn't exactly gotten caught with his hand in the cookie jar, but Claire didn't think it was her imagination that he'd been thinking about putting his hand in the jar.

Or maybe that was wishful thinking on her part.

What wasn't in dispute was that Jodi looked a lot like her. Same hair and eye color. Similar build. Of course, that's where the similarities ended. Jodi was obviously into adventure.

Like Riley.

Which explained why Jodi was his girlfriend.

"Kandahar was wild this time," Jodi went on. "Ended up about thirty miles from there and got some great shots of an extraction by some PJs after an IED shit-bath."

"Sugar," Riley corrected, hitching his thumb to Ethan. "Little pitcher, big ears."

"Oh, right. The kid." Jodi said *kid* in the same tone one might refer to a persistent toenail fungus. "You know me. Not one to watch my language."

Or her hands. They were all over Riley again, and that really was Claire's cue to get the heck out of there. She scooped up Ethan in her arms.

"Nice to meet you, Jodi." She nearly choked on the words, but it was a testament to her upbringing that Claire managed to make it sound genuine.

"Nice to meet you, too, Candy."

"Claire," she corrected, though she figured it wasn't actually necessary.

Either Jodi was playing fifth-grade games with her or she was so genuinely disinterested in Claire that she hadn't bothered to commit to memory anything except the first letter of her name.

"Enjoy your visit," Claire said to no one in particular. She turned, and, with Ethan on her hip, she walked away.

Riley didn't say a word to her. Not even a goodbye.

Claire got a really bad feeling in the pit of her stomach. The feeling she'd gotten when she had lost her lunch money or broken something she really liked. Except this feeling was a thousand times worse than that.

It was the feeling that she'd lost something important.

And that she was never going to get it back.

CHAPTER NINE

RILEY WATCHED CLAIRE walk away. Was it his imagination or were her shoulders slumping? Of course, it could be just the fact she was carrying Ethan so she could lightning-bolt out of there.

He couldn't blame her.

Jodi had done everything except pee on him to mark her territory. Which was strange because Riley hadn't been aware there was territory to mark. Things had always been so casual with Jodi. Or at least the sex had been. But that clearly wasn't a casual look she was giving him now.

"Let's go inside and catch up," Jodi said. She snuggled up to him and got him moving toward the back porch.

She snuggled in just the wrong place against his shoulder, though, and Riley wasn't able to bite back the groan in time. He didn't want to show his pain in front of anyone, including Jodi, but for once the pain worked in his favor. Jodi moved off him.

"Man, you really are hurt," she said as if it was some kind of revelation.

"I'm on medical leave," he reminded her.

"Yeah, but I didn't think you'd actually be in pain. I mean, I've never seen you in pain before." She laughed, nudged him. "Well, unless it was painful pleasure."

Right. "About that…"

But Riley didn't continue until they were inside the kitchen. Considering that the ranch hands had ratted to Logan about his porch-swing nightmares, Riley didn't want them blabbing about how he'd handled this impromptu visit from a fuck buddy.

And that's exactly what Jodi was.

"I'm not in any shape for painful pleasures," he finished.

Jodi looked as if he'd slapped her, and she dropped back a couple of feet. Her gaze lowered to his shoulder and then went back to the window, where Claire was still in sight. She and Ethan were making their way along the back road that led to her house. It would be a half-mile walk for her, and Riley nearly went after her to see if she wanted a ride. She wouldn't, though, of course. Not after what she'd just endured with Jodi.

"I see," Jodi said in that tone that only she and a third-grade teacher could have managed after listening to a student explain why she'd just caught them cheating.

Of course, Riley hadn't cheated. Not in body anyway. But for some moments there, he'd wished... Well, it didn't matter what he wished. The way Claire had hightailed it out of there, she was probably already on the phone, giving Daniel the answer he'd been waiting to hear for more than a decade.

Jodi cursed. And she didn't use *sugar* or any of those other goofy substitutions. "The kid is yours." It wasn't a question, either.

Now Riley cursed. "Why does everyone keep thinking that?"

"He's not?" Jodi inched back closer to him.

"No. I've never been with Claire like that."

Jodi gave him a bit of the stink eye. "You're sure? Because the kid looks just like you, Riley. Who is his father?"

Riley had to shake his head. "Claire won't say."

She coupled the stink eye with a *hmm*. "He's probably one of your brothers' kid then because..."

Jodi kept on talking, pointing out all the similar features between Ethan and him, but Riley had such a sudden roar in his head that he didn't exactly hear what she was saying. That's because he remembered the conversation that Claire had mentioned having. A conversation about sex.

With Lucky.

The sonofabitch.

Logan had enough boundaries and common sense to keep his hands off Claire, and Logan wouldn't have cheated on his longtime girlfriend. But Lucky wouldn't know a boundary if it kicked him in the ass. Which was exactly what Riley planned to do.

"Riley?" Jodi asked. "Are you in pain again? Your face is all red."

"Yeah, I'm in pain," he lied. "If you don't mind, I think I'll grab a shower and see if that helps." And it wasn't a total lie. He'd been handling those horses for hours, and he probably smelled. Plus, the pain would be there the moment he peeled off his shirt.

"Just help yourself to anything in the fridge," he offered and headed toward his bedroom. Riley stopped when he spotted her duffel bag by the front door.

Soon, very soon, he'd need to tell her if she was staying the night, it would have to be in one of the guest rooms. Because sex was out, and he wished he could put all the blame on his injury. But he couldn't. He just wasn't in the mood—or in any shape—to tangle with Jodi.

Riley went to his room, shut the door, and in the same motion he flipped through the numbers on his phone to call Lucky. He didn't have a clue what his brother's hours were these days. Didn't care, either. He stabbed the number as if he'd declared war on it.

"Yeah?" Lucky greeted when he answered. It was followed by a noisy yawn.

"Did you touch Claire?" Riley snapped.

"Excuse me?" Another yawn.

"Did you touch her?" Though it came out a little garbled with his jaw and teeth clenched.

A third yawn. Then a groan. "I'm sure I did at some point over the past thirty years. Are you talking about a good touch or a bad one?"

That was Lucky's usual brand of smart-assed humor, and Riley was so not in the mood for it. "I'm talking about you not keeping your dick zipped up. Is Claire's son yours?"

"What? No!" No yawn or groan that time. His response was really loud, and it appeared to wake up someone who was with Lucky because Riley heard a woman's voice. "No, I'm not talking to you, honey. Just my idiot brother. Why would you think something like that?"

It took Riley a moment to realize that Lucky's question was for him and that it wasn't part of the conversation Lucky was having with his current bedmate.

"Because Ethan looks like us," Riley growled.

More groaning. "According to the woman I'm with right now, so do a whole bunch of actors."

"Hot actors," his bedmate supplied.

"That doesn't mean I fathered any of them," Lucky went on, "and I sure as heck didn't father Ethan." He cursed some more, which was out of the ordinary for Lucky. Despite his hellion, bed-hopping reputation, Lucky usually kept his language fairly clean.

"What's this phone call really about?" Lucky barked a moment later. "Why would you think I'd ever sleep with Claire?"

"You had that sex talk with her, the one where you told her for a guy there was no such thing as bad sex." The moment he heard the words come out of his mouth, Riley felt as if he were back in junior high.

"Say what?" Lucky questioned.

Of course Lucky wouldn't remember talking about sex to a woman since it was probably something he did on a daily basis. He was thirty-three now, which meant he'd had thousands of such conversations. Maybe millions.

"You shouldn't have talked to Claire about sex," Riley settled for saying, mainly because he didn't know what else to say.

"It's not like that between us. Yeah, we're friendly, but she's like a sister to me, Riley."

The fit of temper disappeared just as quickly as it had come, and it left Riley feeling as though he'd just earned the label of the idiot brother.

"It was just something someone said," Riley explained. "And Claire won't talk about it." He paused, figured since he'd already made an ass of himself that he might as well continue. "Has she said anything to you about the father of her son?"

Lucky made an *isn't-it-obvious* sound. "I always figured it was you."

Now it was Riley's turn to shout. "No!"

"Well, my bad, then. The kid does look like you, though."

Riley wanted to reach through the phone, rip off Lucky's dick and beat him senseless with it. Hell, he wanted to beat those hot actors senseless while he was at it.

"Ethan's not my son." Riley was in pain now, not from his shoulder but from his too-tight jaw.

"Too bad. I always figured... Well, never mind."

"Say it," Riley demanded. The temper was making a comeback.

"All right. I always figured that sooner or later Claire would do something to make you forget all about those stupid man-rules."

"They're not stupid." Sometimes they were constricting and frustrating, but they definitely weren't stupid.

"Right. Whatever. You know, for a hotshot special ops guy, you're a turd head. You just don't get it, do you?"

Riley didn't think they were talking about the man-rules just now. "Get what?"

Lucky cursed again before he answered. "That Claire's been in love with you for years."

His brother hung up, leaving Riley to stand there, staring at the phone. He felt a little as if a fully loaded Mack Truck had just slammed into him.

Claire was in love with him?

But wait. He shook off the question before an answer could even form in his mind. Of course she wasn't in love with him. Riley had to consider the source—Lucky—and his brother had never been a font of reliable information. Lucky probably just wanted to put an end to the conversation.

Which he'd managed to do.

Riley considered calling him right back and interrupting another round in Lucky's latest hookup, but the sound of someone talking stopped him. At first he thought maybe Jodi was on the phone, but it wasn't just her voice. He heard two people. And it wasn't a call on speaker, either.

Then he recognized who she was speaking with. Daniel.

Great day. He so didn't need this right now, but Riley wasn't about to hide behind the pain or the frustration that he was suddenly feeling.

He took a minute, steadying his nerves. "Jingle Bells" didn't do squat for nerves, but he had something in his hand that helped. Right there on his phone's screen saver.

Claire's picture.

He'd caught the shot with her partway between a smile and a surprised look. Not exactly a soothing pose, but it had the intended effect.

How long that effect would last was anyone's guess, especially if Daniel had come there to invite him to Claire's and his wedding. Certainly Claire had had time to call him by now, and Daniel had probably scurried right over to tell Riley the *good* news.

Riley made his way back into the living room. There was definitely a celebratory vibe in the air. Jodi and Daniel were both smiling, and even though he didn't know the reason for it, something Daniel said caused her to erupt into a giggle.

They were so involved in their conversation that it took them a couple of seconds to hear Riley and turn in his direction. Jodi would be plenty pleased with the news of Claire's wedding, too, but that still didn't mean he was going to invite her into his bed.

"There you are," Jodi said.

She went to Riley, hooked her arm through his as if that was something they did all the time. It wasn't. Cuddling, romance and the lingering look she was giving him were things that just didn't happen.

Saying hello was Jodi's idea of foreplay.

"You two have met, I see?" Riley nearly groaned.

He couldn't have possibly sounded any more wussy if he'd been dosing up on wuss pills. But he didn't have much of an alternative. He needed to keep this visit pleasant—and short. Punching Daniel wouldn't accomplish that, but hell in a hand-basket, he might burn off some of this restless energy if he punched something.

"Yes, we met." Daniel wasn't just smiling. He was grinning. An ear-to-ear kind of grin. "Didn't know you were involved with anyone."

If that was the truth, then Daniel clearly wasn't in the gossip loop. Riley was certain Trisha had spilled the handful of details that he'd given her about Jodi and then added some details of her own for embellishment. Like maybe Jodi being a substitute for Claire. Which she wasn't.

"Riley and I have been involved for a couple of years now," Jodi explained. "I had a week off before my next assignment, and I decided to nurse him back to health."

A week? Oh, man. He really needed to nip that in the bud. First, though, he had some bud nipping to do with Daniel.

"Was there something I could do for you?" Riley asked. It was better than barking out, *Why the hell are you here anyway?*

Daniel just kept on smiling. "I just dropped by to catch up. But I can see this is a bad time." He checked his watch. "I need to be at Claire's soon anyway."

"Claire?" That perked Jodi up even more. "You mean the woman who was here earlier, the one with the kid?"

That perked up Daniel, too, but not in the same way as Jodi. "Claire was here?" Daniel asked.

Riley nodded. "Logan's doing. He had to go out of town, and he asked her to check on me."

There went the rest of Daniel's smile. "Do you still need someone to check on you? I thought you'd be past all of that now."

"Still healing."

Daniel lifted his shoulder. "Well, it's not as if Claire has any nursing skills. And she stays so busy with Ethan these days and going through all that junk at her grandmother's place. I'm just surprised she had any free time to come over here."

Riley wouldn't dare mention the near kiss. But mercy, he was thinking about it right now. Thinking about that stupid thing Lucky had said, too, about Claire being in love with him.

"I met Claire," Jodi volunteered. "And her son. He was peeing on a tree in the backyard."

Daniel turned his head so fast that Riley was surprised he didn't dislocate his neck. "I hope you stopped him," he said to Riley.

"Wasn't really my place."

Daniel gave him that look, the one that implied he was waiting for Riley to confess what everyone else already knew. That Ethan was Riley's.

"Sometimes, Claire's too easy on him," Daniel finally continued. "Of course, I help her, but Ethan's strong willed. He's already behind other kids his age, and Claire's not making much progress with the Baby Genius packets."

"Ethan's as smart as a whip," Riley argued. "He potty trained himself in thirty seconds."

"By peeing on a tree." Daniel's look was flat. The run-over-twice-by-a-bulldozer kind of flat.

"It worked for Lucky." Which, of course, was a terrible argument. Lucky was as maladjusted as they came.

Daniel huffed. "You clearly don't know much about kids. But I'd have thought you would have at least read some books about it."

"And why would Riley have done that?" Jodi asked.

For seven little words, her question was a powerful gauntlet. Daniel stared at him, waiting for an answer. Jodi stared at him, too. And Riley decided while it might not be very mature, he wouldn't be the one to answer Jodi's question.

Finally Daniel said, "Well, it doesn't matter who Ethan's father is. Even if it's you, I'm the one who's been there for him, and I'll continue to be there for him. And for Claire, of course."

Riley broke his stare when Jodi made a slight gasping sound. "You said the kid wasn't yours. Is he?"

It was the renewed anger over the question that caused Riley to pause and generally look pissed off. But Jodi—Daniel, too—apparently took that pause as a confession.

"Ethan's not my son," Riley finally said. But it was too late. It sounded like a lie.

"Well." Jodi flexed her eyebrows, said another *well*, then did more eyebrow flexing. "You know I have fun with you," Jodi said to Riley, "but this isn't fun. Jodi-rule number six—don't get involved with men who have kids."

Yeah, he knew about that rule. Ironically, it was ahead of the Jodi-rules about her not getting involved with a married man or convicted felons.

"Is there a hotel in town?" she asked Daniel, not him. "I need to get some pictures edited."

Daniel nodded. "There's an inn on Main Street, just up from my office. It's not that far, but you can follow behind me if you like. I'm headed in that general direction anyway."

Where he was headed was to Claire's.

Jodi grabbed her duffel bag and hoisted it up over her shoulder with all the efficiency of a lumberjack and his ax. Riley nearly stopped her. Nearly went on the offensive so he could try to dispel once and for all that he hadn't slept with Claire. But he'd just be wasting his breath.

Besides, he really didn't want Jodi hanging around for a week. The only time they could tolerate each other was when they were in bed, and no way was that happening.

"Be seeing you," Jodi said, patting Riley's cheek.

That was it. Apparently the only goodbye he was going to get after a two-year semirelationship. Of course, Riley wasn't feeling any tugs of his heartstrings, either.

Jodi went out the door and down the porch steps, but Daniel lingered in the doorway. "She might change her mind when she's had a chance to deal with the shock."

No. She wouldn't. But Riley decided not to prolong this conversation, so he nodded.

"I'll check on Jodi later," Daniel went on. "After I see Claire, of course. I'm pretty sure that in the next hour or two, I'll become an engaged man."

"Really? I thought Claire was still thinking about it."

Daniel smiled again. "I talked to her right before I came here, and the thinking is finally over. I'm ninety-nine point nine percent sure that this time Claire will say yes."

CHAPTER TEN

"No," Claire said.

She wasn't sure who was more surprised by the word that came out of her mouth—her or Daniel. She hadn't hesitated, hadn't blinked. She'd put on her big-girl panties and delivered the answer that she should have delivered years ago.

"No?" Daniel asked. He didn't look just thunderstruck. He looked as if he'd been hit with a sledgehammer.

"No," she repeated, and since she was ready for this moment, Claire took his hand and put the engagement ring in his palm. "I'm sorry, but I can't marry you."

His mouth didn't drop open exactly, but it was close. "I thought for sure you'd say yes. Claire, we're so good together, and you know how much I love you and Ethan."

"I know." She glanced at Ethan to see if he was hearing any of this, but he was sacked out on the sofa. Obviously the walk to and from Riley's had worn him out. The tree peeing, too, since he'd repeated that once they made it home.

"Then, if you know I love you, why don't you say yes? I even told people you'd say yes," he amended.

Great. So it was all over town, and it wouldn't be long before she'd start getting congratulatory calls. Calls where she would have to dodge questions about not only why she'd dumped her longtime boyfriend but also whether it had anything to do with Riley.

"Does this have to do with Riley?" Daniel snapped.

Obviously she'd have to deal with that question a little sooner than planned. "No." And that wasn't a lie, either.

Daniel clearly thought it was. "He has a girlfriend, you know?"

She nodded. "I met her." Claire considered adding something polite like that Jodi was lovely, but she couldn't even muster up the effort.

"Then you know they're right for each other," Daniel went on. "They're not like us. They're adrenaline junkies. They want to live their lives on the line. You should have heard the stories she was telling me about some of the missions she's been on with Riley."

Claire didn't want to hear. She saw the proof of one of those missions every time she looked at Riley's face. The pain was right there, and judging from the conversation she'd had with Logan, Riley was still having flashbacks. He might never get over those, and even if he did, Riley would just want to go back into situations where he could be hurt.

Or worse.

It crushed her heart to think of Riley dying. Crushed it even more to know there was nothing she could do to stop him.

"Are you listening to me?" Daniel snarled.

"Of course." Now, that was a lie.

For a moment she thought he might call her on it, but he finally huffed. "Even if Riley and Jodi don't agree on everything right now, they'll be together."

Claire was with him on all but one point. "Uh, what don't they agree on?"

Daniel promptly waved that off. "I don't want to talk about Jodi and Riley. I want to talk about us. Look, I'll give you an extension on the proposal. Take another week to think it over. Just know that this time, I'll expect the answer to be yes."

She took in a long, deep breath. Had Daniel always been like this? Persistent to the point of being a bully?

Maybe.

But she'd been so comforted by the notion that he had a safe job and safe expectations that she'd overlooked that particular aspect of his personality. Well, he'd obviously overlooked one of hers. Her need for a safe, white-picket-fence life didn't mean she was brainless and spineless.

"I don't need a week," she assured him, "because my answer won't change. It'll still be no."

He huffed again, looked ready to gear up for what would be more of the same argument, but Claire took Daniel by the arm and led him to the front door. She hoped to usher him out and then have a huge glass of wine before Ethan woke up. But a quick ushering wasn't in the cards.

That's because Livvy and Riley—yes, Riley—were making their way up the porch steps.

Daniel spun toward her, the accusation all over his face. "What are they doing here?"

"I saw Riley walking this way, and I gave him a ride," Livvy volunteered. "Claire and I have some work to do."

Partially true. Livvy had called her about forty-five minutes earlier to say she had to see her, that they needed to talk. That was possibly work related, but Claire suspected Livvy had come over for what would have no doubt turned into some wine drinking and consoling.

But she didn't have a clue why Riley was there.

"I just need to talk to you," Riley said. That sounded a little ominous. Had he come to tell her he couldn't see her, not even as a friend, because of his relationship with Jodi?

Livvy pulled her into a hug and put her mouth right against Claire's ear. "Don't say anything until we've talked." Heck, that sounded ominous, too.

What was going on?

Daniel looked at all of them as if expecting an explanation.

Riley shrugged. Livvy smiled. Claire stayed quiet, too afraid
to talk after Livvy's warning. Daniel obviously didn't appreciate any of their responses.

"Claire, I'll expect your answer in a week." Daniel slapped the
engagement-ring box on the table next to the door and stormed
out.

"I thought you were going to tell him no," Livvy said.

"I did. I guess he didn't believe me." Claire looked at her
friend, hoping for more clues about that warning, but Livvy
headed toward a still-sleeping Ethan to give him some air kisses
and air cuddles before she started for the bathroom.

"I'll give you two a couple of minutes to talk. Remember
what I said, though."

Claire wanted to throw up her hands. She still had that blasted
engagement ring in her house, which meant she would need to go
another round with Daniel. And now here was Riley, no doubt
ready to deliver news that she didn't want to hear.

"Did Lucky call you, by any chance?" Riley asked.

Okay. That wasn't the news Claire had been expecting. "No.
Why? Is anything wrong?"

He shook his head. Looked relieved, or something. "I was just
wondering." Riley wasn't actually fidgeting, but she thought he
might start at any moment. "I, uh, wanted to apologize for what
happened with Jodi. She can come on a little strong."

"That's okay." No, it wasn't, but Claire did want to be nice
now. This was already going to end on a sour note, so there was
no sense her adding yet more sourness to it. "I think she was
just surprised to see me there with you."

"She was." He didn't exactly spew forth any details, but she
wondered if Jodi had gotten jealous.

Even if Riley and Jodi don't agree on everything right now...

That's what Daniel had said, so maybe that meant he'd witnessed some of Jodi's displeasure.

"Anyway, Jodi's not staying at my house. She took a room at
the Bluebonnet Inn." He rotated his shoulder a little, maybe si-

lently telling her that he'd distanced himself from Jodi because he hadn't wanted to be tempted into having sex.

But Claire wasn't fond of this filling-in-the-blanks stuff. "So, Jodi's planning on staying in town?"

"For a day or two, I think. She's got some work to do. And so do you." He tipped his head to the bathroom, where Livvy was no doubt—*no doubt*—just on the other side, listening to their every word. Claire just hoped after her friend's piss-poor warning that she wasn't saying the wrong words.

"I'll be in touch," Riley said, and he headed out.

Claire shut the door, huffed, but before the huff was even out of her mouth, Livvy was out of the bathroom. She wasn't wearing mile-high heels today, but she teetered toward her as if she were, making Claire briefly wonder if Livvy had permanently altered her arches.

Livvy opened her mouth to say something but then glanced back at Ethan. She motioned for Claire to follow her into the kitchen. *Oh, no.* Since she figured Livvy wasn't there to delve into the juicy details of her latest date, privacy was needed for a different reason. A reason that went along with that cryptic warning.

"Uh, has Lucky McCord called you?" Livvy asked the moment they were in the kitchen.

Claire did throw her hands in the air. "Riley asked me the same thing. Why would Lucky call me?"

The way that Livvy screwed up her mouth, Claire knew this was something she wasn't going to like. "I ran into Lucky at a bar last night," Livvy explained. "And we sort of…"

Claire held up her hands for a different reason. "I don't need to hear the details of that. I don't want them in my head because Lucky's like a brother to me."

"Funny that you mentioned that because Lucky said you were like a sister to him." She went to the fridge, helped herself to some wine. From the bottle.

"How did you and Lucky get on the subject of me? And why did you tell me not to say a word?"

"Riley called him this morning, and I was still there." Livvy stopped, smiled. "Don't you think Lucky looks like one of those hot actors who stars in those action movies?"

Heck, she might as well keep her hands in the air. "What does that have to do with Riley calling him?"

"Nothing. It's just that it also came up in conversation."

"That must have been some morning chat. Lucky's sibling-esque feelings for me. His movie-star looks." Claire took the bottle from her and got in her face. "What aren't you telling me?"

"Well, Riley called because he was mad. He thought Lucky was Ethan's father."

"What?" Since she'd practically burst her own eardrums with that shout, Claire peeked into the living room to make sure she hadn't woken Ethan. Thankfully she hadn't. "Why would he think that?"

"I'm not sure. Maybe it came from Daniel?"

Probably. After all, Daniel had been over there because he'd met Jodi. "What did Lucky tell Riley?"

"That's where the sister part came in. He said he didn't think of you that way." Livvy took back the wine. "Has Riley asked you again about Ethan's father?"

"In a roundabout way. But I can tell he wants me to fess up."

"A lot of people want you to fess up. Don't you think it's time?"

"No." And that wasn't up for debate. "If I tell them...tell Riley," Claire corrected, "it won't make things easier between us. He's got a girlfriend, Livvy."

Livvy made a sound that could have meant a dozen different things, but since this was Livvy, it meant something important. "What else did Riley and Lucky talk about?"

"Well, Lucky didn't put the call on speaker, mind you, so I didn't hear everything." Which meant she'd heard enough.

"What?" Claire pressed.

Claire had never seen a clearer example of hemming and hawing. "Lucky called Riley a turd-head and told Riley that you were in love with him." Livvy said that last handful of words faster than some people ripped off bandages.

Despite the speed of Livvy's speech, Claire had no trouble hearing it. "Lucky said I was in love with him?"

"No, he said you were in love with Riley."

Holy moly. That required her to sit down. "It's not true," Claire managed to say.

But Riley wouldn't believe that. He would think she was in love with him, and that would send him running. That's what his visit had been about. He was putting some distance between them.

Livvy handed her the bottle. "Drink up. I'll get the ice cream from the freezer."

Wine and ice cream. Livvy was bringing out the big guns, and Claire wasn't sure it was at all necessary. "I'm not going to cry," she insisted, but her eyes seemed to have a different notion about that.

Livvy had made it back to her with two spoons and a quart of double-fudge rocky road before the first tear slid down Claire's cheek.

"This is so stupid." Claire fought those tears and sort of won the battle, but she didn't win the battle going on in her heart. "I mean, it's not as if Riley was mine to lose."

"Yeah, he was." Livvy handed Claire the spoon piled high with ice cream. "It doesn't have to make sense. Childhood crushes are like that. They'll always be yours."

"But that's just it. I chose Daniel. I had a list."

"A list you wrote when you were a child. That was then. This is now. You had no idea that Daniel would grow up to be a dickweed."

"He's not. That's just it. Despite his flaws, he loves me. I have no doubts about that."

"Ah, got it." Livvy talked around the ice cream in her mouth.

"You're afraid no one else will ever love you." She didn't wait for Claire to consider it. And confirm it. "Daddy issues again. Your daddy did a Houdini, and now you want to reward Daniel because he wasn't like your dad. He stuck around, and he loves you. Still not a reason he can't have the dickweed label."

Maybe not. But Claire had never wanted to be an old maid. Heck, she'd really wanted that picket-fence life, and Daniel might have been her only shot at getting it.

Livvy nudged her with her elbow. "Want me to go into town, find Riley's girlfriend and start a fight with her or something?"

"No." And Claire couldn't say it fast enough. "You're staying away from her. So am I, and if Riley and she hook up again, then it's just something I have to accept. Besides, she could probably take us both in a bar fight."

Even though she was about the same size as Claire, Jodi looked a lot tougher.

There was a scratching sound at the back door, and Claire didn't have to guess who or what it was. The cat. Since she was running low on milk, she dumped some of the ice cream in a saucer.

"Got a new friend?" Livvy asked, following her to the door. "Whoa," Livvy shrieked when she saw the animal.

"That's what Ethan named her. It," she corrected since Claire still didn't know if it was male or female.

Livvy studied the cat for a couple of moments, actually cringed. "Well, Whoa looks as if he cooks meth. And he brought a friend."

Claire hadn't noticed the second cat until she put down the saucer, and the gray tabby came running toward it. This one was nothing like Whoa and actually looked and sounded like a real cat.

"I think it's Whoa's girlfriend," Livvy remarked.

The newcomer did indeed sidle up to Whoa, and just the sight of the pair caused Claire's eyes to water again.

"Oh, honey." Livvy dragged Claire into her arms for one of

those nipple-bruising hugs. "You know what we need? A girls' night out. Let's plan that for tomorrow night. You get a sitter, and I'll swing by and pick you up."

Claire nodded, mainly because she didn't want to explain to Livvy that there was no way she wanted to go out and party. Her party meter was at zero. Plus, it was short notice for a sitter. In the morning she'd call Livvy and tell her that it was a no go.

"We should get to work," Claire said, moving away from her.

She took her laptop from the living room, and since Ethan was still sleeping, she led Livvy toward the makeshift nursery that Claire had been using as a makeshift office. They went well with her makeshift life.

Which was exactly the reminder she needed that no one liked a whiner.

"Uh, how's the box sorting going?" Livvy asked, the question prompted by the fact that she had to step around a half-dozen boxes to get in the room. There was another half dozen inside.

"I think the boxes are breeding. I found more in the attic behind an old chest of drawers. There were other small boxes inside the drawers."

Livvy sank down next to one, pulling up her long legs in a lotus position, and she started rummaging through the nearest box. "Any sign of that letter yet?"

"None. I'm beginning to think Gran threw it away. Still, I'll keep looking. It might be in one of these boxes or somewhere else in the house."

"Maybe it's in this." Livvy dragged a book from the bottom of the box. "Bet there are some naughty details in there. Always did love your gran's sense of adventure."

Claire's heart and stomach dropped. She snatched the book from Livvy.

"No. It's my mother's journal," Claire managed to say.

"She left a journal? Have you read it? Oh, God. You've read it, haven't you?"

"Just two words." Claire opened to the first page so Livvy

could see those two words, and then she turned that very page back so she could see it again for herself.

The two words were indeed still there.

Fucking kid.

The next words weren't any better. Words like *miserable*, *swollen. Hell.*

"Fudge." Livvy again. "You're sure you actually want to read that?"

Claire wasn't sure at all, but she couldn't stop herself from doing just that. The entry on the first page was dated, and Claire quickly did the math. Her mother would have been eighteen, and after just a few lines, she realized this wasn't the journal of a normal teenager.

"'The baby moved today,'" Claire read aloud. She looked at Livvy. "She wrote this when she was pregnant with me."

"You're sure you want to read that?" Livvy repeated.

It had become a moth-to-flame moment, and Claire frantically skimmed through the next passage.

Rocky broke up with me. The bastard. He didn't even tell me to my face. He just disappeared. What kind of sick bastard does that? Here, I'm carrying his brat kid and he leaves me here in this shit-hole.

Rocky. That was the first time Claire had ever heard her father's name. And it might just be a nickname. It was stupid, but she latched onto that little piece of information as if it were gold.

Rocky-somebody was her father.

"Claire," Livvy tried again. "You're crying. Girl, you need to put that away."

Claire intended to do just that, but she read the next line before she could stop herself.

Tomorrow, I'm getting rid of this kid.
Oh. God. Oh, God. Oh, God.

Claire slammed the journal shut and tossed it into the box marked Trash. She was already feeling raw and bruised, and nothing written on those pages would help. They certainly wouldn't help her understand why her mother had run out on her.

Or why those words still crushed her heart after all this time.

Her mother clearly hadn't ended the pregnancy, but the fact that she'd even considered it nearly brought Claire to her knees.

"Still up for that girls' night out?" Claire asked.

Livvy nodded. "You bet. Set up a babysitter for Ethan, and I'll pick you up tomorrow night. And wear something slutty." She hooked her arm around Claire. "You, my friend, are having sex with the hottest cowboy we can find."

CHAPTER ELEVEN

RILEY ACTUALLY FELT HUMAN. Well, close to human anyway. If he discounted the constant throb in his shoulder, the twinges in his knee, the continuing flashbacks and the crappy feeling he had about how he'd left things with Claire the day before.

So, maybe not that human after all, now that he'd taken inventory.

But at least he had showered, and there were some muscles aching that should be aching. The kind of muscles that got worked by herding horses from the corral to one of the pastures. He hadn't done any heavy lifting—none had been required, and it wasn't possible yet anyway. However, he had twisted and turned more in the saddle than was probably good for his shoulder.

Tomorrow morning he would probably have to take that human feeling down yet another notch when those aching muscles turned stiff. Still, he'd done the job and hadn't violated a man-rule by doing it half-assed.

Not bad for someone who hadn't done real ranch work in more than a decade.

He heard the women, Della and Stella. They weren't quiet women and were even louder since they'd gotten back from their forced vacation. The extra volume was probably to teach him a lesson for trying to make a go of his recovery on his own. Neither had been pleased about that, and Della had let him know that she'd been flat-out insulted. She would have been far more than insulted if she'd seen the mess he had for a shoulder.

She would have been worried.

Stella, too. And that's the reason Riley had demanded they stay away for a while. They still had to see him in pain, but he was getting some home-cooked meals as a trade-off.

Riley followed the sounds of their voices as he made his way to the kitchen. They were gossiping about Trisha and a bad waxing experience she'd had at a salon up in Austin while Johnny Cash and June Carter blared out a duet about pepper sprouts on the radio.

He didn't want to ask about Trisha, especially didn't want to ask what she'd had waxed, but Riley hoped that meant she was back in Austin for good. He didn't want her unveiling that new wax job for him with another surprise visit.

While he was hoping, he added that maybe Jodi had left, too. After the way things had played out, she probably wouldn't have stopped by the house to say goodbye. Heck, she was probably already off on another adventure.

Riley only had one pang that he wasn't on an adventure, too. All right, there were two pangs, but they were slightly overshadowed by the smell of heaven.

Chocolate-chip cookies.

Or rather tookies.

Riley laughed at the reminder of Ethan. Then he cursed himself for the way the kid, and the kid's mom, just kept popping into his head.

"Well, lookie here," Della said when Riley strolled into the kitchen. She stopped stirring whatever she was cooking and made a show of ogling him. "Did a movie star just come walking in the kitchen?"

It wasn't party clothes, but Riley had managed to button up his shirt, tuck it in and put on a belt, all with minimal grunting and wincing. The cowboy boots, however, had required some grunts. They took more tugging and pulling than the combat boots he'd been living in.

"He's joining the other movie star," Stella remarked.

Riley wasn't sure what she was making, but she was punching a basketball-size wad of dough with her fists. She could have knocked out Mike Tyson with the force she was putting behind those wallops.

Riley glanced around to see what Stella meant by that other-movie-star comment, and he spotted Logan at the table. A rare sighting indeed, and he was using the kitchen table to do some paperwork on the horse shipment they'd just received. But heck, Logan did sort of look like a movie in his Texas tuxedo. He'd probably just come from a meeting or was headed to one.

Della plucked a cookie right from the baking sheet that she'd just taken out of the oven and handed it to Riley on the down low as if trying to hide it from her sister and Logan. One bite of it, and it was like being transported back to his childhood. Suddenly, he was six years old again, not a care in the world, and with Della sneaking him cookies while Stella and his mom pretended not to notice.

The sisters weren't gray haired then, and they'd been young, only in their late thirties, but at the time Riley had thought they were old. The first cookie Della had sneaked him was as good as this last one.

Ethan would have loved every bite.

The thought just jumped in his head, causing the childhood memories to vanish. Riley was back to being thirty-one again, feeling partly human, but he still had his cookie. It was warm, gooey and perfect.

"Are you going somewhere?" Logan asked, glancing up from his paperwork.

Riley shrugged, finished off the cookie. "Thought I might go to Calhoun's Pub."

The three froze, looked at him as if he'd just announced a solo expedition to Antarctica.

"You're sure you're up to that?" Della asked. "You looked tuckered out when you came in from dealing with those new horses."

"I *am* tuckered out." Though he hated using that word, *tuckered*. "But I thought I could use a cold beer, maybe see some old friends."

Again more of those stares.

"I'm not really asking permission," Riley finally said when the staring continued and then the concerned looks kicked in. But he stopped. Maybe he didn't need to ask for permission, but he sure needed some information. And some keys. "I need to use a vehicle. What's in the garage?"

Logan got to his feet. "I'll drive you. Wouldn't mind having a beer myself."

Now Riley was the one who stared. "I don't need a babysitter, Logan."

"Good. Because I wasn't offering. You can buy. I'll have one beer—then I'll go to the office and clear out some of this paperwork. When you're done at Calhoun's, you can walk over or give me a call, and I'll drive you home. Consider me your designated driver."

Logan apparently assumed that offer was a done deal because he gathered up his papers and headed to the side door, which led to where he'd parked. Riley considered arguing but realized he'd be doing it just for argument's sake—a constant problem for him when dealing with Logan—but he really did want to just get out and maybe clear his head.

Of Ethan.

Of Claire.

Especially Claire.

"Dinner's ready, but if you're in a hurry to take off, I'll hold some for both of you in the microwave," Della called out to them.

"No need," Logan answered at the same time Riley said,

"Thanks. I appreciate it." Maybe she'd leave him some more of those cookies, too.

Riley followed Logan outside to a big silver truck with the McCord Cattle Brokers copper logo painted on the door. On both doors, Riley realized when he went to get in.

"Thanks for helping today," Logan said.

Riley didn't wait for more praise because with Logan that was about as good as it would get. But Riley didn't need his praise anyway. Hadn't in a long time. He hadn't done the work today for Logan but rather for the family. And for himself.

"I called Lucky earlier," Logan went on as he pulled out of the driveway. "I asked him to come home to help you with the cutting horses. The new trainer gets here tomorrow, and Lucky and you can get him settled. Plus, I need the two of you to go look at some other horses I'd like to add to the inventory."

There was so much wrong with that handful of sentences that Riley didn't know where to start. "You really think Lucky will come home?"

"He should. This is his business, too."

Which wasn't an answer at all, but Riley knew how things would likely go. Or rather not go. Lucky wouldn't be there because he was off doing some rodeo promotion. Riley didn't know a lot of the details because Lucky didn't make it home often enough to share what was going on in his life, but Lucky wouldn't just drop everything—or *anything* for that matter—to attend to family business.

Especially when his twin brother had ordered him home.

But that wasn't the only thing wrong with Logan's decree. "I don't know how much longer I'll be able to help, either," Riley said. "The Air Force should be scheduling my physical soon, and once I'm cleared for duty, I'll be leaving."

Now, normally that gave Riley a nice kick of adrenaline, but tonight it made his stomach feel a little acidy. He'd probably downed that cookie too fast.

"You're sure you'll be cleared?" Logan asked.

"Of course." That was perhaps the biggest lie he'd ever told, but it was a lie that Riley had to hang on to. He couldn't fail at this. He had to go back on active duty.

"What about the flashbacks? Are you still having them?" Logan pressed.

Thankfully Riley didn't have to lie and say no because Logan's phone beeped. A simple little sound to indicate he had a phone call. Judging by what Riley could hear of the conversation, it was about those horses Logan had just mentioned, and the deal apparently wasn't going well, if Logan's terse, one- and two-word replies were any indication.

Too much. Renegotiate. Now.

He said *now* a lot.

Logan was still growling out those replies when he pulled into the parking lot of Calhoun's Pub. He motioned for Riley to go ahead in, which suited him just fine. If he waited around with Logan much longer, his brother would try to rope him into doing something else that Riley was reasonably sure he wouldn't want to do.

It was only a short walk from the parking lot to the entrance, but by the time Riley made it, the sweat was already making his back and neck sticky. Inside wasn't a whole lot better. The place was a converted nineteenth-century barn, and even though it had AC and dozens of ceiling fans, it wasn't cooling off the place much.

Riley figured that was the owner Donnie Calhoun's way of getting people to buy more cold beers.

Since it was a Saturday night, the pub was packed. He'd forgotten how it could be and that it was the only place where folks could unwind at the end of a workweek. Not exactly a quiet place to have a beer with the jukebox blaring, the customers trying to be heard over the music and even the crunch of the peanut shells beneath him. One step, and Riley felt his boots shift a little. Just enough.

As they'd done that day in the sand.

The fan blades whipped through the air above him, somehow cutting through the other sounds but not the heat, and they stirred up the dust. Smothering him. Someone, a man, shouted out something. Maybe his name. But it was just an echo in Riley's head. A cry for help.

Shit.

The sensations all hit him at once, and Riley felt himself being yanked back into the middle of the flashback. *No.* This couldn't happen. Not here in front of everybody.

Jingle bells. Jingle bells.

That didn't work, so he pulled out his phone to look at Claire's picture. Maybe it was the poor lighting or maybe he just hadn't caught it in time, but the picture didn't work. He was going down fast.

Because he could hear the kid.

He could feel the warm blood snaking down his body.

Get the hell out now!

But he couldn't run. The sand was pulling him down, and the pain. *Fuck, the pain. Too much.* And the kid wasn't moving.

Sixty-forty chance if he got him moving, but Riley couldn't lift his feet.

It'd been a huge mistake coming here, and he turned to try to leave—fast—when he saw something. The woman pushing her way through the crowd. Or maybe she was a mirage.

Because it was Claire.

Not a picture on his phone, either. She was wearing jeans and a snug little red top and had a beer in her hand. She was making her way toward him.

"Riley," she said, obviously aware that all hell had broken loose inside his head. Probably because she'd seen him like this on the porch that day. But that was a picnic compared with the roar going on inside him right now.

Livvy was with her, right by her side, but unlike Claire, she didn't seem to notice what was going on because she was smiling in between swigs of a beer.

"Now, there's the hot cowboy Claire's been looking for," Livvy declared.

And Livvy pushed Claire right into his arms.

OH, NO. This wasn't good. Claire knew that look, knew that Riley was about to lose it.

"Come on," Claire said. She slipped her arm around Riley's waist and got him moving toward the back exit. "I'll get you out of here."

Livvy clapped her hands. "Now, that's what I'm talking about."

She no doubt thought Claire was finally taking the initiative with Riley and was hauling him off for a good make-out session. But making out was the last thing on Claire's mind as she worked to get Riley away from the crowd and thought of ways to help him fight these demons that were bearing down on him.

If that was even possible.

Claire had been doing some reading about PTSD and combat flashbacks, and while the websites had given her some useful information, all of that went out the window when it was happening right in front of her. Especially since it was happening to Riley.

"Just put one foot ahead of the other," she instructed, though she had to yell it to be heard over the music. She considered dropping her beer, but that would only cause unwanted attention.

"The sand," he said.

"I'll get you through it." Both the sand in his head and the stuff just out the back door of the pub.

Donnie Calhoun had added several inches of sand to the back so the smokers would have a place to squash out their cigarette butts, but that meant Riley and she were trudging through it while dodging any questions from the gaggle of smokers out there.

Claire had a solution to avoid those questions. It wasn't a good solution, but desperation took over. She knew above all else that Riley wouldn't want anyone to know what he was going through. So she put her mouth on his neck and pulled down his head so that it looked as if they were kissing.

It worked.

They didn't get a single flashback/PTSD/what's-wrong-with-you? question from the dozen or so smokers. Though Riley did get some cheers and dirty suggestions.

Maybe it was the neck nuzzling or those dirty suggestions, but it seemed to get Riley to pick up some speed.

"Sixty-forty if I hurry," he said.

He was still in the nightmare, still clearly fighting it, judging from his steel-hard muscles and the sweat that had beaded on his face. Claire figured that ratio had something to do with his chance of succeeding on a mission. Not ideal odds considering he was probably talking about his life.

"Gotta get the kid out," he said. Each word seemed to be a battle in itself.

One he was losing.

Claire went with something drastic. She poured her beer over his head.

Riley stopped in his tracks, gasping for breath. The kind of gasp someone might make if they'd been underwater too long. And he looked at her, the beer trickling from his hair and down his face.

"You poured your beer on me." His words weren't so shaky now, but Riley did look at her as if she'd lost her mind.

Since they were still in view of the smokers, the beer ploy had gotten their attention, too, and the questions came.

Can't handle her, Riley?

Does the flyboy need some help locating his target?

The questions were punctuated with laughter, some jeering, and Claire shot them nasty glares before she pulled Riley to the side of the old barn. Thankfully, there was no one else here, and there was still enough light coming from the front of the building so she could make sure she wasn't maneuvering them into a fire-ant bed.

"You poured your beer on me," Riley repeated.

She nodded. "All the websites I read said I shouldn't tell you to snap out of it, offer advice or minimize what you've been through, but none of the sites said I couldn't pour a beer on you."

He stared at her. Laughed. It wasn't a 100 percent kind of a laugh. More like that sixty-forty ratio he'd mentioned earlier, and it was short, but at least she could see Riley coming back to her.

"Logan," Riley said, leaning the back of his head against the wall. "He's in his truck in the parking lot."

"You want me to get him?"

"Hell, no."

All right. "I can text him and tell him that I'll make sure you get home." Claire put the empty beer bottle on the ground and fired off a message to Logan. He answered right away, saying that he'd skipped Calhoun's and was at his office.

Good.

Riley definitely wouldn't have wanted to face Logan with his head smelling like beer and the semi-shell-shocked look still on his face. She showed Riley the text response, then put her phone back into her pocket and debated what to do next. Anything she did could cause Riley's walls to go up again, but she wouldn't be much of a friend if she blew this off.

"Now, according to the websites, this is when I should ask you if you want to talk about it?" she tossed out there.

He had his head tipped up to the sky as if seeking some kind of divine assistance. And maybe he was. The websites had suggested that as an option, too. Then, by degrees his chin came back down until they made eye contact.

"I'm getting help," he said. "At the base. I've only been to one session, but there are, well, exercises and stuff. Nothing about beer pouring though. Or neck kissing. But I have to say, that worked pretty well. The kissing, not the beer." He licked some of it from the corner of his mouth.

Now she laughed. "That was my attempt at a distraction. And I didn't actually kiss you. I just wanted to avoid the jerks in that smoking crowd."

"Does the flyboy need some help locating his target?" Riley repeated. "And Jake Banchini offered to lend me a condom if he could join us."

Claire hadn't heard that, but she'd deal with Jake the next time she saw him. Maybe she'd dump a beer on Jake's head, too. For very different reasons.

"You know the gossips will get wind of this," she reminded him.

"Yeah." Definitely no trace of that laughter now, and she hated that she'd even brought it up. "I'm sorry about that."

Claire shrugged. "Either way, we would have given them gossip fodder, but the talk will die down when folks see you with Jodi."

It was such a stupid thing to say, and the trouble was, Claire didn't want to take back the comment.

"Jodi's probably gone by now," he said.

"Oh. Well. How do you feel about that?"

She got the look, the one to let her know that this subject was off-limits. The old, normal Riley was back, not a trace of the flashbacks anywhere on his face. "I don't have my car, Livvy drove me, but I can walk you home if you like," she suggested. It was more than a mile from this part of town, and it was a scorcher of a night, but she didn't want to leave him alone just yet. "Or I can have Livvy take you."

A taxi wasn't an option because the sole taxi driver in the town, Walter Meekins, was home with a gout flare-up. For once, the gossip mill had actually given her some relevant information so she wouldn't bother wasting time calling him.

Riley shook his head. "Let's just stay here a little longer. Then I can walk home."

And she would follow him to make sure he didn't have another episode on the way there.

He wiped his face with his shirtsleeve. "I'm not sure how much of this is sweat and how much is beer. It's hot enough to catch malaria out here."

It was, but he didn't budge. Riley didn't talk, either. He just stood there, looking up at the sky. Claire looked, too. Or rather she tried, but her attention just kept going back to him. Even with the beer-head and wet shirt, he still managed to look, well, mouthwatering.

"This might be the malaria talking, but you're hot." *Uh-oh.* She hadn't exactly intended to say that out loud, and it got Riley's attention all right.

Not 60 percent of it, either.

All of it.

"Want to do something we'll probably regret?" he asked. But he didn't give her a chance to answer.

Riley slipped his hand around the back of her neck, lowered his head and kissed her.

CHAPTER TWELVE

AS REGRETS WENT, it was a damn good one.

Riley had always figured that Claire would taste like something sweet, but he hadn't known just how sweet that sweet could be. Of course, her taste was mixed with some of the beer she'd had before rescuing him, some of the beer on his own mouth, too, but that only added another memory to the one he was making.

It'd be a short memory, though.

Or so he'd thought when he first touched his lips to hers.

He'd thought she would immediately come to her senses and put a stop to this fire-playing game. But Claire upped the memory-making a thousandfold by making a little sound. Barely audible over Garth Brooks, who was now belting out "Friends in Low Places" on the jukebox. But it was audible enough for Riley's ears to catch it.

And have that sound slide right through his whole body.

Not a purr, exactly. More like surprise mixed with a whole lot of heat. Yeah, maybe the malaria had kicked in after all. Or maybe he'd just lost what little of his mind he had left, but that didn't get him to back away.

Riley continued kissing her until lack of oxygen became a

serious issue. They broke the mouth-to-mouth just seconds before they certainly would have passed out.

"Oh," she said, the single word muttered as she gulped in some air.

That was it. Nothing else. And Riley was still trying to gather enough breath to say something even marginally PG-rated or relevant. "Me, man. You, woman" probably wouldn't do it.

She looked up at him as if waiting to see what he would do next. She was still breathing through her mouth, and her warm breath was hitting against his face. Her breath smelled good, too. Again, beer with a whole lot of heat that was zinging between them.

Since Claire clearly wasn't going to do any moving away, Riley figured he should be the one to do it. Really. As in right now. Before he crushed what was left of their friendship.

But that didn't happen.

He was obviously weak and mindless when it came to Claire, and that really stupid part of him behind the zipper of his jeans was encouraging him to go in for another round.

So, that's what he did.

"I didn't regret that nearly enough," he said, right before he kissed her again.

Claire didn't stay passive this time, either. Her hands went to his waist, and she leaned in, not exactly deepening the kiss, but rather deepening something even better.

Her belly landed against the beginnings of his hard-on.

Now, that was something she noticed, and she did pull back. She slid her tongue over her lips, dropped a glance at the front of his jeans, at the intruder that had just popped up between them.

All right. So, that was the end of the kissing.

Or so he thought.

But Claire cursed, caught on to him again and kissed him the right way. She made it French. Made it hard and long—mirroring what was happening in his jeans.

Riley turned her, putting her back against the wall so he

could add some more of that body pressure without ramming his shoulder into her. Nothing would kill the mood faster than if he had to howl in pain.

They grappled for position, not breaking the kiss, and generally acting as if they were starved for each other. This time, it was Riley who stopped, but only because he didn't want to start dragging her to the ground.

"Ouch," Claire grumbled.

It took him a moment to realize she wasn't saying that because of the kiss. She was rubbing her butt, and he hadn't kissed or touched her there.

Not yet anyway.

"I think I got a splinter," she said.

Of all the things Riley had thought she might say, that wasn't one of them. "Where?"

She looked behind her where just seconds earlier her backside had been firmly planted against the wall. "You think it's some kind of sign to get us to stop?"

"I think it's just a splinter."

But that was his hard-on talking, and Riley knew from experience that when his dick was in that particular state, wise words never came out of his mouth. Often, unwise actions followed, too.

The splinter, whether a sign or not, did the trick of getting her out of his arms. Claire signaled the end of this regret-testing/make-out session by putting a couple of inches distance between them.

His hard-on reminded him that a couple of inches was nothing and that it could still reach pay dirt and complete that whole "Me, man. You, woman" thing. But this was Claire, and he really did need to consider the consequences here. For one thing, Daniel's proposal was still on the table.

Literally.

Della had heard that the guy who'd gone to Claire's to collect some stuff for Goodwill had seen the engagement-ring box still on the table in her foyer.

Violate the man-rule.

Of course, that was his hard-on talking again, but Riley still had a brain. Well, for the most part. Plus, there was the other thing to consider here. He wouldn't be in Spring Hill or even Texas much longer. A few more weeks at most. And then he'd have to leave and go wherever the Air Force sent him.

Probably to another deployment.

That wouldn't sit well with Claire's safe-flying ways, and it would drive her crazy knowing he was there, doing the stuff that had given him these nightmares and flashbacks.

"Arguing with yourself?" she asked.

"Yeah," he admitted.

"Who's winning?" She glanced at the front of his jeans again.

"Right now, it's a draw." Not even close. Brainless was still in the lead. "Are *you* arguing with yourself?"

"Not really. I think we both know this can't work out." She paused, shrugged. "But the kiss was, well, really, really, really good."

Riley smiled. He'd gotten a triple really. From Claire.

"Don't grin like that." She hit him on his good arm. "You know we just made things a lot harder on ourselves." Another gaze drop to his jeans. "And I'm not just talking about *that.*"

Yes, he did know. But that didn't stop him from wanting to make things a lot more complicated.

"It's not just us," she went on. "I've got Ethan to consider. If I get close to you, *closer,*" Claire amended, "I have to think about how that'll affect him."

No effect whatsoever. Again, not Riley's brain talking because he knew what she meant. If he insinuated himself into Claire's life, he was also including Ethan in certain parts of that insinuation. Riley didn't know much about kids, but he knew Ethan well enough now to know that when Riley just up and disappeared, Ethan would notice. Might even be confused or hurt.

Riley would rather punch himself in his bad shoulder than let that happen.

"And there's one more thing," Claire went on. She actually touched the front of his jeans this time. "I know what's going on there." Then she touched his head. "But I don't know what's happening in there. I don't know if you're even in a place to think about kissing me again."

Oh, he was in the right place for that, but he heard the logic of what she was saying. He cursed the fucking logic, too.

"You want to know what's going on in my head?" he asked.

She nodded.

All right. Not exactly a shout for more, but Riley would give her what he could.

"I'm scared," he confessed. "And if you don't think it took a lot to admit that to you, think again."

She nodded. "I know it took a lot. Thank you."

Riley figured this could be the jumping-off point for a long conversation. One that he wasn't ready to have with her yet, and if they stayed out here against the barn wall, he'd just end up kissing her again. Besides, he thought he might have softened up enough now so he could walk.

He decided to go with the safer option.

"Come on." He slipped his arm around her waist and got her moving. "Let's go inside. I'm ready for another cold beer. This time, I'm going to drink it."

WELL, CLAIRE WASN'T ready for a beer. After that kissing session, she was ready to haul Riley off to bed. Her body was itching for more, more, more.

But the beer was a much safer option.

She hadn't been just doling out lip service when she'd spelled out her concerns. About Ethan. About Riley's mental health. About their polar-opposite lifestyles. He would be leaving soon, and she would be staying if not in Spring Hill, close enough to still call it home. And she wanted to call it home as much as

Riley wanted to eye the town and his family's ranch in his rear-view mirror as he sped away.

In his uniform.

Headed right back into situations where he could be killed.

Those were all major deal breakers, and still she had to force herself away from him and start the trek back into Calhoun's.

There was a fresh group of smokers at the back now. A small blessing. And they were in the middle of a heated discussion about the high school basketball team, so they barely noticed when she and Riley slipped past them inside.

"You're sure this is okay?" she asked. The crowd seemed even louder and rowdier than earlier.

Riley nodded. No verbal answer. Was that because he didn't want her to hear the lie in his voice? Just in case, Claire decided to stay close to him. However, she hadn't realized just how close that close would be when they started to worm their way through the crowd toward the bar.

Calhoun's wasn't exactly a dance hall, but that never stopped people from doing just that. The dancing started in the center and spread out, sometimes with couples bumping into tables and sloshing drinks. Which was exactly what happened to Riley and her.

Terrence Joe O'Malley and Misty were doing their own version of a boot-scootin' boogie, and they collided with Riley and her. They, in turn, collided with a table filled with pitchers of beer and the Nederland brothers. All three of them. No necks, bear-size shoulders. Low IQs. Beered up.

Never a good combination.

If Riley had been any other man in the place, with the exception of Logan, a fight would have quickly followed, but one of the Nederlands—she didn't know which one because they were like snowflakes, and she couldn't tell them apart—gave Riley a wobbly salute and snapped his fingers to the harried waitress to order another pitcher.

Since there were no open tables for Riley and her to do a finger snap of their own, the bar trek continued. More collisions. Claire got groped. Riley, too. And she prayed the groping didn't extend to his shoulder. He seemed to be making progress with the physical healing, and she didn't want him to have a setback, all because he insisted on having a beer.

"Well?" Livvy said from behind her.

She wasn't sure how her friend had gotten through the crowd at that angle, but Livvy even managed to crook her arm around Claire and yank her closer.

"How was it?" Livvy asked. Of course, she had to shout it.

There was no way Claire could answer that in this place. Probably no way to answer it even when Livvy and she were alone, so Claire just smiled and nodded.

But Livvy wasn't exactly smiling. Even in the filmy light, Claire could see something was wrong. Livvy got Riley's attention by tapping him on the back of the head, and then she motioned for Claire and him to follow her.

Away from the bar.

Too bad because Claire had worked up a thirst, and she needed something to cool her off.

It was impossible to ask Livvy why they were making the detour, and the detour wasn't any faster than their trek to the bar would have been. Livvy kept herding them through the crowd, all the way to the front entrance. It was marginally quieter there but much farther away from the beer.

"Your girlfriend's here," Livvy announced. She pointed toward the bar. Actually, she pointed *on* the bar. And Claire saw the woman dancing there. It took her another moment to realize that it was indeed Riley's girlfriend.

Jodi.

Well, that was a quick reminder for Claire of why she shouldn't have been kissing Riley outside.

"She's been asking for you," Livvy added. Not looking at Riley but rather Claire.

"Me?" Claire asked.

"Her?" Riley asked. "Why?"

"It was hard to hear the details, but I think Jodi believes you stole her man."

Well, good grief. And it wasn't exactly something that Claire could jump to deny. Except she could. The kissing hadn't gone beyond kissing. And an erection. But the erection had been Riley's reaction, of course, not hers.

Riley mumbled some profanity. "Jodi's drunk. She never makes sense when she's drunk. I'll handle this," he insisted and would have started toward the bar if Livvy hadn't stopped him.

"There's more," Livvy said, still looking at Riley now. "Daniel's here, too, and he's accusing you of stealing his girlfriend."

Claire wanted to scream, but instead she blurted out, "Balderdash." A word she'd never used in her life, but it beat screaming and the real profanity she wanted to use instead.

"My advice?" Livvy went on. "Why don't we just go over to the Tip Top and have a drink?"

The Tip Top was the only other drinking place in town, and there'd be no noise or bar dancing there. That was because it was a vegan, organic wine bar, and the only people who ever went there were people over seventy or the occasional drunkard who'd been kicked out of Calhoun's.

If Livvy had had her way, she would have pulled them right out of the pub, but before she could do that, Claire heard a shout. One that was very audible even over the crowd.

"Cindy!" Jodi shouted. "Don't you ignore me!"

And Claire knew the woman was referring to her. "I'll handle this," Riley repeated, and he started toward the bar with Claire and Livvy trailing along behind him.

"Remember Daniel's up there somewhere," Livvy yelled.

In the meantime, Jodi continued to yell, too. "That's right. Come on, Candy." She was facing Claire now and waggling her fingers. "We'll settle this woman to woman."

"You should stay back," Riley warned her.

Of course Claire ignored that. Yes, she was a mother, but that didn't mean she was just going to tuck tail and run. And there was an even bigger issue here if she didn't stand up to this loud-mouth. In addition to the gossips blabbing about Riley and her smooching outside Calhoun's, there'd be new gossip now about Jodi besting her in a showdown. Claire didn't especially want a showdown, but maybe, just maybe, they could get Jodi out of there so they could have a civil conversation.

"Claire," she heard when she got closer to the bar. Not Jodi— the woman wouldn't have gotten her name right—but Daniel. He fell in step alongside her as Riley continued to lead the way.

"You're really here with Riley?" Daniel asked. "I thought that was just a rumor."

"No. I came with Livvy, and Riley and I ran into each other." That was the sanitized version anyway. He'd hear the rest soon enough. Maybe then he'd want his ring back and would stop proposing to her.

They kept moving, and Claire noticed something strange going on. Something more strange than Jodi's slurred, stagger-ing attempts to call her names.

Chloe was her latest attempt.

But the other thing going on was that people were moving out of the way for Riley, Livvy, Daniel and Claire. She had no idea where the people were actually going because there was no room to create the path they were creating. But there it was.

And the now-open path led straight to the bar.

"Carrie!" Jodi shouted, pointing at Claire again. It was much easier for Jodi to see her now that only Riley was in the way. And the woman's glare zoomed right over Riley to Claire.

"She's been drinking," Mr. Obvious—aka Daniel—said. "I should get you out of here."

But Claire held her ground.

Unfortunately Jodi didn't.

She brought back her hand to do another finger point, probably more name-calling, too, but the sudden motion must have thrown her off balance. Jodi let out a loud shriek and fell face forward. If Riley hadn't rushed to grab her, she would have splatted right on the peanut-covered floor.

Riley howled. But his howl was one of pain. No doubt because the rescue had hurt his shoulder. Claire wanted to throttle Jodi for that alone. Jodi must have had throttling on the mind, too, because without any concern whatsoever about Riley, Jodi shrieked out some curse words and launched herself at Claire.

Someone got in the way.

At the exact moment of Jodi's launch, one of the Nederland sisters moved to the bar. Moved into Jodi's path, too. And the fist that Jodi had apparently meant for Claire slammed into the Nederland sister's face.

Oh no.

She didn't know which Nederland sister this was—Claire couldn't tell them apart, either—but there were three of them, all built like their linebacker-size brothers. The sister who'd gotten hit, hit back, and her sisters hurried to join the fray. The brothers, too.

Claire couldn't see much after that. Fists started flying. Chairs, too. A beer bottle went zinging past her, and it smacked her on the head. She would have gotten smacked with a second one if Riley hadn't gotten her out of the way.

"Get Claire out of here," Daniel told Riley. "I'll take care of Jodi."

Riley was still grimacing in pain, but Claire saw the debate he was waging with himself. He didn't want to leave Jodi in the middle of this.

More flying beer—this time in a pitcher—must have ended the debate for him because he caught on to Livvy with one hand, Claire with the other, and began to plow through the chaos.

They were still much too far away from the front door when Claire heard a sound that stopped everyone and everything. Including her heart.

Sirens.

And the Spring Hill Police Department cruiser squealed to a stop right in front of them.

CHAPTER THIRTEEN

WELL, THIS WAS not what Riley had in mind when he'd decided to go to Calhoun's for a beer. Here he was at the Spring Hill Police Department, hauled in for questioning in what had become a full-fledged brawl. Riley wasn't under arrest.

But Claire was.

And so were Daniel and Jodi.

Even though Riley had tried to explain that Claire didn't have any part in starting or finishing the fight, it didn't matter. Whoever had called the cops—apparently before blood was even drawn—had said that Claire and "Riley's crazy-assed girl-friend" were fighting. The cops had gone to Calhoun's looking specifically to break up that fight and had stormed in after Jodi and Claire just as Daniel threw a punch at one of the Nederland brothers. Or maybe it was one of their sisters.

Now there they were. And even though Riley wasn't behind bars with them, he'd decided to stay as close as possible and was sitting on the floor across from the side-by-side cells.

Claire's expression said it all. She was not pleased about any of this. Maybe because she was not only behind bars but was also pacing while holding an ice pack to her head where she'd gotten hit with a beer bottle.

She wasn't alone in that cell, either.

The Spring Hill Police Department only had two holding cells, and the Nederland siblings were in one of them. Riley was convinced all six siblings had glandular issues to make them the size of tree trunks, and when they were drunk—which they were—it wasn't safe to put anyone else in there with them. That's how Daniel, Claire and Jodi had ended up together in the other cell.

"This is all your fault," Daniel growled for the umpteenth time, and his growled words were meant for Riley.

Riley had given up on the notion of defending himself. Besides, it was his fault in a roundabout way. He should have insisted that Jodi leave Spring Hill. She probably wouldn't have listened—Jodi wasn't exactly one to do what people asked of her—but at least he could have tried. Now, here they were in this mess.

"It's her fault," Jodi argued, hitching her thumb in Claire's direction. Jodi winced, probably because she'd bruised her hand when she was trading punches with one of the Nederlands.

Claire gave Jodi a look that could have instantly frozen a vat of boiling water.

"It's your fault," one of the Nederland sisters said to no one in particular. The clan was all stewing but mainly because they hadn't gotten to finish their pitchers of beer before being hauled in.

Livvy stuck her head around the corner and motioned for Riley to get up. "This cop wants you to sign some papers."

That brought Claire to her feet, too. "Does that mean we're getting out?"

"I sure hope so." And Riley did hope that.

The minutes had crawled into hours, and he wanted Claire out of there and home. Daniel and Jodi, too, only because he thought he owed them that much. After that, Riley could go home, as well, and take some pain meds. His shoulder had gone past the throbbing stage and was now screaming at him.

He followed Livvy into the squad room. Such that it was. Crime wasn't a big problem in Spring Hill, so there was only the chief of police, Luke Mercer, two deputies and an admin assistant. Only the chief and one of the deputies were there tonight, and it was Deputy Davy Divine—his real name—who was sitting at the front desk with some papers neatly arranged in front of him.

"It's for their bail," Davy explained. He was a wormy-looking guy who'd never had a date or even a single look from a girl in school, but he'd found his forte with that badge. If Mayberry's Barney Fife and a zombie had managed to have a kid, it would have looked a lot like Davy.

"How much and who do I pay?" Riley asked.

"Five hundred apiece, and you pay here. We take check, debit or credit."

Riley whipped out his MasterCard. "But do you really think Claire and Daniel are flight risks?" He didn't include Jodi in that because she certainly could and would hightail it out of there just for the thrill of it.

"Doesn't matter what I think. The law's the law. Are you paying for the Nederlands, too?" Davy asked.

"No." And Riley couldn't say that fast enough. He needed to get a head start on them in case they renewed their disagreement with Jodi. "Just Claire, Daniel and Jodi." He signed the papers, and Davy took the credit card.

"I'll have to make sure the card is good." Davy examined it as if it were the norm for people in Spring Hill to give him fake credit cards. "Might take a while since our computer's down, and I'll have to call. You can sit back in there with your…friends or wait out here."

"Great. More waiting," Livvy mumbled.

Maybe this time it wouldn't take as long as it had to get the paperwork done. Holding on to that hope, Riley sank down in the chair across from Davy's desk to wait.

"Is Jodi usually like this?" Livvy asked.

"Sometimes. I've never been with her in a bar fight, but she tends to live life on the edge."

Which was exactly what had attracted him to her in the first place. Of course, she was drawn to his desire to live life on the edge, too, but Riley had never mixed that particular side of him with a dose of crazy.

"Claire was supposed to have hot sex tonight," Livvy said, sitting next to him. "Did she?"

It took him a moment to shift gears and absorb what Livvy said. Another moment to decide if he was going to answer at all. "No. Sadly, the closest she came was getting a splinter in her butt." Realizing just how that sounded, Riley gave her a warning glare. "And if you tell anyone that, I will hunt you down."

Livvy held up her hands in mock defense. "No threat needed. I'm not into gossip, and besides, any details I hear, I'd rather get from Claire."

Riley wondered exactly how Claire would catalogue this night. First, she'd had to coax him out of the flashback, then they'd kissed, then she'd gotten arrested. He figured the kiss was going to get lost in all that other mess. But it wasn't lost for him.

Nope.

He stood no chance whatsoever of forgetting exactly how Claire had felt in his arms. How she'd tasted. That sound she'd made. Now, that was a sound and a flashback he actually wanted to experience. With the way Davy was dragging his feet—he'd struck up a conversation with the chief now about whose turn it was to descale the coffeepot—there might be time for a flashback or two.

Riley was still thinking about that kiss when something else popped into his head. "What about Ethan? Who's with him?"

"Claire got a sitter." Livvy checked the time. "If Claire's not out in the next hour, I'll go to her house so the sitter can get home. I figured I'd be spending the night there anyway. Well, unless you're staying."

"I won't be staying."

Riley was certain of that. He was going to need a big dose of the painkillers, and they made him drowsy. They also made him talk in his sleep. Claire had been through enough without hearing about shit he didn't want her to hear about.

He was so caught up in his pain and thoughts that it took him a second to realize that Livvy's tone had changed on her next-to-last sentence.

"Why did you figure you needed to spend the night at Claire's?" he asked.

As Riley had done earlier, Livvy paused, maybe debating if she would answer. Or rather *how* to answer. "When Claire was sorting through a box, she found her mother's journal."

Hell. Riley didn't have to ask what was in it. He knew that if it had anything to do with her mother, it couldn't be good.

"She's torn up about what she read in it, Riley," Livvy added.

Of course she was. Her mother had been dead since she was a kid, and yet she could still put knots in Claire's stomach. "I don't guess Claire burned it?"

Livvy shook her head. "No such luck. She put it in one of the trash boxes, but she's been sorting for weeks, and not one trash box has left the house."

And this one wouldn't go out, either. Claire would end up reading every painful word in it. "Any idea what her mother wrote?"

"I only saw two words, fudging kid, except she used the real *F* word."

Great. He wondered if he could somehow talk Claire into putting it in a real trash bin. One that contained stuff she'd never see again. But he had to be honest with himself. He'd likely lost a lot of clout with Claire tonight. Ironic since they'd had their first kiss.

Second one, too.

But those might be the only kisses they'd ever have. She was probably ready to wash her hands of him and his crazy girlfriend. A girlfriend who would soon become an ex if Jodi didn't know that already. And that was an ex in a forever-and-ever kind of way, too.

Riley heard some movement in the holding cell, and he got up to make sure Claire was okay. Thankfully Jodi was asleep and snoring like a hibernating buffalo. Even Daniel had closed his eyes, and the Nederlands were all knocked out. The movement had come from an ice cube falling out of the plastic bag that Claire had been holding against her head.

"It won't be long now," Riley told her, something he'd been telling her since they arrived.

Even though it was against Deputy Davy's rules, Riley sank down on the floor right next to the cell, instead of across from it.

"You think we tempted fate or something?" she asked. She was still pacing. Not that she could go far. Six steps forward, six steps back. There were definitely no remnants of the heat that'd been between them at Calhoun's, and Riley didn't think the chill in the room was all from the AC.

"I think we just got unlucky," Riley answered.

"Hey, did somebody say my name?" a male voice called out.

Riley recognized the voice, of course, but he was hoping it was some kind of trick brought on by the pain and fatigue.

It wasn't.

With his arms outstretched and that cocky grin on his face, his brother Lucky walked in.

LUCKY HADN'T EXPECTED to see party faces, but this was one notch below the gloom-and-doom stage. It had a whole vibe of one of Dante's levels of hell.

And speaking of hell, Riley brought up the subject right away.

"What the hell are you doing here?" Riley asked, getting to his feet.

"I brought bail money. *Cash.* It'll take Deputy Dweeb out there all night to process a credit card, but he knows how to count money, provided you give him big enough bills so he doesn't have too many of them." Lucky had a little experience with that. "He's getting the keys now to unlock the cell."

Maybe it was the mention of being sprung, but thankfully Claire had a warmer reaction to Lucky than Riley had. She smiled, but that smile didn't win him any brotherly awards with Riley because it only deepened his scowl. That scowl was probably about that phone conversation they'd had a couple of nights ago. The one where Riley grilled him about the sex talk Lucky had had with Claire ages ago.

Riley just liked to hang on to things.

Like beer, apparently.

Lucky got a strong whiff of it when he walked closer. "Jeez, what'd you do? Pour a beer over your head?"

Riley could have sent small children and animals running with that glare. "That look doesn't work on big brothers," Lucky let him know.

Lucky pushed past him to get to Claire and he gave her a cheek kiss through the cell bars. Like his experience with bail money, it wasn't his first through-the-bars kiss. "Are you okay?"

She gave him a flat look, too, but then added another smile. A really small one. Of course, the new smile didn't sit well with little brother, and Lucky wondered if Riley knew it was jealousy driving all these intense feelings. Probably not. Jealousy wasn't covered by one of Riley's man-rules.

"How'd you know we were here?" Claire asked.

Lucky held up his phone and showed her the flurry of calls, texts and voice mails he'd gotten in the past hour. It was the norm for the Nederlands to land in jail, but it was the story of the decade, maybe the century, for Claire to get locked up. Folks just couldn't wait to tell him that Riley had been at the scene of the crime, too.

It was a funny, tenuous thing being a McCord. Having money generated as much admiration as it did sour grapes, and people were always happy to see a McCord come down a notch.

That was one of the reasons Lucky liked to provide such entertainment to the townsfolk. Even though he'd never get any thanks for being labeled the family screwup, it took pressure off Riley, Anna and Logan.

Deputy Dweeb finally arrived with a ring of keys that clanged and rattled as he went through them, searching for the right one. Since there weren't that many doors in the entire town, Lucky had a theory that Davy had scrounged up the extra keys just to make himself look more important. It didn't work. Davy could have had the keys to every door in the world, and he'd still be a dweeb.

The moment the cell door was open, Claire rushed out. She hugged him and then made a beeline for Livvy.

Ah, Livvy.

No gloom and doom for her. Well, not when Lucky had first come in anyway, but it was obvious the woman was ready to get Claire out of there.

Daniel got up, too, and he shook the snoring woman on the cot. This was Jodi, no doubt. Riley's girlfriend and the reason for Claire's incarceration.

Lucky would take that up with his brother later.

"You got one more paper you have to sign," the deputy told Claire.

With Daniel still trying to rouse Jodi, Riley, Claire, Livvy and Lucky all went back into the squad room. And, yes, there was a paper to be signed. Of course, Davy had to find it first. Then he'd have to find a working pen.

Lucky wasn't sure how Davy even made it out of the house by himself.

The wait gave Riley more chances to sling that ugly look at Lucky. "Why are you here in Spring Hill?"

Lucky shrugged. "Logan called and asked me to come home."

No glare this time. Riley looked at him as if he'd sprouted an extra ear. "Logan calls you all the time and asks you to come home. You never do."

"I like being unpredictable." That was his answer, and he was

sticking to it. Of course, Riley would soon figure it out. Unlike
Deputy Dweeb, his brother had a functioning brain. And when
Riley did figure it out, he wasn't going to like it.

This was going to be like the potty training all over again except this time it was going to require more than pissing on a tree.

"Ouch," Claire grumbled, getting all their attention.

Lucky hadn't seen what had prompted her ouch, but in the
aftermath he noticed she was looking at her backside. He made
it to her ahead of Riley, turned her and quickly spotted the
problem.

"You got splinters." He plucked the ones he could see from
her jeans. "That happened to me once. Got it when I was making out with Wendy Lee Keller against the wall outside Calhoun's Pub."

And the silence rolled in like London fog.

So, hell. That's what had happened. Riley and Claire had
made out. Maybe even more. Lucky glanced at them, assessing.

No. Not more.

They would have been more content, or uneasy, if they'd
had sex.

But the making out had been enough. Maybe Jodi had gotten
jealous. Daniel, too. Or as Lucky liked to call Daniel, Dweeb
Two. The Nederlands had likely just been the rocket fuel that
fed all this.

On general principle Lucky wasn't opposed to Riley and
Claire making out. But—and this was a huge *but*—he didn't
want Riley doing that unless he'd come to his senses and realized that playing with Claire's heart was the same thing as giving it a good ass-whipping.

If Riley didn't use his more than half a brain to figure that
out, Lucky intended to spell it out for him.

"I need to sleep," Jodi grumbled from behind them. Daniel
had managed to get her on her feet, barely, and he had finally
gotten her out of the cell. Daniel looked at Riley as if he expected him to take things from there.

Riley didn't budge.

That half brain was doing its job. Lucky didn't know this Jodi, but she had bad news written all over her. And Lucky should know. He was an expert at picking out bad girls. She was far more his type that GI Riley's.

Deputy Dweeb finally made it back with the paperwork, and Lucky provided the pen. One that he'd taken from the dweeb's desk right after he came into the police station. Dealing with the deputy was a little like getting stuck in the movie *Groundhog Day*, and Lucky had learned some shortcuts to speed things up. Like bringing cash and stealing pens. In case it had been needed, he also had some advice on how to descale a coffeepot.

Claire hurried to sign the paper.

"I just got a call from Wilma over at the newspaper," the deputy said. "I think you should know they're running a story on the pub brawl in the morning. There'll be pictures."

"How'd the newspaper get pictures?" Daniel howled. He was apparently the only one in the room who didn't know the answer.

"Cell phones," each of them answered, adding varying verbs and adjectives. Jodi even added a knowing grunt. Anyone who wasn't falling-down drunk would have wanted to snap shots of something like that. It wasn't as if brawls happened in the pub on a daily basis.

More like monthly.

Claire didn't even read the paper Davy gave her. She just signed it and glanced at Lucky. "Thanks for the bail money. I'll pay you back." Then she turned to Livvy. "Please take me home now. I have to get some rest, and makeup concealer, before I do that photo shoot in the morning."

For a moment Lucky thought she was just going to waltz out of there and not even say goodbye. And she did sort of do just that.

"Next time I want a beer, I'll have it at home," Claire grumbled.

Livvy winked at Lucky, gave him the call-me sign with her

pinkie and thumb, and slipped her arm around Claire to get them moving. Claire did look back, though. At Riley this time, and Lucky tried to figure out how to describe the look she gave him. Definitely no Mona Lisa smile moment. More like Munch's *The Scream*. There was no call-me gesture involved.

"She's just tired and upset," Lucky said. And he nudged Riley, as well, and moved him to the big glass window so they could watch Claire and Livvy leave. "But you gotta admit, this proves exactly what I was saying to you the last time we talked."

Riley looked at him as if he'd sprouted another nose to go with that extra ear. "What the hell are you talking about?"

"That." Lucky motioned toward Claire. "That's the face of a woman who's in love with you."

Even though they were in the police station and Lucky knew it would hurt like hell, he let Riley ball up his fist and punch him.

CHAPTER FOURTEEN

CLAIRE FIGURED THAT was the worst photo shoot she'd ever done, but at least she had managed to finish it. Not easy with her head still hurting from the beer and lack of sleep.

Especially the lack of sleep.

After getting home from the bar brawl/arrest ordeal, she had been so wound up that she hadn't slept a wink. She'd finally given up, left Ethan with Livvy and had gotten some pictures edited before leaving hours earlier than necessary for the photo shoot. Now that it was done, she was going to have to face a cold, hard reality.

She had kissed Riley, and she'd liked it. Too much. So much so that it was driving her crazy. And it was just the tip of the frosty little iceberg that was now her life.

She had a police record.

Her face was plastered in the town newspaper.

And, yes, it was there because she hadn't been able to resist glancing at it in the stand when she'd driven past the grocery store. On the front page was a picture of one of the Nederlands flinging Jodi at her. It looked a lot worse than it'd been, which, of course, was exactly why it had gone on the front page. Claire had no doubts, *none*, that by now every copy had already sold out.

Balancing her camera equipment, Claire let herself into the

house, expecting to see Summer Starkley, one of the twins, there with Ethan. But it wasn't Summer or her sister, Savannah. It was Livvy. She and Ethan were at the kitchen table, and judging from the volume of cookies and ice cream in front of them, they were either on a quest to become diabetic or celebrating something.

Claire figured it wasn't the latter because there was nothing to celebrate.

"Summer had car trouble, couldn't come," Livvy said, not addressing the treats. "So Ethan got me as a sitter today."

Both Ethan and Livvy seemed pretty happy about that, but the happiness could have been just a sugar high.

"Thanks for staying with him," she told Livvy.

"No prob. And hey, you did a great job covering up the bruise on your face. I can hardly see it."

That was a very bad lie. The couple that Claire had photographed had noticed it first thing. So had the attendant at the gas station where she'd filled up. And now so did Ethan.

"Boo-boo," he said, pointing right to it.

He'd been asleep when Claire had gotten home from jail— now, that was something she thought she'd never say about herself. *Home from jail.* Anyway, Ethan had still been asleep when she'd left for work, so this was his first chance to see the proof of the bad decisions she'd made the night before.

"Mommy's fine," Claire assured him, and she kissed his cheek. She hugged him, too, despite the fact he was holding a spoon dripping with ice cream. "What's with all the sugar?"

The confused look on Livvy's face let Claire know she needed to clarify. "Sugar-sugar." Not shit.

"Oh, this," Livvy said in the tone of something not even worth mentioning. "Riley dropped by earlier and brought it. Oh, and Ethan peed on the tree in your backyard. Is that okay?"

No, it wasn't. She was trying to redirect his bodily functions in the direction of a real toilet, but since his diaper usage had been cut by half, it was hard for Claire to dispute the temporary potty-training method. However, that wasn't what had her attention now.

"Riley was here?" Claire asked.

"Riley!" Ethan squealed, and he clapped his hand against the drippy spoon.

Livvy nodded. "He brought ice cream, cookies and a new wallpaper scraper for you." She pointed to the scraper on the counter. "He said word around town was you'd broken your other one."

She had but was miffed about how something so mundane had made the gossip factory when there were so many other juicy things for people to discuss.

"Did Riley, uh, say anything else?" Claire asked.

"Sor-ree," Ethan supplied.

"Yes, sorry. Riley did say that a lot," Livvy continued, talking around the egg-size bite of ice cream she'd just stuffed into her mouth. "He really is sorry for what happened at Calhoun's. I think all this was his idea of a peace offering. A sugar-hot peace offering if you ask me."

Yes, it was, but Claire would have liked to have been there for his visit. Or maybe not, she quickly amended. She was embarrassed and not at all sure what to say to him, so maybe it was a good thing she'd been at work.

"Don't worry," Livvy went on. "I had Ethan eat some healthy stuff before he got dessert."

"Ickin, tarrots," Ethan attempted. "Bocci." Chicken, carrots and broccoli. The first two were his favorites, the broccoli not so much, but her son must have known there was sugar and lots of it at the end of the proverbial veggie tunnel.

"Did Riley say anything else?" Claire pressed. The first time she'd asked it, Livvy had barely spared her a glance. But she stared at Claire now.

"He didn't bring up j-a-i-l, and neither did I. Didn't bring up the k-i-s-s-y stuff, either."

Ethan stared at her, too. "K-i-spell-y?"

Livvy cackled with laughter, causing Ethan to laugh, too, and while it normally would have gotten a smile or chuckle from Claire, her funny bone was broken today. She'd left it and her dignity on the floor of Calhoun's Pub.

Riley hadn't mentioned something as huge as jail and the kiss? Of course, Claire hadn't wanted him to talk to Livvy about either of those, but she'd figured he would have mentioned it in a roundabout way. Ditto for the roundabout approach to the kiss since he might have figured that she had already discussed it with Livvy.

She hadn't. Not in detail anyway.

Despite Livvy's best attempts to get her to bare her soul, Claire had only acknowledged the kiss and nothing more. Since Livvy had been the one to get out the final splinter, Claire had decided that baring her butt to her friend was plenty enough for one night.

"There was so much ice cream. Three half gallons," Livvy went on, still eating. "I put some in the freezer for later, and we gave Whoa a scoop of the vanilla."

Sure enough Claire could see the cat through the glass door on the back porch, and he/she and his/her companion were licking away. It probably wasn't good for a cat to have that much sugar, either, but considering this was Whoa, she doubted anything would do much more harm. He didn't just look as if he'd been cooking meth, more as though he had been using it frequently.

"If you want to go over to Riley's and thank him," Livvy added, "I can watch Ethan a little longer."

Claire didn't even consider it. She looked like hell, felt even worse. What she really needed was a bath and a nap.

After some ice cream, of course.

Claire was about to sit down and see if she could start her own journey toward type 2 diabetes when her phone rang. For one heartbeat-skipping moment she thought it might be Riley, and she had to fight back the panic of what or what not to say to him. But it was a different McCord.

Anna.

Oh, no. Had the gossip managed to reach Riley's sister even though she was miles and miles away in Florida? In case it had, Claire stepped into the living room to take the call. She didn't want to have to explain j-a-i-l in front of Ethan.

"I hate to bother you," Anna greeted, "but I wondered if you'd heard from Riley?"

That was such a loaded question that Claire went with one of her own. "What's this about?"

Anna made a sound of frustration. "I just got a call from Lucky, who said Riley had gotten news from the military base. He has to show up tomorrow morning first thing for a meeting with the brass."

"This is the first I'm hearing about it." Claire tried not to be alarmed. However, Anna clearly was. "What's the meeting about?"

"Well, Riley didn't get into a lot of details. He just said it was a meeting about his medical review. Lucky said Riley's expecting good news, that he'll soon be returning to active duty. God, Claire. Is he ready for that? I mean, has his shoulder healed? Has *Riley* healed?"

"He's *healing*," she settled for saying. But it'd been less than twenty-four hours since he'd had a flashback. How would he deal with those if he was right back in a situation that had caused those flashbacks in the first place?

"And Riley thought this meeting would actually put him back in uniform?" Claire asked.

"That's what Lucky was pretty sure he heard, and he said Riley went straight to his room and started packing. Listen, Claire, if you hear from him, let me know. I've tried calling, but it goes straight to voice mail."

Oh, God.

Claire felt stunned. Then furious. Riley could teach her son to pee on a tree, he could bring over a mountain of ice cream, but he couldn't tell her something as important as this?

Then the sickening feeling came. And the heart-crushing ache.

So, maybe the ice cream and cookies hadn't been an apology after all. Maybe that had been Riley's way of saying goodbye.

"CAPTAIN McCORD," the first lieutenant greeted him when Riley walked into the office.

According to his name tag, his last name was Silverman. Riley didn't know him, but he was probably the colonel's exec, which was the military's equivalent of an assistant. Riley hoped this would be the last time he'd ever see him.

Because Riley wanted to walk out of this building with an assurance that he'd be returning to duty, immediately, as a Combat Rescue Officer.

"Colonel Becker will call you back when he's ready." The lieutenant motioned toward some chairs. "You can sit there and wait...with your guest."

Riley certainly hadn't forgotten about his *guest*. Lucky. Apparently, the lieutenant hadn't, either, because he eyed Lucky, who'd not only already sat down but was in his usual lounging pose, slumped in the seat, arms folded over his chest, his jeans-clad legs stretched out in front of him. He was wearing a shiny silver rodeo buckle the size of a child's head. If this wait went on very long, Lucky would probably pull down the brim of his Stetson and take a nap.

Lucky wasn't the ideal person to bring along for moral support, but his shoulder was still giving him trouble when driving in the city traffic during rush hour, and the base was situated right in San Antonio. That's the reason he'd scheduled his PT and doctor's appointments at hours when the traffic wouldn't be so bad. But he hadn't had control of the timing for this meeting.

Riley hadn't wanted to risk showing up while on pain meds, especially since he was weaning himself off them.

"This reminds me of the Spring Hill jail," Lucky remarked.

It would look like that to Lucky. Anything resembling structure and rules would make him feel hemmed in. But when Riley looked at it, he saw the polished tiled floors. The tasteful, patriotic artwork on the walls. The lieutenant's neatly organized desk. Everything was in its place. All the expectations spelled out in black-and-white in the regulations.

Unlike life in Spring Hill.

He was never sure what Logan expected or wanted from him. Claire, either, for that matter. Especially her. He needed to call her soon. Maybe after this meeting was over and things were settled. He owed her a face-to-face apology.

That mentally stopped him.

Was that all he owed her?

After all, he had gotten close to her over the past month. And he'd kissed her. Plus, she'd gotten him through the bad flashback at Calhoun's even if it had taken him a half hour of showering to get the smell of beer off him.

"You're doing some deep thinking." Lucky rubbed his jaw where Riley had punched him. "You're not thinking about hitting me again, are you?"

"No." At least not here. "And you deserved that, by the way."

Lucky didn't argue, which meant he likely knew it was true.

"Claire's not in love with me," Riley mumbled.

Lucky didn't argue with that, either, but damn it, his silence felt like an argument anyway. Or maybe he was just losing it. He needed to get his mind on something else.

"Thanks for driving me," Riley told him. "I didn't think you'd come."

Lucky shrugged. "Didn't think you'd want me to come."

"I didn't," he admitted. "But thanks anyway. I didn't want to have to ask Logan."

"Logan," Lucky repeated. "On the drive over he would have talked you into doing some work for the family business. Not that he needs you specifically to do it. Or me. He's got people who know that business better than I know my own toenails. I've got a theory, though, that Logan wants us involved because it gives him validation."

Riley wasn't following him. "Validation for what?"

"That he did the right thing by staying behind and building the company." Lucky shifted in the seat so he could face him. "You see, part of my theory is that he'd like to be off doing things we're doing."

Riley never considered Lucky the model for human logic, but he might be on to something. Either that or Logan just wanted McCord Cattle Brokers to grow, grow and keep on growing. Sometimes, it was a uniform—or a silver rodeo buckle—that fueled people, but maybe at the root of it, all three of them were just running from being ordinary. And in their own varying ways, they had succeeded.

At least Logan and he had. Riley wasn't sure about Lucky.

"Logan will still try to suck you back in before you manage to run for the sandy places where you rescue people," Lucky continued. "My advice—don't let him bully you into doing anything you don't want to do."

Bully was sure a harsh word. Logan had more of the make-'em-feel-guilty approach. "He bullied you into coming back," Riley reminded him.

"No. I didn't come back because he asked me. I came back for *you*."

Riley turned toward him so quickly that it caused the lieutenant to look up from a file he was reading.

"For me?" Riley shook his head. "How'd you figure that?"

"I knew Logan would be coming at you with guns loaded. That's a metaphor," Lucky added, glancing at the lieutenant in case he was still listening. "I thought you could use somebody on your side to make sure you get to live the life you want to live. When it's time for you to go, just go. I'll deal with these horse trainers that Logan keeps pissing off. Will deal with the horses, too. Heck, he pisses them off, as well. I get along with horses, women and trainers just fine."

"Does that mean you're moving back home?"

"Heck, no." Lucky didn't hesitate, either. "But Logan's not the only one with sneaky skills. I've got a rodeo up in Abilene in a week, and I'll be there."

Riley didn't doubt it, but all this talk made him realize he really didn't know much about Lucky's life. Or Logan's for that matter. Logan had a longtime girlfriend—perfect, of course. Helene.

Well, perfect for him anyway.

Beautiful, polished, business savvy. She'd look good on those magazine covers Logan was always appearing on. Riley figured one day they'd get married and be the perfect couple together, on and off the magazine covers.

But Lucky was a different story, and Riley had his own theory about Lucky's future. Definitely not picture-perfect by most people's standards.

Of the four McCord kids, Lucky had been the closest to their mom. Losing her and their dad had been hard on all of them, but that's when Lucky had started to pull away from the family. And the pulling away had only caused Logan to try to herd them all back together. Logan had stayed and been the responsible one. Lucky had joined the rodeo, which was a Texan's version of running off to join the circus.

"Are you happy?" Riley asked his brother. It wasn't something guys usually asked each other, but he figured this might be as close to a heart-to-heart as he'd ever get with Lucky.

"Sure." But it took Lucky too long to answer. "Don't know how much longer I'll be able to bull ride though. There's only so much ball-busting a man can take before the balls start to protest."

Lucky didn't change his expression, but Riley heard it in his brother's voice. The fear of losing what made him Lucky Mc-

Cord. Yeah, Riley got that. His uniform was like that rodeo buckle that Lucky was always trying to win.

Before Riley could ask more about that sneaky skill set, a skill set Riley might want to learn, the colonel's door opened, and he motioned for Riley to go inside his office.

Unlike the lieutenant, this was an officer that Riley did know. Colonel Becker had visited the base during Riley's second deployment, and Riley had escorted him into a classified area for a briefing. The colonel hadn't changed much in those couple of years. A little more gray at his temples. Maybe an extra wrinkle or two, but he was someone Riley trusted to give it to him straight.

Riley only hoped that *straight* was good news.

However, judging from the colonel's expression, maybe it wasn't as good as Riley had hoped for.

Riley reported in by saluting. "Captain McCord reporting as ordered." He held the salute until the colonel saluted him back and then lowered his hand. With the formalities over, Riley took a seat when the colonel gestured for him to sit.

"You didn't pass your physical," he told Riley right off.

Riley nodded. Not exactly a news flash. "But the shoulder's improving, and I should be able to pass the next one. The physical therapist said I could up my home exercises to three hours a day."

Colonel Becker looked him straight in the eyes. "Can you pass a physical in two weeks?"

"Sure."

Riley didn't have a clue if that was true or not. But it was something that was partially in his control. He was doing all the physical therapy exercises and then some. He was up to five hours a day with what he was doing at PT and at home. And convincing the mental health folks was doable, as well.

If he didn't mention the flashbacks, that is.

However, it was possible the exercises still wouldn't be

enough to get him through the physical. His shoulder simply might not be able to take the weight that he'd be required to lift.

That didn't mean he wouldn't try. Hell, yes. He'd try. That's why he'd gone ahead and packed because when he got orders, he wanted to be ready to go.

"The flight surgeon doesn't think you can pass the physical," the colonel went on. "Not even in a month, much less in half that time. He thinks your injury will give you limitations—permanent ones. Ones that you can't have and still be a Combat Rescue Officer."

Riley sure hoped he didn't look as bad as he suddenly felt. Each word was like a punch from a fist.

"You personally talked to the flight surgeon?" Riley asked.

The colonel nodded.

Good. Riley continued, "And did he or she give you odds as to whether or not I could pass that physical in two weeks?"

Colonel Becker blew out a long breath. What he didn't do was answer.

"Was it fifty-fifty?" Riley pressed. "Because I can win if it's fifty-fifty."

"Maybe when it comes to extractions in the desert, but this isn't a fifty-fifty kind of situation."

"Then what is it?" Riley insisted.

"Twenty-eighty at best."

Oh, hell. Yeah, that was bad, but he'd won with odds that bad before, too. *Once.* But if he had been able to do it then, he could do it again.

The colonel put his elbows on his desk, leaned closer. "Look, you know how this works, Captain. A Combat Rescue Officer has to be a hundred percent. If not, you put your whole team, your extractions and the mission at risk."

"I know that." Riley hadn't intended to snap while talking to a superior officer, but he did. "But I have to be a CRO. There's no other choice."

The colonel made a sound to indicate otherwise. "If you fail the physical, you'll either have to retrain into a different career field, one less physically demanding—"

"I don't want a different career field." And yeah, he snapped again.

"Then you'd have to resign your commission."

To a civilian, those words might not mean much, but they sure as heck meant something to Riley. Resigning his commission would mean getting out of the Air Force.

He'd be ordinary again.

"I'm telling you all of this because you should prepare yourself for the worst," the colonel added. "I'll see you in two weeks."

Riley went on autopilot, standing, then saluting the colonel before he did an about-face and walked out of the room. It felt as if his entire world had come crashing down on him.

Lucky stood when he saw his face, and his brother mumbled something Riley didn't catch. Lucky went to him and gave him a pat on the back.

"Come on," Lucky said. "I think you need some therapy. Not that kind of therapy," he corrected when Riley just stared at him. "My version of therapy. In a couple of hours, I promise you that things are going to look a whole lot brighter."

CHAPTER FIFTEEN

THINGS DIDN'T LOOK brighter at all, but Riley had to admit that things weren't feeling as shitty as they had. The shots of tequila had helped with that, but underneath the tequila haze, Riley knew this was a temporary lull. Tomorrow, he'd have to face a cold, hard reality.

But that was tomorrow.

Tonight, he was back at Calhoun's Pub, drinking his troubles away.

Lucky had brought him here after they'd gotten back from the base. They'd made a quick trip to the house just so Riley could change out of his uniform. Lucky had said something about not wanting to disgrace it, and Riley had agreed.

He figured he'd get a full glass of disgracing tonight.

With several of the Nederlands cheering him on, Riley bit into the lime, took a shot of tequila and finished the ritual by licking the salt. At first all of this had felt very frat-party-ish, but after multiple bites, shots and licks, Riley wasn't sure he cared. Neither did the Nederlands, who were doing two shots for Riley's every one.

Of course, they were double his size, so it probably took that much tequila for them to get the same buzz that was going on in Riley's head.

There'd be no brawls tonight—mainly because he was now drinking with the brawlers. Plus, there really wasn't anyone to start any trouble. Other than the now-friendly Nederlands, there was just Lucky, him, the bartender and the petite blonde waitress who was flirting with Lucky. Naturally, Lucky was flirting back. Except it had moved past the flirting stage, Riley realized, when Lucky kissed her.

Seeing that kiss brought it all back. Not the flashback, thank God, but what had happened with Claire outside this very building. *Oh, man.* He could still taste her. Could still remember everything about those moments.

And he wanted more.

Of course, the tequila could be playing into that desire, but Riley didn't think so. He didn't need alcohol to make him want Claire. Plus, he did owe her that apology.

"Think I'll go for a walk," Riley said to no one in particular.

Lucky tore himself away from his flirting/kissing with the cocktail waitress and looked at him. "You want me to drive you?"

"No. I'll be fine."

Lucky tore himself away even more. "You're not driving, are you?"

Not a chance. He was well past his limit, and he wasn't stupid.

"Nope. It's a nice night for a walk." Maybe it was. Riley didn't have a clue. But he didn't want Lucky driving him to Claire's. That would feel more like junior high than a frat party.

Besides, Claire's place wasn't far, and he could get there, apologize. Maybe kiss her good-night. And then head on home. If there ended up being more than one good-night kiss, even better.

Seven would be ideal. That would equal the amount of tequila shots he'd taken.

It turned out, though, that it really wasn't a good night for a walk. It was still hot, and he'd drank so much that he was sweating tequila by the time he made it the handful of blocks to her place. When he saw her lights were still on, Riley took that as a good sign, especially since he'd forgotten to check the time. It could have been anywhere between eight at night and three in the morning.

He made it up the steps of her porch, knocked and did a breath test by blowing against his palm. On the first attempt, he missed his palm and had to do it again. Too bad he didn't have a mint or something, but maybe the lime would mask the tequila.

Or not.

Claire opened the door, cautiously, as if she expected Jack the Ripper to be on her porch. She took one look at him. One whiff, too. "You're drunk?"

It was possible that it wasn't even a question, but Riley chose to put a question mark at the end of what she'd just said.

"Tequila shots with Lucky," he explained.

"Of course," she said as if this were a normal occurrence. She glanced behind him. "How'd you get here?"

Now, that was a question. "Walked from Calhoun's." Was he slurring? *Hell.* Yeah, he was. "I wanted to say I was sorry."

She folded her arms over her chest and that's when Riley realized she was wearing just a T-shirt and nothing else. It was a longish T-shirt that hit her midthigh, but the arm folding hiked it up a bit.

"You packed your clothes. Are you here to tell me goodbye?" she asked. Now, that was a real question.

Because his head was suddenly whirling, it took him a moment to wrap his mind around what she was saying. "No. I'm here to apologize and to kiss you seven times." The last part was something he shouldn't have said aloud. "Sorry. That was the tequila talking."

"Obviously." She huffed, unfolded her arms so she could put her hand on his waist and led him inside.

No kiss, though, and Riley was so dizzy, he wasn't even sure if he could locate her mouth. Any attempt at this point might result in an ear kiss.

"Is Ethan up?" he asked.

"No. It's ten thirty. He's been in bed for hours."

Ten thirty didn't sound that late to him, but he'd forgotten that Claire's schedule probably included turning in early so she could then get up early with Ethan. Did that mean he'd woken her? Maybe. But there were some boxes in the living room so maybe she'd been doing more sorting.

He wondered if she'd tossed the journal. Wondered, too, if he was sober enough to work that into the conversation.

No, Riley decided. He wasn't sober enough for that.

She led him to the sofa, had him sit. She disappeared into the kitchen and came back with a bottle of water. "What happened? Did you have another flashback?"

"No. I was at the base, got some…news."

"Bad news?"

"Twenty-eighty." Riley didn't expect her to get that, and maybe she didn't, but she made a sound that could have been one of understanding.

"You can stay in the guest room," she said, motioning for him to follow her. "And I can drive you home in the morning. Logan's at your house, and I doubt you want to run into him tonight. Not like this anyway."

Riley didn't. He didn't want to know the things he'd say to his big brother while under the influence of Jose Cuervo. "How did you know Logan was there?"

"He called earlier to find out if I knew where you and Lucky were. He mentioned he was at the house and that he'd be spending the night because another shipment of horses is scheduled to arrive in the morning." She paused. "What's he doing with all those horses anyway?"

"Making money, I'm sure. And setting a trap to snare Lucky and me into adding a cutting-horse empire to the cattle empire he already runs."

Of course there was more to it than that. Their father had always wanted to bring in cutting horses, and maybe that's what was fueling Logan. Maybe he wanted to keep being Daddy's good boy. It was hard to know since Logan wasn't the feeling-sharing type.

One thing for certain—Logan was the money-sharing type. Even though he ran the business, he split the profits four ways. Riley had never touched his portion. It was in his accounts being invested and reinvested by Logan's financial gurus. But Riley always figured if he touched it that it would obligate him to do a lot more than he wanted to do—like stay in Spring Hill.

Riley knew where the guest room was. He'd helped Claire's grandmother haul some old furniture out of there when he'd been about sixteen or so. Despite the other changes in the house—stripped wallpaper and some fresh paint—the room hadn't changed in all that time. Even with the tequila messing with his head, he thought maybe that was the same quilted bedspread. And because the tequila was messing with his head, Riley had no choice but to drop down on it.

Claire didn't drop down, though. She pulled back the covers for him on the other side of the bed and started helping with this boots. Good thing, too, because Riley wasn't sure he could see his boots, much less take them off.

He made a mental note to avoid all forms of bite, drink and lick in the future. Tomorrow, he probably wouldn't remember that mental note, but he was certain his head would remind him.

Certain that Claire would, too.

"I don't suppose Lucky or you will fall in to this trap Logan is setting?" she asked.

"Not a chance." He chuckled but quit when he saw that it wasn't funny to her. Just the opposite.

"Anna said you packed your things when you heard about the meeting at the base," Claire tossed out there.

Hell's bells. "Anna called you, too?"

Claire nodded, pulled off the second boot. "She's worried about you. Everyone's worried about you."

"Does that include you?" he asked.

"I thought I made that pretty clear when I said *everyone*." And she didn't sound at all happy about that.

This sure wasn't going the way Riley had thought it would. A shame. Since Claire looked darn amazing in that old *NSYNC T-shirt. And that wasn't the tequila talking. She always looked amazing.

Always looked kissable, too.

"Sleep," she insisted. "We'll talk in the morning." Then she did something else amazing.

Claire kissed him.

Not on the cheek, either. It was full on the mouth.

Well, he got the good-night kiss after all, but Riley wasn't in any shape to do anything about it. Nor did Claire wait around for him to do anything about it. She pulled the covers over him, turned off the lights and walked out.

"Tookie?"

The word seemed to come out of nowhere, and it forced its way into Riley's dream. Not a nightmare. He was dreaming about Claire. Specifically, Claire kissing him, and he wanted to hang on to that dream as long as possible.

The jab to his cheek put an end to it, though.

Riley forced open his eyes, caught a glimpse of Ethan and was so glad he was able to bite back the profanity that was trying to leap out of his mouth. The pain shot through his head. Not the other kinds of pain he'd been feeling, either. This was fresh, new and raw. Really raw. Added to that his mouth felt as if skunks had nested in it.

In short, he had a hangover.

And Ethan was there, holding a cookie under Riley's nose.

It took Riley a couple of seconds to realize that Ethan and the cookie weren't part of the dream. They were real. And so was the bed he was sleeping in. Claire's bed. Or rather the bed in Claire's guest room. It all came rushing back to him then in perfect detail. He'd gotten drunk, shown up at her house and she'd put him to bed to sleep it off.

"Tookie?" Ethan offered him again. He had two, both half-eaten, and he was offering Riley one of the halves.

"Ethan, you'd better not be into those cookies again," Claire called out.

For a kid who didn't talk much, Ethan certainly had no trouble communicating. His eyes widened, and he knew he was in a boatload of trouble. Probably because Claire didn't want her son to eat cookies for breakfast.

Or rather lunch.

Riley checked his watch and nearly bolted from the bed. Hell, it was almost noon. He hadn't slept that late since he'd gone in the military. He was usually an up-before-the-sun kind of guy. That only reinforced his vow never to touch tequila again—and never to go drinking with Lucky.

"Ethan?" Claire said, the sound of her footsteps headed right toward the guest room. It was probably a violation of some parenting rule, but Riley took both cookie halves from Ethan and started eating the evidence.

His stomach protested right off, but he kept eating. However, he wasn't finished when Claire poked her head around the doorjamb. She didn't have to say words, either, for her expression to scold Ethan.

"He brought me some cookies for lunch," Riley volunteered.

Claire looked skeptical. Ethan looked skeptical, too, probably knowing that his mom wouldn't buy the little white lie that Riley had told. But Claire didn't address the white lying. That's because she was hopping around, trying to put on her shoes. No more *NSYNC T-shirt or mussed bedtime hair. She was wearing a slim blue skirt and top. Makeup, too.

"An engagement photo shoot had to be moved to today," she said, "and I have to head out like—" she did a watch check, as well "—now. The sitter can't be here for another half hour so I was wondering if you could watch Ethan until she arrives?"

Ethan looked as skeptical as Riley felt. Instead of expressing that, he said to Claire, "Of course. No problem."

"You're sure? I wouldn't want to interfere with the PT exercises you've been doing."

Even with the fuzzy head, Riley knew what that meant. One of his siblings had no doubt told her about the hours of exercises he'd been doing each day. If it had been Anna doing the telling, she would have gotten her info from Della or Stella, and the sisters would have told his own sister that he was overdoing it.

"I'll have time," he assured her. Later, he'd call each of his siblings and tell them to quit blabbing to Claire.

"Good. Thanks so much for this. If you need to go to the bathroom, you should do that now while I'm still here."

She was talking to him, Riley realized. And he hobbled off to do as she suggested. When he got back, Claire scooped up Ethan, kissed him. "Be a good boy for Riley."

Ethan rattled off something that Riley didn't catch, and ran out of the room. That was Riley's cue to get moving, too. But he didn't exactly move with the same speed and enthusiasm as Ethan. Riley finally caught up with them in the living room.

"Ethan's had his lunch," Claire said, hurrying to the front door. "No more treats, though. I think those cookies you two shared are more than enough dessert."

So, Riley had been right about the cookie eating not fooling anyone. He'd upset his stomach for nothing.

"Plus, if Ethan has too much sugar," Claire went on, snatching up her purse, camera bag and keys, "you'll have to peel him off the ceiling. Oh, you already have my cell number, but I left the number of where I'll be. The sitter's and Livvy's, too, along with the contact info for Ethan's pediatrician on the table by the door. There's a cup of coffee for you, too."

With that, Claire blew a kiss—Riley decided to claim that one for himself—and hurried out. Riley went straight for the coffee. It wouldn't cure his hangover, but it might stop the woodpecker that had set up shop in his head. It also might wash out that family of skunks in his mouth.

Ethan looked at him as if sizing up not only him but this situation. "Tookie?" Ethan asked.

"Sorry, buddy. That ceiling's too high for me to reach to peel you off it." But then, what did you do with a two-year-old other than dose him up on sugar?

Ethan solved that problem for him. He dumped out a huge basket of cars in the middle of the living room floor. Riley had seen Ethan play with cars before, and as expected, the crashes started almost immediately. Normally, a few toy crashes wouldn't have caused him to lift an eyebrow, but with the other things going on in his head, Riley's brain must have thought it was an okay time for a flashback.

No.

Not this, not now.

But it didn't come in that dark, sandy wave like it usually did. This was just a flash of the kid.

The *other* kid.

The extraction. Riley got just a glimmer of him, and his trick-playing mind decided to impose that glimmer right over Ethan's face.

Ethan laughed, snapping Riley back, and Riley realized he was humming "Jingle Bells." However, he didn't think it was the song that'd worked for him that time but rather Ethan's laughter. Maybe he could record that laughter to take with him when he went back on duty. He refused to put an *if* anywhere in that. He would get back in uniform as a CRO.

Some movement on the coffee table caught Riley's eye. It was the slideshow screen saver on the laptop that Claire had left there. Pictures of Ethan scrolled by, and when it got to the beginning, he saw Ethan as a newborn. Claire was in a hospital bed, Ethan bundled in her arms, and she was smiling. The kind of smile that made him smile, too. Riley went closer for a better look, and he sank down on the floor next to the coffee table.

"Me," Ethan announced pointing to the picture.

The next photo popped on the screen. Ethan, still a newborn, this time asleep in a bassinet. "Me," Ethan said, and the *me* continued with each photo.

Riley remembered Claire saying she took at least a photo a week of her son, and it was all here, scrolling for him to see. Ethan crawling. Ethan walking. Even Ethan playing with Crazy Dog at the ranch. Claire was in a few of the shots, Livvy, as well. There was even one of Riley in the background of the Crazy Dog picture. But there was definitely someone missing.

Ethan's father.

Other than Riley, there wasn't a man in any of the shots. Not even Daniel. Of course, Daniel had already said he wasn't Ethan's father, and Riley's mind latched onto that now. Where was the man responsible for Ethan?

And then Riley got a thought that turned his stomach far more than wolfing down the cookies had.

Had the jerk abandoned Claire the way her own father had? That had to be it. No way would Claire want everyone to know she had a broken heart, but if Riley ever got his hands on the turd, he was going to have a word or two with him. Seriously, how could a man abandon a kid like Ethan and a woman like Claire?

Except that was sort of what he was doing.

But Riley's situation was different. Ethan wasn't his son. Claire wasn't his lover. And he'd made a commitment to himself and the uniform.

With those thoughts still stewing in his mind, Riley's phone beeped, indicating he had a call, and he fished it from his pocket.

Logan's name popped up on the screen.

Riley hadn't had nearly enough coffee yet to deal with his big brother so he let it go to voice mail. That's when he saw the other voice mails. Some from Anna and more from Logan. He'd missed those while in his tequila-induced stupor, but when

Logan immediately called him back, Riley had a bad feeling. Had there been some kind of family emergency?

"Are you okay?" Logan asked when he answered. "Della said you didn't come home last night. She was worried about you."

All right, so no family emergency after all. Riley didn't want to tell Logan that he was at Claire's, though the news would probably reach the gossips before too long, depending on who the sitter was. The sitter would see Riley there and perhaps start blabbing. But Riley wasn't interested in explaining to his big brother what had gone on the night before.

"I was worried, too," Logan added a moment later.

There was something in Logan's voice, something he wasn't saying, but something that Riley heard loud and clear. "Lucky told you about what happened at the meeting at the base?"

"No. I guessed something didn't go your way. If it had, you would have cleared out by now."

True. Riley had left his packed duffel bag on the bed. "It'll all work out," Riley assured him. "I'll make it work out."

Twenty-eighty was still a shot.

Ethan must have gotten bored with the pictures of himself and saying "Me," and went back to playing with his cars. Since Riley's leg was now in the traffic pattern, Ethan used it as a hill.

"By any chance have you heard from Lucky?" Logan asked.

"No, not since last night. But he did mention something about registering for a rodeo in Lubbock that's tomorrow and then he'd be going straight from there to the one in Abilene."

"Of course, he did."

There it was again, something in Logan's voice, but Riley didn't think this had to do with him. "Anything wrong?" Riley asked.

"Yes. It's the negotiation for some cutting horses I want to add to the program. Things aren't going well. The owner is a retired military guy. Army, I think. And I thought maybe you could talk to him."

Sneaky for Logan to mention the Army part. He probably

thought it would hook Riley's attention. "I've got a lot of physical therapy—"

"This wouldn't take long. Maybe just a single phone conversation."

Yeah, or maybe sixteen conversations, some visits and formal mediation with lawyers. Riley huffed. Still, he needed to do something in between the physical therapy and this weight pressing down on his mind, and it was probably a safer alternative than lusting after Claire.

Of course, he'd probably still lust after her, but this would give him something to distract him from the lust.

"When do you want me to call him?" Riley asked.

"Tomorrow if possible. I'll email you the file with all the info. Thanks." And Logan hung up.

Riley didn't have time to decide if he'd just made a mistake because there was a knock on the door, and a second later it opened. The sitter. One of the big-busted Starkley girls.

"Riley," she said, letting herself in. "Claire mentioned you'd be here. Sorry I missed you the night of your homecoming."

Well, Riley wasn't sorry about that at all. He hadn't been in much of a visiting mood that night. Still wasn't. And he didn't like that his time with Ethan was about to end.

"Mind if I hang around a while longer and spend some time with Ethan?" Riley asked her.

"Of course not." She held up a thick book that prompted Ethan to say his version of "book" and then go running out of the living room. "I've got a chem test tomorrow and an art project due, and I need to study."

"Then, study away."

Riley got up, not easily, and with his coffee cup in his hand, he went in search of Ethan. He didn't want the kid getting into those cookies, but Ethan wasn't in the kitchen. He was in the room that Claire was using as a nursery, and the kid was pulling out a blue book from one of the boxes.

"Book," Ethan announced handing it to him. Maybe it was a homemade storybook that Claire had read to him.

Except it wasn't.

According to the name inside, it was her mother's journal. Riley didn't mean to read the first page, but his attention went there anyway. Then to the next page.

Ethan lost interest in the book, thank God. Even though he wasn't anywhere close to being able to read, Riley didn't want him near this piece of toxic shit. Too bad Livvy hadn't been able to talk Claire into burning it or putting it in the trash.

Riley sat back down on the floor, unable to stop himself from turning the page.

Tomorrow, I'm getting rid of this kid.

Mercy, it hurt to read that, and if Claire had read it, too, it must have crushed her. He went to the next page, then the next. When he was about ten pages in, something slipped out.

Some kind of dried flower.

And he could tell from the way the image was pressed into the page that it hadn't been opened in a long time. That probably meant Claire hadn't made it this far. *Good.* Livvy had said Claire was shaken up about it, so maybe she'd just quit reading.

Riley, however, didn't.

Yeah, it was a violation of privacy, but Claire's mother was long dead, and her privacy didn't matter to Riley anyway. The only thing that mattered now was how this would affect Claire.

He found a comment about the flower. It was just something she'd picked that reminded her of the prom corsage she'd always wanted. A prom she hadn't been able to attend because she'd been pregnant with Claire.

Her mom definitely wasn't happy about that.

Riley kept reading, wanting enough fodder to convince her to destroy this particular family heirloom.

And he soon found it.

Shit.

Riley had to slam the journal shut. There was no way he was going to let Claire read *that*.

CHAPTER SIXTEEN

CLAIRE HATED THAT she was going to miss seeing Ethan before bedtime, but she was so late that there was no way he'd still be up. Or if he was, he'd be so grumpy that Claire would wish that he was asleep. Still, she'd be able to sneak in a kiss or two before collapsing into her own bed.

Most engagement shoots were fun, being with the happy couple and trying to capture that love and happiness in the photos. Not this one, though. Both sets of parents had been there. It had involved four different locations, including an abandoned drive-in movie theater where one set of the parents had met. Claire was sunburned and had a few fire-ant bites, and she knew without a doubt that she hadn't captured much happiness in those shots.

She definitely hadn't made any fantasies come true today.

Claire unlocked the front door and froze. No sitter. But Riley was still there. He was asleep on the floor, Ethan asleep next to him. There was a junkyard of cars and toys scattered all around them.

What the heck had happened here?

And where was Summer?

There was a car parked in the back part of the driveway, and Claire had assumed it was Summer's vehicle. Claire soon figured out what was going on when she saw the note on the table next to all the phone numbers she'd left.

Riley said he'd stay with Ethan, so I cut out early to study. Riley paid me. Summer

Claire didn't groan, but that's what she wanted to do. She wasn't sure she had the energy to deal with Riley. But then his eyes opened, he lifted his head and he gave her a lazy, half-asleep smile that made her nether regions go warm.

So maybe she did have the energy to deal with him after all. But that didn't mean she should.

She repeated that to herself.

Riley stood, scooping up Ethan in his arms and tiptoeing—yes, tiptoeing because he was barefoot—to the nursery. He eased Ethan into his crib as if he'd done it a thousand times. After Claire kissed her son, whispered a good-night, Riley motioned for her to go back into the living room with him.

"Why did you stay?" she asked, also in a whisper.

He shrugged. "After I did my workout at home and showered, I decided to come back. Summer has a chemistry test and an art project due tomorrow."

All right, that was a good reason, she supposed, but then he dodged her gaze, and Claire knew something other than her nether regions were up to something funny.

"Ethan brought me your mother's journal." Riley pointed to the blue book he'd put on the mantel.

That was all he needed to say before it felt as if the world had dropped out beneath her feet. Riley was right there to take hold of her, and as gently as he'd handled Ethan, he had her sit on the sofa.

"You read it?" she asked.

"Some. How much did you read?"

"Some," Claire settled for saying. "But I want to read more. I want to know if it got any better for her."

"You don't need to read more. There's stuff in there that you don't want to know, trust me."

"Stuff? What do you mean?" There were plenty of bad things on those pages, but Riley seemed to be referring to something specific.

But he didn't go the specific route. "Just crap stuff. You need to burn the damn thing and put this behind you."

She knew that. Knew now, too, that there was something worse than what she'd already read. God, something worse.

The tears came. She cursed them, blinked them back, but they came anyway. "I can't put it behind me. Maybe if I read it all, I'll either be at peace or else be so fed up with all this old baggage that I'll toss it once and for all."

Because the tears were already there, the razor-sharp emotions, too, Claire got up, snatched the journal from the mantel, and before he could stop her, she opened it to the page that she'd already read.

Tomorrow, I'm getting rid of this kid.

"Obviously, she changed her mind," Claire said.

"Yeah." Riley didn't look anywhere near tears, but the anger was there. He pulled her beside him, still treating her with kid gloves, and he turned the page. "If you're going to do this, read with me here. Then I can hold you, kiss you, sleep with you or whatever hell else it takes to help you get through it."

Whatever was in there must be pretty bad for him to offer to sleep with her. Did that stop her? No. Neither did her tear-filled eyes. Claire read the page he'd opened.

Didn't go to the clinic after all. Call me chickenshit, but I guess I'll carry this kid after all. Mom says she'll help, of course, but she's bat-shit on a good day. Besides, I know she doesn't want to get stuck with another kid either.

Riley stabbed the last sentence with his index finger. "That's not true. Your grandmother loved you."

"I know." Still, it made her breath so thin for her mother to say something so horrible. Her grandmother had indeed loved her, and she'd loved Claire's mother, too.

Riley cursed. "I didn't want you to see that. I didn't want it in your head."

She looked at him, met his gaze. "Everything on these pages is already in my head, Riley. I don't have to read it to imagine it or even something much worse. After all, I know how this ends. My mother left me."

Claire doubted she'd convinced him, but she went to the next entry. It was dated a week after the last one.

The kids at school know I'm knocked up. It's all over town. Bitches spread gossip. Mom says I should go back, that I can graduate in just three months, but in three months I'll be as big as a whale. Once this kid is out of me, I'm out of this shit town for good.

"Sometimes I forget just how young she was," Claire said.

Too young. Claire had been twenty-nine when she was pregnant with Ethan, and she couldn't have imagined doing that at eighteen. No wonder her mother had been so angry, and the anger was there all over the other pages.

Especially the next one.

A shit-hole of a day. I wish Mom and this kid was dead. I made a mistake keeping this brat.

Dead. There it was. More of the little knives slicing away at her. Her mother was obviously on an emotional roller coaster, and now Claire was, too, because she was reliving this.

"I didn't want you to see that," Riley said, his voice strained.

She hadn't wanted to see it, either, but she couldn't stop herself from continuing, either. With Riley right next to her, Claire kept reading, and she prayed that it would get better.

Rocky isn't coming back. I know that now, and even if he did, I would kick his sorry excuse for an ass. What kind of man just knocks up a girl and then runs out on her?

Yes, what kind of man did that?

"Do you feel that way about Ethan's father?" Riley asked, but he waved it off just as quickly as it left his mouth.

"No," she answered. It wasn't a lie, but judging from his expression, Riley didn't believe her.

"I'm sorry," he said.

She wasn't sure exactly what the apology was for. Claire wasn't sure of much at the moment except that she was going to have to take him up on that kissing and holding he'd offered.

But he beat her to it.

Riley hauled her to him, pulling her onto his lap, and he kissed her first.

RILEY WAS CERTAIN he'd lost his mind. With all the energy zinging between them, the last thing he should be doing was kissing Claire. But it was the only thing that made sense to him right now.

Not much sense, though.

But enough that it didn't stop him.

He'd already known how she tasted, but this was even better than the kisses outside Calhoun's Pub. Maybe because there wasn't sweat and beer running down his face, and they weren't plastered against a splintery wall. They were on a soft couch, behind closed doors.

And Ethan was asleep.

This was as dangerous of a situation as going into enemy territory, but knowing that still didn't stop him. He deepened the kiss, dragging Claire closer and closer.

"Your shoulder," she mumbled.

At least that's what he thought she said, but his shoulder wasn't the problem here. The problem was that in just a matter of seconds, the kiss had already gotten hotter than wildfire and was spreading just as fast. This certainly wasn't the holding/kissing comfort session she'd likely been expecting. Nor was it what she needed.

That stopped him.

Riley pulled back. "We might need to rethink this."

"I'm tired of thinking." And she went right back into the kiss.

Obviously, that meant she was no longer considering Daniel's proposal. This was the part where a smart man might have made sure she was telling the truth, or that it wasn't just the lust or hurt talking, but apparently he was no longer a smart man.

Riley kept kissing her, and he added some more trouble to this brew by slipping his hand beneath her top. His fingers brushed across bare skin, and that was all it took for his body to go into serious overdrive.

Man, he wanted her.

And since wanting her would almost certainly involve getting naked, he scooped her up and headed to her bedroom. There was a baby monitor in there. He'd already spotted it earlier, and this way if Ethan woke up, they'd hear him. Yes, it was a miracle that he could consider such a thing at a time like this, but Riley was used to considering many factors when it came to a mission.

And what a mission it was.

He closed the bedroom door behind them and placed Claire on her bed; the feather mattress swelled around her, giving way to her weight when her body landed against it. Her top slid up a little, exposing the part of her he'd just touched.

So, Riley touched some more.

With his mouth this time.

It was a much better experience, not just for him but apparently for Claire, too, because she lifted her hips and made that hot little sound of pleasure.

Riley figured the grunt he made wasn't nearly as sweet sounding, but he didn't make it for long. He kept kissing her, sliding up the top to reveal more and more that he kissed, too. Soon though, that wasn't enough, and he pulled the top off her and went after her bra.

How many times he'd dreamed of doing this. Too many. Claire had been a steady source of dream fantasies for years, and now here she was in front of him.

He unclipped her bra, taking her breasts into his hands so he could kiss them. The only thing that would have made it more pleasurable was for him to have two mouths, but Claire seemed to be happy with his one-mouthed attempt.

She fisted her hand in his hair, dragging him closer. Not that he could get much closer, mind you, and they grappled, kissed and generally drove each other crazy until something had to be done.

Riley went after her skirt next.

He skimmed it off her, not intending to remove the panties just yet, but he did. And with a toss of her clothes, he had a naked Claire on the bed in front of him.

Oh, mercy.

He'd been working up an erection since the first touch of her mouth to his, but now he went rock hard. He was ready to take her and fulfill all those fantasies that'd been in his dreams, both the sleeping and the waking ones. But first he wanted more kissing. On her belly.

Her thighs.

The inside of her thighs.

Then the center.

That got a really good reaction from her. She bucked beneath him and fought to drag him back to her so she could start a war with his shirt. She wasn't winning, mainly because she was trying to kiss him while she undid the buttons. Riley stopped his kisses to help her.

There was no longer a bandage on his shoulder, and for a moment he considered that Claire would freak when she saw the scar. She didn't. She kissed it, too, a lot more gently than he'd kissed her thigh region.

That got him much hotter than he thought it would, but it was lukewarm compared with her going after his zipper. He had to help her again so she could remove his jeans, making sure he didn't bang his shoulder in the process. No sense working themselves up to this point if he couldn't finish it.

It was the thought of finishing this that had everything inside him freezing.

And Claire noticed. She levered herself up on her elbows, her attention on his shoulder. "What's wrong?"

Riley really hated to have to tell her this. "I don't have a condom. Do you?"

No freezing for her. Claire groaned and dropped back down onto the mattress. "No. And I'm not on the pill, either."

Riley wasn't ready to give up just yet, and it was desperation that made him ask the next question. "You don't think your grandmother left any condoms?"

All right, it was a horrible question and a way to kill the mood. Almost. The mood was definitely still there with him, pressing against the fabric of his boxers.

Riley decided to look at this as a different kind of mission. Things went wrong all the time, and he often had to improvise. He could go to the pharmacy and get some condoms. Except it was closed by now.

That left the gas station/convenience store on the edge of town. It'd be open, might even have condoms, but if he hurried in there, it would be all over town that Claire and he had done the dirty—especially when coupled with any gossip Summer would spill about Riley spending most of the day with Ethan. After the pub brawl/jail incident, Claire didn't need that kind of talk going around.

Claire shook her head and moved as if to get off the bed. "Maybe this is fate—"

Riley didn't let her finish that. He stopped her with a kiss. Stopped her from moving off the bed, too. No way was this fate. It was just bad preparations on his part. He should have stuck a condom in his wallet. Of course, when he'd decided to spend the day with Ethan, he hadn't exactly had Claire and condoms on his mind.

And now he needed to improvise.

"We're finishing this," he insisted. Which was more or less the truth. He would finish Claire anyway.

Riley started a trail of kisses that went from her mouth to the exact spot where he could finish her. Not with his hard-on, which was begging to get in on this. Nope. He used his mouth, and he kissed her, kissed her and kissed her until Claire *finished*.

She wasn't a screamer but rather a moaner. Good thing because the sound wouldn't wake up Ethan, and her soft moans went with the ones Riley was making. Both pleasure and pain, as life so often was. His erection was throbbing, but the throbbing that Claire was doing was certainly pleasurable to watch.

As backup plans went, it wasn't ideal, but at least one of them would sleep better tonight. And it wouldn't be him. Claire pulled him down to her, the glow of the orgasm all over her face. She was happy, smiling, and he'd already noticed the glowing part.

All in all, it was amazing to see. Just as he'd thought it would be if he ever got to do anything remotely sexual with her.

But when the glow had run its course and the morning came, Riley didn't have to guess what the percentage was for this complicating the hell out of both his and Claire's lives.

This would fuck things up between them 100 percent.

CHAPTER SEVENTEEN

RILEY'S ALARM CLOCK—the one in his head—went off at 6:00 a.m. Not that he'd actually needed it to wake him. He hadn't done much sleeping with a naked Claire beside him in bed. He was probably in pain, too, but it was hard to tell because his body was giving him some mixed signals.

On the one hand, he was feeling slack and sated after a couple of rounds of oral sex with Claire. Riley had been on both the receiving and giving ends, and he wasn't sure which one he liked better. All right, he was sure, but both had been mind-blowing.

And terrifying.

Because with her in his arms like this, it only reminded him that he had crossed a bridge that he would soon have to leave behind. Yeah, it was a bad metaphor, but when the lust had been clouding his head and judgment, he hadn't thought to see this to its possible conclusion.

Claire could get hurt.

That was the very thing Lucky had warned him about, and even though Riley never thought he would hear himself say this, for once Lucky had given him good relationship advice. Ironic since the advice had come from a man who'd never had a relationship last more than a week.

Riley eased out of the bed, trying not to wake Claire, but just the slight shift of the mattress caused her to open her eyes. She smiled at him, kissed him and then went back to sleep. *Good.* Conversation was best left for when they both had clearer heads. Of course, after her head cleared, she might be ready to throttle him.

Claire had been at a seriously low point after reading that asinine journal. Riley had known that. He'd seen the tears in her eyes, and he figured those tears had played into her decision to kiss him.

All over his body.

In a way, it was as if he'd taken advantage of a drunk woman. Something he never did. Well, not before last night anyway.

He made another attempt to get out of bed, and this time she didn't wake up. Riley dressed. Not easily. There was pain now, and while he wouldn't medicate it, he would need to start his exercises to get rid of some of the stiffness. Too bad the exercises wouldn't take care of the stiffness of the brainless part of him in his boxers. No, the best cure for that was to quit looking at a naked Claire and get the heck out of her bedroom before Ethan woke up.

Riley tiptoed out of the room, checked on Ethan. The kid was still sacked out. He went to the living room to put on his boots. Claire's note was still there, the one with the phone numbers, so Riley added his own note to it.

"I'll call you later," he wrote.

He considered adding something else, but anything he could come up with would only complicate things. Definitely no "love, Riley" at the end of it. And no hearts or some other doodling to trivialize what'd happened.

Besides, he wasn't even sure what had happened.

Was this an oral fling? Or was Claire expecting a whole lot more?

With those questions on his mind, Riley put on his boots and slipped out the front door. He locked it behind him and made his way to the car he'd parked on the side of her house. He rounded the corner and immediately had an ah-shit moment.

Because Daniel was there.

Leaning against Riley's car.

Riley so didn't want to deal with Daniel this morning, but since Daniel was right against the driver's-side door, he was going to have to speak at least one word to him.

Move was the first word that came to mind.

"We have to talk," Daniel insisted.

Daniel took a drag off a cigarette—Riley didn't even know the man smoked—and he flicked the cigarette butt on the ground, crushing it with his shoe. That's when Riley noticed there were multiple butts there. At least a dozen. Which meant Daniel had been out there most of the night.

Riley didn't think Daniel was perverse enough to peek through Claire's bedroom window, but he wouldn't have actually needed to peek. Given the hour and after one look at Riley's walk-of-shame wrinkled clothes, Daniel had likely guessed what had gone on.

Or rather what he thought had gone on.

"You broke your own man-rule," Daniel tossed right out there.

Yeah, and it didn't matter that it hadn't been fully broken. Riley wasn't going to mention anything about a condom holding him back because the intent of man-rule number three had indeed been violated.

Don't take anything that wasn't his.

While he didn't believe that Claire was Daniel's girl, not anymore, Riley also knew she wasn't his for the taking.

"Are you happy with yourself now?" Daniel snarled, and there was no doubt about it—it was indeed a snarl.

Riley huffed. Certain parts of him were happy, but he wasn't giving those parts a vote in this. "None of this was planned."

Which, of course, was the worst excuse of all worst excuses.

"So, what happens now?" Daniel lit up another cigarette, his right eye squinting from the coil of smoke. "You leave town to go do your military thing, and Claire is stuck here to pick up the pieces."

As much as he hated the way Daniel had put it, that pretty much summed it up. It wouldn't do any good to repeat to him, or Claire, that this hadn't been planned. Though it hadn't been. Still, there were consequences, and Riley had to accept that things would never be the same.

He might even lose Claire's friendship.

"I don't want her hurt," Riley said. Yet another stupid comment, but he meant it. It wasn't nearly enough, though.

Daniel cursed. "You should have thought about that before you slept with her." He cursed some more and used the cigarette to point at Riley. "I'm going to try to fix this. I'll help her put the pieces back together. You do know that she still has my engagement ring, right?"

Riley did know that, and he hadn't been worried about it until now. "She told you no, that she wouldn't marry you."

"She's still thinking it over. Why else would she have kept the ring?"

Riley certainly couldn't think of a reason. Not a good one anyway.

Well, hell. For Claire to have been with him like that while still mulling over Daniel's proposal meant she hadn't been thinking straight. As in not one tiny bit of thinking straight. That journal must have shaken Claire even more than Riley had realized— and it had shaken her a lot.

Of course, he was hearing this from Daniel, and it was possible, likely even, that Claire's answer to the proposal was still going to be no.

But it should have been no before she ever got into bed with Riley.

"I love her," Daniel went on. "I want to stay in Texas and marry her. That's all Claire's ever wanted—a man who would be here for her and not run off like her father did."

It was indeed what she wanted. And it was something Riley

had always known he couldn't give her, not with those Texas-deep roots of hers. Heck, Riley didn't even doubt that Daniel loved her.

"I don't want you taking any of this out on her," Riley insisted. "Everything that happened was my fault."

Daniel made a face as if thoroughly insulted by that. "I wouldn't take anything out on her, and I'll forgive her. That's what I'll tell her, that I love and forgive her, and that I'll be here as long as she needs me."

As mission statements went, it was a powerful one. Daniel was like the Texas heat. He would always be around. And that's exactly what Claire and Ethan needed. Even if it made Riley feel like shit.

"I'm sorry," Riley said, and that encompassed a lot of things.

"I sure hope so." Daniel ground out the cigarette he tossed. "Because now I've got to go in there and clean up this mess."

Daniel didn't exactly ask permission, and Riley wasn't in a position to stop him. Heck, he didn't know what his position was, but Claire certainly didn't have an engagement ring from Riley in her house.

Riley got in his car and drove off. As he did, he made the mistake of checking the rearview mirror, and saw something that he was sorry he'd seen. Claire had opened the door to Daniel and was letting him inside her house.

CLAIRE KNEW THERE would be a price to pay for what she'd done with Riley, but she just hadn't expected to start paying so soon. The only reason she'd opened her door when she heard the knock was because she thought it was Riley, that maybe he'd forgotten something.

Like a kiss goodbye.

But no Riley. It was Daniel. He was sporting a scowl, a scowl that deepened when he looked over his shoulder at Riley driving away.

Oh, no.

She was betting that hadn't been a friendly conversation. Nor was the one she was about to have with Daniel. That's why Claire had him come inside. Best to air her dirty laundry behind closed doors.

"What did you say to Riley?" she demanded.

Better yet, what had Riley said to him? Because Riley certainly hadn't said much in the note he'd left her.

Since Daniel wasn't battered and bruised, there probably hadn't been any punches thrown. Daniel wasn't the punch-throwing type anyway. But she was betting there had been a man-pissing contest with their war of words.

"Where's Ethan?" Daniel asked, looking at the car and toy mess on the floor.

"Still asleep, but since he'll be waking up any minute, let's finish this conversation before he does. What did you say to Riley?" she repeated, expecting an answer this time.

Daniel eyed her the same way he'd eyed the toy clutter. She'd put on some clothes, but she probably still looked as if she'd just climbed out of bed with a man. Plus, she hadn't showered yet and had Riley's scent all over her.

"Riley and I talked," Daniel finally said. "I made him understand that what he did with you was wrong."

"What?" she practically shouted, probably waking Ethan. "You had no right to do that. None." And Riley didn't have to listen to any of it.

When Ethan called out for her, Claire went to him before he tried to climb out of his crib.

Daniel followed right behind her.

"Of course I had a right," Daniel argued. "I love you. I want to marry you."

Despite her suddenly surly mood, Claire managed to scrounge up a smile and a kiss for Ethan, but he was the grumpy boy this morning, and he gave her a scowl that matched Daniel's. Or maybe Ethan was actually scowling at Daniel. It was hard to tell anything other than obviously her son didn't want to be awake yet.

"For what it's worth," Daniel went on while she changed Ethan's diaper, "Riley agreed with me. He's not going to be in town much longer. We all know that. And you don't need him playing with your heartstrings."

Well, it hadn't been her heartstrings that Riley had played with, but she wasn't getting into that with Daniel. She finished the diapering, and while still smiling at Ethan and pretending nothing was wrong, she carried him into the kitchen.

Daniel followed her there, too.

"Also for what it's worth," he repeated, "it didn't take much to convince Riley to leave this morning."

She tried not to let that sting. But it did. Because it was likely the cold, hard truth. The night before she and Riley had been caught up in the heat of the moment, but now that the heat had been satiated, he might be seeing a lot clearer than she was.

Yes, Riley was leaving.

But Claire still wanted him.

That heat had satiated much for her, but it might be the only taste she ever got of Riley McCord. After all, they'd never gotten around to discussing how his meeting at the military base had gone. It was possible he'd spent that day with Ethan, and that night with her, as a way of saying goodbye.

She put Ethan in his high chair, poured some Cheerios right on the tray and fixed him a sippy cup of milk. All of that while her heart felt as if someone were stomping on it. If Ethan noticed the tension in the room, he didn't react. He dove right into the cereal.

"I reminded Riley you still have my engagement ring," Daniel added.

Claire had been about to put some fresh blueberries on Ethan's tray, but Daniel's words stopped her. "You told him that?"

"Of course. Because it's true."

"It's only true because you wouldn't take it back." Claire certainly hadn't meant to yell, but even a hard-of-hearing person would have labeled it as a shout.

Ethan stopped munching and started watching them. It was for her son and her son alone that she forced herself to calm down. If Ethan hadn't been there, she would have let Daniel see, and hear, just how upset she really was.

Damn.

Now Riley probably thought she'd done all those things with him in the bedroom while she was still keeping Daniel on the hook. Well, Daniel was about to get dropped from that hook right now.

She hurried into the living room, took out the ring that she'd shoved into the foyer table drawer. Thankfully, this time Daniel didn't follow her, and when Claire returned to the kitchen, he was standing there, the look on his face indicating he'd just stepped in something he was going to regret.

Claire took his hand, slapped the box in his palm. "If you try to leave it again, I'll flush it down the toilet. Understand?" She didn't give him a chance to answer. "And there won't be any more proposals or any more conversations with Riley about me. Got that?"

Daniel looked at the ring. Then at her. "You'll never find another man who loves you as much as I do."

"I know." And that broke her heart.

The first tear made it down Claire's cheek before he even walked out the door.

RILEY HAD DONE something to get his mind off Claire. And it had actually worked better than he'd thought it would.

Of course, nothing was going to erase Claire from his mind. She was in every corner of it. However, for a couple of hours he'd felt as if he had done something that he hadn't screwed up.

"Well done," the text from Logan had said.

High praise coming from Logan, and Riley knew it hadn't been just lip service. Riley had negotiated a much better deal for the new cutting horses—championship lines, at that—than even Logan had anticipated. And Riley had played the military card to help him do it.

The owner of the horses, Frank Doolittle, had been Army all right. A Ranger, which made him special ops just like Riley. The first hour of their conversation had been about missions, and they'd discovered that Riley's first mission and Frank's last one had overlapped. They'd been in the same area, assisting with the same situation.

Small world.

That small world had bulldozed through some barriers that Logan had put up with his less than warm-and-fuzzy demeanor. Riley hadn't been exactly warm and fuzzy, but the shared camaraderie of being with a fellow serviceman had no doubt played into Frank giving a sweet deal to McCord Cattle Brokers. With this deal, Logan just might have to change the name to Cattle and Horse Brokers.

The next step would be for Riley to interview some new cutters, the slang term for the cutting horse trainers. Frank had given him a few leads on that. Good thing, too, because the last couple that Logan had hired had already quit. Lucky had managed to talk one into staying before his brother took off, but with this new group of horses Riley had just bought, they'd need at least three more cutters.

Riley would work on hiring those cutters after his usual hours of PT. Between the work and the PT, he might actually be able to deal with the hurricane of thoughts and worries over Claire and his upcoming physical. He had to reduce those twenty-eighty odds.

For the physical anyway.

He wasn't sure there were any odds when it came to Claire.

Riley would give her a few more hours and then call and…

Well, he wasn't sure what he would say to her yet. But maybe the right words would come to him during a long, sweaty workout.

Riley turned into the driveway that fronted his house, and

he cursed when he saw a familiar car—Trisha's. *Oh, man*. He hoped she hadn't shown up half-naked again. But if she had, then she'd probably given Della and Stella an eyeful since they were home, too.

Steeling himself, Riley parked, went inside, but he was the one who got a shock. It was Trisha all right. Fully clothed, thank goodness. But she wasn't alone. She was in the living room, sitting on the sofa and chatting with Jodi.

Both women stood and looked about as uneasy as Riley felt.

"Walter Meekins is still out with a gout flare-up," Trisha said. "So I gave Jodi a ride."

Yes, Riley knew all about Walter and his medical problems, but that didn't explain why the women were here.

"Trisha was kind enough to drive me," Jodi continued. "Daniel introduced us."

That still didn't explain much. Of course, Daniel had driven Jodi to the inn. Maybe to Calhoun's, too, and since Trisha was clearly still in town, maybe they'd run into each other. And then proceeded to come to his living room together.

"I'll wait outside," Trisha added.

Uh-oh. There was only one reason for her to do that. Because she knew Jodi wanted to talk about things that Riley wasn't sure he wanted to hear. Still, after all the time he and Jodi had spent together, he owed her a least a listening session.

Jodi didn't say a word until Trisha was out the door. "Trisha said you've been spending time with Claire."

Well, that put a quick end to the listening session. Riley groaned. "Is that really why you're here—to ask me if I'm seeing Claire?" He hoped not because he didn't know the answer to that himself.

But thankfully Jodi shook her head. "No, that was my attempt at small talk. I'm here to apologize for the bar brawl. For getting Claire and Daniel arrested, too." She drew in a long breath. "I was just blowing off steam and some frustration over not getting to spend time with you."

He groaned again but didn't get to elaborate on that groan because Jodi continued. "No, it's not like that. I'm not hung up on you or anything. Not my style. But I'm going to be around town a couple more days. I sublet my condo in DC, don't have any other travel plans and I need to get some work done. I decided Spring Hill was just as good of a place to do that as anywhere else."

No, it wasn't, and his expression must have conveyed that because Jodi chuckled, patted his cheek. "This isn't about you, Riley. I just wanted you to know that I'd be around in case we ran into each other. But only for a couple of days. Then I'll be out of your hair for good."

Riley figured after all this time, he should feel something. This was confirmation of their breakup. All he felt was regret that it hadn't ended better between them, but what he couldn't do was be sad that it was over.

"Be safe," Jodi whispered to him, kissing him on the cheek. "And if you can't be safe, then it means you're probably having fun."

Always the party girl. She dropped another kiss on his cheek, her mouth lingering there a moment as if to see if he was going to do something about her mouth being so close to his.

Riley didn't.

"Goodbye, Jodi," he said.

She flexed her eyebrows, looked disappointed for a couple of seconds and left. "Ready to hit Calhoun's now?" she asked Trisha on the way out.

Apparently, Jodi had found a new friend. *Good*. Riley wished her only the best.

Feeling as if he'd lost some of the happy air he'd walked in with, Riley headed to his room to get his workout clothes. However, he didn't make it far when his phone buzzed, and he saw the name on the screen.

Claire.

Part of him felt that tug in his stomach. A happy tug. But another part of him didn't know what to say to her. Still, he wasn't going to dodge her.

"Don't say anything," Claire said the moment he answered the call.

Well, good. That worked in his favor.

"I'm calling to invite you to dinner tomorrow night," she continued. "Around seven. Can you come?"

That seemed like a trick question. Or one that could make this situation even messier than it was. For that reason alone, Riley knew he should say no.

He didn't.

"I'll be there," he said.

And maybe by then he'd know what the hell he was going to do.

CHAPTER EIGHTEEN

CLAIRE DIDN'T REMEMBER being this nervous before her first date. And this wasn't even a date-date. It was dinner with Riley. But she couldn't stop herself from shaking. Couldn't keep the nerves at bay.

It was possible she was going to throw up.

She'd already gone over all her lists. Not just the ones for the dinner itself and what to wear but also her conversation list. She needed to tell Riley that she no longer had Daniel's ring. Nor was his proposal still on the table. She'd ended things with Daniel with absolutely no hope whatsoever that it meant anything for Riley and her.

Well, other than it meant she hadn't gotten into bed with Riley while still in a semirelationship with Daniel. She didn't need to have a woman-rule about that. It was just something she wouldn't have done, but Riley perhaps thought she had.

She checked the roast again. The temp was right where it should be and would be ready to take out at six-fifty. Ten minutes from now, which meant there were still twenty minutes before Riley was due to arrive.

Too much fidgeting time.

She paced to the bathroom to check her hair again and feel for razor stubble on her legs. It was something she'd been obsessing about all day, though she doubted Riley would get his hand within touching distance of her legs. Still, it was something she would allow her slight OCD tendencies.

The knock at the door nearly caused her to shriek, but it wasn't Riley. She looked through the glass sidelight window and saw someone she certainly hadn't expected to see tonight. Lucky.

"Did Riley send you?" Claire asked the second she threw open the door.

Lucky gave her a look for a second or two before he shook his head and pulled something from his shirt. A ball of yellow fur. "I brought something for you. This house just isn't the same without a cat."

Claire gave him a look, too, and it lasted for more than a second or two. "I'm already feeding a stray." Which was a reminder that she'd have to figure out what to do with Whoa before she sold the place. "And my condo in San Antonio is pretty small."

"The kitten's pretty small, too, and I sort of saved her. She was on kitty death row at the pound."

Claire was horrified that something so fluffy, tiny and...yes, cute, could have been on death row. But then, this was Lucky, and he had a silver tongue when it came to putting a spin on things.

"All right, I confess." He put the fur ball in her hands. "I went there to chat with a friend, saw this little girl and thought she'd be perfect for Ethan. You can show her to him when he gets back from Livvy's tomorrow morning."

"How'd you know Ethan was at Livvy's?" But she huffed to dismiss that question. Livvy and Lucky had slept together, and maybe they'd extended their one-night stand for another time or two.

"I might not be able to keep her," Claire said, but Lucky was already bringing in something off the porch. A litter box, food, bowls and treats. He'd even included a scooper.

"Give her a trial run," he suggested. "Keep her a couple of

days, and if it doesn't work out, call me, and I'll see if my partner can take her."

Claire knew his partner in the rodeo-promotion business.
Dixie Mae Weatherall. A very colorful woman who dressed like
Dolly Parton. She was built like her, too, but doled out profan-
ity like a sailor's cursing coach. Dixie Mae was originally from
Spring Hill and had returned to town a time or two to visit her
granddaughter who'd gone to Spring Hill High School. While
Claire didn't know the woman personally, Dixie Mae didn't
look like the cat-cuddling type.

"So, why would you think Riley had sent me?" Lucky sniffed
the air. "He's coming over, isn't he? And you made him roast
beef, those little baby potatoes, a salad and some key lime pie."

"You can't smell the salad." She gave him the stink eye not
just for the kitten that she couldn't resist but because he'd likely
heard all about the menu from Livvy. Though Claire couldn't
imagine that would make good pillow talk.

"Well, I just figured you'd serve some kind of green vege-
table," he answered, "and since I didn't smell one, I guessed."

Her timer went off, and she put the kitten on the floor so she
could hurry to wash her hands and take out the roast.

"Don't ask me about Riley," she added. Best to cut him off
at the pass. "Don't ask why he's coming over, either."

He paused, watched her fuss with the roast, basting, rebast-
ing, poking at it with a fork. "How about Daniel?" Lucky went
on. "Can I ask about him?"

"No," Claire answered.

Lucky made a sound as if everything was suddenly very clear,
and then he went back into the living room and glanced out the
window. No doubt checking for Riley. So did Claire.

"Riley and I had a chance to talk when I was driving him to
and from his appointment at the base," Lucky threw out there.

This was tricky territory. If she asked if Riley had talked
about her, that would be opening up the conversation for her
to talk about Riley. And she didn't want to do that. For a man,

Lucky was perceptive—she figured that was why he was so good with women. But she wasn't ready to bare her heart just yet, so she just waited for him to continue.

"When he came out of that meeting with the colonel, Riley was pretty messed up. It took me a while to get it out of him, but he's got two weeks to get his body and head together. If he can't pass a physical then, they'll give him some kind of review board. He didn't explain what that was exactly, but judging from his expression, it's the medical version of a firing squad."

Oh. She'd known the meeting hadn't gone well because Riley had ended up at her house. Drunk, no less.

"Two weeks," she repeated.

Not much time at all, although it was better than she'd thought after Anna had called. After talking to Riley's sister, Claire had thought Riley was already on his way out the door.

Instead of just being partially out.

"Of course, Riley's all geared up to pass that physical," Lucky continued. "He's pushing himself."

"Too much?" she asked.

Lucky shrugged. "It'd be the pot calling the kettle black if I said it was too much. After all, for fun I climb on the back of a seventeen-hundred-pound bull with an attitude problem and let him sling the crap out of me. Not literally," he added with a wink.

Lucky had already moved from shrugging to winking and smiling, which meant he was trying to soften the news he'd given her.

Two weeks.

And Riley would do whatever it took—even if it would sling the crap out of him—to make sure he passed that physical.

Lucky still had a half smile when he reached out, rubbed her arm. "I'm worried about you if he passes whatever tests the Air Force will give him. Worried about him if he doesn't. Picking up pieces isn't my strong suit, but…"

He didn't finish, didn't have to. Someone was going to get

hurt in this. Probably her. In fact, she wanted it to be her. She could heal from a broken heart. After a while, at least. But for Riley, failing this physical would crush him.

"I'm not sure picking up pieces is my strong suit, either," she said.

"Yeah, but you've got a huge advantage. You can make things better just by being around him. For Riley, I mean. Not for you. Just know that no matter how this all shakes out, you can call me."

No wonder the women flocked to him. Claire didn't have an ounce of attraction in her body for Lucky, but he wasn't just a charmer; he was a good listener and someone who cared more than he liked to let people know.

He also brought stupid gifts.

The kitten had stopped its sniffing and exploring and was now jetting around the living room at supersonic speed. No way could she keep it, but if she did, Bullet would be a good name for it.

When Lucky moved his hand from her arm, his attention landed on the mantel. And the journal. Judging from his suddenly tight mouth, Livvy had told Lucky about that, too.

Sheez, it was a wonder they had time for sex with all this talk about her.

What they wouldn't have been able to talk about was the almost sex that she'd had with Riley. That's because Claire hadn't told Livvy. And Livvy had given her the full-court press, too, to get details in not one but three phone calls. If Claire had spilled and then pinkie-sworn Livvy to secrecy, Livvy would have taken it to the grave. But Claire hadn't wanted to share any of it.

When things crashed and burned between Riley and her, Claire didn't want to have to explain why she'd done something as stupid as inviting him to her bed.

"What are you going to do about that?" Lucky asked, tipping his head to the journal.

"I don't want to burn it." Not yet anyway, but it did bring her to something she wanted to ask him. "Did you ever hear anyone mention a man named Rocky?"

It didn't take him but a couple of seconds to piece together why she had mentioned that particular name. "That's your father?"

She nodded. Shrugged. "I think he could be. If my mother was telling the truth in the journal."

"You want me to ask around and find out if anyone's ever heard of him?"

Did she? It suddenly seemed like a huge can of worms to open, and her heart was already on shaky ground. Still, Claire nodded again.

"All right," he agreed. "I'll ask but will be discreet. I'll say it's someone Dixie Mae used to know."

That was the good thing about Lucky; he usually got it without having to be told. With the exception of kittens, that is. His boundaries were a little less defined when it came to totally inappropriate gifts like that.

He glanced out the window again. "I need to get out of here because Riley's coming."

Sure enough Riley was driving up.

Her heart thudded against her chest.

"I don't want to spoil the mood," Lucky said. "So, I'll just head out back." He took something from his pocket, put it in the drawer of the foyer table and hurried out the back before she could see what it was.

A cat toy probably.

She pulled open the drawer and looked. No cat toy.

It was a condom in a pretty gold foil wrapper.

Claire didn't know whether to go after Lucky and throttle him or tell him that he was a couple of days late with this particular gift. But she didn't have time for either because Riley knocked on the door. She slammed the drawer, catching her thumb. Cursed. Danced around while she tried not to curse some more. But she was sure her face was still a little screwed up when she opened the door.

However, Riley wasn't looking at her. He was admiring the new paint job on the exterior of the house. "It looks great."

So did Riley. Of course, he always looked great so that was nothing new, but what was new was that she'd seen just how great he looked naked. Those memories came back to her now. All warm and glowing.

Exactly the feeling she got whenever she thought of what Riley had done to her in the bed. He'd given new meaning to a memorable kiss.

"You're really whipping this into shape," he said.

Because her mind was on that special kissing, it took her a moment to switch gears. "Thanks." At least she had that part of her life under control. The rest of her was suspect, along with being warm and glowing.

"I thought about bringing you flowers," he said, "but, well, that didn't feel right. But I did bring you this." He took something from his pocket. A picture.

Of a kitten.

It was yellow and fluffy and looked exactly like the one that came running through the living room and nearly collided with the wall.

"It was a gift," she said but then immediately realized that Riley might think the gift had been from Daniel. "Lucky brought her, him, it." Claire scooped up the kitten, had a look at its bottom. "Her," she amended.

Judging from the way Riley stared at her, he wanted a bit more of an explanation than that.

"Lucky said he rescued her from the pound, that she was on kitty death row." Claire set the kitten back down, and it took off again.

Riley frowned. "There's a wait list for the kittens. Lucky must have sweet-talked Mary Alice into giving him one." He took back the picture. "Well, I reserved one for Ethan, but I didn't want to just bring it without asking you first."

That was the difference between Riley and Lucky. Impulse control.

"I'm not sure I can keep this one," Claire explained. "But thanks for thinking of Ethan."

Riley slid the picture back in his pocket and came in, eyeing the cat and the interior paint job. No more blue floral wallpaper. It was now a tasteful shade of beige, a good color for prospective home buyers. Or so Daniel had told her. Which was a reminder that she'd need to find a different real estate agent when it went on the market.

"So, when was Lucky here?" Riley asked.

"Earlier."

Another stare, another silent request for more info. "He's worried about you," Claire settled for saying. "How's the PT going?"

"Great. And I closed on a horse sale for Logan."

She'd already heard about that from the clerk at the bank and the cashier at the grocery store. It was the buzz of Spring Hill, and the consensus was that it was Riley's last hurrah and a way of appeasing Logan before he headed back out.

Riley did more glancing around. "Where's Ethan?"

"With Livvy. Once a month he spends the night at her place." That was almost the truth. Ethan's sleepover with Livvy wasn't due for another two weeks, but Claire had moved it up.

"So, it's just us?" he clarified.

She couldn't tell if he was happy about that or if, like her, he wanted to fidget. Claire resisted, but the only way she managed it was to do some controlled fidgeting. She led him into the kitchen so she could check the food that in no way needed checking, and she poured them each a glass of wine.

"Smells good in here. Looks good, too." His gaze skirted over the roast, the potatoes and the pie.

And then settled on her.

Oh, my. Those bedroom eyes of his were in full force tonight, or maybe that was just the way her body was interpreting it. Riley used those bedroom eyes to stare at her as if he were about to tell her something important, but there was something important she had to tell him, too.

"I broke things off with Daniel. Gave him back his ring and told him there'd be no more proposals. We're finished."

She didn't think it was her imagination that he looked relieved. Or maybe that was wishful thinking.

"I saw Jodi yesterday," he said.

God. Had her heart skipped a beat? Claire tried not to jump to conclusions. She failed. Had Jodi managed to lure Riley back into her arms—and into her other places? Claire was too afraid to ask.

"Things are over between me and her," he added.

Her heart skipped even more beats. Much more of this and she'd end up in the ER on an EKG machine. Claire just took some deep breaths and waited for Riley to continue.

"But Jodi will still be around town for a while so she can get some work done," he added. "I thought you should know in case you ran into her."

"I won't be going to Calhoun's." Or into town for that matter. Claire wasn't opposed to a confrontation, but after what'd happened with those special kisses, Claire was certain she wouldn't be able to keep a straight face around the woman. One look at her, and Jodi would know.

And worse, Claire would want her to know.

It wasn't a neener-neener kind of thing, either. All right, maybe it was. A little. But Claire had always had a thing for Riley, and that thing had just gone to another level. The question now was just how far did she want those levels to keep going?

Far, she decided.

She hadn't known what decision she would make, but looking at him now, she realized she knew exactly what she wanted to do with Riley.

"Do you want to have sex?" Claire asked.

IT WAS ONLY pure blind luck that Riley didn't choke on his wine. Definitely not the reaction he wanted to have. But then neither was the instant hard-on he got from Claire just asking that question.

Asking a man if he wanted to have sex was akin to asking if he wanted that air he was breathing. Air that suddenly seemed a little thin right now.

Of course he wanted sex. This was Claire, and he'd wanted to have sex with her since about the time he'd gotten his first hard-on. In fact, she'd been the cause of that first one. But then Riley had pushed his feelings and hard-ons for her aside because she'd chosen Daniel.

However, she seemed to be choosing *him* right now, and while Riley wanted to jump on that, jump on her, too, he needed to take a step back. "Well, do you?" Claire pressed.

Her breath was thin, as well, judging from the way she was sucking it in, and it was coming too fast. Not exactly an erotic come-on. More like the beginnings of hyperventilation.

Riley took hold of her arm and had her sit at the table. He sat, too. Not easily. But he managed it. "Of course I would."

He'd barely gotten out the words when she came out of the chair and kissed him. Now, that was a nice slam of heat. Of course, he didn't need that slam because it messed with his head. Other parts, too. And even though it pained him to admit it, they should talk about this first.

Then jump into bed.

Maybe he could make it a short talk.

"I just want to make sure—" he started, but his question ground to a halt when she kissed him again.

"I'm sure," Claire insisted. And judging from the way she'd bit his lip at the end of that kiss, she was.

Well, Riley was as sure as that and then some, but he needed to hang on to that clear head a little longer.

"Did, uh, anything happen to make you decide to do this?" he asked.

Was that a blank look she gave him? Well, if it was, it only lasted a couple of seconds before she huffed. The lip biting was gone but not the scalding attraction that was still heating up the kitchen. Riley didn't think it was leftover heat from the oven, either.

"Look, I know you'll be leaving soon," she said. "Lucky told me about the physical you needed to pass, and since I know you, I also know you'll pass it."

Twenty-eighty flashed in his head. But with all the exercises he'd been doing, he had to be up to twenty-two–seventy-eight by now. And while he wanted to believe with all his heart that those odds would improve in his favor, Claire clearly had more faith in him than he did.

However, this was more than faith.

"Then, you know I'll be leaving," he said though Riley knew she hadn't forgotten that part.

She nodded.

Okay, he'd expected a bit more of an explanation than just a nod. Preferably, a short explanation that actually made sense.

Claire was a sensible woman, and he seriously doubted she was the fling-having type. Even after what'd happened between them two nights ago. They'd been caught up in the heat of the moment then, no time to give it much thought. She'd clearly given it some thought since, though.

"All right, let's just say we do this," Riley speculated. "Then what? I leave and you just accept that?"

"More or less."

Riley frowned. She wasn't totally killing the mood, not much could do that, but he wanted to know more about that less.

"I don't want you to get hurt," he clarified.

She drew in another of those quick breaths. "I won't. I've been doing a lot of soul-searching about this, and I'm not offering you a white picket fence at the end of these two weeks. I'm offering you sex with no strings attached."

Soul-searching, huh? Riley was reasonably sure this was the first time those words about sex with no strings attached had ever come out of her mouth, but she didn't give him a chance to remind her of that.

"Making fantasies come true," she blurted out. "That's the motto of my and Livvy's business, and it's what I want from you. Starting tonight."

Oh, she looked so hot. Sounded so confident. But Riley could see the nerves just below the surface. They were simmering there with all that heat.

"Tonight? I didn't bring a condom with me."

That was a lie. He had one in his wallet. All right, he had two. But he hadn't exactly felt good about putting them there. It had seemed, well, calculated, as if he were doing something that would lead Claire down the path to a broken heart.

Unless...

Maybe her feelings for him didn't go past this attraction. Oh, and friendship. But maybe that was it, and who was he to argue with a woman who seemed to know her own mind? One who had done some actual soul-searching. Clearly, she was set on doing this.

The little voice in his head, though, wasn't convinced.

"You're sure?" he asked one more time.

She nodded. "And it doesn't have to happen tonight. I'll give you a day or two to think it over, and—"

Claire was possibly going to say something important, but Riley made the decision that this was going to happen no matter what else she had to say. He kissed her.

CHAPTER NINETEEN

EVEN AFTER PRACTICALLY throwing herself at Riley, she still hadn't seen the kiss coming, but Claire sure felt it. *Oh, my.* Riley was so good at this, and despite all that oral foreplay the night before last, her body was aching for a real fix.

Claire refused to think about if this was a mistake or not. She'd already been doing too much thinking, and she was tired of waffling, whining and especially aching. Even if this turned out to put an end to Riley's and her friendship, then so be it. For tonight, she was getting that fantasy.

With just a few of Riley's kisses, the memories of their other encounter came washing over her. Of course, the fire was there, that was a given, but this felt like so much more. Good thing they hadn't become lovers in high school or they might not have ever gotten anything accomplished—including graduation— because Claire suddenly felt as if she'd missed something incredibly good.

Livvy was right about not grading sex on a curve.

Never again.

Of course, that might mean she'd never have sex again, either, but that was a bridge she would cross when she came to it. For now, she just wanted Riley. And she got him. His mouth, his hands, pretty much the rest of him when they landed body to body.

She was mostly responsible for that because Claire hooked her arms around him and kept pulling him closer until she had him where she wanted him. He didn't put up any resistance to that maneuvering, but it was clear he was more interested in the kissing than he was the jockeying for position.

Claire was interested in both.

Taking a step back, she took Riley with her, heading toward the bedroom where she'd stashed the condoms she'd bought. Of course, the one Lucky had given her was closer, so if they didn't actually make it to the bed, she could use that as a backup.

Which she might have to do.

That became clear with the next step when she landed against the freshly stripped and painted wall. It was all smooth and cool now, and Riley pressed her back against it when he took her mouth as if it were his for the taking. He certainly wasn't having any second thoughts about this, thank goodness. For a moment, she wondered if he would, but that thought flew right out of her head when he shoved up her top and kissed her breasts.

Mercy.

The man had a magic mouth.

She'd worn a pink lacy bra, and she thought maybe the grunt he made was one of approval. Yes, approval. He made another sound, and then their gazes connected when he looked up at her and took her nipple into his mouth. Claire perhaps lost consciousness for a couple of seconds when the pleasure shot through her.

"I want you naked," Riley insisted.

An excellent plan. She'd worn her good panties, too, but this time it was going to be a mutual stripping off because she got a great deal of pleasure from seeing him naked. That's why she went after his shirt, but she was mindful of the injury. In fact, she tried not to even look at it...too late. She looked.

"You're sure you're up to this?" she asked.

Without breaking the nipple kisses, he latched on to her hand and put it to the front of his jeans where she felt him not only "up" but rock hard.

"Ha-ha." Except she was moaning when she said it so it didn't sound like a fake laugh.

Still, Riley had proven his point. And she got to feel that proof when he made his way back up from her breasts to her mouth. At first Claire couldn't figure out why he was backtracking, but then she realized it was because it put him in a better position to yank off her top.

She did some yanking, too. His shirt came off. So did her bra, and when he sent it sailing, it landed in the baby potatoes. *Oh, well.* A cream-sauced bra was a casualty of the hot need that was making them both a little crazy and affecting their aim.

His shirt went in the recycling bin.

Riley turned her so fast that she nearly lost her balance, but he was right there to steady her. He leaned against the wall so he could go after her skirt next. She wasn't sure where it landed, but her panties soon followed, and Claire realized she was stark naked in her kitchen.

It occurred to her that she should suggest going to the bedroom. Where she'd put out some candles and washed the sheets. But then Riley did a trail of tongue kisses back down her body, and she knew the candles and clean sheets would have to wait.

He lifted her leg, putting her knee on his good shoulder, and he gave her more of those kisses and nibbles that would bring her to a really fast orgasm if she didn't do something about it. Not that she would have balked too much about a fast orgasm from Riley's mouth, but this time she wanted to make it the main course and not an appetizer.

"I've got condoms, and we're going to use them," she mumbled.

She caught on to his hair, pulled him back up, and in the same motion, Claire went after his jeans.

"How many condoms?" he asked.

A whole box. "Three," she said instead. A whole-box confession would make her seem slutty instead of just frugal. The box had been on sale.

"Good. I brought two with me," he said. "I lied about that earlier."

All right, so they had fifteen counting the one Lucky had left. Claire wouldn't mention that one, either. Fifteen condoms had to be more than enough to quell this raging heat. Riley unzipped his jeans, came back to her for another kiss while they got them off him. Not easily. She was all thumbs and crazy now. She blamed that on the kisses he kept dropping on various parts of her body.

So Claire turned the tables on him.

Literally. She pushed him against the table, anchoring him in place so she could kiss his neck. His chest. And because she felt that she owed him a little payback, she went down on her knees, too. She took him into her mouth.

He cursed.

But she thought that was a good thing. However, he didn't let those bubblegumming kisses go on for long. Still cursing, he fumbled through his pocket, located a condom and somehow managed to get it on despite the fact she was *helping*.

More payback for driving her crazy and allowing her to go years and years without having him. Claire intended to make up for some of those years in the bed.

Or on the table.

Riley turned her, leaning her against the table and stepping between her legs. Of course, he didn't wait long before thrusting inside her.

Good gravy.

The pleasure just sort of burst through her head to toe and especially to the parts in between. Big and hard wasn't overrated. At all.

Despite being on the table and sticking her hand in the key lime pie, it was somehow perfect. Riley found just the right rhythm, the right everything down to the sweet kiss he gave her that sent her flying. He flew, too, and then he landed against her, their bodies slick with sweat.

Parts of their dinner, too.

It took him a few seconds to get back to earth, and when he did, he licked the key lime from her hand.

"Hungry?" she asked when she finally caught her breath.

"Yeah, but not for that yet." Riley scooped her up and headed for the bedroom.

"HOW'S YOUR SHOULDER?" Claire asked. She leaned in to have a look for herself.

Riley wasn't exactly comfortable having her examine the scar. It was still raw and ugly. Maybe it always would be. But thankfully Claire didn't have the same horrified expression as she had the first time she'd seen it.

"It's fine." No lie this time. The muscles still twinged and pulled when he moved it, but sex hadn't aggravated it, and even if it had, Riley doubted he would have noticed.

He wasn't noticing now, either.

He was admiring the view. Riley was sure he'd never had dinner in bed and certainly not while he was naked. While Claire was naked, too. And while they were still wearing some of that food.

"I could heat up the roast," Claire offered, kissing him.

Riley shook his head. That would only require her to get up again, and while he'd have a good show of her coming and going, it really wasn't necessary. The food was just to stave off starvation.

In addition to the key lime pie that Claire had gotten on her hands, Riley had somehow managed to get potatoes on him. That was probably why sex should never happen on the dinner table, but at the time it'd seemed like his only option. He'd had to have Claire right then, right there. And he had managed to do just that. However, with the heat temporarily sated and his stomach getting there, as well, he had to wonder.

What now?

She smiled at him around a forkful of key lime. A smile that seemed genuine, maybe even a little giddy, but he knew Claire well enough to know that there could be nerves behind it, too.

Yeah, Claire had offered him no-strings-attached sex, but he wondered if she'd even thought it through. He certainly hadn't, but Riley was certain he'd be doing a lot of thinking about it in the days to come.

There was a crashing sound, and Claire practically tossed the rest of her pie on the nightstand, flung back the covers and was out of the bed before Riley could get up. He seriously doubted it was a burglar. And it wasn't.

It was the kitten.

It had somehow managed to topple a basket filled with Ethan's toy cars. Riley certainly hadn't forgotten about the gift from his brother. A gift he'd discuss with Lucky first chance he got. Lucky had something up his sleeve.

Claire scooped up the kitten, redirected it to its own toys. No doubt gifts from Lucky, too, and she dumped some of the kitten food into the bowl. While she was doing that, Riley set up the litter box. All while they were stark naked. She noticed him naked, too. He noticed her naked. And all that noticing began to feel a little like foreplay. He wasn't sure he was up for another round so soon.

Yes, he was.

He was always ready for Claire even if his shoulder disagreed.

But Claire no longer seemed ready. That's because her attention landed on that damn journal again.

Riley huffed. "I wish you'd let me burn that thing for you."

She made a sound that could have meant anything, and she kept looking at it. Not as if it were a coiled rattler ready to strike but as if it were a new pie that she wasn't sure she'd like or even wanted to try.

"I think I should read it," she said.

"Shit. Sugar," he automatically corrected even though Ethan wasn't around. "Why would you want to do that?"

Claire looked at him, and he knew why. Because it was there. It was from her sorry excuse for a mother, and Claire needed to know what the woman had written.

Part of Riley got that. If he were in her shoes—or in this case, her naked body—he would want to read it, too. But he also wanted to protect Claire from the woman's venom.

"Tomorrow," she said. "I can read it when Ethan's napping."

"No way. If you're going to read it, do it while I'm here." Riley didn't have to think about that.

She shook her head. "It's not fair to you. You came over for a night of dinner and sex. You don't need to have a course of old baggage to go with all that."

Actually, he'd come over just for dinner. Hadn't had a clue about the sex course. And while old baggage wouldn't be nearly as tasty a dessert as Claire or the key lime pie, if those long-ago written words caused her to fall apart, and they almost certainly would, Riley wanted to be there to pick up the pieces.

And despite the fact there would be pieces, Riley didn't stop her when she went to the mantel and picked up the journal.

FOR SOME STUPID reason it didn't feel right reading the journal while she was naked. Maybe because she already felt exposed just by holding it in her hands. Claire grabbed a T-shirt and put it on despite Riley grumbling something about losing a great view. That caused her to smile.

Which was probably why he'd said it.

He put on his shirt and boxers, and after losing that view, Claire was rethinking her decision. This wouldn't just put a damper on the evening; it could ruin it. But the wounds inside her seemed to keep festering with each passing minute that the journal stayed around. She needed to think of it as a bandage that should be ripped off so the old wounds could finally heal.

Not that she expected to find anything healing on those pages.

No, she had no hopes of that whatsoever. But if she dealt with them all at once, the pain wouldn't be piecemeal.

"You want me to read it first?" Riley offered.

It was such a sweet gesture that Claire paused to kiss him. Of course, she hadn't needed a sweet gesture as an excuse. She planned to kiss him a lot throughout the night in case this was the last chance she got to do that. For now, they were still basking in the aftermath of the sex glow, but in the morning light, Riley might decide to turn down any future sessions of casual sex.

But she'd deal with that later, too.

Claire took the journal back to bed. Riley joined her, of course, not sitting so close that he was reading over her shoulder but close enough to be there if she needed him. Then, he handed her the fork that he'd used to eat the roast beef.

"I want you to use it to stab the page whenever you read something hurtful," he instructed. "That probably means multiple stabs on every page."

She smiled, took the fork and yes, kissed him again. "Do you remember ever seeing her?"

He shook his head. "But I remember a picture of her. Your grandmother used to have it on the mantel."

Claire remembered that picture, as well, but wasn't sure where it was. Maybe with the mystery letter that she hadn't been able to find.

"Deep breath," Riley coached. "And get the fork ready."

She did. Claire leaned her back against the headboard and flipped past the first couple of pages that she'd already read. Still, she took a moment to stab them. It felt surprisingly good even if it did leave a little au jus on the old pages.

When she got to an unread page, the first thing that jumped

out at her was the profanity. She had so few memories of her mom, but she hadn't remembered her using profanity every other word. Claire could almost feel the anger jumping off the page.

So she stabbed it.

"How bad?" Riley asked.

Claire shrugged. "More bitching about being pregnant and Rocky leaving her. I don't think she ever figured out she was better off without a man who ran out on her."

Even though Riley hadn't moved, she thought maybe he went still. No doubt because he thought Ethan's father had done the same to her. He hadn't. But she didn't want to get into that, not with the emotional powder keg in her hands.

The next pages were filled with comments about doctor's appointments, gaining weight, swollen ankles and the boring homework she'd been given by the school so she could graduate. Claire wasn't sure if her mother had ostracized herself or if the school had had a policy back then of not allowing pregnant students to attend.

"Remember, you can stop at any time," Riley reminded her.

She nodded, thanked him for his concern and kept turning the pages. Thankfully, after a while the profanity-laced entries became numbing, and it occurred to Claire that she had done plenty of whining in her own diary. But she'd had the good sense to destroy it before she headed off for college so that no one would ever see it.

The next date was one she instantly recognized because it was Claire's birthday. One word took up half the first page.

Hell.

That was just the beginning of her mother's profanity. Since Claire had gone through childbirth, as well, she knew it was painful. However, so were the words her mother had put in bold block letters:

I thought that fucking kid would never come out. My poor body won't ever be the same. Neither will my fucking life.

Claire stabbed the page twice with a fork and nearly bolted from the room. She needed to hold Ethan. She needed to tell him that she loved him.

She needed to breathe.

But Riley caught on to her and pulled her back into his arms. It was the right thing to do. Claire didn't bolt but stayed put in his arms. "Why couldn't I find the letter instead of this?" she mumbled.

Did Riley go still again? No. He was probably just trying not to remind her that she'd been wrong to read this.

"My question is why didn't your grandmother just throw away the journal?" he asked.

"I know the answer to that one. Gran didn't throw away much of anything. The proof is in all the boxes and drawers. There were over a hundred twisty ties from bread bags. It was as if she was prepping for doomsday and a twisty-tie shortage."

Riley chuckled, kissed her head again. "Now can you throw the journal away? With those fork marks on it, the next page would be hard to read anyway."

True. She'd stabbed it so hard, the tines had gone straight through the paper. Still… "There isn't much more of it."

He grunted, and it had a hint of disapproval to it, but Claire turned the page. The date was the day after she was born.

> Mom put Claire Marie on the kid's birth certificate. The nurses kept bugging me about a name so I said Clover Lane, but Mom said she was going to put Claire Marie, and I told her I didn't give a shit, that she could name the kid whatever she wanted. The nurses are giving me shit about not holding the kid, too. I told them they're getting paid to hold her, I'm not.

That hurt, too, so she stabbed it. *Clover Lane?* That sounded like a 1960s rock band or a stripper. "I spent months picking out Ethan's name. Months decorating his nursery. I held Ethan the moment he was born and didn't want to let go of him. She didn't do any of those things."

"But your grandmother did," Riley pointed out.

She nodded. It wasn't as if she hadn't felt loved. She had. However, Claire could never understand why her mother had felt this way, especially after seeing or holding her child. Of course, she hadn't held Claire, so maybe that was at the core of this latest page filled with bile.

"Gran didn't talk much about it, but my mom left Spring Hill with me when I was four and a half. But there aren't enough pages left in the journal for her to get into that."

"You don't have any memories of those six months or so you were away from here?" he asked.

"Some. I remember a man, but I don't know his name. I guess he was her boyfriend because they slept in the same bed. They yelled a lot." Thankfully, there were only bits and pieces of that, like the car accident that'd taken Riley's parents.

"Did either of them ever hurt you?" A muscle flickered in his jaw.

"No. No physical abuse." But her mother had indeed hurt her.

He paused a long time. "You think it'll help if you know the reason your mother left town with you and then came back?"

She nodded. "I think it would."

Another long pause, and Claire could practically see the debate he was having with himself. "Lucky remembers Della and Stella talking about it. Your mother met some man in San Antonio, took you and ran off with him. Take this with a grain of salt, but they say he was wanted by the law."

Well, that would explain why her mother had left. Of course, it was just as likely that six months of motherhood had been more than enough. So, her mother had come running back to Spring Hill in order to dump Claire and take off again.

She reached to turn the page, the last one, she realized, but Riley put his hand over hers. "Let me read it to you."

Claire was instantly suspicious. "I don't want you to sugar-coat it. After the other pages, I can take one more." She hoped.

"No sugarcoating."

She believed him, but it still took Claire a couple of long moments to let go. Riley took it. And the fork.

"Last page," he verified. "It was two days after you were born." He took a deep breath. "'Finally got out of that hellhole hospital and am home. It sucks but not as much as the hospital. Those nurse bitches! They made me hold the kid before I could leave. Blackmail! So, I held her—Claire—not a bad name, I guess. It suits her.'"

He stopped, looked at her. "Are you okay?"

Dang it. There were tears in her eyes and all because her mother called her by her name. Such a simple thing. But she held on to the half compliment as if it were a lifeline.

"I'm fine," Claire insisted. "Keep going."

Riley read ahead, silently, and she saw some sort of emotion in his eyes. What exactly, she wasn't sure, but he didn't look ready to stab the page. Instead, he handed it to her.

"You should finish this," he said.

All right, so it must not be too bad for him to offer that. Still, her heart was racing. Her mind, too. And while Claire wanted to finish it and put it behind her once and for all, finishing it also meant they'd come to the last link she had with her mother. After learning that her mother had considered ending the pregnancy and then wishing her dead, she only hoped there wasn't anything else so painful.

Claire did take the journal, but she also took the fork back, just in case. Not much was left at all, just a few sentences, and before she read them, she had a horrible thought. This was literally the last page in this particular journal, but what if there were others? That was a stomach-churning thought.

"Deep breath," Riley reminded her.

She took two of them and started reading.

Claire doesn't look like Rocky. She looks like Mom and
me. That's good. Looking at her won't remind me of him.
I don't want to think about him ever again. I just want to
get on with my life. That means getting on with my life
with Claire. God, she'll never know how scared I am. I'm
so going to screw this up.

There it was. The end. Ironic, since it had been the beginning.
And her mother hadn't sounded bitter but rather scared. Claire
had felt the same way about Ethan. She'd desperately wanted
and loved him, but she'd been terrified, too. It was strange to
know her mother had felt the same way.

Riley slipped his arm around her, pulled her close. "What do
you want to do with the journal now?" he asked.

That required more deep breaths. Ninety-nine percent of the
journal was filled with anger and profanity—most of it directed
at Claire and Rocky. There was no way Claire wanted to go back
through that again.

But she tore out the last page.

This one she'd keep.

She got up and took the rest of it to the fireplace. It was a
good night to put some things in her past to rest.

RILEY COULD SMELL the fire in his dream. But it wasn't an ordinary fire. It was from the explosion. From the IED. He'd heard
IEDs go off before. Never this close, though.

Never.

Get the hell out now!

He had to get out of there. Sixty-forty. That had been the
kid's odds. Good odds. But that was before the last IED. Before
Riley had felt the blood and the pain. Before the extraction had
become a kid in his arms.

The kid moaned. Still alive. Riley held him even tighter, hoping the pressure would stop the bleeding—both his and the kid's.

Hoping he'd get back in time to the Pave Hawk. Hell, hoping he'd find the damn thing and that it hadn't been blown to bits.

The fire and smoke were all around him now. Blobs of fiery debris left over from the IED. God, he couldn't hear. The blast was still ringing in his ears.

Couldn't see, either, because of the sand.

But he could think, and he went through all the things he'd learned in his training. Hadn't it been about this anyway? Needing to take evasive measures. Doing whatever it took to finish the mission.

Sixty-forty.

Get the hell out now!

Riley forced himself to move, one foot ahead of the other, and he made the mistake of looking down. He was leaving a trail of blood on the sand. His own blood.

There was too much of it.

But since he was moving, his odds were better than the kid's. Riley's blood type was on his name tag. If the medic was still alive, he'd see it and would be able to give him whatever he needed to stay alive.

The kid was a different matter.

Kids didn't wear their blood types on their clothes. Sure as fuck-hell shouldn't have been in this place, and Riley couldn't let him die here, either.

Sixty-forty.

One step ahead of the other.

He thought of his brothers. Of Claire. Why had she popped into his mind? He wasn't sure, but it was a welcome memory. Of Claire in the marching band on the football field of Spring Hill High School. Her stiff blue uniform that made her look like a soldier. The memory of her, the sound of the clarinet she was playing was weaving in and out of the sand so Riley marched with her.

Get the hell out now!

Claire said his name. Except he hadn't remembered her doing

that that day of the extraction. In the memory, she'd been playing her clarinet. No talking. She certainly hadn't called out to
him. Nor had she touched him. But she was doing that now.

"Riley?" she said. Claire was shaking his good arm. "You're
having another nightmare."

His eyes flew open, and it took a moment to pull himself
from the dream and figure out where he was. Hell. He was still
in Claire's bed, which would have been a good thing if he hadn't
had the nightmare. She'd already seen him have one on the porch
swing and the flashback at the pub. Two experiences too many.
Riley didn't want her seeing any more of that.

Too late.

He saw the worry in her eyes. Easy to see it since the sun-
light was already streaming through the window. Riley sat up,
scrubbed his hand over his face.

"Sixty-forty?" she asked.

Mercy, he'd obviously talked in his sleep again. His breath
was still gusting, and it took him a moment to gather himself.
"What else did I say?"

"My name." Claire paused. "Was sixty-forty your odds of
getting out of there alive?"

"No." That was all he was considering saying, so why he said
more, Riley didn't know. "Mine were better."

"Those were the *kid's* odds," she said on a rise of breath.

"Yeah." At least they had been before the last IED. Riley
wasn't sure what they were after that.

He could see the question in her eyes—she wanted to know
if the kid made it—and Riley considered using a personal evasive measure. After all, Claire and he were practically naked
in her bed, and if he just started kissing her, she wouldn't be
able to talk.

But that didn't seem right.

It didn't matter that Riley wanted to protect her from this,
because he couldn't. Claire had already heard too much. Had
also seen too much with the scars on his body.

"Two of the crew and an airman didn't make it," Riley said. "But the kid did."

The tears were in her eyes, and she didn't even try to blink them back. "He's alive because of you."

It hadn't all been because of him. Riley had just gotten him out, had given him a fighting chance. The medic and then the doctors had done the rest. But the bottom line here for him was something that'd gotten lost in all the pain and the flashbacks.

The kid had made it.

All those steps through the sand. All the blood he'd left behind. The pain. The loss of the other crew members. All of it had brought him to this one realization.

The kid had made it.

And so had he.

It was somehow that journal all over again. Tough to take and with an ending that wouldn't necessarily make everything right. And Riley decided to do what Claire had done.

He mentally tore out the last page—*the kid had made it*—and pitched the rest of the nightmare into the fire.

CHAPTER TWENTY

SMILE, CLAIRE REMINDED HERSELF.

If she didn't do that Livvy would think something was wrong. Too late. One step outside her car, and Livvy's attention zoomed straight past the weak smile and to Claire's eyes. Livvy didn't exactly look crestfallen, but she didn't look so eager to ask for juicy details of Claire's night with Riley.

"I didn't bring wine," Livvy called out, "but I brought something better." She scooped up a giggling Ethan like a football and ran with him to the porch.

Since Livvy was teetering on mile-high heels again and wobbling, to Ethan it must have felt a little like being on a carnival ride.

"How'd he do last night?" Claire asked.

"Good as beans." Whatever that meant. "But I bought him some pull-ups."

Despite the fact Ethan was still tucked under Livvy's arms, he pulled down the waist of his jeans for her to see. "Ull-ups."

He seemed very proud, though Claire couldn't imagine what'd prompted Livvy to buy them. Or how the heck she'd found them in the store. Livvy wasn't exactly a pro at buying baby supplies. Once Claire had asked her to buy wipes, and Livvy had come back with eye-makeup remover pads.

"He kept peeing on the fake rubber tree I have in the living room," Livvy explained. "And each time he undid his diaper to do that, I couldn't get the tape to stick so I took him to the store and asked one of the moms I saw shopping what I should get."

Good choice. These had smiling toy cars on them. Ethan's selection no doubt. Though Claire would need to scold him for peeing on the rubber plant. Later, she'd sit him down and talk to him about that.

Claire took him from Livvy the second they made it to the porch, and she managed to steal some kisses before Ethan wiggled out of her arms. That's because he saw the kitten on the other side of the screen door, and he scrambled to get inside.

"Van Gogh," he said with perfect clarity. Though Claire had no idea why until she realized the kitten did indeed look like one of the gold-star blobs in the painting that she'd been showing him for weeks.

"Is it a gift from Riley?" Livvy asked, following Claire inside.

"From Lucky. He brought it over before Riley got here last night."

"No. I mean that." Smiling and winking, Livvy touched the spot on Claire's neck.

The very spot that was doused with every drop of concealer that Claire had been able to squeeze from the tube. Between the bruise from the pub brawl and the love bite, she'd gone through more concealer in a week than she had in the past six years.

"That was an accident," Claire explained.

But she was sorry she'd even offered that small bit of an explanation. Because now Livvy would want more. And Claire had no intention of sharing. But the "accident" had involved her learning that the spot on her neck was very sensitive and whenever Riley kissed her there, she was within a heartbeat of having an orgasm.

So he'd kissed her there.

A lot.

And when coupled with "other things" he'd done to her, the orgasm did indeed happen.

"Van Gogh, van Gogh," Ethan repeated. He sat on the floor, and the kitten crawled into his lap. It was instant love. She could see it all over her boy's face.

Claire sighed. Because it meant they were keeping the kitten. Now, she was feeding the gray tabby and Whoa, and if she included the one Riley had reserved for her at the pound, she was well on her way to being a crazy cat lady.

With a hickey.

Ethan couldn't take his eyes off van Gogh and Livvy wouldn't take her eyes off Claire's neck. "I'll tell you about my date if you'll tell me about yours," Livvy said.

"You didn't have a date. Ethan stayed at your place last night."

"I meant the date the night before. The one with Lucky."

"That wasn't a date." Claire leaned in to whisper the rest. "That was hot monkey sex. Wasn't it?"

"Always is with Lucky. But, no, there's nothing serious between us. Not like with Riley and you."

Of course, Ethan latched on to that. "Riley?"

"He's not here, baby," Claire answered.

Ethan looked disappointed, and Claire knew exactly how he felt. It'd been hard for her to see Riley fully dressed and walking out her door. Hard because she might not get a night like that with him again. Yes, she'd offered him no-strings-attached sex, but after the mixed bag of stuff that'd gone on, he might decide sex with her could never be string-less.

"It is serious now between you two, right?" Livvy asked.

"No. Of course not. Last night wasn't about getting serious. It was about, well…" She might as well just call it what it was. "Fudging."

"Well, fudging can become serious. With the right person," Livvy added. "And I'm pretty sure R-i-l-e-y is the right person."

Claire wasn't sure of that at all. "It takes two people for it to be right." And Riley wasn't on board for anything that would take him away from the military. "He saved a kid when he was over there. That's how he got hurt."

"That's what you talked about last night?" Judging from her tone and the face Livvy made, she guessed that had been a real mood killer.

And in a way, it had been when it came to the sex. But in other ways, it'd been incredible. She had watched Riley's mind heal right in front of her eyes.

"His body's healing, too," Claire continued. "I was amazed at what he could do."

Livvy grinned. "Do tell."

"I didn't mean s-e-x-u-a-l-l-y." Not completely anyway, though he had been especially good at all that. "He lifted me up like I weighed nothing, and after all that apology ice cream I've been eating, you know that couldn't be farther from the truth."

Livvy made a sound of agreement, patted her stomach. She'd been eating some bowls of Riley's I'm-sorry offerings, too.

"I think he might have had some pain a time or two," Claire went on, "but it was nothing like it was when he first got home."

Livvy studied her a moment. "You don't exactly sound happy about that."

"No. I am." Claire couldn't say that quickly enough or mean it more. "I hated seeing him in pain." Of course, there was a *but* coming.

One that Livvy had no trouble interpreting. "But it means he'll pass that physical."

Yes. Mercy, that was selfish of Claire to even think otherwise. She wanted Riley to pass the physical, wanted him to be happy and free from those horrible flashbacks, and she wanted that even if it meant she couldn't have him.

"I think the old adage applies here," Claire said. "I made my bed, and I can sleep in it." *Alone.*

She didn't say the alone part aloud, but Livvy had no trouble picking up on it. Her hug tightened around Claire. "But at least you had a great night with him," Livvy reminded her. "And you have a kitten. The place is looking better every time I come over. Soon, it'll be ready to go on the market."

Yes, soon, and for some reason that caused her stomach to churn. "I still want to find the letter, though."

"And what about that sugary journal from your sugary mother?" Livvy asked.

Claire tipped her head to the ashes in the fireplace. "Gone. Well, gone except for the one good part. I kept that."

"Good. Because it's time for your mind to heal, too."

Yes, it was, and Claire was certain she was almost there. Almost. But she wasn't exactly doing a victory dance. Because even if all the final pieces fell into place—selling the house, finding the letter and having some peace that her mother maybe hadn't hated her with every fiber of her being—it all suddenly seemed a little hollow.

Because she'd have none of those things with Riley.

RILEY TOOK HIS TIME walking through the pasture. Why, he didn't know. It was too hot. He was tired after helping the new cutter with the horses. Considering he'd gotten less than an hour of sleep, he should be hurrying to catch a nap before dinner. Still, he didn't rush.

He'd seen his father do this a hundred times, stroll through the pasture as if soaking it all in. Riley supposed that's what he was doing now. His mind had slowed down enough for him to be alone with his own thoughts and not be sickened by what was in his head.

The kid was alive.

That would replace "Jingle Bells" if the flashbacks threatened again. Everything he needed to remember about what had happened in that wall of sand was that he'd done his job. The kid was alive.

He tested the shoulder. Stiff and sore. But considering the workout he'd given it the night before with Claire, he was surprised it felt as good as it did. Ditto for him. Sex with Claire had been everything he'd thought it would be, but he hadn't managed to keep the regrets at bay.

Yes, he was already having regrets.

Without the night of sex, leaving Ethan and her would have been hard, but now he'd taken hard to a whole new level. Which had pretty much described his dick most of the night.

Hard-dick thoughts aside, Riley wasn't sure how this was all going to work out with Claire, but he didn't see a white picket fence in their future. Still, that didn't mean he wasn't going to enjoy the short time they had together. That's what Claire wanted.

Or rather what she'd said she wanted.

While that might have been wishful thinking on her part, Riley was feeling too at peace, too content, too happy to question it. By damn, he was putting on a pair of rose-colored glasses for a while, and he whistled on the walk back to the house. Only the horses and Crazy Dog were around to notice that he was acting like a giddy fool.

Lucky, too, he realized when Riley saw his brother coming out of the house.

Riley stopped whistling when he spotted him. For one thing he didn't want Lucky picking up on his good mood and asking him about how his night had gone with Claire, and for another Lucky's own mood seemed to be several steps past the riled stage. Lucky cursed, threw his hat on the porch and picked it up only to throw it again.

"Should I ask?" Riley offered as he approached him.

"No."

With that, Lucky started to pace. It only lasted a couple of seconds. Lucky wasn't known for doing long stretches of anything, and it was the same this time. He headed off the porch and in the direction of his truck.

Riley huffed, followed him. "Did something happen between Logan and you?"

It wasn't exactly a guess. Lucky's fits of temper were rare.

For the most part, Lucky was a lover. However, his occasional clashes were usually with Logan.

"He's three minutes older than me," Lucky snarled.

Yeah, definitely Logan. "He's decades older than you, than both of us," Riley pointed out.

Lucky opened his truck door, but he didn't get in. "Is that some kind of an old soul reference? Because an old asshole would be a better label for it. No matter what I do, it's not enough. Well, you know what? I don't want to do enough to make it enough. Understand?"

Maybe. Riley thought he had mentally worked his way through all those *enough*s. "Does this have to do with the other horse trainer who'll be coming in?"

"You bet it does. I called in a friend for that job, and Logan fired him on the spot. Well, if he didn't trust my judgment, why ask me to do it in the first place?"

Riley didn't have an answer for that, but it did bother him that Logan had fired the guy. They had nearly fifty horses thanks to the deal he'd made with the Army Ranger and only one trainer.

"You know what Logan wants?" Lucky continued, but he decided to answer his own question. "He wants me to train them. He wants me to drop everything I'm doing and work a program I was against from the beginning."

Riley hadn't been around for those *discussions* about the cutting-horse program between Lucky and Logan. Riley's first reaction was that it was a good thing. That was his usual reaction anyway. Stay uninvolved. Hear about all the spats after the fact and not give a damn about any of it.

But the breakthrough he'd had about those flashbacks must have softened his brain because Riley had a new thought. If he had been around for those discussions, he could have soothed them over. A stupid thought because it wasn't his place to do that.

He frowned.

Of course it was his place. These were his brothers, and while more times than not, he wanted to punch them in their faces, it was still his place to smooth things over.

Hell.

He wasn't sure he liked all these revelations.

Lucky's fit of temper seemed to leave him as quickly as it had come. "Dixie Mae's sick," Lucky threw out there, and judging from the way he dodged Riley's gaze, that admission was at the heart of his anger. Not the run-in with Logan.

Riley knew Dixie Mae, of course. Lucky and she were rodeo promoters together. But Dixie Mae was old. *Really* old. Like maybe past ninety. Riley would have been more surprised if Lucky had said the woman was in stellar health.

"Is there anything I can do?" Riley asked.

Lucky looked at him then, the corner of his mouth lifting in what Riley had heard some women say was Lucky's panty-dropping smile. "Not a thing, but thanks for offering."

Lucky moved again as if to get into his truck, but he apparently had something else to discuss with Riley because he kept his boots on the ground. "You're spending more time with Claire."

Ah, that. "So are you. You gave her a cat."

"One that was on death row. Maybe it wasn't right at the moment, but if no one had adopted it within the next three months, it would have gone on death row."

"There was a waiting list to adopt it and the other two in the litter," Riley pointed out.

But Lucky just shrugged. "I thought her boy would like it."

Riley was sure Ethan would. In fact, that was why he was so anxious to get back over to Claire's—to see Ethan's reaction. One of the reasons anyway.

"I know you stayed with Claire last night," Lucky went on.

Riley felt a lecture coming on. Lucky was protective when it came to Claire, and he was looking at Riley as if he'd just defiled her. He hadn't. Well, that depended on Lucky's definition of defiled, but he hadn't done anything that Claire hadn't wanted him to do.

Multiple times.

"Daniel still wants to marry her," Lucky went on. So, no lecture after all. "He told Maude Kreppner that when he was checking out at the grocery store."

If Daniel had told Maude, then he wanted it to get around town since Maude was the top spiller of gossip.

But why had Daniel done that?

Riley had to shake his head. "Claire turned down his proposal."

"This time, yeah. But Daniel's thinking that once you're out of the picture—and you will be soon—that he'll be there to help Claire finally get over you for good."

Riley wanted to believe that wouldn't happen, but he had to be realistic. Claire was an attractive young woman. Great in bed. She wouldn't live like a nun just because he was back in uniform. And she did want a home, a family. Daniel just might end up wearing her down with the lure of giving her those things.

"Something to think about, huh?" Lucky said.

No, it wasn't something Riley wanted to think about at all. He definitely didn't want any images in his head of Daniel and Claire.

Too late.

They were there, and he might have found a new use for "Jingle Bells."

Lucky took out a piece of folded paper from his pocket. "Before I go, Claire asked me to ask around about a guy named Rocky."

"Her father," Riley said.

Lucky nodded. "Anyway, I asked Maude since she seems to remember every dribble of gossip and news that's ever spread through town. We don't need archives with Maude around. She remembered his last name and the rest of the stuff I jotted down there." He paused. "You can decide whether or not it's a good idea to give to Claire."

Shit.

If it was good, Lucky would have no doubt done the honors himself, and after the journal experience, Riley wasn't sure she was ready for anything bad.

"It wouldn't be right to keep it from her," Lucky added, and this time he did get in the truck. That's when Riley noticed he already had his bag inside. Packed. It was stuffed to the point of bulging.

Riley couldn't argue with Lucky about it not being right, but it might not be right to put her through another emotional wringer, either.

"One more thing." Lucky started the engine, shut the door and finished what he was saying through the open window. "If you break Claire's heart, I'll have to punch you, hard. Like, right in the nuts."

Yes, he knew that. Lucky would consider it his duty to punch him.

And Riley would let him.

"You do know I will hunt you down if you hurt Claire," Livvy said.

For Riley it was a déjà vu moment because Livvy's threatening call had come less than an hour after Lucky's nuts-punch-threatening goodbye. At first Riley hadn't been certain why the woman was calling him, but Livvy hadn't wasted even a greeting before she'd launched right into the reason.

"I don't want her hurt," Riley assured her.

"Wanting and making sure it doesn't happen are two different things. Claire's vulnerable right now."

"I know. But unless she's told you something different, she wants to be with me. No strings attached."

"Bullocks. She'd take those strings in a second if you offered them to her. And, no, I know you can't, but you can do this the right way."

"Then tell me what the right way is." Riley was serious, too. He'd never thought he'd ask for love advice from Livvy, but he was open to suggestions.

"Offer her an out. She won't take it, but it'll remind her that you're worried about how deep this shit is you're both stepping in and tracking all over her life."

An out? Instead of asking Livvy to tell him the right way, maybe he should have said he was open to *good* suggestions. That didn't sound like a good one since Claire had been the one to put this sex pact together. If he offered her an out now, she might interpret that as his thinking she sucked in bed.

And she didn't.

Nor did she suck on the kitchen table.

"If you hurt her," Livvy went on, "I'm coming after you with a set of rusty pliers, and I won't be using them on your teeth."

Riley couldn't help it. He winced. But thankfully he didn't have to listen to the details of what Livvy planned to do with those pliers because she hung up, leaving Riley to sit there and wonder if every single human being on the planet knew he'd slept with Claire.

And that latest threat wasn't the end to the unpleasant parts of what had otherwise been a pleasant day. Riley had some manning up to do. He needed to talk to Daniel about Claire, but the question was—how should he do that?

He'd have to do this face-to-face, which was the reason Riley had stopped in town when he'd seen Daniel's car in front of his real estate office. He'd parked up the block, though, to give himself a few minutes to figure how to work this out. It was getting late, well past eight, so it was possible Daniel was in there doing paperwork and not with a client. Riley hoped so anyway. This wasn't something he wanted to discuss in front of an audience.

There wasn't a man-rule about manning up, but Riley didn't need a rule to let him know that he had to own up to having slept with Claire without actually saying he'd slept with her. Something like that was Claire's to tell, but Riley also knew he'd have to let Daniel know the other man-rule had been broken.

Don't take anything that wasn't his.

Claire hadn't been his, but then she hadn't exactly been Daniel's, either. Not after turning down his proposal.

"Need a drink before you go in there?" someone asked. Trisha.

Hell. With all his special ops training, Riley should have heard a woman in high heels walking up to his car. He needed to get back to par with his observation skills because if he had heard, he could have avoided this conversation with Trisha by going straight into the office.

Riley lowered the window and hoped this would be a short conversation. But Trisha leaned against his car. Thankfully, that wasn't a come-and-get-me look in her eye. More like sympathy.

Great.

That meant she'd likely heard about Riley staying the night with Claire. Maybe she even knew about both times. Of course, he hadn't expected something like that to stay quiet. Anyone driving by Claire's house would have seen his car. Or Daniel's for the first overnight stay.

"Daniel's upset, you know," Trisha said. "I probably should be, too. After all, I thought you were with Jodi. Jodi thought you were with her, too, but it turns out we were both wrong."

And she waited for Riley to verify something he had no intention of verifying. Instead, he got out of the car.

"I'll be seeing you, Trisha," he said.

But she trailed along beside him. "You should probably wait a day or two before talking to Daniel. I heard from Maude that he wasn't taking this well. He especially didn't take it well when he found out Claire had bought that deluxe box of condoms on sale at the convenience store."

Riley didn't stop walking, but that slowed him down a bit. Claire hadn't mentioned the box of condoms, probably because he'd brought one, but damn it, just the thought of her doing such a thing nearly gave him a hard-on.

Coupled with Lucky's threat to punch him, his own threat to punch himself if he did indeed break her heart, Riley wasn't sure what the hell he was going to do. Have sex with her again and then beat himself up? Sadly, that was the best solution he could think of because he wasn't going to be the one to end the sex pact with Claire. She would have to do that.

"The clerk said he'd never seen Claire buy condoms before," Trisha added. She paused, but Riley stayed mum.

"If you don't mind, I think I should talk to Daniel alone," Riley told her.

"You're sure? I mean, if it comes to blows, I could be there to stop it. I don't want you to hurt your shoulder."

Neither did he, but if Daniel started throwing his fists, Riley didn't want an audience for that. Especially an audience who would blab it to Claire before Riley could even make it to her house.

"I'm sure," Riley insisted, and he waited for Trisha to leave before he finished walking to Daniel's door.

The building was an old midcentury glass front so it was easy to see inside through the wall of windows. There was a desk where it looked as if a receptionist would usually be. No receptionist now, though, but there was an office just behind the desk. Riley went inside and headed there. Since the door wasn't fully closed, he pushed it open.

And got a big eyeful.

Earful, too.

Daniel shrieked, a very unmanly sound, probably because his bare ass was facing the door. Probably, too, because there was a naked woman beneath him on the desk. She didn't shriek, but she did curse, and it was both a profanity and a voice that Riley recognized.

Jodi.

Daniel got up, scrambling to get dressed. Jodi didn't scramble. Despite the fact that she was naked, too, she got up off the desk as if doing a leisurely stroll in the park.

"You should have knocked," Daniel growled.

Riley gave him a flat look. "You should have locked the door. Or at least closed it all the way."

However, Riley could see how this had all played out because something similar had played out between Claire and him the night before. He'd taken her on the kitchen table, which wasn't that much different from a desk.

Huffing and puffing enough to blow a house down, Daniel got dressed and then took Riley by the arm to lead him back into the reception area. He shut the door between them and Jodi.

"What happened in there wasn't planned," Daniel said, removing his hand from Riley so he could fling it back toward the office where he'd left a naked Jodi. "Jodi came by to comfort me because I was upset."

"About Claire and me. I heard. That's why I came, too. To tell you in person that the man-rule had been broken. But now it appears it's been doubly broken."

"How can you say that? Jodi and you broke up."

"So did Claire and you," Riley reminded him.

"That's temporary."

"What if it's temporary between Jodi and me?" It wasn't, but Riley was making a point here.

Point taken judging from the way Daniel's face got red and sweaty. Of course, that could have been from the sex on the desk.

"So, we're at a stalemate," Daniel concluded.

Were they? Riley had enough unresolved situations without continuing this one with Daniel. So, no, it wasn't a stalemate.

"The man-pact is null and void because I'm seeing Claire again," he told Daniel, and he spoke slowly enough so that neither Daniel nor Jodi would miss a word. Jodi was almost certainly listening at the door. "And I'll continue seeing Claire as long as she wants. Or until I leave, whichever comes first. In fact, I'm headed to her place now."

"To use all those condoms she bought at the convenience store." Daniel's face got redder. "I'll bet she didn't tell you they were on sale."

Riley wasn't sure what that had to do with anything and was afraid to ask. It was time for him to get out of there.

"You'll just break her heart," Daniel said as he was walking away.

"So I've heard," Riley mumbled.

"And you know what I'll do to you if that happens."

Riley did know. He'd just punch him, but Daniel would apparently have to wait in line to do that—behind Lucky's fist and Livvy's pliers. God knew how many people were ready and willing to maim him for Claire's sake.

Finally, Riley started back toward his car, and that meant he'd see Claire in just a matter of minutes. However, the thought alone must have tempted fate because his phone rang. He glanced at the screen and cursed.

Hell.

What now?

WELL, THIS WAS not what Claire had in mind when she'd offered Riley sex. She'd expected him to take her up on the offer, and he had. For one night anyway. Two if she counted the no-condom night before the offer. But she hadn't heard a peep from him since he'd left that morning.

Of course she thought the worst.

But in her mind, there were several worsts, including but not limited to that he was dead in a ditch somewhere. She wasn't certain why her mind always paired unexplained absences with ditches and death, but she did.

Ditches and worst-case scenarios aside, she had another problem. One that she hadn't actually thought through when she'd started this affair with Riley—if one and a half times could be considered an affair, that is. And what she hadn't thought through were the logistics of having hot sex with a toddler in the house. Certainly, parents had figured out a way to accomplish an orgasm or two, but they must have adjusted.

Definitely no sex on the kitchen table.

Probably minimal moaning, too. Claire hadn't realized until she'd been with Riley that she was a moaner.

"Riley?" Ethan asked.

Had she said Riley's name aloud again? If so, she needed to watch that. Because now that Riley was paired with sex in her mind, Claire didn't want any naughty words tumbling out of her mouth when Ethan was around.

"I don't think Riley's coming tonight," she answered, and Ethan seemed to understand that. He frowned, kept playing his newly created game of chase van Gogh—or just Gogh as he was now calling the kitty—with a toy van while he chanted, "Go, go, go."

Claire was sure she frowned, too, and nearly broke her hand reaching for the phone when it rang. Not Riley. Livvy. Claire moaned again, but this time there was nothing orgasmic about it.

"Has he called yet?" Livvy asked.

Livvy didn't have to clarify the *he* or the *yet* because this was Livvy's third call of the evening to see if Riley had shown. Something was up, and while Claire had been too preoccupied with her ditch-and-death fears, she hadn't noticed that Livvy was on edge. But she noticed it now.

"All right, what's up?" Claire demanded.

Silence. Never a good thing with two-year-olds, kittens or best friends.

"I might have scared Riley off earlier," Livvy finally answered.

Her stomach went to her kneecaps. "You did what?"

More silence. "I called him and told him he'd better not break your heart. I might have implied a threat."

Claire groaned. "Not the rusty pliers again." It was one of Livvy's favorite threats when a guy dumped her. She'd never go through with it, of course, but it couldn't have been fun for

Riley to hear. But it was just a threat. "That alone wouldn't have scared Riley off," Claire insisted.

"No, but I'm pretty sure Lucky threatened him, too. And maybe Daniel."

Sheez. Lucky she understood. It was a brotherly thing to do. But Daniel? "When did Daniel see Riley?"

More silence. "Uh, how much gossip do you want to hear?"

Claire wasn't sure. "Is the gossip related to Riley?"

"Yes."

She debated it. Gossip rarely left her feeling good, and her mood already sucked. "All right, spill it but only if it really relates to Riley. I don't want to hear any sidelines like bad wax jobs or crabs."

"Crabs?" Livvy latched right on to that. "Who has crabs?"

According to the gas station attendant, apparently one of the Nederlands did, but Livvy had already missed the point. "That's not related to Riley or me. Or you."

Another round of silence, but Claire figured that was because Livvy was only trying to pick through whatever it was she'd heard. There was a lot of gossip floating around at the moment.

"According to Trisha," Livvy finally continued, "Riley caught Daniel fudging Jodi in his office. On his desk."

Her heart nearly tumbled out of her chest. That was definitely relevant gossip. "Did they get in a fight? Is Riley hurt?" And better yet, was Riley crushed that he'd caught Jodi with another man?

That was really the key point here. The next key point was that Claire was having trouble picturing Daniel and Jodi together that way... *Nope.* She pictured it, and she wished she hadn't. Not because she cared if Daniel had sex with Jodi, but because she didn't want the naked image in her head of them having sex on a desk.

And here Daniel usually kept his desk neat as a pin.

She'd never be able to look at that desk again, or his office, without that image popping up.

"There was no fight that Trisha could tell, but she was watching from a distance. Maybe even through binoculars since she said she couldn't tell what they were saying because she doesn't lip read."

Claire nearly asked for more as to how Trisha knew all of this, but she already had too many details to sort through. "So, if there was no fight, then what happened?"

"Trisha said Daniel and Riley talked, or rather they argued. She said Daniel's face got all red, and after they talked for a while longer, Riley stormed out."

Stormed? That meant he was upset. Maybe upset about Jodi having sex with Daniel. Maybe upset about whatever Daniel had said to him. For the first time since she'd become aware of the gossip epidemic in Spring Hill, Claire wished Trisha had gotten more info.

"What was Jodi doing during all of this?" Claire asked.

"Getting dressed. Trisha said she didn't come out and talk to Riley after he found Daniel and her bare-assed naked."

Poor Riley. Even though he had broken off things with Jodi, that would have given him a jolt. Ditto for the argument he would have no doubt had with Daniel. No wonder he'd stormed off.

"Are you okay?" Livvy asked. "Want me to come over?"

"No. I'm fine."

"You're sure? Because I can cancel my date with the actor."

Despite her own troubles, Claire caught that last word. "You have a date with an actor?"

"A wannabe actor," she clarified. "It's a match from the dating site. But I can cancel it—"

"No. Go on your date and have fun. I'm fine. Bye, Livvy." And she hit the end call button before Livvy could keep arguing.

Livvy would know that she wasn't fine and just might show up anyway. Too bad because Claire thought it would make her feel a smidge better if one of them wasn't miserable. Thankfully, Ethan hadn't noticed that his mommy was in the miserable mode. He kept playing the go game with Gogh.

Claire stared at her phone, wondering if she should just call Riley and ask him about his encounter with Daniel and Jodi. Of course, then she'd have to mention the gossip she'd heard, and he would feel obligated to talk about it. If they'd been in a real relationship, that would have been okay. But with a relationship based purely on no-commitment sex, he probably wouldn't want to discuss finding his ex with another man.

Especially since Jodi might not stay his ex.

She had to be realistic about this. If Riley went back overseas, he'd likely run into Jodi again. Hadn't he said something about them being together for years and that their paths crossed often? Their paths would cross again when they were back to their normal lives.

When Claire wasn't in the picture.

And that ex status might go right out the door of the helicopter. Claire knew Daniel was banking on that, too. He'd chatted up the store clerk about how he still wanted to marry her. She doubted Daniel was thinking about that when he was fudging Jodi on his desk.

Maybe the cosmos was actually tuned in to her tonight because Claire stared at her phone so long that it dinged. A text message.

From Riley.

Before she'd heard the sex-on-the-desk gossip, she would have jumped to look at the text, but she took her time, and a few deep breaths, before she touched her phone screen so she could read it.

It didn't take long.

Something's come up, Riley texted. Will call you tomorrow.

Oh, no. That definitely didn't sound like good news. Still, she kept her reply short.

OK, she texted back.

But it wasn't okay. Claire felt as if an elephant and a dozen of his biggest friends had just sat on her heart.

CHAPTER TWENTY-ONE

IF LIVVY KEPT UP her ice-cream therapy, Claire was going to have to buy some bigger clothes. Still, it was hard to fault something that worked. She no longer felt as if she had elephants sitting on her heart; they were now on her stomach.

Just as Claire had thought, Livvy had ditched her date and dropped by the night before, and she'd brought lots of sugary goodies and wine with her. After a pint of Ben & Jerry's Karamel Sutra and a wine so sweet and cheap that it was only one step above Kool-Aid, she and Livvy had collapsed into a sugar coma.

When her alarm had gone off the following morning—the alarm being Ethan calling out for her—Claire had felt like jumping right out of bed. The sugar coma hadn't left her wrung out and bloated. Claire had gotten up ready to finish sorting through the rest of the boxes.

Therapy to keep her mind off Riley.

Livvy knew that, of course. Thankfully, Ethan didn't. While Claire sorted and fought off the bad thoughts, her son was teaching Gogh to color.

On the van Gogh painting.

Since Claire had decided to cut her losses and toss the Baby Genius packet, she figured Ethan might as well get to do something FUN! with them. And he was. Gogh, too. Ethan added more gold blob stars to the painting while Gogh batted the crayons around like elongated soccer balls.

Livvy wasn't quite into the coloring activities, the crayon batting or the box sorting. She hadn't dodged the sugar-coma bullet. She was on her back on the floor, her body stretched out like a corpse, and she had a washcloth on her face. She occasionally mumbled something about drinking the Kool-Aid.

What Livvy hadn't brought up was Riley.

But Trisha had.

Apparently, Trisha thought she hadn't spread the story of Daniel and Jodi to enough people because at 8:01 a.m., she'd called Claire to offer her *sympathies*. Or so Trisha had said. Claire wouldn't have minded the call if Trisha had managed to give her any useful information about Riley, but the only revelation Claire had gotten from the woman was that Jodi had skedaddled—and yes, Trisha had used that particular word—shortly after Riley left. It was possible that Jodi was going after him.

That information wasn't useful.

It only added to the gloom and doom Claire already felt. Thankfully, the contents of the boxes were giving her short distractions. A ball of rubber bands. Some old construction paper. And a stack of valentine's cards that Claire had gotten when she was in third grade. They were the kinds of cards that came twenty-five to a pack. One was from Riley—it had combat robot–looking things on it. There were four from Daniel. All of those had kittens and hearts.

She hoped the number ratio wasn't some kind of omen for her future, that Daniel cared for her four times more than Riley did.

Claire moved on to another box. It was the next to the last, and while she went through that one—more Valentine and Christmas cards—Ethan finished his coloring project and decided to help. He tipped the final box on its side, spilling the contents on the floor and on Gogh. Gogh treated that like an adventure, too, and started batting everything including her own tail.

Then Claire saw it.

The cigar box. It'd been her "treasure" box from her child-hood, and she'd painted it purple and had glued sequins on it. The sequins had long fallen off, but she could still see the glue bits. Could also see where she'd written her name and *keep out* in permanent marker.

Claire shoved the other things aside to get to the cigar box, and all that shoving alerted Livvy because she sat up. "Did you find something?"

"Maybe."

With Ethan and Livvy both watching her, Claire opened the cigar box, and the first thing she saw was a picture. It was of Daniel, Riley and her. With her in the middle, of course. Riley's mother had snapped the shot while they were at the county fair and had had an extra print made for Claire. It was the very photo Claire had studied years later as she'd chosen between the two.

And, yes, Riley was hot.

Not just in that picture but also the ones beneath it. There were six photos in all. One was of them eating watermelon on the Fourth of July. Another was of them at the Christmas parade, all bundled up with knit caps and heavy coats. Claire hadn't even remembered putting the pictures in the box, but she was glad she had. It was like a little time capsule.

She rummaged through the box and found other treasures. The cheap heart-shaped necklace Daniel had given her in fifth grade. A pretty blue river rock that Riley had found one time when his dad had taken them all fishing. A dried flower she'd picked on that trip.

Claire worked her way through all the bits and pieces and nearly missed the white envelope. That's because at first it looked like the bottom of the cigar box. It wasn't.

"Is that what I think it is?" Livvy asked. "*The* letter?"

"Maybe." She certainly didn't remember putting a letter in the box, mainly because she'd never gotten a letter. And maybe she still hadn't. Because this one wasn't addressed to her.

But rather to her grandmother.

However, her gran had put a sticky note over the top of her own name and had written three words: "Keep for Claire."

"Is it from your mother?" Livvy didn't scoot closer, but she was volleying glances between the envelope and Claire.

Claire shook her head. "It's not the same handwriting as the journal." Which meant this could be from her father.

Oh, God.

Was she ready for this? Especially since it might be another rant about the pregnancy, and therefore a rant about Claire herself.

"Want me to read it for you?" Livvy volunteered.

Did she? Claire was still debating that when she heard the knock at the door. *Riley.* And despite the fact that she had just found the very thing she'd been searching for, seeing Riley felt a lot more important.

Claire hurried to the door, threw it open and wished she'd checked out the window first. She still would have opened the door, but she would have steeled herself up first.

Because it was Jodi.

"Punch me," Jodi greeted her, outstretching her arms.

Claire glanced around the porch to see if the woman was alone. She was. Then Claire looked at her to try to figure out what the heck was going on.

"Go ahead," Jodi prompted. "Punch me."

Claire actually considered it. For a very brief moment anyway. But only because she was still jealous about that earlier thought of Jodi and Riley getting back together. However, it was a fleeting notion that Claire resisted. She'd already been in a pub brawl and didn't want to add a fistfight to the list of her life regrets.

Livvy hurried into the room. "I'll punch her for you," she volunteered.

But Claire waved her off. "Can you make sure Ethan doesn't get into anything in those boxes?"

Livvy hesitated, but Claire knew in the end that watching Ethan would win out when it came to punching Jodi's face. *Barely.* Livvy might still try a face punch later, though. Unlike Claire, Livvy didn't mind adding such things to her own life experiences.

"I was with Daniel," Jodi said, her arms still outstretched and waiting for that punch.

"I heard." Claire pushed down the woman's arms because she didn't want to hear the kind of gossip that it would create if anyone saw her. Trisha could be out there somewhere with her binoculars.

"Then you know you have every right to punch me," Jodi concluded.

"Uh, no. Daniel's free to have sex with whomever he wants."

Jodi frowned, pulled back her shoulders. "You're sure about that? Daniel said you two were probably getting back together."

At least Daniel had remembered to include the *probably.* "We're not getting back together."

And the fates aligned again to remind Claire—and hopefully Jodi, too—as to why that wasn't happening. Riley pulled his car into the driveway.

Claire immediately saw the concern on his face, and he didn't exactly run to the porch, but it was close.

"Everything okay?" he asked.

Claire nodded. "Jodi was just here so I could punch her for sleeping with Daniel. I declined," she added.

Maybe Riley heard what she said, but if he did, he didn't show it. Instead, he hooked his arm around Claire, pulled her to him and kissed her into the middle of next week.

RILEY HADN'T PLANNED on kissing Claire at the door. He'd planned on doing that later. But he realized this was his chance to clarify to Jodi how things were.

Or at least how Riley hoped they were.

He'd missed Claire, and even though their relationship was

temporary, it was best for Jodi to understand that he was with Claire, not her. And Jodi got it all right. When Riley finally broke the lip-lock with Claire, he saw the thunderstruck look in Jodi's eyes. Maybe because he'd never kissed her like that. Heck, he'd never kissed any woman like that. Claire was looking a little thunderstruck, too.

"Um, I just came to apologize to Claire," Jodi said, "but I'll be going." She didn't just go, though. She stared at them, and while still staring, she made her way down the steps. Walking backward so that she kept her eyes on them the whole time.

Riley didn't wait to watch her drive away. That kiss with Claire had been so good that he pulled her inside for another one. A much shorter one this time because Livvy, Ethan and the kitten were there, all staring at Claire and him.

"Riley!" Ethan squealed, and he raced toward them. Riley broke his grip on Claire so he could scoop him up. And so he could give him the toy car in his pocket. A 1967 yellow Firebird that was the same color as the kitten. The moment Riley had spotted it online, he'd ordered it with rush delivery.

Ethan rattled off his version of thank you, smacked a kiss on Riley's cheek and then took off running the moment Riley set his feet back on the floor. No doubt to add the car to his stash.

"I'll just check on him," Livvy said, going off after Ethan. With all the gossip that was no doubt going around about Daniel and Jodi, Livvy probably thought Claire and he needed to talk privately. But what he really wanted to do was just kiss Claire again.

So, he did.

Oh, man. She tasted good, like birthday cake and Christmas candy all rolled into one. She looked just as good, too. Well, with the exception of some dust in her hair and a bit of concern in her eyes. Concern no doubt caused by how he was reacting to the gossip.

"I can't stay long. I have something I need to do for Logan. But I wanted to tell you that I'm over Jodi," he let her know right off. Although he and Jodi had never been serious enough for him to have to get over.

She nodded. Whether she actually believed him was anyone's guess. "Trisha saw what happened, and she's been spreading the *news*."

Of course. Riley should have guessed that Trisha would have hung around, waiting to see how things played out between Daniel and him, and that glass front on Daniel's office building would have given her a good view. Heck, Trisha might have even seen Jodi and Daniel go in before Riley arrived, and then stood back and waited for the chaos to begin. And she'd likely been disappointed that there hadn't actually been any chaos.

"What about you?" he asked. "How are you handling this?"

She kissed him. It was such a great way of communicating, and Riley wished he had time to deepen this communication in bed. That wouldn't happen with Livvy and Ethan around. Plus, the new cutter would be arriving at the ranch soon, and Riley needed to be there to show him around.

Claire paused the kiss, looked up at him. While standing really close to him. Like with her body right against his. "I was worried when you didn't come by last night. I thought maybe Daniel and you had gotten into a fight."

"No fight. I've been at the hospital all night with Lucky."

The concern in her eyes quadrupled. So did the body contact. She went right into his arms.

"Lucky's okay," Riley explained. "His business partner had a heart attack, and Lucky was shaken up. He called and asked me to stay with him. Dixie Mae's out of the woods. The doctor's pulled her through."

Some of that concern turned to relief. "I'll call Lucky later and see if there's anything I can do."

That was Claire. Kind, thoughtful. Soft. Her breasts were right against his chest so he could feel two good examples of that softness.

"So, what have you been doing all morning?" he asked. "Other than kissing me and getting visits from Jodi?"

He expected her to say something sexual. Something naughty, even. Because if she didn't, Riley certainly intended to do that. Not that he could do any of those naughty things. He had fifteen minutes at most, and that wasn't enough time to drag Claire off somewhere. But the new look she got in her eyes wasn't remotely naughty, and she pulled back to make eye contact with him.

"I found the letter," she said.

The letter. The one that hadn't been on Riley's radar because he was too busy building a sex fantasy with Claire.

"I haven't read it yet," Claire continued, "but I'm positive it's the one Gran mentioned on the calendar."

So was he, and he wanted to come clean. Not just about the letter but also the note Lucky had given him about her father. But that would have to keep. And, no, it wasn't because it would ruin what was left of the sexual fantasy. It was because after they talked about those things, Claire would likely fall apart.

Fifteen minutes wasn't enough time to fix that.

"Any chance I can cook you dinner?" he asked. And talk to her. And sleep with her. "It's Della and Stella's night off. Lucky will be at the hospital, and Logan will be at his loft in town. You and Ethan could maybe even stay the night."

Yes, he was blatantly offering her sex along with that package deal. Just in case she didn't pick up on that, he kissed her again.

Message received.

At least it was until Livvy cleared her throat. "I'm taking Ethan out for ice cream."

Ethan clapped. "Ice cream!"

"How about just going to the farmer's market for some fruits and veggies instead?" Claire said.

Ethan wasn't enthusiastic about that at all.

Livvy nodded. "Veggies first and then a small cone. How does that sound?"

Ethan clapped again. Livvy grabbed her purse, Ethan's hand and headed out the door.

Later, Riley would thank Livvy, but for now, he didn't want to waste a single moment of those remaining fifteen minutes. Or waste a footstep. He shut the door, locked it, and with Claire and he already grappling to get closer, Riley pulled her to the living room floor.

CHAPTER TWENTY-TWO

OTHER THAN THE rug burns on her butt, there was a lot to be said for quickie sex.

A lot not to be said for it, too.

No cuddling, and since the quickie had taken nearly twenty minutes, that meant Riley had been late for his appointment with the horse trainer. He'd dressed and hurried out of the house, leaving her with a smile but also wanting a whole lot more.

Like maybe a second orgasm for starters.

Plus, they hadn't really had a chance to talk about the letter. She'd wanted his advice about whether or not she should read it. She hadn't wanted to turn her feelings about reading it into how she felt after reading most of her mother's journal. But if it was bad, then why would Gran have made a note to give it to her?

Of course, Gran hadn't actually given it to her, and maybe she had done that because she'd known it would upset her.

And it still might.

However, while Livvy was off with Ethan on their ice-cream run—which might or might not include veggies—Claire decided to woman-up and read it. If it caused her to crumble, then so be it, but the quickie sex hadn't just given her an amazing orgasm, it had also apparently made her fearless.

She went back to the sorting room/nursery and picked up the

letter. Her fearlessness took a little dip when she actually had it in her hands, but she opened it anyway. One page. Handwritten. Not her mother's handwriting. Probably not her father's, either. This was a child's scrawl so her attention zoomed to the signature on the bottom on the page.

Riley McCord.

Riley had written the letter? Riley? Like Claire, he would have been just ten years old at the time, so why had he written Gran a letter? Riley and Gran saw each other almost daily. Anything he wanted to say, he could have said to her in person.

Couldn't he?

Claire's fearlessness turned to shock, and she sank down on the floor to read it.

Dear Mrs. Davidson,

I feel real bad about Claire not having any folks. I know she loves you, but it's not the same as having a mom and dad, like me. So, I talked to my mom and dad, and we all think they could be Claire's mom and dad too.

Oh.

The tears came. So did the warm feeling that blanketed her from head to toe. Claire certainly hadn't seen this coming, and she kept reading, eating up each word that Riley had written two decades ago.

If you don't mind and if you think Claire would like that, I want her to be part of my family. What do you think? Check yes or no.

The tears had filled her eyes, but Claire could see that Riley had drawn four sets of square boxes. Each set had a yes and no box. The first set was for him.

Which he had checked yes.

The second set was for his mom and dad. Another yes check.

The third was for Gran. And she had checked yes, too.

The last set of boxes was for Claire. It was empty and waiting for her.

There was only one more line at the bottom after Riley's signature.

PS: Don't give this to Claire until her birthday.

But Gran hadn't given it to her. Why? Had she simply forgotten about it?

No.

It was a lifetime ago, but Claire's mind went back to that birthday. That was around the time Daniel's parents had started including her in more of their family gatherings. In fact, his parents had given her a tenth birthday party. Since Riley had gone to that party, maybe he'd thought the offer of his parents was no longer necessary. Too bad. Because that would have been an incredible birthday present.

Still was.

Riley had obviously cared for her a long time. Of course, as a child she hadn't been able to see it, but she could certainly see it now.

She tucked the letter in her pocket and went to the door when she heard Livvy and Ethan coming up the steps of the porch. Judging from the volume and intensity of the giggling, no veggies had been consumed today. But that didn't matter. Smiling, Claire walked to the door, not in a hurry, but rather taking her time to look at the wallpaper-free walls. The floors that she'd finished. The fresh coats of paint.

The house itself.

People had always said the house had good bones, and it did. But it had a whole lot more than that.

Livvy opened the door cautiously as if concerned Ethan and she would walk in on a naked mommy and Riley. No nakedness. Just Claire smiling. Her smile must have looked a little off balance, though, because Livvy looked concerned.

"He only had one scoop," Livvy said, motioning toward the smears of chocolate ice cream around Ethan's mouth. Ethan took off running after Gogh.

"It's okay." Claire couldn't help it. She kept smiling. It felt as if everything had suddenly become crystal clear.

"Well?" Livvy asked, bobbling her eyebrows.

Normally, Claire didn't like to spill any sex details to Livvy, but she'd make a small exception this time. "It was great."

Perfect in fact. Despite her butt burns, those twenty minutes had been amazing. Better yet, she was going to get more than twenty minutes of amazing tonight when she went to Riley's for dinner.

Claire wasn't sure how long their sex agreement would last, and she decided not to worry about it. She couldn't hog-tie Riley and make him stay, but now that she knew just how much he cared about her, how much he'd always cared, she would just enjoy every minute she had with him.

"That's a big smile," Livvy observed. "Did something else happen? Like maybe a marriage proposal?"

Claire waved that off. "I read the letter."

That got rid of some of the joy and speculation on Livvy's face. "You what? You did that while Riley was here?"

"No. After he left. But it's okay, Livvy. Everything's okay." Claire looked around and knew exactly what she wanted to do. "I've decided not to sell the house. I'm moving back home."

THERE WAS ONE last thing Riley needed to do before his hot date with Claire, and it wasn't something he especially wanted to do. However, he had to give Claire the note from Lucky, and Riley didn't want to wait and have her have to deal with it during dinner. Best to clear it out of the way rather than risk having it spoil the entire evening.

Of course, she'd be surprised to see him so soon after their sex-by-the-door encounter. Even more surprised when she read the note. But Riley hadn't imagined there'd be a surprised look on his own face when he arrived at her place.

Surprise from seeing Daniel's car in front of her house.

Not now. He'd already had too many doses of Daniel in the past couple of weeks.

Riley spotted his old friend right away because Daniel was on the porch. Claire, in the doorway. Well, it didn't appear to be another proposal unless Claire was signing a prenup. Or maybe a restraining order. Judging from the glare Daniel gave him, it was the latter.

"She's not selling the house," Daniel snarled, and he took the clipboard of papers from her and hurried off the porch.

"I'd done some initial paperwork with him for the listing," Claire explained, motioning toward a fleeing Daniel. "I had to cancel it, and that required my signature. Or so he said."

Ah. Maybe Daniel had tried to use it as an excuse to sneak in another proposal after all.

"You're really not selling?" Riley asked at the same moment that Claire asked, "What are you doing here?"

"I just dropped by to give you something," he answered. "But you're really not selling the place?" Riley repeated.

"Nope." And she seemed pretty happy and sure about that, too. *Good.* Then Riley was happy for her, as well.

"What about your business, though?"

"Not a problem. I can run it from here just as well as San Antonio. Ethan's not here," Claire added when Riley looked around. "Livvy took him and the kitten home with her."

"Again?" Riley hated to sound so disappointed, and then he remembered he was cooking dinner for Claire at his place so this was a good thing. She opened her mouth to say something, but he kissed her. This was really shaping up to be a great day, and Riley hated to ruin it, but this was something she needed to know.

"Lucky asked me to give you this," he said, taking the note from his pocket.

He didn't have to clarify. Claire took one look at the note, another look at his expression, and any trace of her smile disappeared. "It's about Rocky, my father."

Riley nodded. "Lucky said you wanted him to ask around. He did, and that's what he found."

"It's bad?" she asked, studying his eyes.

He lifted his shoulder. Nodded.

She handed him back the note. "Just tell me what it says, then."

All right. Riley wished there was a good way to say this. There wasn't. "Maude remembered Rocky. She thought his last name was Lambert, but Lucky did some checking, and it was Landrum. Rocky Landrum. He had cousins in the county but never lived here."

"Was, had, lived," she repeated. She paused, gathered her breath. "He's dead?"

"Yeah." Riley gave her a moment to let that sink in. "But there's some good news in this. Possibly good," he amended. "Rocky got a job working on an offshore oil rig when he found out your mother was pregnant." Riley had to pause. "He was killed his first week out there in a freak accident. No one told your mother because she wasn't listed as his next of kin."

Claire stayed quiet a moment. "That's why he never came back."

Yes, and all her mother's anger over being abandoned was for nothing. Because Rocky hadn't abandoned her, or Claire, after all. In fact, it appeared Rocky had gotten the job so he could support Claire and her mother. Riley hoped she would see the silver lining in that, but the bottom line was her father was dead.

She tried to smile, stepped back and held up her finger in a give-me-a-second gesture. "I'm okay," she insisted. "Knowing is better."

In a day or two, she might actually believe that.

Riley was about to try to hug her again and to ask if she needed a rain check on their dinner plans but his phone rang, and he fished it from his pocket. His heart stopped a moment when he looked at the screen, and he saw the number for Colonel Becker.

"I'd better take this on the porch," Riley said, and he went outside. "Captain McCord," he answered.

"Just got a call from your new commanding officer, Colonel Hagan. You need to report to the base at fifteen thirty today for a physical."

Fifteen thirty? That was three thirty civilian time and just two hours from now. "The physical was scheduled for next week," Riley reminded him. Eight more days. Eight more days that Riley needed to get ready.

"Sorry, but there was a change in plans. Someone put the wrong date on your medical leave. The flight surgeon will do the physical, and if you pass it, be ready to report to duty ASAP."

The colonel didn't say good luck or any other farewell. He just hung up, leaving Riley to stand there, stunned, with the phone still pressed to his ear.

He finally turned, ready to tell Claire the news, but she was in the doorway, her hands bracketed on each side of the jamb. She wasn't crying, but it seemed to him that she was blinking awfully fast, maybe to stave off some tears. Maybe because she just didn't know how else to react.

"I heard," Claire said.

CHAPTER TWENTY-THREE

THERE WERE PLENTY of thoughts going through Riley's head. The physical that he'd just taken. The results that were in a computer file, a file that he'd know all about as soon as Colonel Hagan briefed him.

Whenever that would be.

It was already past normal duty hours, but the colonel was apparently still tied up with meetings. His exec officer had told Riley to wait in the outer office, that the colonel would see him as soon as he was free.

There were so many questions about his future. So much riding on what was going to happen in the next half hour or so. But the one thing that Riley consistently kept seeing was the look on Claire's face when she'd overheard his phone call. In a way her overhearing it had made it a little easier.

Because Riley hadn't had to say the words aloud.

Hadn't had to answer her questions, either, because she hadn't asked any. Claire had simply kissed him goodbye and asked him to call her when he had any news. It was a polite, no-pressure kind of comment.

Sort of like their sex pact.

But Riley figured she had started crying the moment he left. Hopefully she'd called Livvy to bring Ethan home, too. Riley really didn't want her being alone right now. He was, and he knew that sucked.

He had considered calling Lucky, but he was still at the hospital with Dixie Mae. He hadn't bothered trying to get in touch with Logan, but Riley had told Della and Stella where he was going. Of course, they'd guessed, too, when he'd come out of his bedroom wearing his uniform.

His phone dinged with a text, a reminder for him to turn it off, but he checked the message first. It was from Logan. *Anything yet?*

So, Della and Stella had already told him. Riley didn't answer because the colonel's door finally opened, and the exec—a young captain—ushered him in. The colonel wasn't alone. Colonel Becker was there. The hospital commander, as well.

Hell. This couldn't be good. It felt more like a firing squad than a meeting.

Riley reported in, and Colonel Hagan immediately asked him to sit. Only Hagan had papers in front of him, which meant the other two had likely been briefed already as to what was going on.

"You didn't pass the physical, Captain," Hagan said. Without any warning or fanfare.

Oh, man. Hearing that nearly knocked the breath right out of him. Riley fought to gather what breath he needed just so he could speak.

"I can retake it," Riley insisted.

The trio mumbled some variation of no. *No*s that went straight to his gut. "The PT and the flight surgeon don't believe you're going to regain the mobility necessary for you to remain a Combat Rescue Officer," Hagan informed him.

There was a term in the Air Force, military bearing, that meant maintaining an outward appearance of being professional, being a serviceman in uniform. Usually it wasn't a big deal to keep his military bearing, but Riley was sure struggling with it now. It took everything he could muster up just to stay seated and not shout out how wrong this was.

"We've already discussed some of this," Becker continued. "It would endanger your crew if you didn't have the mobility needed for your job."

"My experience could make up for it," Riley argued. "And the mobility issue is temporary. I've been working out. The exercises are helping."

"This isn't up for discussion," Hagan snapped. But then his expression softened. "Look, we know this isn't the news you want to hear. We didn't want to hear it, either, but we can't keep you in the Air Force as a Combat Rescue Officer."

The flashbacks came. Probably because his pulse was galloping and his breathing was too fast. But Riley fought them back. *The kid was alive.*

Because of him, the kid was alive.

"You have options," Hagan went on, the words droning in Riley's head. "You've fulfilled your active duty service commitment so you can get out, of course. We hope you won't do that. As you said, you have experience you can pass on to others, and that's where the options come in."

Riley didn't want options. He wanted to be a CRO with a shoulder the way it'd been before that damn IED. Because that was repeating in his head now, too, Riley missed the first part of what Hagan said. He didn't miss the second part though.

"You can become an instructor."

There it was. One of those soul-crushing *options*. The Air Force's version of putting him out to pasture.

"Of course, you'd have to continue your physical therapy," the hospital commander said. "You'd still have to pass the standard fitness tests."

"I don't want to instruct," Riley said.

Hagan hardly reacted. Maybe because he'd anticipated it. Maybe because he just didn't give a shit. Riley wondered how the colonel would feel if someone had just told him to give up being what he was.

If someone told him he'd have to be ordinary again.

"There are other career fields," Becker said. "With your aptitude scores and security clearances, you could choose whatever you want."

No, he couldn't. Riley didn't go into the broken record mode and repeat himself, but there was no other job he wanted. No other job that wouldn't feel ordinary after being a CRO.

"Another option would be for you to transfer to the reserves," Becker continued. "You couldn't be a CRO, of course, but you could stay in the local area where I understand you have family."

Weekend Warrior. No, thanks. It was still a huge step down from what he'd been doing.

"We can give you some time to think about it," Hagan said a moment later. "But not much. We'll need to have your decision in the next twenty-four hours."

Somehow Riley nodded. And got to his feet. Somehow he saluted Colonel Hagan and made it to the door.

Keep your military bearing.

He was succeeding, for the most part, until he opened the door and saw Lucky there. Lounging as usual, and he was chatting up a blonde lieutenant who quickly excused herself when she took one look at Riley's face.

"Wanna go get drunk and raise some hell?" Lucky asked, getting to his feet.

"No." There was only one place Riley wanted to be right now, only one person he wanted to see.

Claire.

CLAIRE FORCED HERSELF not to pace while she waited for news. Besides, it wasn't as if she didn't have things to do. The last of the boxes had been sorted, and she needed to find places for the stuff she was keeping. The rest she had to haul to the curb for trash pickup. All in all, it felt like the same thing she'd been doing with her life.

Daniel was out forever.

She was keeping Gran's house, except it'd be her house now. Ethan's and her home. She'd come to a peaceful place with her mom and dad. Not a perfect place. Never would be. But it didn't cut and gnaw at her as it'd done in the past.

In short, things were perfect.

Except for Riley.

She was the one who'd invited him in to her head and bed, and Claire had known right from the start that this day would come. Riley wanted to be back in uniform, and he would be. That would leave her to pick up the pieces of her heart—something she would do.

Somehow.

And that somehow was coming sooner rather than later, she realized, when she saw Riley's car coming up the road to her house. Claire put the box she'd been carrying on the curb and watched him as he got closer and closer. One look at his face, and she knew the physical hadn't gone as he'd wanted.

He parked, got out and walked to her. Without saying a word, he slipped his arm around her waist and got her moving back into the house.

"They want me to retrain into a different career field or become an instructor," he said, looking her straight in the eyes. "Or get out." He paused, his jaw muscles stirring. "I have until tomorrow to make a decision."

Claire only saw this playing out one way. Just one. "You've already made your decision."

He didn't look surprised. Didn't argue. Because it was true. One of the first two things would happen—he'd stay in uniform and become something else. But he wouldn't get out. And that meant he'd be leaving.

Soon.

Riley pulled her closer, brushed a chaste kiss on her forehead. "I'm sorry."

Claire did know he was sorry—for hurting her. But not for the decision he'd made.

"You were up-front with me and everyone else right from the start," she reminded him. "I knew this day would come."

She just hadn't known that it would hurt this much. God, someone had clamped a fist around her heart and wouldn't let go. Still, she had only a matter of hours to spend with Riley, and she didn't want to be crying, moping and aching from the heart crushing.

That would come later. And possibly last a really long time.

"Is Ethan still at Livvy's?" he asked.

Claire nodded. She'd considered having Livvy bring him and Gogh back, but Claire figured if she was going to have a breakdown, she didn't want anyone around to witness it. Or say I told you so. Livvy wouldn't have actually said the words, but it would have been in her friend's eyes.

"Can you stay for a while?" she asked. "Or do you need to tell your family?"

"Lucky knows. He'll tell the others. I have until morning." He gave her another chaste kiss. "But I didn't come here for this to be a drive-by sex call."

Claire tried to be brave. Not that she had an alternative other than that. If she fell apart, Riley would leave knowing he'd done that to her. She preferred him leaving with much better memories. Which meant she'd have some memories to hold on to, as well.

She locked the door. Forced a smile. "Too bad. I've never had a drive-by sex call and was looking forward to it."

Riley shook his head, no doubt ready to tell her that this didn't feel right. Or some other such nonsense. Of course, it didn't feel right. But it soon would. Sex with Riley could make everything feel all right. For a while anyway.

Before he could say anything, Claire slid her hand around his neck and pulled him to her for a kiss. One touch of his mouth, and things were instantly better. A little better anyway. So she kept kissing him until she felt the stiffness ease from his muscles. Until she felt some of her own dark thoughts turn warm and dreamy.

Riley could do that. With just some kisses.

Heck, he could do that by breathing.

She felt the exact moment that he surrendered. Mainly because he took charge of the kissing. He snapped her to him, deepening the kiss until Claire almost expected him to lower her to the floor again.

He didn't.

She and Riley stood there while he lowered the kisses to her neck. *Oh, yes.* To that spot that made her crazy. Maybe that's why he'd put a love bite on it, so he wouldn't have any trouble finding it again.

No more just warm and dreamy. Claire wanted him in her bed. Maybe she even said it aloud because Riley picked her up, and without breaking the neck-kissing assault, he headed there.

"You're sure?" he asked, easing her onto the mattress.

She took out the deluxe box of condoms and slapped them on the nightstand. "I'm sure."

It got the exact reaction she wanted. A smile. Perhaps a little fear.

Claire could have relieved that possible fear by telling him she didn't expect them to go through the whole box, but he kissed her again, and she was beyond something as complex as human speech. The only thing she could do was feel.

And Riley made sure she did plenty of feeling.

This was their fourth time together, and he'd learned all her good spots, not just the one on her neck. He kissed her in each one of them until she could take no more. She almost hated the frenzy inside her as much as she loved it because the frenzy— the need—made her want to rip off their clothes and end this all too fast. Of course, anything, even a snail's pace, would have been too fast.

Because it was the last.

Claire pushed that dismal thought aside. It wasn't hard to do because Riley took off her top and delivered some of those kisses to the very spots he'd kissed seconds earlier through her clothes.

Without the clothes, it was better.

But it built more of that frenzy until Claire couldn't help herself. She got rid of his shirt. Went after his jeans, too, and through it all she tried to grasp on to each memory. The way he looked.

Amazing, by the way.

The way he felt in her arms. His taste. Amazing, too.

She wanted to keep all of that, but at the same time her body was begging for release.

Riley knew what to do about that release thing. He got her naked. One of Claire's favorite parts, and despite what had to be a frenzy in him, too, he slowed down, sliding off her jeans inch by inch, and admiring the view along the way.

Maybe he was trying to hang on to this, as well.

And drive her insane.

Because despite the jumbo box of condoms, he pushed her legs apart and kissed her in the very spot that would indeed make this end too soon. He flicked his tongue in her, causing Claire to curse him. Pull her hair. And try to hold on for the ride. Just when she thought he would finish her this way, Riley surprised her again by stopping and getting one of those condoms.

Thankfully, he was fast at putting it on because Claire no longer wanted to hang on. Or so she thought. When he pushed inside her, she changed her mind for just a second. She did want it to last for more than the couple of seconds that her body was urging her to last. Too bad she couldn't bottle this sensation and then she could walk around with a goofy look on her face all the time.

Too bad she couldn't bottle Riley.

He kissed her when he moved inside her. Slowly at first. No urgency. As if they had years to finish this. Of course, slow was still effective, and the urgency came. Riley made sure of that with those maddening strokes, his erection hitting her in the exact spot she needed to fly.

So that's what she did.

Claire tried to cling to it. Failed. But instead she held on to Riley. For now, she was his, and he was hers.

For now.

And that's when she allowed herself to admit something she'd known for most of her life.

That she was in love with the man who'd just given her that orgasm.

RILEY KNEW IT was time for him to go. Claire was already up, fixing him breakfast. And Livvy was on the way to drop off Ethan before she started work for the day. He didn't want Ethan to find him naked in his mommy's bed, so Riley used that to get him up and start gathering his clothes.

He tried not to think of each step as the last time. The last time he'd be naked in Claire's bed. The last time he'd get dressed here at her house. Or have a love bite that she'd put on his chest near his scar. He was going to have fun explaining that to the physical therapist.

Was going to have fun remembering it, too.

But in the back of his mind he couldn't help wondering if he should have just turned down this sex pact. It would have certainly made this goodbye a whole lot easier. Then again, Riley had never chosen the easy path.

And he wouldn't now.

He'd say goodbye to Claire and Ethan. Kiss them. And report to the base to begin the process for his retraining. It wasn't the job he wanted, not by a long shot, but it's the job he'd take to keep him in uniform. There was even a small consolation prize.

Even though he could no longer be a CRO, he could always wear the badge on his uniform since he'd earned it.

That gave him an uneasy jolt.

It was sort of like those has-been high school football stars who continued to wear their letter jackets.

With that gloomy thought on his mind, he took a quick shower, dressed and went into the kitchen. The smell of coffee lured him there, and while he was desperate for a cup, he took a moment to admire the view.

Claire wearing those cutoff shorts. Maybe the same ones she'd worn the morning after he'd first arrived home with his bum shoulder, full of flashbacks and a bad attitude. The flashbacks were gone. The shoulder, not so bum. The attitude, not so bad. But he didn't get that giddy feeling this time when he saw her hips swaying as she scrambled some eggs.

Hell.

This was hard.

She turned, looking at him over her shoulder. Smiling. It didn't look like a fake smile, either, but Riley bet she had to remind herself to do it. He sure had. He went to her, kissed her. Not one of those deep French kinds that was the start of foreplay. A morning kiss.

"Hungry?" she asked.

"Starved," he lied.

He helped himself to a cup of coffee as she dished up a plate of eggs. She didn't pause even a second when she put the plate on the table. Claire headed to the fridge and took out the OJ.

That's when Riley stopped her by taking hold of her arms.

That's when he made another mistake, too. He kissed her. Really kissed her. Not one of those morning deals, either. This one had goodbye written all over it, and Claire knew it, too, because when Riley finally pulled away from her, he saw the tears in her eyes.

"I'm not gonna cry," she insisted. Maybe trying to convince him. Or convince herself.

Her attempt to blink back those tears would have likely failed if she hadn't heard the quick knock on the front door, followed by someone opening it. Followed then by Ethan's giggle and hurried footsteps. Ethan bolted into the kitchen—where did the kid get all that energy this time of morning?—and he made a beeline for Claire.

She scooped him up and showered some kisses on his smiling face. Riley was betting Ethan hadn't had to remind himself to smile because it was the real deal.

The moment Claire set him down, Ethan ran to Riley, and the whole process repeated itself. Riley got some kisses, too, and a big hug from Ethan.

Something he definitely wouldn't be getting from Livvy.

Livvy came into the kitchen, and she volleyed some uneasy glances between all three of them. Maybe Claire had already told her friend that he was leaving, or perhaps Livvy just picked up on the vibe in the room. Either way, she gave Riley a scowl, and he looked to make sure she didn't have those rusty pliers in her hand.

"Sorry, but I gotta run," Livvy said. "Got an appointment in under an hour. But I can come back later if you want."

"I'll be fine," Claire assured her. She put Ethan at the table, busied herself with dishing him up some eggs. "Really," she added when Livvy didn't budge.

"I'll come back later," Livvy insisted, giving Riley another glare. That glare was the last he saw of her as Livvy left.

Ethan gave them some uneasy glances, too, even after Claire set the plate of eggs in front of him. The kid was only two, but Riley figured there was a lot going on in that little head.

"It's okay if you don't eat," Claire said, and it took Riley a moment to realize she was talking to him not Ethan. Probably because Riley hadn't even picked up his fork.

He did eat some, but not too much since anything, including the coffee, was causing his stomach to churn.

"You need to say goodbye to Riley," Claire prompted Ethan.

She turned back toward the stove, and Riley hoped she wasn't crying. He already felt like an asshole, and tears would only make him feel worse.

But Ethan didn't say goodbye. He bolted from the chair, heading toward the living room, and a few seconds later, he came back with a toy. It was another of those defender action figures. This one looked a little like Cher on steroids.

"For you," Ethan said. Or rather he said something similar to that.

Riley considered telling him to keep it, especially since it was a toy that Ethan played with often. But Riley wanted it. He wanted to be able to look at it and think of Ethan. Not that he didn't already have enough memories in his head.

Enough memories of Claire, too.

"And I have something for you, as well," Claire said. She handed him a five-by-seven envelope. "Don't open it yet. Go through it in a day or two."

When he'd be gone from Spring Hill.

Riley nodded. Since it was probably a goodbye letter, he wasn't sure he wanted to read it just yet anyway.

"It's the day for gifts, I guess," Riley told her. "Well, it's not really a gift, more like a project. But it's not ready yet. Summer Starkley will be bringing it by when it's finished."

Maybe the project/gift would cause Claire to smile. A real one.

He kissed the top of Ethan's head. Kissed Claire one more time because he couldn't stop himself. And before Riley could say or do something that would only make this worse, he headed for the door.

CHAPTER TWENTY-FOUR

RILEY FINISHED DRESSING and checked himself in the mirror. It'd been a while since he had worn his full dress blues, but he was glad he'd brought them with him. Everything fit and was aligned the way they should be. All his medals, his Combat Rescue Officer badge and his name tag.

This one didn't have his blood type on it. Only his last name.

That would have to be enough.

He checked the time. Nearly noon. He'd already said all his goodbyes so there was no reason to hang around the house. Lucky had already left for Abilene. Logan was at the office. Claire and Ethan were at their place. Della and Stella were around, but they were so accustomed to saying goodbye to him that they weren't even upset. Ditto for Logan and Lucky.

Even though he'd already done it once—okay, twice—he went through his duffel again to make sure he had everything. He did. Including the envelope that Claire had given him. The one she'd said not to open for a day or two. Vague instructions for something that might not be so vague because it was almost certainly a goodbye letter. Maybe one where she poured out her heart. Or maybe she would just let him know that it was all right for him to head out again.

It was probably the latter, he decided.

Claire wouldn't make this harder on him even if in doing so, it made it harder on herself.

Riley opened it.

And a picture fell out.

Not a recent one, either. This was a shot of Claire, him and his parents on a fishing trip. Lucky was behind Claire and had lifted up her ponytail so that it looked like a blond palm tree on her head. However, Claire wasn't paying any attention to Lucky. She was looking at Riley. All four of them were smiling. And it made Riley smile, too.

So did the next one. It was a shot of Daniel, Claire and him at a picnic. She was looking at him in that picture, too. And smiling. They must have been ten or so, long before she'd chosen Daniel and set that man-rule into motion. Long before Riley had had sex with her and broken her heart.

Since that was such an unsettling thought, he moved on to the final thing in the envelope. Not another photo but rather another envelope.

One that he recognized.

Because it was the one he'd sent Claire's Gran more than two decades ago.

Of course, Claire had said she'd found it, but they hadn't discussed it. Probably because there hadn't been anything to discuss. Heck, it was possible that she'd been disappointed when she had finally found it because Claire had believed it would be from her father or mother. Not from some ten-year-old kid with a silly notion of how to make her happy.

Riley turned the envelope to open it and saw that Claire had written something on the back.

Thank you for sharing your family with me.

Maybe she hadn't been completely disappointed after all.

He opened it, though, like the contents of his duffel, Riley already knew what was inside. It had taken him nearly a week to write and rewrite that letter, and the words were permanently stuck in his head. Still, he groaned when he saw what his ten-year-old self had produced.

Not his best effort.

So, I talked to my mom and dad, and we all think they could be Claire's mom and dad too. If you don't mind and if you think Claire would like that, I want her to be part of my family. What do you think? Check yes or no.

Below the letter were the boxes for everyone to check yes or no. Not exactly original, but he saw some new additions to the letter. Her gran had checked the yes box.

And so had Claire.

It was just a little check mark, like the others. His, his parents', her gran's and now hers. Riley had to smile. Then shrug. Since his parents were long gone, he hadn't expected her to check no.

Actually, he hadn't expected her to check anything.

He looked through the letter again, wishing that Claire had added a note here instead of just on the envelope. Something he could read and reread when he started missing her.

Like now.

Too bad she hadn't put something in that theoretical note that would let him know just how she felt about him leaving. How she felt about *him*.

Of course, Claire wouldn't have done that because she wouldn't have wanted to say or do anything that would make him feel guilty about going. Again, that was Claire. Always thinking about others' feelings.

Even though the minutes were ticking off, Riley kept looking at that check mark. Maybe that was her version of a note. Her way of saying something she didn't really need to say.

Because it was all there.

In those pictures. The way she had been looking at him. *Hell.* The way she still looked at him.

Claire was in love with him.

Oh, man. That hit him like a punch to the gut. How could he have missed it all this time?

And better yet—what was he going to do about it?

"RILEY PEE-PEE," Ethan said.

That got Claire's attention, and she hurried to the living room where Ethan was playing to make sure he wasn't trying to get outside to pee again. But he wasn't at the door but rather the window, and he was pointing at something.

"Riley pee-pee," he repeated.

She couldn't imagine what had prompted Ethan to say that, but she sincerely hoped no one was outside peeing.

Claire rushed to the window, nearly tripping over Gogh and the car menagerie on the floor, and she saw something she darn sure hadn't expected to see.

A man carrying a toilet.

And he was walking toward her house.

She couldn't see the man's face because of the way he was holding the toilet, but at first she thought it might be Lucky. But not Lucky.

Riley.

Why was he here? They'd already said their goodbyes. But it was indeed Riley, wearing a blue uniform, and he was apparently bringing her a toilet.

Maybe it was some kind of weird goodbye gift, but if so she wasn't sure she was up to the gift or another goodbye. The last one had left her wrung out, and the crying jag afterward had only made it worse. Besides, she didn't want Riley to see her with her face all puffy and red like this.

Ethan tried to open the door, and Claire helped, though she did wonder if Riley had intended just to leave the "gift"—hopefully, with a note explaining why he'd chosen it—and then he could have just taken off. Again. After all, the minutes to his twenty-four-hour deadline were ticking away.

Keep it light, Claire.

But she wasn't sure she could deal with ripping open wounds that hadn't even had a chance to heal.

"I took a chance you'd be home," Riley said, smiling. He made it sound as if that explained everything. It didn't.

"And you walked here with that?" She tipped her head to the toilet.

"It wouldn't fit in the car. It's for Ethan."

That obviously wasn't enough explanation, either. Well, it wasn't until Riley set it down in the foyer for her to see inside the toilet bowl.

There was a painted tree inside. Similar to the peeing tree in the backyard at Riley's house.

Ethan giggled, clapped his hands and would have dropped his pants and peed in it right then, right there if Claire hadn't stopped him. Clearly, he'd picked up on the abstract concept right away. But Claire was still dealing with her own abstract concept of why Riley had brought it over. And why he wasn't at the base.

"When I found out she was an art student, I hired Summer Starkley to do it," Riley added. "She was supposed to bring it by, but she got sick, and I decided to do it."

So it was a goodbye gift. An amazing one. "Ethan loves it. So do I. The neighbors, too, I'm sure. It'll stop him from peeing on the tree out back and Livvy's fake plants."

"Then it's well timed." He took out a piece of paper from his pocket. "When you want it installed, just call that number and make an appointment with the plumber. It's already paid for. All you have to do is let him know a good time for you."

She nodded, tried to think of something clever and funny to say. She failed.

Claire burst out crying.

Ethan looked stunned. Riley, even more stunned. Claire was mortified.

This was the last thing she wanted. Heck, she would have taken Ethan peeing in the unconnected toilet over this. And the sudden unstoppable string of words that started coming out of her mouth.

"I used artificial insemination to get pregnant with Ethan. And the reason he looks so much like you is because I chose a donor who looks like you." God, she couldn't stop. It was like a seizure or something. "Your hair, eye color, height, weight. I saw a picture of him, and he even had your smile."

Even though there was no way Ethan could have understood that, he continued to look stunned. Riley continued to look even more stunned. And the mortification on her part went up a huge notch.

And the blasted verbal lava flow just kept on coming. "I just thought you should know that I've never believed you were ordinary, and I wanted my son to look, and be, just like you."

Mission accomplished. Seeing them side by side, gaping at her, Ethan was a little version of Riley.

But that wasn't the end of her word eruption. "I kept it a secret because I didn't want you to know. Because I thought maybe it would make you feel… I don't know…obligated or responsible or something. You might have also thought I was obsessed with you."

Riley finally did something to stop the babbling. He kissed her. Probably just to shut her up, but it worked.

"Are you…obsessed with me?" he asked.

There was no smart answer to this. If she said yes, it might cause him to say that goodbye even faster. Of course, the same could happen if she said no. So, for the first time in the past two minutes, she went silent.

Ethan broke that silence. "Pee-pee now?" he asked, and he was dancing around while holding his crotch.

Since that was his way of letting her know he had to go

potty, Claire scooped him up and hurried toward the bathroom. It wasn't a tree-toilet, but he lifted the plain white lid, shoved down his jeans and pull-up, and took care of business.

"Good boy," she praised, but her attention was on Riley. This was hardly the moment or the situation for her to answer his question, but Riley was apparently waiting for an answer.

Claire went with a question of her own. "How much time do you have?" she asked. "When do you have to leave for the base?"

Riley walked closer, took her hand. "I asked first."

Indeed he had, and even though she'd had a couple of long moments and a potty break to give her time to come up with an answer, Claire still didn't know what to say. She decided to go with another lava approach. She opened her mouth and waited to see what would come out.

"Yes," she admitted. *Oh, no.* Now, she had to explain. Or else she could just get angry with herself for the confession. She went with the second option. "I am obsessed with you. There. Satisfied?"

Riley frowned. "Well, I was until you got pissed. Angry," he corrected for Ethan's ears. But Ethan wasn't listening. Triumphant from his accomplishment, he hurried back into the living room, not washing his hands and also leaving the toilet lid up.

That was clearly something they'd have to work on.

But Riley was working on something, too. He pulled a piece of paper from his pocket. Paper that she recognized.

The letter.

"I didn't want you to see that until after you were gone," she reminded him.

"Yeah. And I'm guessing that's because you didn't want to discuss it with me. Well, we're discussing it."

He unfolded the letter, pointed to the box at the bottom. "If you don't mind and if you think Claire would like that, I want her to be part of my family," he read. "You checked yes. Did you mean it?"

Well, that wasn't a question she'd seen coming. "Uh, of

course. Your parents treated me like I was one of their own kids."

"No. Did you mean it?" he repeated.

Claire studied his expression, trying to figure out what was going on here, but she was either dense or Riley was. "Of course?" she repeated, this time adding a different inflection. "What's this all about, Riley?"

He certainly didn't develop a case of verbal lava. Riley stood there, staring, breathing too fast and generally looking as if he might lose his lunch instead of his mind.

"Because I want you to be part of my family," he finally said.

"All right. It won't be much of a stretch. I'm over there a lot so Ethan can play with Crazy Dog, and Lucky drops by whenever he's in town—"

That obviously wasn't the right answer because Riley took hold of her, snapped her to him and kissed her. This wasn't one of those goodbye pecks he'd given her earlier in the kitchen. This was the real deal. The kind of kiss that would have made her think about carting him off to bed if Ethan hadn't been in the house.

The kiss went on for a while. Too long and too short at the same time, and when he finally let go of her, Claire immediately felt the loss, or something. It was as if she was in the wrong place with him standing there and not touching or kissing her.

"I'm not leaving," Riley said.

Claire nodded, figuring he meant he was staying until they talked this out. Whatever it was they had to talk out. But it was obvious that Riley had something on his mind.

"I mean, I'm not leaving," he repeated.

Maybe it was the look in his eyes or the addition of his own inflection, but Claire thought she knew what he meant. But he couldn't mean that.

Could he?

"You're not leaving?" she clarified. "But what about being in the Air Force? What about being ordinary?"

He shrugged. "I'm leaving the service. I'm staying here in Spring Hill."

She checked his eyes to make sure he meant it. He did. But she shook her head. "I don't want you doing this for me."

"Nope. I'm doing it for me. My mind's already made up."

"Are you sure? What about—"

"You said you never believed I was ordinary," he interrupted. "And that you believed that so much that you wanted Ethan to look and be just like me. Was that true?"

"Absolutely." She couldn't say it quickly enough.

Riley gave a crisp nod. "Along with that checked box on the letter, there's only one thing missing."

Since he kissed her after that, Claire couldn't imagine anything was missing. Until Riley spoke again.

"I'm in love with you," he said.

There it was. Magic words indeed. Words that she had held in her heart for so long that they slipped right out of her mouth.

Claire gave those right back to Riley. And ditto for the kiss.

* * * * *

Lone Star Nights

To my wonderful editor, Allison Lyons

CHAPTER ONE

THE DYING WOMAN'S misspelled tattoo bothered Lucky McCord. Not nearly as much as the dying woman, of course, but seriously, who didn't know the rule about putting *i* before *e* except after *c*?

The tattoo "artist" who'd inked that turd of a misspelling onto Dixie Mae Weatherall's forearm, that's who.

It was a shame the inker wasn't anywhere around to fix his mess so Dixie Mae could finish out her last minutes on God's green earth with a tat that didn't set people's teeth on edge.

While the nurse adjusted the tubes and needles going in and out of Dixie Mae, Lucky stayed back against the wall. Man, he hated hospitals. That smell of disinfectant, lime Jell-O, floor wax and some bullshit—literal bullshit—from his own boots.

Lucky hadn't had time to clean up before he'd gotten the call from the doctor telling him that Dixie Mae had been admitted to Spring Hill Memorial Hospital and that it wasn't looking good. The doctor had said he should hurry. Lucky had been thirty miles away in San Antonio, just ten minutes out of an eight-second bull ride that'd lasted only four seconds.

A metaphor for his life.

The bull ride, or rather the fall, had left him with a bruised tailbone, back and ego. All minor stuff, though, compared to what was happening here in the hospital with Dixie Mae.

Hell.

He'd always thought Dixie Mae was too tough to die. Or that she'd at least live to be a hundred. And maybe she was pretty close to that number.

Most folks estimated Dixie Mae's age anywhere between eighty and ninety. Most folks only saw her gruff face, the wrinkles on her wrinkles and her colorful wardrobe that she called a tribute to Dolly Parton, the rhinestone years.

Oh, and most folks saw the misspelled tattoo, of course. Couldn't miss that.

When Lucky looked at her, he saw a lot more than just those things. He saw a very complex woman. By her own admission, Dixie Mae subscribed to the whack-a-mole approach to conflict resolution, but she was one of the most successful rodeo promoters in the state.

And hands down, the orneriest.

Lucky loved every bit of her ornery heart.

There'd been so many times when Lucky had walked away from her. Cursed her. Wished that he could tie her onto the back of a mean bucking bull and let the bull try to sling some sense into her. But he'd always gone back because the bottom line with Dixie Mae was that she was the only person who'd ever believed he could be something.

Powerful stuff like that would make a man put up with any level of orneriness.

The petite blonde nurse finally finished whatever she was doing to Dixie Mae and stepped away, but not before giving Lucky that sad, sympathetic look. And a stern warning. "Don't give her any cigarettes. She'll ask but don't give her one."

Lucky had already figured that out, both the asking part and don't-give-her-one part. He didn't smoke, but even if he did, he wouldn't have brought her cigarettes. A shot of tequila maybe, but that would have been to steady his own nerves, not for Dixie Mae.

"She bribed the janitor," the nurse added. "And she called

a grocery clerk to offer him a thousand dollars to bring her a pack, but we stopped him before he could give them to her."

"Assholes," Dixie Mae declared. "A woman oughta be able to smoke when she wants to smoke."

Lucky just sighed. It was that way of thinking that had put Dixie Mae in the hospital bed. That, and the other hard living she'd been doing for decades. And her advancing years, of course. Besides, since there was an oxygen tank nearby, it was possible the staff hadn't simply wanted to deny her a smoke for her health's sake but rather because they hadn't wanted her to blow up the place.

"Are you close to her?" the nurse asked him. According to her name tag, she was Nan Watts.

"Nobody's close to me," Dixie Mae snarled. "But Lucky's my boy. Not one of my blood, mind you, but my own blood son's an asshole." She added a profanity-riddled suggestion for what her son could do to himself.

The nurse blushed, but maybe Dixie Mae's cussing gave her some ideas because on the way to the door, Nan Watts winked at Lucky. He nearly winked back. A conditioned reflex, but he wasn't in a winking, womanizing kind of mood right now.

"Boy, you look lower than a fat penguin's balls," Dixie Mae said after the nurse left. She waggled her nicotine-yellowed fingers at him, motioning for him to come closer. "Did you bring me a cig?"

"No." He ignored the additional profanity she mumbled. "Why are you here in Spring Hill?" Lucky asked. "Why didn't you go to the hospital near your house in San Antonio?"

"I was here in town seeing somebody."

Since Dixie Mae had been born in Spring Hill, it was possible she had acquaintances nearby, but Lucky doubted it.

"I'm worried about you," Lucky admitted. He went to her, eased down on the corner of the metal table next to her bed.

"No need. I'm just dying, that's all. Along with having a nicotine fit. By the way, that's a lot worse than the dying." She had to stop, take a deep breath. "My heart's giving out. Did the doc tell you that when he called?"

"Yeah." Lucky wanted to say more, but that lump in his throat sort of backed things up.

He touched his fingers to the tat.

"I know. It bothers you," Dixie Mae said. Each word she spoke seemed to be a challenge, and her eyelids looked heavy, not just from the kilo of electric-blue eye shadow she had on them, either. "Have you thought maybe you're all over the tat because you don't want to think about the rest of this?"

There was no *maybe* about it. That's exactly what it was. It was easier to focus on something else—anything else—rather than what was happening to Dixie Mae.

Lucky nodded. Shrugged. "But the tat really does bother me, too."

She waved him off. Or rather tried. Not a lot of strength in her hand. "I was shit-faced when I got it. So was the tattoo guy."

"*P-e-i-c-e-s* of my heart," he read aloud. Complete with little heart bits that had probably once been red. They were now more the color of an old Hershey bar. And Dixie Mae's wrinkles and saggy skin had given them some confusing shapes.

When he had first met Dixie Mae, Lucky had spent some time guessing what the shapes actually were. Not a disassembled United States map as he'd first thought.

But rather a broken heart.

With the way Dixie Mae carried on, sometimes it was hard to believe she even had a heart, and she'd never gotten around to explaining exactly who'd done such a thing to her. Or if the person had survived.

Lucky doubted it.

"I wish there was time to get it fixed for you." He traced the outline of the heart piece that resembled the map of Florida but then drew back his fingers when he realized it could also be a penis tat. "I wish there was time for a lot of things."

Like more time. This was too soon.

"No need. Besides, it's not even the worst of the bunch. When I was younger, I got drunk a lot. And I went to the same tattoo guy," Dixie Mae admitted. "You should see the one on my left ass cheek. I didn't realize he needed a dictionary for the word *ass.*"

It wasn't very manly to shudder, but Lucky just had this thing about misspelled words and didn't want to see other examples of them, especially on her ass. Besides, there wouldn't be many more moments with Dixie Mae, and he didn't want to waste those moments on a discussion about the origins, shapes and locations of bad tats.

Dixie Mae dragged in a ragged breath, one that proved beyond a shadow of a doubt that she was a two-packs-a-day smoker. Unfiltered, at that. "We've had a good run together, me and you. Haven't we, boy? Made each other some money. Had some good times when I wasn't kicking your butt or boxing your ears."

"We've made some money all right," he agreed.

As for the good times, Lucky would have to grade those on a curve.

She'd started sponsoring him in bull-riding events when he was nineteen, just a couple of weeks after his folks had died. When he'd turned twenty-five, Dixie Mae had allowed him to buy into her company. Lucky was nearly thirty-three now, and they were still partners. He did indeed help her run Weatherall-McCord Stock Show and Rodeo Promotions, but he hadn't given up bull riding, mainly because he was better at it than the business side of things.

"I'll miss you," Lucky added. He cursed that lump in his throat again. Because it was true. He would miss her.

"Awww." She dragged in another ragged breath. "That's monkey shit, and we both know it."

"No. It's not. I will miss you." And he meant it. He'd never thought he could love someone this much, not since his mother had passed, but he loved Dixie Mae.

Lucky couldn't be sure, but he thought maybe her eyes watered a bit. Then she was back to her usual self. There was something comforting about that.

"I do have a favor to ask you," she said. "That's why I had the doc call you."

Lucky nodded. "I'm here, and I'm listening."

She patted his cheek. "The girls do like that pretty face of yours, but rust up your zippers a little. Or wear a bigger rodeo buckle. Might slow you down a bit so you can take time to enjoy something other than a woman's secret place. Besides, some of those women you see don't keep their *places* so secret."

"Neither do I," Lucky reminded her. Then he winked. It was a good use of what might be the last wink he'd ever give her.

"Don't get fresh with me, boy. I don't fall for monkey shit like that."

He figured she was saying that just to take away the tension in the room. But then again, it was her normal, surly mood and one of her normal, surly sayings.

"Now, to that favor," Dixie Mae went on. She took an envelope, one that had a couple of cigarette burns on it, from beside her on the bed and handed it to him. Her hands were shaking now. "I got nobody else to ask, but I need some help. And before you think about saying no, just remember this is my dying wish. A man wouldn't be much of a man to deny an old dying woman her last wish."

Yeah, a man like that would indeed have to be missing a pair. "I'll do whatever you want. Anything."

Lucky started to open the letter, but Dixie Mae stopped him by taking hold of his hand. "No. Don't read it now. Save it for later. Let's just sit here, take in the moment together."

And she smiled.

Not that evil smile Lucky had seen her give before she'd thrown something at somebody, threatened them with bodily harm or cursed them out. This smile seemed to be the genuine article. She'd saved it just for him.

"Tell me about your ride today." Her voice was a hoarse whisper, and her eyelids drifted all the way down.

Lucky's own voice didn't fare much better. "Not much to tell, really. The bull won."

"The bull usually does," Dixie Mae whispered. She smiled again, then both her grip and the smile began to melt away.

And just like that, Dixie Mae Weatherall was gone.

Lucky tried to hold it together. Tried not to give in to the grief that felt heavy and cold in his chest. He brushed a kiss on her cheek, gathered her in his arms, and Dixie Mae's "boy" cried like a baby.

CHAPTER TWO

CASSIE WEATHERALL FOUGHT back the tears. Fought for air, too.
Breathe.

She couldn't actually say the word aloud. She couldn't speak yet, but she repeated it in her head and hoped that it worked.

It didn't.

Her heart continued to race, slamming so hard against her chest that she thought her ribs might break. Her throat closed up, strangling her.

This was just a panic attack, she reminded herself. All she needed to do was calm down and breathe.

That reminder still didn't work so Cassie tried to force herself to think this through logically. She had enough adrenaline pumping through her to fight a bear. Maybe six of them. But there were no bears to fight here at Sweet Meadows Meditation and Relaxation Facility. Other than the grizzlies in her head anyway, though sometimes, like now, they felt worse than the real thing.

And speaking of her head, Cassie was no longer sure it was on her shoulders. Too much spinning. Wave after wave of panic. She couldn't let anyone see her like this. Couldn't let them know that she was broken and might never be fixed.

She went old-school and put her head between her knees. Of

course, that meant sitting down, and while the path was good for walking and running, the small rocks dug into her butt and legs. Good.

Pain was good. Pain gave the adrenaline something else to battle other than the bears.

Breathe.

It was all about the breathing. All about taking in the right amount of air. Releasing the right amount, too. Cassie managed that part, but then the darkness came. The shaking. And her feet and hands started to go numb. That dumb-ass bear was going to win if she didn't get hold of this right now.

She heard the sound of someone approaching, and Cassie struggled to get to her feet. *Please, you can't see me like this.* But thankfully the footsteps stopped just on the other side of the path. There were thick shrubs between her and the person who'd made those footsteps.

"Miss Weatherall?" someone called out. Not a shout, but a soft, tentative voice.

Orin Dayton. The office manager at Sweet Meadows.

Cassie considered not answering him, but that would no doubt just prompt him to walk the twenty or so feet around the row of shrubs that divided her suite from the running trail. And then he would see her with her head between her knees, sweating, crying.

"Yes?" she forced herself to say.

"Uh, is something wrong, Miss Weatherall?" he asked.

"No. I overdid my run, and I'm a little queasy." The lie was huge. So huge that Cassie looked up at the afternoon sky to make sure a lightning bolt wasn't coming at her.

"All right," he finally said. He used the tone of a person who wanted to believe the malarkey she'd just doled out. "A Dr. Knight from Los Angeles called a couple of minutes ago."

Andrew. He was the only person other than Cassie who knew why she was really here at Sweet Meadows.

"I rang your room," Orin went on, "but when you didn't

answer, Dr. Knight said to get you a message. That Dr. Stan Menger from a hospital in Spring Hill, Texas, is trying to reach you."

Spring Hill. Her hometown. But Cassie didn't know this Stan Menger. "What does Dr. Menger want?" Please not something that required her immediate attention. Not while she was battling a panic attack.

Orin paused again. "I'm afraid it's not good news."

Great. First, bears. Now, bad news. Since she'd already used what little supply of air she'd had left in her lungs, Cassie didn't say anything else. She just waited for him to continue.

"There's been a death, Miss Weatherall," Orin said. "It's your grandmother. Dr. Knight said you shouldn't go home, though, that it wouldn't be good for you right now. Dr. Knight said just to stay put and that he'll take care of everything."

But Orin was talking to himself because Cassie punched the last of the bears aside, got to her feet and ran to her room to pack.

DIXIE MAE DESERVED a lot better send-off than this. But considering she didn't have a friend other than him in the tristate area, Lucky figured he shouldn't be surprised there were only four people at her memorial service. Five, if he counted his brother Riley who'd dropped by earlier. Six, if he counted the sweaty-faced funeral director who kept popping in and out.

Lucky decided to count them both.

Dixie Mae's driver, Manuel Rodriquez, was at the back of the room that the funeral home had set up. He was glaring at the flower-draped coffin, and the glare only got worse when-ever his eyes landed on the four-foot-by-four-foot glossy pic-ture that Dixie Mae had arranged to be placed beside her. No smile in this one, just a steely expression, as if she were pick-ing a fight from beyond the grave.

Judging from Manuel's glare, he'd likely been on the receiv-ing end of too many of Dixie Mae's fight-pickings.

Other than Manuel, the funeral director and Lucky, the only other guests were two women.

And Lucky used that term loosely.

It was hard to tell their ages, probably in their early twenties. Purple hair, purple nails, purple lips and boobs practically spilling out of their purple tube tops. Yet another loosely used term because the tops were more like Band-Aids.

Since Dixie Mae's only child, her estranged son, Mason-Dixon, owned a strip joint on the outskirts of town, it was possible these two were his *employees*. Perhaps he'd sent them to see if his mom had left him some kind of inheritance.

Good luck with that.

Dixie Mae had probably figured out a way to take every penny to the grave. Or skip the grave completely. Plus, Dixie Mae wasn't exactly fond of her son and would have given her money to his strippers rather than the man she'd called her shithead spawn.

Lucky hadn't been able to get in touch with Dixie Mae's only other living relative, her granddaughter, Cassie, though Lucky and Dixie Mae's doctor had left her a couple of messages at her office in Los Angeles. Whether she'd show up was anyone's guess.

He heard someone come in and turned, hoping it was a mourner who'd make this memorial service actually look like one. But it was only his twin brother, Logan.

Logan and he were identical in looks, but that was where any and all similarities ended. Logan was the responsible, successful tycoon who ran the family business, McCord Cattle Brokers, and had been in charge of it since their parents had been killed in a car wreck fourteen years ago. Lucky was the screwup. Considering their other brother had been an Air Force special-ops super troop and his sister was the smartest woman in Texas, it meant all the good family labels had been taken anyway.

Screwup suited him just fine.

Fewer expectations that way.

After having a short chat with Manuel, Logan came to the front where Lucky was standing. Even though Logan ran a cattle-brokerage company—and ran it well, of course—there were no bullshit smells coming from his boots that thudded on the parquet floor. With his crisp white button-up shirt and spotless jeans, he looked as if he were modeling for the cover of *Texas Monthly* magazine.

Logan had done exactly that—a couple of times.

"Are those Mason-Dixon's girls from the strip club?" Logan hitched his thumb to the pair in the back.

Lucky shrugged. "Don't know for sure. I introduced myself when they arrived, but the only response I got was a grunt from one of them." He'd been afraid to ask anything else since even the smallest movement might cause those tube tops to explode.

"Did Dixie Mae go peacefully?" Logan asked.

"As peacefully as Dixie Mae could ever go anywhere. Thanks for coming. She would have appreciated it."

"No, she wouldn't have, but I didn't come here for her. Are you okay?"

The funny thing about having an identical twin was being able to look into eyes that were a genetic copy of Lucky's own. The other funny thing about that was despite the screwup label, Logan's eyes showed that his question and his concern were the real deal.

"I'm fine." Lucky patted his back jeans pocket. "Dixie Mae gave me a letter right before she died."

"What does it say?" Those genetically identical eyes got skeptical now. So did Logan's tone. Lucky couldn't blame him. Dixie Mae brought that out in people.

"Haven't read it yet. Thought I'd wait until this was over." Until after he'd had a little more time to deal with her death. A few shots of Jameson, too. "I know it's hard to believe, but I'll miss her."

Lucky didn't see Logan's hand move before he felt it on his back. A brotherly pat. Just one. It was more than most folks got.

"What will you do with the rodeo business now that she's gone?" Logan asked.

"Dixie Mae and I talked about it. She wants me to keep it going." It was her legacy in a way. His, too, since the name of the company was Weatherall-McCord Stock Show and Rodeo Promotions. "But it's a lot of work for one person." He poked Logan with his elbow. "Want to help me?"

Logan shrugged. "We could incorporate it into McCord Cattle Brokers. That way you could use the administrative staff I have in place. Plus, there's an office already set up for you here in Spring Hill."

Considering that Logan hadn't even paused before that suggestion, it meant he'd been giving it some thought. Well, Lucky had, too, and the rodeo business was his. He didn't know how he was going to run it all by himself, but he wasn't going to be lured back to Spring Hill and be under Logan's thumb.

That thumb might also be a genetic copy of Lucky's own, but it had a way of crushing people.

"I need to get back to the office," Logan added, already looking at the exit. "We've got a cutting-horse trainer coming in today, and I could use some help. Maybe when you're finished here, you can come on home?"

Most of his conversations with Logan went that way. There was always something going on at either the office in town or at the ranch where Logan stashed some of the livestock he bought. And Lucky would indeed make an appearance, maybe try to smooth over things with the horse trainer Logan was sure to soon piss off if he hadn't already. Logan was good with four-legged critters and paperwork. People, not so much.

"I'll be there later," Lucky told him.

After he read the letter from Dixie Mae, he'd probably need to get drunk. Then sleep it off. Of course, after that he had a rodeo all the way up in Dallas. Even though he didn't spell that out to Logan, his brother must have tuned in to that twin telepathy thing that Lucky had never experienced. But Logan seemed to know exactly what Lucky had in mind.

"Also, remember the wedding and the Founder's Day picnic next month," Logan added. "You should at least put in an appearance."

Lucky nodded. He'd make an appearance all right. For both. His brother Riley and his bride-to-be, Claire, were getting married at the family ranch and then having the reception at the picnic so that everyone in town could attend. It made sense since the McCords hosted the event. That not only meant they footed the bill, but that the entire family was expected to show up and have fun. Or at least look as if they were having fun. It'd been much easier to do that when Lucky was a kid, and his mom and dad had been running the show. Now it was just another place for him to have memories of things he didn't want to remember.

Still, he'd be there. Not just because of Logan and Riley, either, but because the picnic was something his mother had started, and despite the bad memories it would bring on, the event was her legacy.

Logan went to the guest book and signed it before he left, his boots thudding his way to the exit. That's when Lucky noticed the purple-tube-top girls were gone. Manuel, too. Heck, even the funeral director had ducked out again.

Lucky sank down in one of the creaky wooden chairs, wondering if he should say a prayer or something. Dixie Mae had left specific instructions with the funeral home that there would not be a service, music or food. No graveside burial, either, since she was to be cremated. The only thing she'd insisted on was the creepy picture of her that would ensure no passerby would just pop in to say goodbye to an old lady. However, she hadn't said anything about a guy praying.

Footsteps again. Not boots this time. These were hurried but light, and he thought maybe the tube-top visitors had returned. It wasn't them, but it was a woman all right. A brunette with pinned-up hair, and she was reading something on her phone. That's why Lucky didn't see her face until she finally looked up.

Cassie.

Or rather Cassandra Weatherall. Dixie Mae's granddaughter.

She practically skidded to a stop when she spotted him, and he got the scowl he always got when Cassie looked at him. He got his other usual reaction to her, too. A little flutter in his stomach.

Possibly gas.

Lucky sure hoped that was what it was anyway. The only thing he'd been good at in high school was charming girls, but nothing—absolutely nothing—he'd ever tried on Cassie had garnered him more than a scowl.

"You're here," Cassie said.

Lucky made a show of looking at himself and outstretched his arms. "Appears so. You're here, too."

She slipped her phone into the pocket of her gray jacket. Gray skirt and top, as well. Ditto for the shoes. If those shoes got any more sensible, they'd start flossing themselves.

But yep, what he'd felt was a flutter.

Probably because he'd never been able to figure her out. Or kiss her. He mentally shrugged. It was the kiss part all right. When it came to that sort of thing, he was pretty shallow, and it stung that the high school bookworm with no other boyfriends would dismiss him with a scowl.

He'd considered the possibility that she was gay, but then over the years he'd seen some pictures she'd sent Dixie Mae. Pictures of Cassie in an itty-bitty bikini on some beach with a guy wrapped around her. Then more pictures of her in a party dress, a different guy wrapped around her that time. So apparently she liked wraparound guys. She just didn't like him.

"Is your dad coming?" he asked.

Her mouth tightened a little. Translation: sore subject. "Probably not. He hasn't spoken to Gran in twenty years."

Lucky was well aware of that because Dixie Mae brought it

up every time she got too much Jim Beam in her. Which was often. According to her, twenty years ago she'd refused to give Mason-Dixon a loan so he could add an adult sex toy shop to his strip club, the Slippery Pole, and it had caused a rift. Or as Dixie Mae called it—the great dildo feud.

Still, Lucky had hoped that her only child could bury the hatchet for a couple of minutes and come say goodbye to his mom.

"My mother won't be here, either," Cassie went on.

Yet another complicated piece of this family puzzle. Cassie's folks had divorced before she was born. Or maybe they had never actually married. Either way, her mom preferred to stay far, far away from Spring Hill, Mason-Dixon, Dixie Mae and Cassie.

Cassie walked closer, stopping by his side. She peered at the casket. Hesitating. "That's not a very good picture of her," she said.

Lucky made a sound of agreement. "Her doing. All of this is. She did try to call you before she passed. I tried to call you afterward."

Cassie nodded, seemed flustered. "I was at a…retreat on the Oregon Coast. No cell phone. I didn't get the news until yesterday afternoon, and I caught the first flight out."

"Shrinks need retreats?" Lucky asked, only half-serious.

"I'm not a shrink. I'm a therapist. And yes, sometimes we do." There seemed to be a lot more to it than that, but she didn't offer any details. "Were you with Gran when she died?"

Well, heck. That brought back the lump in his throat. It didn't go so great with that flutter in his stomach. Lucky responded with just a nod.

"Was she in pain?" Cassie pressed.

"No. She sort of just slipped away." Right there, in front of him. With that smile on her face.

Cassie stayed quiet a moment. "I should have been there with her. I should have told her goodbye."

And the tears started spilling down her cheeks. Lucky had been expecting them, of course. From all accounts Cassie actually loved Dixie Mae and vice versa, but he wasn't sure if he should offer Cassie a shoulder. Or just a pat on the back.

He went with the pat.

Cassie pulled out a tissue from her purse, dabbed her eyes, but the tears just came right back. Hell. Back-patting obviously wasn't doing the trick so he went for something more. He put his arm around her.

More tears fell, and Lucky figured they weren't the first of the day. Nor would they be the last. Cassie's eyes had already been red when she came into the room. As much as he hated to see a woman cry—and he *hated* it—at least there was one other person mourning Dixie Mae's loss.

Lucky didn't hurry her crying spell by trying to say something to comfort her. No way to speed up something like that anyway. Death sucked, period, and sometimes the only thing you could do was cry about it.

"Thanks," Cassie mumbled several moments later. She dabbed her eyes again and moved away from him. That didn't put an end to the tears, but she kept trying to blink them back. "Did she say anything before she died?"

Lucky didn't have any trouble recalling those last handful of words. "She said, 'The bull usually does.'"

Cassie opened her mouth and then seemed to change her mind about how to answer that. "Excuse me?"

"I don't know what it means, either. Dixie Mae asked about the rodeo ride that I'd just finished. I told her the bull won, and she said it usually does."

She blinked. "Does it usually win?"

"Uh, yeah. About 70 percent of the time. But I got the feeling that Dixie Mae meant something, well, deeper."

Heck, he hoped so anyway. Lucky hated to think Dixie Mae had used her dying breath to state the obvious.

Cassie glanced at him from the corner of her eye. "So you're still bull riding?"

The question was simple enough, but since it was one he got often, Lucky knew there was more to it than that. What Cassie, and others, really wanted to ask was—*Aren't you too old to still be riding bulls?*

Yep, he was. But he wasn't giving it up. And for that matter, he could ask her—*Aren't you too young to be a shrink?* Or rather a *therapist*. Of course, her comeback to that would probably be that they were the same age and that she'd just managed to cram more into her life than he had.

"Are you okay?" she asked. "You seem, uh, angry or something."

Great. Now he was worked up over an argument he was having with himself.

"I'm still bull riding," Lucky answered, knowing it wouldn't answer anything she'd just said. "And you're still, well, doing whatever it is you do?"

She nodded, not adding more, maybe because she was confused. But Dixie Mae had filled in some of the blanks. Cassie had gotten her master's degree in psychology and was now a successful therapist and advice columnist. Cassie traveled. Wrote articles. Made regular appearances on TV talk shows whenever a so-called relationship expert was needed.

Bull riding was the one and only thing he'd been good at since adulthood. Ironic since he failed at it 70 percent of the time.

Cassie took a deep breath. The kind of breath a person took when they needed some steeling up. And she got those sensible shoes moving closer to Dixie Mae's coffin. So far, Lucky had kept his distance, but he went up there with Cassie so he could say a final goodbye.

Dixie Mae was dressed in a flamingo-pink sleeveless rhinestone dress complete with matching necklace, earrings and a half foot of bracelets that stretched from her wrists to her elbows. Sparkles and pink didn't exactly scream funeral, but Lucky would have been let down if she'd insisted on being buried in anything else. Or had her hair styled any other way. Definitely a tribute to Dolly Parton.

Too bad the bracelets didn't cover up the tattoo.

"I loved her." Lucky hadn't actually intended for those words to come out of his mouth, but they were the truth. "Hard to believe, I know," he mumbled.

"No. She had some lovable qualities about her." Cassie didn't name any, though.

But Lucky did. "Right after my folks were killed in the car wreck, Dixie Mae was there for me," he went on. "Not motherly, exactly, but she made sure I didn't drink too much or ride a bull that would have killed me."

More of that skeptical look. "Your parents died when you were just nineteen, not long after we graduated from high school. She let you drink when you were still a teenager?"

"She didn't *let* me," Lucky argued. "I just did it, but she always made sure I didn't go overboard with it."

"A drop was already overboard since you were underage," Cassie mumbled.

Lucky gave her one of his own looks. One to remind her that her nickname in school was Miss Prissy Pants Police. She fought back, flinging a Prissy Pants Double Dog Dare look at him to challenge her until Lucky felt as if they'd had an entire fifth-grade squabble without words. He'd be impressed if he wasn't so pissed off.

"You can't tell me you didn't love her, too," he fired back.

At least Cassie didn't jump to disagree with that. She glanced at her grandmother, then him. "I did. I was just surprised you'd so easily admitted that you loved her."

Easy only because it'd dropped straight from his brain to his mouth without going through any filters. That happened with him way too often.

"Men like you often have a hard time saying it," she added.

"Men like me?" Those sounded like fighting words, and he was already worn-out from the nonverbal battle they'd just had. "I guess you're referring to my reputation of being a guy who likes women."

"A guy who sleeps around. A lot." She hadn't needed to add *a lot* to make it a complete zinger.

"Rein in your stereotypes, Doc." While she was doing that, he'd rein in his temper. And he'd do something about that blasted tat.

Lucky grabbed the felt-tip pen from the table next to the visitor's book, and he got to work.

"What are you doing?" Cassie asked.

"Fixing it." Not exactly a professional job, but he made a big smudgy *i* out of the *e* and an *e* out of the *i*.

Cassie leaned in closer. "Huh. I never noticed it was misspelled."

Lucky looked at her as if she'd sprouted an extra nose. "How could you not notice that?"

She shrugged. "I'm not that good at spelling. I mean, who is, what with spell-checkers on phones and computers?"

"I'm good at it," he grumbled. So that made two skills. Spelling and bull riding. At least he succeeded at the spelling more than 30 percent of the time.

Cassie stepped back, looked around the room. "I need to find the funeral director and then call the hospital and find out if Gran left me any instructions. A note or something."

Lucky patted his pocket. "She gave me a letter."

Cassie eyed the spot he'd patted, which meant she'd eyed his butt. "Did she say anything about me in it?"

"I'm not sure. I haven't read it yet." And darn it, the look she gave him was all shrink, one who was assessing his mental health—or lack thereof. "I was going to wait until after the service." Except it was as clear as a gypsy's crystal ball that there wasn't going to be an actual service.

"Well, can you look at it now, just to see if she mentions me?" She sounded as though she was in as much of a hurry as Logan.

Lucky wished he could point out that not everything had to be done in a hurry, bull riding excluded, but he was just procrastinating. Truth was, as long as the letter was unread, it was like having a little part of Dixie Mae around. One last unfinished partnership between them.

He huffed, and since he really didn't want to explain that "little part of Dixie Mae" thought, he took out the letter and opened it. One page, handwritten in Dixie Mae's usual scrawl.

Cassie didn't exactly hover over him, but it was close. She pinned her chocolate-brown eyes to him, no doubt watching for any change in expression so she could use her therapy skills to determine if this was good or bad.

Dear Lucky and Cassie...

That no doubt changed his expression. "The letter's addressed to both of us." He turned it, showing her the page. "Dixie Mae didn't mention that when she gave it to me at the hospital."

Cassie took it from him, and Lucky let her. Mainly because he really didn't want to read what was there since it hadn't gotten off to such a great start.

"'Dear Lucky and Cassie,'" she repeated. "'I need a favor, one I know neither of you will refuse. I've never asked either of you for anything, but I need to ask you now. Call Bernie Woodland, a lawyer in Spring Hill, and he'll give you all the details.'"

Cassie flipped the letter over, looking for the rest of it, but there was nothing else. "What kind of favor?"

Lucky had to shake his head. He'd figured it had something to do with the rodeo business, but now that Dixie Mae had included Cassie, maybe not. Cassie had never participated in the rodeo, or in her grandmother's finances for that matter.

He was also confused as to why Dixie Mae would have used Bernie for this. Dixie Mae no longer lived in Spring Hill. Hadn't for going on ten years. Her house was in San Antonio, and she had a lawyer on retainer there. Why hadn't she used him instead of Bernie?

"Did she say anything when she gave you the letter?" Cassie asked.

It wasn't hard to recall this part, either. "She said a man wouldn't be much of a man to deny an old dying woman her last wish."

Remembering her words had Lucky feeling another flutter. Not a sexual one like with Cassie, but one that sent an unnerving tingle down his bruised spine and tailbone.

If it had been a simple request, Dixie Mae would have just told him then and there on her death bed, rather than using her final breath on the bull remark. Instead she'd used the dying card to get him to agree to some unnamed favor, and that meant this could be trouble.

Cassie must have thought so, too, because some of the color drained from her cheeks, and she pulled out her phone again. "I'll call the lawyer."

She stepped away from the coffin. Far away. In fact, Cassie went all the way to the back of the room, and, pacing behind the last row of chairs, she made the call.

Lucky was about to follow and pace right along with her, but his own phone buzzed. Because he was hoping Cassie would soon have some info on the favor, he was ready to let the call go to voice mail, but then he saw the name on the screen.

Angel.

What the hell? He wasn't the sort to believe in ghosts and such, but if anyone could have found a way to reach out from beyond the grave, or the coffin, it would have been Dixie Mae.

Lucky hit the answer button and braced himself in case this was about to turn into a moment that might make him scream like a schoolgirl.

"Lucky," the caller said. It was a woman all right but definitely not Dixie Mae. This voice was sultry, and he was about 60 percent sure he recognized it.

"Bella?" he asked.

"Who else?" she purred.

Well, she hadn't been at the top of the list of people he expected would call themselves Angel, that's for sure. Bella was more like a being from the realm opposite to the one where angels lived. Lucky had met her about three months ago after a good bull ride in Kerrville, but he hadn't seen her since.

"I expected you to call me before now. Naughty boy," Bella teased.

Now, that label fit. They had engaged in some rather naughty things during their one night together. But he'd never intended for it to be anything other than a one-nighter. And Lucky had made that clear, with very specific words—*just this once*.

He glanced back at Cassie. She was still talking on the phone. Or rather listening, because she didn't seem to be saying much at all. Unlike Bella.

"Did you hear me?" Bella asked.

No, he hadn't, but Lucky had his own stuff to ask her. "How'd you get my number? And who's Angel?"

"Angel's my stage name, remember?"

Oh, yeah. Now he did, thanks to her memory jogging. Bella aka Angel Bella was a wannabe actress moonlighting as a cocktail waitress at the Blue Moon Bar.

"When you were asleep, I added my number to your contact list," she explained. "And I put your number in my phone to make sure we stayed in touch. Like now, for instance. I remember you saying you're from Spring Hill, and guess who's passing through town right now?"

Lucky didn't think that was a trick question. "Look, Bella, this isn't a good time. I'm at a friend's funeral."

"Oh." She paused and repeated that "oh" again. "Well, darn. I'd really hoped to see you. Maybe in an hour or two? I could... console you."

He bit back a groan. "Sorry, but I'm just not up to a good consoling."

Especially Bella's version of it. And especially not now. Cassie had started to talk, and though body language could be deceiving, he thought she might be arguing about something.

"I can see you tomorrow, then?" Bella pressed, and even though Lucky couldn't see her face, he sensed she was doing a fake pout thing with her mouth.

Lucky was about to come up with a couple of excuses, but then he saw Cassie slide her phone back into her pocket. She didn't come hurrying to him, though, to tell him about her conversation with Dixie Mae's lawyer. She just stood there, her back to him.

"I gotta go," Lucky said to Bella, and despite the woman's howling protest, he hit the end-call button and made his way to Cassie.

"So what's the favor Dixie Mae wants us to do?" Lucky asked.

Cassie took her time turning around to face him, but she didn't actually look at him. Instead, she tipped her eyes to the ceiling as if seeking divine help.

Then Cassie uttered a single word. A word that Lucky was afraid summed up this mess that Dixie Mae had just dumped on them from the grave.

"Shit."

CHAPTER THREE

CASSIE HATED TO rely on profanity to express herself, but she didn't know what else to say after the conversation she'd just had with Bernie Woodland.

Why in Sam Hill had her grandmother done this?

"Do I want to know what Dixie Mae's lawyer had to say?" Lucky asked.

That was an easy question to answer. "No."

Apparently, though, Lucky wanted her to expand on that a bit. And she would. But first, Cassie had to locate the nearest chair and sit down. Sometime during that conversation with Mr. Woodland, her knees had lost all their cartilage.

Lucky cursed. It was a much worse word than *shit*, and he dropped down in the chair next to her. "Tell me what's wrong."

Cassie nodded, swallowed hard. "There's no need to panic. It's something we can work out, I'm sure."

Though the lawyer seemed to have a different notion about that last part. Still, he was wrong. He had to be.

"What's the favor Dixie Mae wanted us to do for her?" Lucky pressed.

Best just to put it out there and let Lucky work through his own version of panic. Then they could go to Mr. Woodland's office and talk some sense into him.

"Apparently, my grandmother left us custody of some children," Cassie said.

Lucky stared at her. Stared some more. Then he laughed. Not the hysterical laugh of someone panicking, either. He thought this was some kind of joke.

"Custody of some kids?" More laughter from him. It was so hard he appeared to get a stitch in his side because he clamped his hand there for several seconds. "Right. Like I'm daddy material."

Cassie agreed with him on that point. Lucky was about as un-daddy-ish as a man could get. He was more the sort to practice making babies than to tend to them. That was something she hadn't especially wanted to notice about him.

"Never took Dixie Mae for one to pull a prank like this," Lucky added when he finally quit ha-ha-ing.

She hated to say this, but it was something he had to hear. "It's not a prank. Mr. Woodland said Grandmother had him draw up papers, and she signed them the day before she died."

Because Lucky was so close to her, just inches away, Cassie watched that sink in. Slowly. Word by stupid word. It didn't sink in well.

A muscle flickered in his jaw. Then another. It didn't take long for the shock and anger to set in after that.

Lucky snapped to his feet with military precision. "Those darn papers can just be *unsigned*. Come on. Let's go to the lawyer and get this straightened out right now."

If he hadn't caught onto her arm and wrenched her from the chair, Cassie might have had trouble getting her legs to work. But Lucky had no such trouble. He lit out of there with her in tow while he fished through his jeans pocket for his keys.

Snug jeans.

That hugged his butt just right.

Cassie was dumbfounded that she'd even noticed something like that. Then again, she always noticed things like that when it came to Lucky. She made a mental note to talk to a therapist about it. Of course, she had plenty of other stuff to bring up considering her grandmother had obviously lost her mind and Cassie hadn't picked up on that until it was too late.

"What kids?" Lucky snapped.

Throughout most of her life, Cassie had gotten accustomed to Lucky giving her heated looks. Or maybe that was just the way he normally looked when his attention landed on a woman. However, that kind of heat was gone now, and in its place was a whole lot of confusion.

"I'm not sure, but according to the lawyer, Grandmother had custody of them for the past several months."

"Impossible. No one in their right mind would give Dixie Mae kids to raise. *Any* kids. What do you know about them? Who are their idiot parents? And why didn't Dixie Mae ever mention anything about them?"

Three good questions. She had fewer good answers. In fact, Cassie had no answers at all.

"Mr. Woodland didn't know. Grandmother didn't give him any details, only that she was transferring guardianship to the two of us. He was going to call us when the children arrived at his office—which should be any minute now."

Just saying the words aloud caused the anxiety to swell in her chest again. Her nerves were already prickling beneath the surface, what with Dixie Mae's death, and her other *problem*, but the prickling was well on its way to being full-blown panic. *Breathe.*

Not that guppy breathing, either. That would cause her to hyperventilate again. Nice, normal, slow breaths. At the end of a few of those, Cassie's head finally began to clear.

"It has to be a misunderstanding," she said more to herself than Lucky, but he latched right on to the idea as if it were a true beacon of hope.

"You're right. And Bernie Woodland will tell us that." Possibly a lie, but she needed a beacon of hope, too.

Lucky practically stuffed her into a sleek red truck and peeled out of the parking lot. Even though she didn't need any proof whatsoever of his bad-boy reputation, she got it right away. He sped down Main Street, violating at least three traffic laws while getting the attention of every single female they passed along the way. Two gave him "call me" hand gestures.

Because Spring Hill was a small town by anyone's standards, it didn't take Lucky long to get to the lawyer's office. Only a couple of minutes. He screeched the truck into one of the tight parking spaces and threw open the door in the same motion that he turned off the engine.

Cassie had to run to catch up with him. Thankfully, that was easy to do since she was wearing her traveling shoes and not her usual heels. She made it in behind him by only a few seconds. During those seconds, though, Lucky had already managed to get the attention of the receptionist, Wilhelmina Larkin.

Wilhelmina was sixty if she was a day but obviously still wasn't immune to Lucky McCord and his crotch-framing jeans. She stood, twirling a coil of her hair around her finger and smiling in a coy way that made it clear she appreciated the view in front of her.

"I need to see Bernie," Lucky insisted. His tone was hard enough, but he returned Wilhelmina's smile as naturally as he drew in his next breath.

"He's busy with a client right now," Wilhelmina said.

The woman actually batted her eyelashes. Good gravy. If Cassie hadn't already had enough to sour her stomach, that would have done it. With the way women threw themselves at Lucky, it could possibly turn out that these children in question might be his offspring after all.

Lucky leaned in, his hands landing on Wilhelmina's desk. "*Un*busy Bernie. We want to talk to him right now. It's important."

Maybe it was because Lucky quit grinning or maybe it was because he no longer sounded like the hot cowboy women drooled over, but either way, Wilhelmina nixed the eyelash batting and actually slid her gaze toward Cassie, apparently noticing her for the first time.

"Oh," Wilhelmina remarked. "This must be about Dixie Mae. What's going on anyway? Bernie wouldn't get into it with me. Dixie Mae's orders, he said. Dixie Mae thought I'd gossip about it. That's what she said to Bernie—that I would gossip about it—so Bernie typed up the paperwork himself. Didn't even know he could type."

Lucky gave her a flat look, and Cassie thought he might repeat his order to see Bernie. He didn't. He stormed passed Wilhelmina, heading up the hall. There were several offices, but Lucky seemed to know exactly which one belonged to Bernie because he opened the door without knocking. Bernie was with someone all right.

Cassie's father.

Mason-Dixon Weatherall.

Cassie stumbled to a stop, her father's and her gazes colliding like two unconnected burglars who'd broken into the same place at the same time. Instant guilt.

Well, guilt on her part anyway.

She'd distanced herself from him years ago because of the way he treated her, and he'd distanced himself from her because of the distancing. Cassie was betting, though, that her father felt no guilt whatsoever about that, what with his my-way-or-the-highway approach to life.

It was the first time she'd seen him in nearly ten years, and her immediate thought—once she got past the question as to why he was there—was that he looked so old. He was still dyeing his hair the color of crude oil, still wearing clothes straight out of the sixties, but there were a lot more wrinkles on his face than there had been during their last meeting.

Her father eased himself to his feet. "Cassie," he greeted.

"Dad," Cassie greeted back with the same caution of those two theoretical burglars.

Lucky volleyed some glances between them. "Does your dad have anything to do with this *shit*?"

"Do you?" Cassie asked her father.

"You'll have to be more specific," he snarled. "I deal with lots of different kinds of shit."

Bernie stood then, tugging off his glasses and dropping them onto the desk. He was about the same age as her father, but it was night and day in the apparel arena. Bernie was wearing conservative clothes similar to hers. Actually, the jacket was identical to hers.

Something that made her frown.

"Mason-Dixon doesn't have anything to do with the letter Dixie Mae left the two of you," Bernie clarified.

"The old bat left you a letter, too?" But her father didn't wait for them to confirm it. "She left me six fucking cats. Six! She arranged to have her driver drop them off at the club this morning. Them, and their litter boxes, which hadn't been cleaned in days. They're going to the pound as soon as I leave here."

"No," Cassie practically shouted, and it got everyone's attention. "Grandmother loved those cats."

Her father's fisted hands went on his boney hips. "Then why the hell did she leave them to me?"

Yet another of those questions that Cassie couldn't answer. Maybe Dixie Mae had indeed gone insane.

"I'll take the cats," Cassie volunteered. "Just give me a couple of days. I've got my own problems to work out." A laundry list of them, and that list just kept growing.

Her father looked at her. Then at Lucky. "Did you knock up Cassie or something?" he asked Lucky.

While Lucky was howling out a loud "no," Cassie fanned her hands toward her clothes. Then toward Lucky's. "Does it look as if we could be lovers?" she asked.

Her father did more glancing and shook his head. "Guess not."

It was yet something else that made her frown. Maybe she needed to start shopping at a different store.

"So, you'll take the cats?" her father clarified.

Cassie nodded but didn't have a blasted clue how she was going to make that happen. Her condo in LA didn't allow pets. Still, the shelter here in Spring Hill probably wasn't no-kill, and she couldn't risk her grandmother's precious cats being put down—even if it had been a lamebrain idea for Dixie Mae to leave her pets to a man who'd been on her bad side since she'd given birth to him.

Her father moved closer and gave her *the look*. The one he'd been giving her since she was a kid. "Just know that I expect something other than cats from Dixie Mae's estate. Whatever she had, I get half."

"I'm pretty sure you won't," Lucky spoke up. "Dixie Mae didn't like you, and she always told me that she had no intention of giving you any money. She wanted her money to go to Cassie."

"Cassie will share," her father insisted. The look intensified, and suddenly she was six years old again and getting sent to her room because she was acting too prissy.

Lucky moved in front of her father, getting right in his face. "I'm thinking that'll be Cassie's decision."

"We'll see about that." Her father started out, then stopped when he was right beside her. "If those cats aren't gone in two days, they're going to the pound. The goddamn things are chewing the feathers in the girls' costumes."

That seemed very minor compared to being given children, but as Cassie had always done with her father, she held her tongue. And took a few steps away from him. She'd spent her entire adult life trying not to get embroiled with him and his smutty lifestyle, and she didn't want to start now.

Cassie didn't say goodbye to him. She merely shut the door once her father was gone and then whirled around to face Bernie. Now, here was someone she would confront. Except Lucky beat her to it.

"Say it's not true," Lucky demanded. "Tell me that Dixie Mae didn't give us custody of some kids."

Bernie sighed, causing his pudgy belly to jiggle. He pulled open his desk drawer, cracked open a bottle of Glenlivet and downed more than a couple of swigs. "She did indeed leave Cassie and you custody of two children," Bernie confirmed.

Of course, the lawyer had already told her that, but hearing it face-to-face gave Cassie a new wallop of panic. No. This couldn't happen now. She couldn't lose it in front of Lucky. In front of anybody.

Lucky, however, didn't seem to notice that she was cruising her way to a panic attack. He was apparently coping with the anxiety in his own way. By cursing a blue streak in an extremely loud voice.

"How the hell could you let Dixie Mae do something like that?" Lucky yelled. "You should have stopped her."

"Really?" Bernie challenged. "You believe I could have stopped Dixie Mae? Were you ever able to stop her from doing something she insisted on doing?"

"No, but that's beside the point. Dixie Mae and I differed on rodeo stuff. Business. If she'd mentioned giving me custody of some kids, trust me, I would have stopped her."

Judging from the groan that followed, Lucky knew that was a partial lie. He would have indeed *tried* to stop her, but Dixie Mae would have just found a way around it.

The same thing Cassie had to do in this situation.

"Neither Lucky nor I knew that Dixie Mae had anything to do with any children," Cassie started. "When did it happen? *How* did it happen?" she amended.

"I'm not sure of all the details," Bernie answered. "Until Dixie Mae showed up here, it'd been years since I'd seen her. She said she wanted me to do the paperwork because I was local."

Local? Cassie figured there was more to it than that. Maybe Dixie Mae's usual lawyer didn't handle situations like this. Or maybe her grandmother had just tried to be sneaky because her lawyer in San Antonio perhaps would have contacted Cassie to let her know something fishy was going on. And this definitely qualified as fishy.

"Dixie Mae said a couple of months ago an old friend of hers got very sick," Bernie continued. "This friend was taking care of her grandkids and asked Dixie Mae to step in for a while."

All right. There was the out Cassie had been hoping for. "You can contact the grandmother and tell her to resume custody."

Bernie shook his head. "The grandmother died a short time later, and the grandkids' parents aren't in the picture. They're both dead. That's why Dixie Mae took over legal custody."

Lucky shook his head, too. "Well, she must have hired a nanny or something because Dixie Mae never had any kids with her when she came to work."

"She did have a nanny, a couple of them, in fact," Bernie went on. "But they quit when they butted heads with her so Dixie Mae arranged for someone else to watch them temporarily. She didn't give me a lot of details when she came in and asked me to draw up papers and her will. And right after we finished with it, she got admitted to the hospital."

Cassie latched on to that. "Maybe there's something in her will about Lucky and me being able to relinquish custody to a suitable third party."

Lucky tipped his head in her direction. "What she said. Find it."

But Bernie didn't pull out a will or anything else. "The will didn't address trusteeship of the children, only the disbursement of Dixie Mae's assets. I'm not at liberty to go over that with you now because she insisted her will not be read for several weeks."

Cassie doubted there was a good reason for that. But she could think of a bad reason. "This was probably Grandmother's attempt at carrot dangling. If Lucky and I assume responsibility without putting up a fuss, then we'll inherit some money. Well, I don't want her money, and I'm putting up a fuss!"

"So am I," Lucky agreed. "Fix this."

Bernie looked around, clearly hesitating. "I guess if you refuse, I can have Child Protective Services step in."

All right, they were getting somewhere.

Or maybe not.

"Of course, that's not ideal," Bernie went on. "The children could end up being placed in separate homes, and foster care can be dicey." He scratched his head. "Dixie Mae was so sure you two would agree to this since it was her last wish."

Her grandmother had no doubt told Bernie to make sure he reminded them of that a time or two. Especially after what Dixie Mae had said to Lucky: *A man wouldn't be much of a man to deny an old dying woman her last wish.*

"I smell a rat," Lucky mumbled.

So did Cassie. Dixie Mae had practically duped Lucky into saying yes, and the old gal had figured Cassie wouldn't just walk away, leaving him to hold the bag.

Damn it.

Cassie couldn't just walk away. But that didn't mean she was giving up without a fight. She wasn't in any position to raise children. Especially not with Lucky.

Heck, who was she kidding?

He'd probably be a lot better at it than she would be. At least he wasn't an emotional mess right now and hadn't just checked out of a glorified loony bin. As a therapist she probably should have considered a better term for it, but loony bin fit. Too bad she hadn't had her grandmother there with her so she could have had the chance of talking Dixie Mae into making other arrangements for the children.

"How do we get around this?" Cassie asked Bernie at the same moment Lucky said to him, "Fix this shit. And I don't mean fix it by putting some innocent kids in foster care. Fix it the right way. Find their next of kin. I want them in a home with loving people who know the right way to take care of them."

Good idea. Except Bernie shook his head again. "I started the search right after Dixie Mae came in. No luck so far, but I'll keep looking. In the meantime, Cassie and you can take temporary custody, and if I can't find any relatives, I'll ask around and see if someone else will take them."

That wasn't ideal, far from it, because "asking around" didn't seem to have a deadline attached to it. "How long would we have them?" she asked.

"A couple of days at most," Bernie said.

Perhaps that was BS, but Cassie latched on to it and looked at Lucky. "Maybe we can figure out something to do with them just for a day or two?"

Oh, he so wanted to say no. She could see it in his eyes. Probably because *he* didn't want to stay anywhere near Spring Hill. It was no secret that Lucky had a serious case of wanderlust. Along with the regular kind of lust.

"Two days is too long," Lucky said, obviously still mulling this over and perhaps looking for an escape route.

Two days, the exact amount of time she had to do something about those feather-chasing cats at the strip club. Cassie tried very hard not to think bad thoughts about her grandmother, but she wished the woman had gone over all these details before she'd passed away.

"You'll need to work out something faster than two days," Lucky insisted. "I've got to be at a rodeo day after tomorrow."

Yes, she had things to do, as well. Things she didn't want to do, but she wouldn't be able to wiggle out of them the way that Lucky was trying to wiggle out of this.

"I can try," Bernie said, not sounding especially hopeful. Too bad, because Cassie needed him to be hopeful. More than that, she needed him to succeed.

"I'll call the Bluebonnet Inn," Bernie added, "and get the girls a room there."

Lucky seemed to approve of that, but Cassie wasn't so sure. She, too, had planned to stay at the Bluebonnet Inn, mainly because it was the only hotel in Spring Hill. That meant Lucky would likely expect her to be with the children 24/7.

But Cassie wasn't having this all put on her shoulders. Nope. She was packing enough baggage and problems as it was so she'd also get Lucky a room at the inn.

"Where are the children?" Cassie asked.

Bernie checked his watch. "They should be here any minute now." He pushed a button on an old-fashioned intercom system. "Wilhelmina, when the Compton kids arrive—"

"They're already here," Wilhelmina interrupted. "Want me to send them back?"

"Sure." Bernie took his finger off the intercom button and drew in a long breath, as if he might need some extra air.

A moment later, Cassie saw why.

The air sort of vanished when the door opened and Cassie saw one of the children in question. And this time, she wasn't the one to say that one all-encompassing word. It was Lucky.

Shit.

They had apparently inherited custody of a call girl.

CHAPTER FOUR

THERE WERE ONLY a handful of times in Lucky's life when he'd been rendered speechless, and this was one of them.

The "girl" walking up the hall toward him was indeed a *girl*. Technically. She was female, nearly as tall as Cassie, and she was wearing a black skirt and top. Or perhaps that was paint. Hard to tell. The skirt was short and skintight, more suited for, well, someone older.

"This is Mackenzie Compton," Bernie said.

Cassie blew out a breath that sounded like one of relief. Lucky had no idea what she was relieved about so he just stared at her.

"This isn't a child," Cassie explained, relief in her voice, too. "So obviously there's no need for us to take custody."

Right. "What Cassie just said," Lucky told Bernie.

However, Bernie burst that bubble of hope right off. "Mackenzie just turned thirteen."

Maybe ten years ago, she had. But she wasn't thirteen now. "Can she prove that?" Lucky blurted out.

Mackenzie didn't say a word. Didn't have any reaction to that whatsoever. She just stood there looking like a both-arms-down Statue of Liberty who'd been vandalized with black spray paint. She had black hair, black nails, black lipstick and stared at them as if they were beings from another planet. Beings that she didn't want to get to know.

Good. The feeling was mutual.

But thirteen?

"I can prove her age," Bernie supplied. "I have her birth certificate and school records." Bernie handed him a folder. "Her sister, Mia, is four."

Four. Well, hell. Now, that was a child, though he still wasn't convinced Mackenzie was a teenager. Maybe if she scrubbed off that half inch of makeup, there'd be some trace of a girl, but right now he wasn't seeing it.

However, he was seeing something. An extra set of legs. Either Mackenzie had four of them, a pair significantly shorter than the ones wearing that black skirt, or her little sister was hiding behind her.

Mackenzie took one step to the side, and there she was. A child. A real one. No goth clothes for her. She was wearing a pink dress with flowers and butterflies on it, and her blond hair had been braided into pigtails. She had a ragged pink stuffed pig in the crook of her arm.

If there had been a definition of "scared kid" in the dictionary, this kid's photo would have been next to it. Mia was clinging to her sister's skirt, her big blue eyes shiny with tears that looked ready to spill right down her cheeks.

Lucky took a big mental step back at the same time that he took an actual step forward. He didn't have any paternal instincts, none, but he knew a genuinely sad girl when he saw one, and it cut him to the core. He went down on one knee so he could be at her eye level.

"I'm Lucky McCord," he said, hoping to put her at ease. It didn't work. Mia clung even tighter, though there wasn't much fabric in Mackenzie's skirt to cling to.

Mia. Such a little name for such a little girl.

"Do either of them..." Cassie started, looking at Bernie. But then she turned to the girls. "Either of you, uh, talk?"

Mia nodded. Blinked back those tears. Her bottom lip started to quiver.

Well, hell. That did it. Lucky fished through his pocket, located the only thing he could find resembling candy. A stick of gum. And he handed it to Mia. She took it only after looking up at her big sister, who nodded and grunted. What Big Sis didn't do was say a word to confirm that she did indeed have verbal communication skills beyond a primitive grunt.

"The girls have had a tough go of it lately," Bernie said as if choosing his words carefully.

Lucky added another mental *well, hell*. He'd probably said *hell* more times today than he had in the past decade. He'd always believed it was the sign of a weak mind when a man had to rely on constant profanity as a way of communicating his emotions, but his mind was swaying in a weak direction today.

And he didn't know what the hell to do.

"Where have they been staying since my grandmother's death?" Cassie asked. "Gran passed away two days ago."

Good question, but Lucky didn't repeat himself with another *what she said*.

"With Scooter Jenkins," Bernie answered.

Lucky had to do it. He had to think another *hell*.

"You know this man?" Cassie asked him.

"Scooter's a woman." At least Lucky thought she was. She had a five-o'clock shadow, but that was possibly hormonal. "She's one of the rodeo clowns."

Spooky as all get-out, too. While Scooter had worked for Dixie Mae as long as Lucky could remember, she was hardly maternal material. Nor was she exactly Dixie Mae's friend. The only way Scooter would have taken the girls was for Dixie Mae to have paid her a large sum of cash.

"Ten grand," Bernie said as if anticipating Lucky's question. "The deal was for Scooter to keep them until after the funeral and then transfer physical custody to Cassie and you."

Since Scooter was nowhere to be seen, that meant she'd likely just dropped off the kids. Lucky would speak to her about that later. But for now, he needed to fix some things.

Apparently, Cassie had the same fixing-things idea. "Why don't Bernie and I go in his office and discuss some *solutions*?" Cassie said to him. "Maybe you can wait in the lobby with the girls?"

Lucky preferred to be in on that discussion, but it wasn't a discussion he wanted to have in front of Mia. Not with those tears in her eyes.

"Please," Cassie whispered to him. Or at least that's what Lucky thought she said at first. But when she repeated it, he realized she had said, "Breathe."

Oh, man. Cassie looked ready to bolt so maybe her talking to Bernie was a good idea after all. While the two of them were doing that, maybe he'd try to have the kids wait with Wilhelmina so he could join the grown-ups.

Cassie and Bernie went to his office. Cassie shut the door, all the while repeating "Breathe." Lucky went in the direction of the reception area.

Where there was no Wilhelmina.

Just a pair of suitcases sitting on the floor next to her empty desk. But there was a little sign that said I'll Be Back. The clock on the sign was set for a half hour from now. It might as well have been the next millennium.

Mia was holding on to the gum and pig as if they were some kind of lifelines, all the while volleying glances between her sister and him. Since it was possible there'd be some yelling going on in Bernie's office, Lucky motioned for the girls to sit in the reception area.

He sat.

They didn't.

And the moments crawled by. The silence went way past the uncomfortable stage.

Lucky didn't have any idea what to say to them. The only experience he'd had with kids was his soon-to-be nephew, Ethan.

He was two and a half, and Lucky's brother Riley was engaged to Ethan's mom, Claire. Too bad Ethan wasn't around now to break the iceberg.

"So, what grade are you in?" he asked, just to be asking something.

Mia held up the four fingers of her left hand—the hand not clutching the gum but rather the one on the pig. Since he doubted she was in the fourth grade, he figured maybe she was communicating her age. So Lucky went with that. He flashed his ten fingers three times and added three more. Of course, she was way too young to get that he was thirty-three, but he thought it might get a smile from her.

It didn't.

He tried Mackenzie next. "Let me guess your favorite color. Uh, blue?" He smiled to let her know it was a joke. The girl's black-painted mouth didn't even quiver.

And the silence rolled on.

Oh, well. At least Bernie had said this so-called custody arrangement would only last a day or two, and they weren't chatter bugs. Mia's tears seemed to have temporarily dried up, too. Plus, Cassie was likely jumping through hoops to do whatever it took for them not to have to leave here with these kids. Lucky was all for that, but he wasn't heartless. He still wanted to leave them in a safe place. Preferably a safe place that didn't involve him.

What the heck had Dixie Mae been thinking?

"Bull," someone said, and for one spooky moment, Lucky thought it was Dixie Mae whispering from beyond the grave.

But it was Mia.

Those little blue eyes had landed on his belt buckle, and there was indeed a bull and bull rider embossed into the shiny silver. Lucky had lots of buckles—easy for that to happen when you rode as long as he'd been riding—but he had two criteria for the ones he wore. Big and shiny. This was the biggest and shiniest of the bunch.

"Yep, it's a bull," Lucky verified.

Mia didn't come closer, but she did lean out from sour-faced Big Sis for a better look.

"I ride bulls just like that one." He tapped the buckle, and hoped that wasn't too abstract for a four-year-old. Of course, she had clearly recognized it as a bull, so maybe she got it.

And the silence returned.

"So, what was it like staying with Scooter?" he asked.

That got a reaction from Mackenzie. She huffed. Not exactly a sudden bout of chatter, but Lucky understood her completely. What he didn't understand was why Dixie Mae had left them with Scooter in the first place. But then, there were a lot of things he didn't understand about Dixie Mae right now.

"How about you?" he asked Mia. "Did you like staying with Scooter?"

She pinched her nose, effectively communicating that Scooter often smelled. Often kept on her clown makeup even when she wasn't working. The only thing marginally good he could say about the woman was that her visible tattoos weren't misspelled.

"Do we gotta go back with Scooter?" Mia asked.

Lucky wasn't sure who was more surprised by the outburst of actual words—Mackenzie or him. It took him a second to get past the shock of the sound of Mia's voice and respond.

"Do you want to go back with her?" he asked.

"No." Mackenzie that time. Mia mumbled her own "No." Judging from the really fast response from both girls, and that it was the only syllable he'd gotten from Mackenzie, he'd hit a nerve.

A nerve that affected his next question. "So, where do you want to go?"

Now, this would have been the time for both girls to start firing off answers. With friends, relatives, rock stars. To a goth store, et cetera. He got a shrug from Mia and a glare from Mackenzie.

What had he expected? Bernie had already told him their parents were out of the picture. Orphans. Something that Lucky more than understood, but he'd been nineteen when his folks died. Barely an adult, but that had *barely* prevented him from having to stay with a clown.

Though there were a couple of times when Lucky had called Logan just that.

More silence. If this went on, he might just take a nap. Lucky went with a different approach, though. "Is there a question you want to ask me?"

Mia looked up at her sister, and even though Mackenzie's mouth barely moved, Lucky thought he saw the hint of a smile. The kind of smile that had some stink eye on it.

"Have you ever been arrested?" Mackenzie asked. Yeah, definitely some stink eye. "Because Scooter said you had been."

"I have," he admitted. "Nothing major, though, and I never spent more than a few hours in jail."

Except that one time when there'd been a female deputy who'd come on to him. But that time he'd stayed longer by choice. Best not to mention that, though. In fact, there was a lot about his life he wouldn't mention.

"What'd you get 'rrested for?" Mia asked.

Lucky smiled, not just at the pronunciation but the cute voice. Cute kid, too.

"Drinking beer." Like Bernie had earlier, Lucky chose his words wisely. At any rate, beer or some other alcohol had usually been at the root of his bad behavior.

Mackenzie made a *hmmp* sound as if she didn't believe him. Lucky didn't elaborate even though there was no telling what Scooter had told them.

"Don't drink beer," Mia advised him in a serious tone that made him have to fight back another smile.

The little girl came closer, leaving her sister's side and not even looking up for permission. She climbed into the seat next to him, tore the gum stick in half and gave him the bigger of the two pieces.

"Thanks," Lucky managed to say.

Mia then offered half of her half to her sister, but Mackenzie only shook her head, grunted and deepened her scowl. Much more of that and she was going to get a face cramp.

"Is Lucky even your real name?" Mackenzie again. "Because if it is, it's a stupid name."

Such a cheery girl. "It's a nickname. My real name's Austin, but nobody ever calls me that."

Heck, most people didn't even know it.

"My grandpa McCord gave me the name when I was just three years old," he explained. "I somehow managed to get into the corral with a mean bull. And despite the fact I was waving a red shirt at him so I could play matador, I came out without a scratch."

Lucky, indeed. His grandpa could have just called him stupid considering the idiotic thing he'd done.

"What about the lady doctor?" Mackenzie asked, clearly not impressed with his story. She folded her arms over her chest. "Has she been arrested, too?"

"Can't say," Lucky answered honestly. "But I doubt it." Though something was going on with Cassie. Those *breathe* mumblings weren't a good sign.

"Is she gay?" Mackenzie continued.

"No," he said, way too loud and way too fast. He paused. "Why do you ask?"

"Her shoes and clothes," Mackenzie quickly supplied.

Lucky groaned. "It's never a good idea to stereotype people." That was the second time today he'd given such a warning, though Mackenzie probably didn't have a clue what that word meant. She didn't seem the sort to work on building her vocabulary.

He cursed himself. Huffed. He needed to take his own advice. Yeah, stereotypes weren't a good idea.

"Are you two together, then?" Mackenzie asked. "The lady doctor and you?" she clarified, though her question needed no such clarification.

Lucky almost preferred the silence to this. "No. I was business partners with Cassie's grandmother, Dixie Mae, and Cassie and I went to high school together."

"I know who her grandmother is," Mackenzie snapped. *"Was,"* she added, also in a snap. She didn't offer more on the subject of Dixie Mae, but since Mackenzie didn't complain about her, maybe that meant she'd gotten along with the woman.

That would be a first, but hey, miracles happened. Lucky had found a way to love the woman so maybe Mackenzie and Mia had, too. Or rather just Mia, he amended when Mackenzie's scowl deepened.

"I just thought you and the lady doctor were…" Mackenzie said, but she waved it off. "It was just something Dixie Mae said."

That got his attention. "What'd she say? Specifically what'd she say about Cassie and me? Because if this is Dixie Mae's way of matchmaking from the grave—"

He stopped. Wished he hadn't said it because of the look it put on Mia's face. Little name, little girl. Whopping big ears. She'd already been shuffled around too much, and she didn't need to hear that she might go through another shuffling all because Dixie Mae wanted her granddaughter and her "boy" to end up together.

Something that wouldn't happen.

Cassie had already made that plenty clear.

"We need to get one thing straight," Mackenzie continued a couple of seconds later. "If you hurt my sister, I'll punch you and the lady doctor right in your faces."

"Kenzie doesn't mean it," Mia whispered behind her hand. She unwrapped her piece of gum, tore it in half again. One piece she put in her mouth. The other, in her pocket.

"I do mean it," Mackenzie insisted. "Nobody hurts my sister. *Nobody.*"

"I understand. I've got a kid sister of my own. Her name is Anna." Because he thought it might give them some common ground, he started to tell her about Anna, that she was a college student in Florida, that he'd walk through fire for her. But Lucky stopped.

And he silently said another *hell*.

Had someone hurt Mia before? Was that why Mackenzie had doled out that threat? And for the record, he did think she meant it.

Mackenzie clammed up again, and even though he looked at Mia to see how she was dealing with all of this, she was swinging her legs, humming to herself and rolling the silver foil from her gum into a little ball. Lucky would have pressed Mackenzie for more info, or rather *any* info, but he heard the footsteps coming up the hall.

Finally.

He stood, moving in front of the girls in case Cassie and Bernie had to tell him something that wasn't meant for those big ears. But selective muteness must have been catching because Bernie sure wasn't talking, and Cassie dodged his gaze.

"Well?" Lucky finally prompted in a whisper. Probably not a soft enough one because Mackenzie and Mia weren't doing any gaze-dodging at all. They had their baby blues pinned to him.

"We reached a solution," Cassie said.

"Good?" And, yes, it was a question. One they didn't answer. "All right, where are they going?"

Bernie and Cassie exchanged uneasy glances. "Home," Bernie answered, looking right at Lucky. "With you."

CHAPTER FIVE

"HOME, WITH ME?" Lucky said.

All in all, Lucky took the news about as well as Cassie had expected. He added, "No." And he kept on adding to that no. "It's crazy there now what with Riley and Claire's wedding coming up. They're getting married in the house."

She knew Riley and Claire, of course. Had even heard about Riley leaving the Air Force and getting engaged to Claire. But Cassie hadn't known about the wedding planning. Still, their options were limited here.

"It'll only be for a day or two," Cassie reminded him. She also tried to keep her voice at a whisper, but there wasn't much distance between them and the kids. It didn't help that Mackenzie was glaring at her.

"You don't know that," Lucky argued. "*He* doesn't know that." He flung an accusing finger at Bernie. "I'll get us all rooms in the Bluebonnet Inn—"

"I've already tried," Cassie explained, "and they're all booked for the high school reunion, class of 1948." Some might cancel because they weren't spring chickens and might not be able to make it, but Cassie couldn't count on that.

"We can all go to Dixie Mae's house in San Antonio, then," Lucky suggested.

Cassie really hated to be the bearer of more bad news. "She's already sold it. The new owners apparently closed on it earlier today."

"When did Dixie Mae arrange that?" he snapped.

Cassie had to shrug. Apparently, her grandmother had been up to a lot of things that Cassie and Lucky hadn't known about, but from what she could gather, these buyers had agreed to purchase the place months ago and had already done all the paperwork in advance.

Lucky stayed quiet a moment, but the quietness didn't extend to his eyes. There was a lot going on in his head right now, including perhaps a big dose of panic. "Another hotel, then. Or are you going to tell me every hotel in the state is booked?"

"Told you they wouldn't want us," Mackenzie mumbled.

Good grief. This was exactly what Cassie was trying to avoid so she took hold of Lucky's arm to pull him down the hall. "Watch the girls," she told Bernie.

Lucky didn't exactly cooperate with the moving-away-from-them part. "That's not true," he told Mackenzie, surprising Cassie, Mackenzie, maybe even himself. "This isn't about wanting or not wanting you. It's about, well, some other stuff that has nothing to do with you and Mia."

Cassie tugged his arm again, and this time she managed to move him up the hall and hopefully out of earshot. "All right, what's the real problem here?" Cassie demanded. "I mean, other than you don't want to be home, and this would require you to be. Is it because I'd be there, too?"

He looked at her as if she'd just spontaneously sprouted a full beard on the spot. "What?"

Since that question could cover a multitude of things, Cassie went with the one most obvious to her. "I've resisted your advances for years, and you hate me. Now you don't want me anywhere around you."

More of the sprouted-full-beard look. "I don't hate you, and you might not have noticed, but I quit *advancing* on you a long time ago."

Ouch. Well, that stung, a lot more than it should have. And it was stupid to feel even marginally disappointed. But there had been something about Lucky's attention that had made her feel attractive, especially in those days when no other guy was looking her way.

"I don't hate those kids, either," Lucky went on. "In fact, the little one's a sweet girl." He paused, not exactly hemming and hawing, but it was close.

"Is it because there aren't enough rooms in your house?" Cassie asked. "Because it looks huge to me."

"It is huge, and there are plenty of rooms. That's not the point." But it still took Lucky a while to get to what the point was exactly. "Logan's at the house," he finally said. "His loft apartment in town's being renovated so he'll be staying there until it's finished. Heck, he's probably there right now."

She waited, hoping for more of an explanation. Cassie had to wait several long moments.

"Logan and I don't exactly get along," he admitted.

"Okay. That's a valid argument. I understand not getting along with relatives." Mercy, did she. "But there are advantages to being here in Spring Hill, since it's where Bernie is. We could be right in his face every day to make sure he's doing everything he can to resolve this."

Lucky kept staring at her. Then he turned the tables on her. "What's really going on here with you?"

Perhaps all those years of seducing women and being seduced by them had honed his perception. Or maybe he had ESP. This definitely wasn't something she wanted the girls to hear so she pulled Lucky back into Bernie's office.

"Dixie Mae told Bernie that she thought Mackenzie might be suicidal." Cassie didn't add more. Didn't want to add more. She especially didn't want Lucky or anyone else to see that just saying those words felt as if someone had clamped on to her heart with a meaty fist and wouldn't let go.

Breathe.

"If she's suicidal, why isn't she in a hospital or someplace where she can get help?" he asked.

"Because she doesn't have an official diagnosis. That was only Dixie Mae's opinion. I've asked Bernie to try to get Mackenzie's medical records, but that'll take a while. By then we should have found their next of kin or made other arrangements." God, she hoped so anyway.

"There's something you're not telling me," he pressed.

Yes. Something she wouldn't tell him, either. Cassie somehow had to get past this so she could try to work out things in her head. If that was even possible.

"I just don't want Mackenzie to slip through the cracks," Cassie added. That was true, but it had nothing to do with what she was holding back. "No matter how she dresses or how she acts."

Though the dressing part did push Cassie's buttons. Again, old baggage, because it reminded her of her trashy-dressing mother.

"Agreed," Lucky said right away. "But stating the obvious here, I don't know squat about kids. Much less ones who might or might not be suicidal."

Cassie knew more about the suicidal part than she wanted to admit. "If you have another option about where to take them, I'm listening."

Lucky had no doubt already gone through the options, and it wouldn't have taken him that long. Because other options didn't exist. With no next of kin, that left foster care, and while it could be a good thing for some kids, it could spell disaster for someone like Mackenzie, especially if she got placed in a separate home from her sister. Worse, once Cassie signed over the temporary custody, she wouldn't even have any legal right to check on the girls and make sure they were in good homes.

The muscles in Lucky's jaw started stirring. "And you really think it'll only be a day or two at most?"

"I sure hope so. You're not the only one who'd rather not be here."

His eyes met hers, and she halfway expected him to ask if he was part of the reason she didn't want to be there.

He was.

Lucky had a way of stirring things inside her that shouldn't be stirred. Along with heating parts of her that should remain at room temperature. She had enough bears chasing her without adding Lucky McCord to the furry mix. But adding him was something she was apparently going to have to do.

At least for this guardianship facet of her life anyway. No heating or stirring allowed.

"With the Bluebonnet Inn booked, I don't have a place to stay," Cassie added. "And I need some office space. I have a client I have to see. It can't wait, and she'll be flying in to San Antonio in the morning. I can have her come to the house, or I can leave you with the girls while I go to San Antonio and meet—"

"You're not leaving me with the girls. Especially when one might be suicidal. You can have your meeting at the house. There are two offices. My brother Riley's been using one, but the other one should be free."

"Thanks." Of course, office space was really only a minor part of this. "You'll need to keep the girls away from this particular client."

That put some concern on his face. "What kind of client is this?"

"The worst kind. A person who's a celebrity only because she's a celebrity."

Lucky really didn't show any interest in this client anyway, but he probably would when she arrived tomorrow.

"Other than being with this client, you're not to let Mackenzie out of your sight. Agreed?" Lucky pressed.

"Agreed. Well, except that I'd like to go back over to the funeral home and say a proper goodbye to my grandmother."

Certainly, he couldn't deny her that. Even though he looked as if he would do anything to avoid being alone with the girls.

"All right," he finally said.

"I also left my rental car there," she added. "My suitcase is in it."

"I can have one of the ranch hands pick it up if you need it before you can make it back over to the funeral home."

So, they had worked out the immediate details, but maybe this pact wouldn't have to last long. And there were some things she could do to make sure it didn't. Like hiring some private detectives to speed up the hunt for the girls' next of kin.

"I'll call ahead to the housekeepers and tell them to get a couple of guest rooms ready. I'll also need to get another vehicle since my truck won't hold all four of us. And I need to cancel out of the rodeo I'm supposed to be leaving for in the morning." He reached for his phone but stopped when they heard the voice.

"Uh, we got a problem," Bernie called out.

"What now?" Lucky grumbled, and he hurried toward the reception area with Cassie right behind him.

Bernie wasn't in the hall where they'd left him. He was at the front door of his office, and he had a thunderstruck look on his face.

"The girls are gone," he said.

"HURRY UP," Mackenzie told her sister.

But Mia didn't listen. She was poking along, looking back over her shoulder at the lawyer's office. "Lucky was nice," Mia insisted.

Sometimes, her sister could be so dumb. "It's an act," Mackenzie said. "He's only being nice because he has to be, because he wants to get money or something."

"How'd he get money or something?" Mia asked instead of hurrying.

Mackenzie ignored her. It wouldn't be long now before the lawyer looked out and spotted them. Well, it wouldn't be long if he ever managed to finish that text he'd been pecking out on his phone. Sheez. Old people and their fat, slow fingers!

"How'd Lucky get money or something?" Mia repeated, and since she probably wouldn't shut up—or hurry—until she got an answer, Mackenzie ducked into an alley with her so they'd be off the sidewalk.

"Dixie Mae had money, stupid. Lucky and the lady doctor will probably get it if they have us. People leave that sort of stuff in wills."

She nearly said *shit* instead of *stuff,* but Dixie Mae had said it wasn't a good idea to cuss in front of little kids, that it could make them get into trouble. Dixie Mae had said that it happened to her. Since Mia was a little kid, Mackenzie had tried to cut back just in case Dixie Mae was right.

"I'm not stupid," Mia protested.

Great. Now she was about to bawl again. "I didn't mean it. Just quit asking so many questions and keep walking. Your feet don't move fast when you keep saying things."

"Where we going?" Mia asked less than two seconds later.

"Away from here. We're not staying where we're not wanted."

Of course, they hadn't been wanted in a long time, not since their grandmother had gone to heaven—and Mackenzie was sure that's where she'd gone. Maybe Dixie Mae had, too, but maybe it was a different part of heaven from where Granny Maggie had gone because Dixie Mae probably wouldn't like living with angels, nice people and shit. Plus, she wouldn't be able to smoke up there and cuss.

Mackenzie led Mia to the other end of the alley and was about to cross the street when she spotted the Spring Hill Police Department. She definitely didn't want to go in that direction, and if the lawyer had finally finished that text, he might have noticed they were missing. He could have already called the cops.

Or maybe he wouldn't call anybody at all.

Those three beep-heads—that wasn't the name Mackenzie really wanted to call them, but she was trying to think with less cussing, too—anyway, maybe the three would be glad Mia and she were gone so they wouldn't have to upset their pretty little lives.

Mackenzie waited a sec to make sure the police weren't going to come storming out of the building. No storming so far, though. But just in case that happened, she took Mia up the street and to the right, away from the police department.

She'd paid attention when Scooter had driven them in from San Antonio to Spring Hill, and there was a bus station just on the edge of town. If they could get there, she had enough money for two bus tickets to San Antonio. From there they could get to Dixie Mae's house. As big as the place was, they could hide out there until Mackenzie could come up with something better. With the cash she had stuffed in her shoe, they could get by for maybe a whole week as long as they ate just French fries.

They passed in front of the grocery store, and Mackenzie tried to keep her head down, tried not to get noticed. But people noticed all right. Probably because of her clothes. Nobody dressed like her in this hick town. Too bad she hadn't had anything else to put on. All her clothes were black.

Just ahead, Mackenzie spotted something that balled up her stomach. A cop wearing a blue uniform. And he had a gun. Jail might be better than going with Lucky and the doctor, but being locked up would probably just make Mia cry. A lot of things made her cry.

Mackenzie turned around, took a side street and tried to remember how to get to the bus station. She didn't dare stop and ask, but maybe there was a map or sign or something.

"Looking for somebody?" a man asked from behind them.

"Just walking," Mackenzie answered without even looking back at him. But he was walking now, too, and it didn't take him long to catch up with them.

Her heart jumped so high she felt it in her throat.

Because it was Lucky.

Except he'd changed clothes real fast because he was wearing a suit jacket, and he didn't have on that big rodeo buckle that had caught Mia's eye. And he was standing in front of a big building. Probably once it'd been somebody's house because it sort of looked like Dixie Mae's place, but this one had a sign on the front of it.

McCord Cattle Brokers.

Mackenzie didn't know what a cattle broker was, but McCord was Lucky's last name. Maybe it meant he owned the place.

Mackenzie thought about taking off running, but he looked fast. A lot faster than Mia would be anyway. Mackenzie could get away on her own, but there was no way she'd leave her little sister behind.

"Are you ladies, uh, girls, lost?" he asked as if he didn't even know them.

Mia looked at Mackenzie, probably for her to explain this. Maybe Lucky had got hit on the head or something and had amnesia, like what happened on the TV show that Dixie Mae watched.

"We were just headed to the bus station to meet one of our friends," Mackenzie explained.

"What happened to the bull?" Mia asked before Mackenzie had even finished the lie.

"What bull?" Lucky asked.

Yeah, amnesia all right. Or maybe he could just be pretending that he didn't know them so he wouldn't have to take them. Grown-ups played all kinds of stupid games to get out of doing things they didn't want to do.

"The shiny bull that looks like this." Mia opened her hand and showed him the silver ball she'd made from the gum wrapper.

Lucky got a funny look on his face. He also glanced around before he tipped his head to the big building. "Why don't you come in, and I'll draw you a map to show you how to get to the bus station."

Mackenzie didn't like the sound of that at all. She'd met Lucky, but he was still a stranger, and if he got her into the house, he might call the police. Or try to do something even worse.

She stepped in front of Mia. "I already told you I'll bust your face if you try to hurt my sister."

Lucky held up his hands. "Wouldn't dream of it." He mumbled something Mackenzie didn't catch. "Let me guess—you two know my twin brother, Lucky?"

Twin? Mackenzie eyed him, trying to figure out if that was true, but she didn't have time to decide because someone called out her name.

The lady doctor.

She was running toward them, and she wasn't alone. Lucky was with her. At least it was a guy wearing a shiny bull buckle. Maybe there were three of these men who looked alike.

"Why did you run off like that?" the lady doctor asked at the same time Lucky asked, "What the heck were you thinking?" Both seemed to be aiming those questions at Mackenzie.

"So, you do know my twin brother, Lucky," the other man grumbled. "Please tell me you have this, *whatever this is*, under control," he said to Lucky.

"No, I clearly don't." Lucky knelt down in front of Mia. "Are you okay?"

Mia smiled and handed him the silver ball. It was just a gum wrapper, but it also made him smile. People usually smiled around Mia. But Lucky didn't give Mackenzie a smile when he stood back up. Didn't give his twin one, either.

"Remember that letter Dixie Mae gave me?" Lucky said to him. He didn't wait for an answer. "Well, Cassie and I need to take these girls for a day or two."

"Cassie," the twin said in the same friendly way some people said hello. He didn't look angry at her, only at Lucky.

"We need to take them to your house," Cassie explained. "But they slipped out of Bernie's office while we were trying to make arrangements to get them there."

The twin glanced at all of them, like he was the boss or something. Even the boss of Lucky. He pulled Lucky aside, the way the lady doctor had at the lawyer's office.

"Are these your kids?" the twin whispered to Lucky. He probably thought he was saying it soft enough, but Mackenzie had good ears.

"We're not," Mackenzie told the question-asking twin.

But Mia must have heard it, too. "Our daddy and mommy die-did," Mia said.

"Died," Mackenzie corrected. She huffed.

The twin had actually thought they were Lucky's? No way. Of course, Lucky seemed to feel the same about them. In addition to her good ears, Mackenzie had also learned to pick up on that kind of stuff.

The boss twin studied them a few seconds longer as if trying to decide if that was true or not. Then he finally tipped his head to a fancy silver car next to the fancy building. He took some keys from his pocket and handed them to Lucky.

"Use my car," the twin told him. "I'll have somebody drop me off at home later. Good to see you again, Cassie. I'm sorry for your loss."

Lucky made an I'm-watching-you gesture with his fingers, pointing to his eyes first, then aiming those pointed fingers at Mackenzie. He stooped down when he made eye contact with Mia.

"Will you promise me you won't run off again?" he asked her.

Mia nodded. Smiled, even. "Yes, I promise."

Lucky turned to Mackenzie next. "And now I need that same promise from you."

She hated having to do what anyone said, but she wasn't in a good position here. Not with these two staring at her.

"Say it, Kenzie," Mia pressed, giving her skirt a tug.

So Mackenzie did because she knew if she didn't that Mia would just keep at it. "I won't run."

It wasn't a lie. Next time she wouldn't run. Mackenzie would somehow get a ride to the bus station or else just walk. But first chance she got, she was getting Mia and herself out of there.

CHAPTER SIX

THREE CARS AND four trucks. That's how many vehicles Lucky spotted in the large circular drive that fronted the ranch and house. Obviously, he was not going to be able to make a quiet entrance with Cassie and the girls.

"It's really big," Mia said, looking up at the place as Lucky drove closer.

Yeah, it was. Too big. Or at least it had been after his folks died and after both Anna and Riley had moved away. Of course, Lucky had moved even before that, and despite the pretty exterior, he didn't see a home, not anymore. It was just a house where he used to live with his family.

Oh, man.

He tried to push all that back down into the pit of his stomach. It would churn there, but it was better than dealing with it now. Especially when he had a crap-load of other stuff to deal with.

"You told them we were coming?" Cassie asked.

Her nerves were showing. Her mouth was tight. She was gripping her purse. Of course, the nerves likely had more to do with all the things ahead of her rather than walking into what appeared to be some kind of gathering. Things like him. Dealing with Dixie Mae's death. Their temporary custody of these kids.

But especially him.

Cassie had always had this oil/water thing when it came to him, and she wasn't going to like being under the same roof. Lucky wasn't going to like it much, either, not because she was under the same roof with him, but because he was under this roof, period.

"I told the housekeeper Della we were coming," Lucky answered.

Della and her sister, Stella, had started working for his family when Lucky was just a kid, and the pair would make sure those guest rooms were ready. Lucky just hoped that the rooms wouldn't be needed that long. Two nights max. He didn't want this drawn out. Mia and the Runaway Goth Girl had been jacked around enough and needed some place permanent to stay, and this definitely didn't qualify as permanent.

From the looks of it, Cassie had been jacked around, too.

"As soon as you're settled into your room," Cassie said to the girls, "we can talk. Would that be okay?"

Of course, Mia nodded right away. Mackenzie was practicing her "I suck lemons frequently" face. The thick makeup helped with that because it appeared to be cracking in places like meringue on a pie. It was amazing she'd perfected both the expression and the art of pancake makeup at such a young age.

"We gonna talk about Miss Dixie Mae?" Mia asked.

Cassie seemed a little surprised by that. "Would you like to talk about her?"

"Sure. I miss her. She was sparkly."

Yeah, she was, and it only reminded Lucky that he had something else on his plate: grieving for Dixie Mae. He'd planned on having a date with some hundred-proof by now to help ease his pain, but booze would apparently have to wait. Although he might need a shot to get through this next hour.

"Dixie Mae die-did," Mia said, sounding as sad about that as Lucky felt.

"Yes, she did," Cassie confirmed. Heck, she sounded sad, as well. Lucky hoped they didn't start crying, or there'd be several sets of wet eyes in the car. Mackenzie's wouldn't be one of them, he was betting. But his sure would be.

"What about you, Mackenzie?" Cassie asked. "Do you miss Dixie Mae?"

The look on her face intensified to "I suck lemons, and limes, too."

"She misses her," Mia said. "She just doesn't like to say it."

Wise words from such a little one. Too bad this package deal hadn't included only Mia because Lucky wouldn't have minded spending a day or two with her.

Okay, and maybe Cassie, as well.

That blasted attraction was still there, and he was positive now that it wasn't just gas. Too bad. Because attractions like that usually got him in trouble.

"Lady Doctor?" Mia said, reaching up to tug on Cassie's sleeve. "Will you be staying with us?"

"Yes. And call me Cassie." She stopped. "Or maybe Miss Cassie. All right, just Cassie."

It wasn't a good sign that she still seemed to be waffling about what the girls should call her considering they had some whopper obstacles in front of them. Like finding the girls' next of kin. And getting enough washcloths to remove all that makeup from Mackenzie's face.

He parked Logan's car right in front of the house. Like Logan, the Jag had too many bells and whistles, and it took Lucky several minutes—yes, minutes—to figure out how to pop the trunk to get to the luggage. However, before he could even step from the car, the front door of the house opened, and Della and Stella came out. Judging from the gleeful looks on their weathered faces, they were excited about the possibility of kids staying with them. Or maybe they were just excited about the possibility of Lucky being responsible for the kids.

Responsible for anything, for that matter.

"Cassandra Weatherall," Della greeted, pulling Cassie into

a hug. "You haven't changed a drop. Well, except you're dressing more comfortably these days. Nothing wrong with that."

Cassie frowned when she looked down at her skirt and shoes. Something she'd done several times in the past hour. Of course, her clothes were catwalk-ready compared to Mackenzie's.

"I was so sorry to hear of your grandmother's passing," Della added to Cassie. "Dixie Mae always did treat Lucky all right, so that made her all right in my book, too."

"Thank you." And Cassie repeated the process when Stella hugged her and offered her own condolences.

Lucky hadn't been aware that the housekeepers would even remember Cassie since to the best of his knowledge, Cassie had never been to the house. Still, it was Spring Hill, where everybody knew everybody.

Along with everybody's business.

By now, what had happened would be all over town—along with some embellishments to the gossip. Lucky didn't care about that gossip when it came to himself, but he doubted Cassie would appreciate it, what with her status as a celebrity therapist.

"It's about time you came home," Della said, looking at him.

That was the only scolding he got because Della turned her attention to the car's back door when it opened. She gave a big, welcoming smile when Mia stepped out. As did Stella. He could practically see the fantasy they were weaving in their heads about him, Cassie and the cute kid.

Then Mackenzie stepped out.

Della and Stella actually dropped back a little, and just as fast as their mental fantasy had come, it went. Good thing. Lucky didn't want anybody playing matchmaker here, and Della and Stella were prone to that since they often said he didn't choose wisely when it came to female companionship. Which he didn't. And he intended to keep on choosing unwisely.

"Uh, I thought you were getting sisters," Stella said. "Children sisters," she clarified.

"They are children," he assured her. He still intended to check

Mackenzie's birth certificate, though. "This is Mia Compton," Lucky said pointing to her. "And that's her sister, Mackenzie. This is Miss Della and Miss Stella. They pretty much run the place." Something they managed to do even when Logan was there.

Della recovered from the shock before Stella did, and she managed an inkling of the smile that she'd had before her eyeballs had been widened by Mackenzie's appearance. "Well, welcome to the McCord Ranch. I hope you feel right at home here." She extended that to Cassie.

Then to Lucky.

It was a nice chain-yanking kind of reminder that he should come home more often. Lucky expected to hear that a lot in the next twenty-four hours. He grumbled that he wasn't very pleased about it, but then because he knew it would make her smile, he winked at her. It worked. Stella smiled, then giggled.

"What's with all the vehicles?" Lucky asked, hauling out the girls' suitcases.

"Wedding stuff. Claire, Riley, Ethan and Livvy are here. Plus, Riley's having a meeting with the horse trainers in the office. Oh, and there are two fellas from a magazine, and they're taking some pictures and talking to Riley about an article they're doing on Logan."

The latter seemed to be a monthly occurrence, but maybe the other things were temporary. In other words, maybe they'd all be leaving soon.

"Riley is Lucky's brother," Della went on, talking to the girls now. "He's marrying Claire, and Ethan's her little boy. Claire's a wedding photographer."

Mackenzie showed no interest whatsoever, but Mia seemed to hold on to every word.

"She's got a little boy?" Mia asked.

Della nodded, tapped Mia's nose. "Cute as a button, just like you."

"Right," Mackenzie grumbled. "Because all buttons are sooooo cute."

Since that sounded like something Lucky would have said twenty years ago, he tried not to laugh.

"Oh, and Livvy's here," Della added. She glanced at Cassie. "She's Claire's business partner."

Livvy was also one of Lucky's ex-lovers, and with the side glance that Cassie gave him, it seemed she'd already picked up on that. Then again, she would probably give him a side glance because she thought he'd slept with every woman in town but her. He hadn't, but that particular gossip thread had been exaggerated at lot.

"Are they nice ladies?" Mia whispered to Lucky.

"Very nice. But they might make you eat vegetables. Is that okay?"

Mia gave it some serious thought. Nodded. But it garnered some disapproval from Big Sis. "She doesn't have to eat anything she doesn't want to eat," Mackenzie declared like gospel. "And I don't want her compared to a stupid button."

Lucky had no idea how he was supposed to respond to that, but *sounds good to me* probably wasn't the way to go here. Even though that had been his philosophy about life for a while now. Don't eat anything you don't want to eat. Don't do anything you don't want to do.

Don't be like his brothers.

It kept things simple and meshed with his smart-ass outlook on life.

Lucky braced himself for the chaos he was sure to find inside. Good thing because there was indeed chaos. The moment he stepped in, Ethan zoomed past him, running so fast that he was practically a blur, and it took Lucky a moment to realize the toddler was chasing a cat. Judging from the looks of it, it was the same cat Lucky had given him three months ago. It had grown almost as much as Ethan.

He saw Livvy next. She was teetering in needle-thin heels

on a stepladder. She was as skinny as a zipper except for those massive boobs. Today, her hair was turtle green with tiny gold star decorations scattered over her head. Most women couldn't have pulled off the look, but Livvy had the personality to pull off anything. Including his clothes.

Something that wouldn't happen again, of course.

Now that Riley and Claire were getting married, it seemed too risky to sleep with a woman so close to his brother's wife. A two-night stand was one thing, but a long relationship had a hundred percent chance of failing, and Lucky didn't want any bad blood lingering around that he'd have to face every time he came back to town.

It took Lucky a couple of seconds to spot Claire. She was holding some kind of chart-looking thing while studying the layout of the living room furniture. "I think we're going to have to move everything out of this room."

Livvy made a sound of agreement, went up another step on that ladder and clicked off some pictures with her camera phone. But there was another guy there, too, taking pictures—of Riley and one of the horse trainers—and he had a real camera, not just his phone. The man chatting with them had to be a reporter.

"Well, looky who's here," Livvy called out. "Lucky McCord, you look good enough to—"

But she froze when she saw Cassie. Maybe because Livvy thought they were together. Or maybe she stopped because of the girls. In any case, it probably wasn't a good idea for Livvy to finish saying what she thought he looked good enough to do.

"Lucky!" Claire squealed when she saw him. She hurried to him, waving her hands in the air until she reached him, and then she hugged him. "Welcome home."

Leave it to Claire to make it feel as if that welcome were marginally true. Riley was getting one in a million with Claire, and Lucky was glad his usual fool of a brother had come to his senses and seen that. Of course, Riley had had to get out of the Air Force to make all this happen, and Lucky still wasn't sure how he was dealing with that, but once he had Claire wedded, things would all fall into place.

Riley was definitely the marrying sort. Anna, too. Logan was more in the to-be-determined group. And Lucky fell into the no-way-in-hell category. At least with Riley and Anna, Della and Stella would get those "grandbabies" they were always clamoring about.

Lucky had to give it to Claire, she didn't step back or look shocked when her attention landed on the girls. She greeted them, even Mackenzie, and Cassie with the same warm smile she'd given him.

"Cassie." Claire hugged her just as Della and Stella had done. She offered her condolences, too. Since Claire had lost her own grandmother only months earlier, Lucky was sure she knew how Cassie must feel.

"Sorry about all of this," Claire said. "We'll be out of your way soon. I hope," she added when she glanced at Riley. He didn't exactly look comfortable with whatever the reporter and photographer were saying to him. "It's his first big interview."

But not his last. Lucky knew Riley had gotten sucked into Logan's hamster wheel of building McCord Cattle Brokers, making it as big as could be.

"So, when is this wedding again?" Lucky asked. Though he already knew the date. "And am I invited?" he added with his customary wink.

"Of course, you're invited. It's next month, the same day as the Founder's Day picnic. It'll be small, informal," Claire added.

"Semi-informal," Livvy corrected. "I talked Claire into doing the princess dress."

Claire made a face. "That was a compromise, but I nixed the tiara and the glass slippers."

"Nixed for now," Livvy said. "But there's plenty of time to change your mind about those. Also about the wand and hair glitter."

The look on Claire's face let Lucky know there'd be no re-considering those things.

"You gonna be a princess?" Mia asked Claire.

"For an hour or so anyway. Want to be a princess, too? You can be a princess flower girl if you want, and wear the tiara. The hair glitter and slippers, as well. Ethan's going to be a *car boy*. Instead of rose petals, he'll be dropping toy cars from a basket." Claire paused, seemed a little worried. "We'll have to work on him not throwing them at the guests, though."

"I could be a princess?" Mia pressed, sounding in awe and hopeful at the same time.

"Of course. All of you are invited," Claire added looking at Cassie and Mackenzie. "And you can be one, too," she said to Mackenzie.

"We're not staying here that long," Mackenzie grumbled.

"Oh. Well. I'm sorry to hear that. If you have a change in plans, though, the invitation stands." Claire sounded genuine about that. "And what about you?" she asked Cassie.

"I'm afraid I'll have to miss it. I'll need to be back at work as soon as we've figured everything out with the custody, but I'm sure the wedding will be lovely. I always thought Riley and you would make a great couple."

Mackenzie huffed. Why, Lucky didn't know. Maybe because she'd gone more than a minute without doing it. Sort of like a pressure cooker letting off steam, but in this case Mackenzie was letting off some surliness so that she wouldn't explode.

"She's got stars," Mia whispered to her sister. She nudged Mackenzie and pointed to Livvy.

That was Livvy's cue to pluck one from her hair. It was apparently a stick-on, and she gave it to the little girl. "It's magic," Livvy declared. "But it'll only give you one wish so use it wisely."

Mia looked as if she'd just been handed a miracle, one that she'd have to give a lot of thought.

"I like your shoes," Mackenzie said to Livvy. And she actually sounded, well, human. Human enough to be envious anyway.

"These?" Livvy pranced around like a ballerina. "Want to try them on?"

Mackenzie hesitated. Nodded. But then shook her head, probably because she sounded interested, which would have been equal in her mind to committing manslaughter. "No thanks."

Livvy made a suit-yourself sound. "I buy them online, and I'll give you the website." She plucked another gold star from her hair. She offered it to Mackenzie, but the girl only shook her head.

"I don't believe in magic," Mackenzie declared.

"Too bad. Because magic's how I got these." Livvy glanced down at her massive boobs. Then at Mackenzie's rather flat chest.

Mackenzie didn't take the gold star, so Livvy stuck it in the girl's spiky black hair. Livvy looked at Cassie next. No offer of a gold star, but she did extend her hand for Cassie to shake.

"I'm Livvy Larimer, and I've seen you on TV," she said. "All those hot celebrities. Would love to get you drunk and see what kind of secrets you'd share."

"No secrets," Cassie assured her. Now Cassie's gaze drifted to Lucky. Perhaps she was implying that extended to Lucky himself, but Livvy didn't seem to be buying it. Livvy gave him a thumbs-up, apparently approving of a choice that Livvy thought he'd made. A choice to get in Cassie's pants.

Cassie glanced down at Livvy's shoes. "Though I would like the website for those."

"Sure. Of course. I'll email the link to Lucky and he can give it to you."

Great. Now he was involved in the fuck-me-heels buying loop. A loop and link he'd never share with Cassie.

Thankfully, Della saved the day. "I'll show the girls to their rooms," she offered.

"We'll go with you," Lucky said at the same time Cassie said, "I'll go, too."

Mackenzie rolled her eyes because she no doubt knew this was about the running-away thing, and she took both her and Mia's suitcases from him. "You can't babysit me all the time," Mackenzie grumbled, and she made it sound like a threat.

Lucky made a mental note to make sure someone did indeed watch her 24/7.

"You can spend some more time with your family and friend," Cassie said to him. "I'll go up with Della and the girls. I need to make a phone call anyway, and maybe I can do that in the guest room."

All of that sounded, well, like something a visitor might say, but there was something wrong. Something other than the obvious. But Lucky couldn't quite put his finger on it.

While Della led the three of them—Mia, Mackenzie and Cassie—up the stairs, Lucky was about to say goodbye to Claire and Livvy and head toward his own room just off the hall. But he didn't get far because someone else called out his name.

Riley.

His brother stepped away from the others and went to him. Livvy and Claire must have realized a brother talk was about to happen because they suddenly got very busy with a discussion of where to move the furniture. Riveting stuff, apparently, judging from the speed at which the women moved away from him.

"Am I about to get lectured?" Lucky asked Riley right off.

"Not by me. Maybe by Della or Stella, though. By now they've probably figured out this doesn't mean you're settling down and moving back home."

Probably. Of course, the pair would just come up with another dream of marrying him off. Hard to do that, though, whenever they went by his bed and saw the saddle he kept there. Lucky didn't actually use the saddle, didn't bring his lovers to the house, either. For that matter, he didn't sleep in the bed much at all but he liked to keep the saddle there as a reminder to Della and Stella that he wasn't into conventionality.

"You don't seem surprised by any of this," Lucky said.

Riley shrugged. "When I heard Dixie Mae had left you a letter, I figured something was up. I was thinking you were getting the cats, though. Word around town is that she had a dozen or more."

"Just six. And no, Mason-Dixon got those." Lucky was the one shrugging now. "Cassie might end up with them, though, before the dust settles."

Which made him wonder why Dixie Mae had left them to her son in the first place. Certainly she must have known he wouldn't keep them. Maybe this was like leaving a nickel tip to a bad waiter? Mason-Dixon would know she hadn't forgotten him but had simply not been pleased with the sour direction their relationship had taken. Still, it was a crappy thing to do.

The photographer walked closer, his attention on his camera, and he held up one of the screenshots for Riley to see.

"I think that's the photo we'll use for the magazine," the photographer said. "We can put you side by side with the shots that we've already taken of your brother. That'll be the cover."

"Cover?" And yeah, Lucky put some smart-ass attitude on that.

It earned him a jab on the arm from Riley's elbow. "It's good for business." And he nodded to the photographer. "Thanks."

"Are you okay with all of this?" Lucky asked him when the photographer stepped away. Both the reporter and he started packing up to leave.

"Yes. I am. Surprised?

"A little." A lot. Just months ago Riley had feared that working the family business would make him ordinary. That he would be selling out, even. Clearly, that had changed. "Having Claire has probably made things a little sweeter."

Riley looked in his fiancée's direction. Smiled. Yeah, nothing ordinary about that look on his brother's face. The look extended to Ethan when the boy zoomed through the room again in pursuit of the cat. He had a gold star in his hair, too. No doubt a magic gift from Livvy.

If Lucky thought for a second they actually worked, he'd ask for one for himself.

"Definitely. Claire has made everything sweeter," Riley said. "And Ethan. He's a good kid." Riley's gaze drifted toward the stairs. "How about them? Are they good k-kids?" He stuttered on the last word. Or maybe he choked.

Since it was pretty much the same reaction Lucky had had when he first saw them, he couldn't fault his brother. "I'm pretty sure Mia is. I'm not sure about the older one, Mackenzie."

Riley made a sound of agreement. "Mackenzie reminds me of you."

"Me?" Riley couldn't have surprised him more if he'd hit Lucky with a magic wand. "I never dressed like that."

"Same attitude. Except you winked and smiled more than I bet Mackenzie does."

It would be hard to wink with all that mascara. Her eyelids might permanently stick together.

"I'm nothing like her." Lucky shook his head. "Too bad, though, because if I were I might know what to do. At this point about the best I can hope for is that she continues to mope and doesn't do anything stupid." And Lucky knew a little about stupid because he'd managed to do some stupid things in his life.

That still didn't mean Mackenzie and he were anything alike. Heck, she probably wasn't even good at spelling.

Riley gave him a pat on the back. Unlike with Logan, Riley gave him two. It also didn't feel as if Riley couldn't wait to get off to some appointment and therefore get away from him.

"You'll do okay," Riley assured him. "Kids are a lot tougher than they look. Besides, it's just for the night, right?"

"Maybe two. Bernie's looking for their next of kin."

Riley made another sound, not of agreement this time, and even though he didn't explain the sound, Lucky knew what it meant. In fact, he could have an entire conversation with himself about it, but the bottom line was this—Why hadn't the next of kin already come forward? According to Bernie, Dixie Mae had had the girls for a couple of months after their grandmother passed. Certainly, Dixie Mae had searched for their next of kin. Lucky hoped Bernie had better luck than Dixie Mae.

"The girls might end up in foster care," Lucky had to admit. That'd been a hard enough pill to swallow before he'd met Mia. Now it was like swallowing a pregnant elephant.

Another sound from Riley, also not one of agreement. "I'll ask around and see if anyone in town is looking at adoption."

"Thanks." And Lucky meant that. However, it did feel as if he was trying to get out of this guardianship deal ASAP.

Which he was.

The less time he was with the girls, the less chance there was of screwing this up. It was okay when he screwed up his own life—that had become the norm for him—but it was a different thing for that to spill over to two kids who obviously needed a heck of a lot more than he could give them.

Lucky heard the footsteps on the stairs, and he turned to see Mia making her way toward them. Not poking along, either. She was running.

"Come quick, Mr. Lucky," Mia insisted. "It's Miss Cassie. I think she's about to die-did."

CHAPTER SEVEN

OH, GOD. THE BEARS were back, and judging from the way Cassie's heart was thudding in her chest, they had brought along some friends.

Cassie opened her purse. Or rather she attempted to. Her hands were already shaking too hard, and all the shaking caused her to drop it. The contents, including the bottle of meds, scattered across the floor of the guest room. She'd left the door open just in case Della had a question about the girls. It had seemed a good idea at the time, but that open door meant anyone could see her losing this fight with the bears.

And someone did.

Mia.

She appeared in the doorway of Cassie's room. Cassie shook her head, trying to tell the little girl that everything was all right, but the only thing that came out of her mouth was hot air. Literally. Heaven knew how bad she must have looked and sounded to Mia because the little girl took off. Maybe running for cover rather than running for help. Cassie didn't want help.

She crawled across the floor, her spotty vision nailed to that amber bottle of meds. The bears got in the way, of course, blurring her vision even more and thinning her breath to the point she thought she might pass out. Heck, passing out would be a relief right now. And unavoidable, she quickly realized. When you couldn't breathe, you passed out.

The world just floated away from her.

But not for long.

"Cassie?" Lucky said. He tapped her cheeks. Then he shook her. "Call an ambulance."

That got through the bear fuzz in her head just fine, and Cassie forced open her eyes. "No ambulance. I'm fine."

Considering she was sprawled out on the floor, it was no wonder Lucky gave her a skeptical look. But thankfully Mia and Della, who were in the doorway, didn't jump to call that ambulance he'd requested. This was already bad enough without word spreading around town, and if an ambulance came, it'd be all over the state, perhaps the entire country, before she even got to the hospital.

Cassie maneuvered herself into a sitting position. Pulled down her skirt when she realized her panties were showing. It was a true testament to how concerned Lucky was about her that he didn't even seem to notice that. Or maybe compared to the gold-starred, busty Livvy, she wasn't even worthy of a notice.

Which was a good thing, Cassie assured herself.

"I'm fine, really," she repeated when the trio just kept staring at her.

Soon, though, it wasn't just a trio. It was an octet. Lucky, Mia, Mackenzie, Della, Stella, Claire, Riley and Livvy. The woman who'd almost certainly been Lucky's lover. The fact that Cassie would remember that was an unwelcome thought.

It meant she'd given way too much thought to Lucky's love life.

And it wasn't as if she didn't have her own life to think about. Especially right now. Somehow, Cassie had to convince the octet that she hadn't gone bat-shit crazy. While she was at it, maybe she could convince herself of that, too.

"I usually wear much better shoes than this," Cassie said.

All right. That wasn't going to convince anyone of her san-ity. But she did own some beautiful heels. Nothing like those stilts that Livvy was wearing, but still nice ones, in fashionable styles and colors. She had a pair in teal for heaven's sake.

"Uh, you want that ambulance now?" Lucky asked her.

"No." Cassie couldn't say that fast enough. She considered lying and saying she'd had an epileptic seizure. People usually seemed more open to that. Not so much to panic attacks, though, especially ones coupled with chatter about shoe choices. "I just need a minute."

Cassie didn't say she wanted that minute to be solo, but Lucky seemed to pick up on that. He stood, motioned for everyone to leave the room.

"Please keep your eyes on them," he said to Della and Stella while motioning to the girls.

And Lucky shut the door. What he didn't do was go into the hall with them. He stayed right there in the room with Cassie. Not only that, he picked up her medicine bottle, handed it to her and sank down on the floor next to her.

Breathe in, breathe out, she reminded herself.

In doing so, she took in Lucky's scent. That didn't help.

Cassie also added some nonsense sayings like, *Take it one second at a time and you'll get through this.* Of course, she had to take it one second at a time. She couldn't time travel and take it from a second at a time to a minute at a time. And as for the getting through this—of course, she would.

It just didn't feel like it at the moment.

"Panic attack?" Lucky asked.

Cassie wasn't sure if she'd actually used the words *panic attack* when she was prone on the floor or if it was just a good guess on his part.

"One of my ex-girlfriends used to have them," he explained. So not really a guess after all. "It happened every time she... Never mind."

Maybe it was because she wanted to focus on something else, anything else, but Cassie latched right on to his "never mind."

"Did it happen during sex?"

"Uh, no. It happened during bad weather, especially lightning strikes. Why would you think it would have anything to do with sex?" But he waved that off. "You think the only thing I do is have sex. Well, it's been three months. Satisfied?"

He looked as thunderstruck at having admitted that as Cassie had at her shoes revelation. Of course, Cassie probably looked thunderstruck, too. Heck, why had she brought up anything like that with Lucky?

"Why would you think I'd be satisfied over the fact that you've been without sex for a quarter of a year?" Cassie hadn't intended to ask that question aloud, but what with the breathe mantra and the other stuff whirling around in her head, it had just slipped out.

Lucky lifted his shoulder. "Some people like to think of me being brought down a notch or two."

"Not me." She hadn't intended to say that, either. Especially not in a breathy voice. It sounded like some kind of invitation for him to do something about that dry spell. With her.

Cassie took a pill while she waited for him to question her about that breathy invitation. He didn't, though.

"So, how did your ex get through a panic attack?" she asked.

He smiled. It was what the girls in high school had called his pantie-dropping smile. Thankfully, she was immune to it.

"Sex," he answered.

"Of course." What else? He probably used it as a cure for all sorts of things, but apparently he hadn't needed such a cure in the past three months.

"Sex wouldn't work for me," she assured him.

He made a sound that could have meant anything. Or a sound that meant he didn't buy that for a second.

"Since I'd like to stop you from having any more panic attacks without the use of my man parts," he said, "why don't you tell me what triggers them?"

The last question was easy to answer. "Stress triggers them."

And memories. But it was the stress brought on by the memories that flipped her switch and sent her from being Cassandra Weatherall, therapist, to an asthmatic-sounding woman sitting on the floor with a bad-boy bull rider.

"Stress, huh?" He scrubbed his hand over his face. "Well, you don't have much of that right now, do you?" He nudged her arm. Winked.

There it was. The bra-dropping wink. It was an example of the charm that'd coaxed many women into bed. Onto floors, too, probably. And up against walls. It was a lethal combo, with that smile, his looks and that scent. He must be wearing some kind of pheromone aftershave.

"We'll get all of this worked out," he went on. "The girls will land in a good home, and we'll both go back to doing whatever we normally do."

The first two parts of that were the absolute right things to say. The last part not so much. Cassie wasn't sure she could go back to what she'd normally been doing. Not without it triggering more of these bear attacks anyway.

"Don't tell anyone about the panic attack please," she said.

"I won't," he agreed, "but that doesn't mean it won't get around."

Yes, even without an ambulance ride, that was possible. Likely, even. All it took was a slip of the tongue, and there were plenty of tongues that could slip since the octet had seen her at her worst.

"I know it sounds silly," Cassie went on, "but I have this image I have to keep so I don't want people to know I get like this."

Lucky looked at her. "What kind of image?"

"Someone not on the floor having a panic attack." And someone who didn't talk about having a panic attack. Or about shoes. Cassie groaned. "I have to get myself together. That client's coming in tomorrow. Plus, the girls. And I need to go to the funeral home."

All those things were true, but Cassie left off one big item. The main reason that she was actually having panic attacks. No way could she tell Lucky about that.

"I can stay with the girls while you go to the funeral home," he said.

It was a huge offer, and they both knew it. The kids terrified him as much as they did her. "Why are you being so nice to me?"

Lucky slipped his arm around her. "We both lost Dixie Mae. So did the girls."

Cassie made the mistake of turning her head to look at him, and since they were sitting side by side, that meant their mouths were way too close. And Lucky noticed, too. He glanced at her mouth. Then it became more than a glance. It became a lingering look.

It became a mental kiss.

Oh, mercy. She felt it, too, all the way to her toes. And it didn't help with the remnants of the panic attack. She was losing some of that breath she'd just started to gather.

Cassie stood and started gathering the things that had fallen out of her purse. "I'm okay now," she lied. "Just give me another minute to make that call to a PI I know, and then I'll join you and the others downstairs."

Lucky got up from the floor as well, and he did it without taking his eyes off her. For a moment she didn't think he was going to leave, but he finally started for the door. But there was a knock before he even reached it. A very soft knock. When Lucky opened it, she saw Mia standing there.

"Did Miss Cassie die-did?" she asked. She now had the gold star stuck in her hair.

"No, sweetheart. I'm fine." Cassie went closer to show her, and she reminded herself to smile.

Mia studied her face but didn't look totally convinced she was telling the truth. Still, she took Cassie's hand and dropped something into it. A piece of a cookie. She gave another piece to Lucky.

"Ethan gave it to me," Mia explained. "But you might wanna eat it later because I'm supposed to tell you that you gotta come downstairs now because we got some trouble."

"What happened?" Cassie asked, but she didn't wait for an answer. Good grief, had Mackenzie run away again?

Lucky no doubt thought the same thing because he hurried after her, but when Cassie reached the bottom of the stairs, she saw Mackenzie right away. The girl hadn't run after all.

Then Cassie saw the *trouble*.

A cop. One she recognized. Deputy Davy Divine. She'd known him in high school, and he hadn't changed a bit. Still very thin. Still very much resembling his nickname of Davy Dweeb.

"10-23," Davy said to whoever was on the other end of the walkie-talkie he had in his left hand. "That means I arrived at the residence of the perp," he clarified for them, though no one asked him for that information. The person on the end of the line didn't respond, either.

"Cassie," Davy said, adding a crisp nod. "Lucky." Davy was holding a pair of handcuffs. "I'm here to arrest one Mackenzie Compton."

"You're not arresting anybody," Riley insisted. Lucky echoed the same when he stepped in front of Mackenzie.

Davy tapped his badge, one that Cassie was certain he polished daily if not more often. Some people were just born to be cops. Sadly, Davy wasn't one of those people, but the badge gave him some of the respect that he'd never gotten in school. At least he seemed to think so.

"Why are you here?" Lucky asked Davy.

"I already said—to arrest her." He used the cuffs to point at Mackenzie. "She committed a 211."

This time someone did ask what the heck that was. "Robbery," Davy said as if the answer were obvious.

It wasn't. They all just stared at the deputy.

"She stole money from Wilhelmina Larkin's purse," Davy added.

All of them turned to Mackenzie, but the girl just shrugged. Definitely not a denial of guilt.

"Did you take the money?" Lucky asked her.

Another shrug. And Mackenzie suddenly got very interested in staring at the floor.

"Of course she stole it. Wilhelmina said she left her purse under her desk when she went out for her break, and that the only people in the room were these two." Davy pointed to Mia and Mackenzie. "Wilhelmina's pretty sure she's the one who took it." This time, he only pointed to Mackenzie.

"Did you take the money?" Lucky repeated to her.

"Of course she did." Davy, again. "Wilhelmina said she's missing five twenty-dollar bills, and that I'll know it's her money because there are red devil horns on the corners of the bills."

All of them turned from staring at Mackenzie to staring at Davy.

"The bills are her alimony payment from her ex, Tommy," the deputy explained, "and he always pays her in cash, always draws horns on the twenties with a magic marker. Sometimes, he writes voodoo curses on them, but she said he didn't do that this time. That he just drew the horns."

And here Cassie thought *she* had a complicated relationship. A relationship that Lucky likely didn't know about. She should probably mention it to him in case someone blabbered about it before she got a chance to explain.

Since Mackenzie hadn't answered Lucky, Cassie decided to give it a try. She was about to ask again if she'd taken the money, but then Cassie remembered the girl's reaction to Livvy offering to let her try on those heels. Mackenzie had wanted to do it, Cassie had seen that in her eyes, but she'd declined.

"Is the money in your shoes?" Cassie asked.

Silence.

All except for a huff from Davy. "I have the right to search her," he insisted.

"No, you don't," Lucky insisted right back. "She's a minor, and besides, Mackenzie's going to give back the money. Aren't you?" he added through clenched teeth.

The next couple of seconds crawled by. Finally, Mackenzie mumbled some profanity and pulled the money from her right shoe. All five twenties did indeed have devil horns on them. Devils, too. Apparently, Tommy Larkin had spent some time preparing his alimony payment.

Davy put away the handcuffs so he could put on a pair of latex gloves before he took the money and counted it. Twice. Then he put the bills in a plastic evidence bag that he'd taken from his pocket.

"I still have to arrest her," Davy insisted. He shoved the bag and gloves back in his pocket so he could take out the cuffs again.

"You're not taking a thirteen-year-old to jail," Cassie insisted.

Davy just stared at her in disbelief. "If she's thirteen, I'm a camel."

"Then you're a camel," Lucky said, his voice flat.

Livvy mumbled something much worse—"You're a dick-weed." Cassie agreed with her but hoped the girls hadn't heard that. Claire apparently had because she pulled her business partner aside.

"Duckweed," Claire whispered, tipping her head to Mia, then to Ethan, who had apparently finished his cat-chasing adventure and was now falling asleep on the floor.

Livvy nodded, apparently agreeing with the kid-friendly word substitute.

Davy volleyed glances between Mackenzie and the cuffs. "I can arrest minors," he said.

Livvy was about to say something else, but Claire took hold of her arm and moved her away.

Mia stepped forward, maneuvering her way through the group to get to the deputy. She plucked the gold star from her hair and offered it to Davy. "It's magic, and I want to use my one wish so that my sister don't have to go to jail."

Oh, mercy. Could the child get any sweeter? It was as if she'd sucked up all the sweetness from Mackenzie, who wasn't doing anything remotely sweet at the moment. She was glaring at all of them.

Of course, later Cassie would need to clarify to Mia that there was no such thing as magic. She didn't want Mia trying to use that gold star to get out of a serious situation, only to learn the hard way that it was just a piece of foiled plastic with a sticky back and came in packets of a hundred.

Davy did more of those volleyed glances at all of them, obviously not sure what to do about that. But Lucky did.

Lucky knelt down to face Mia. "Save your magic star for something else," Lucky told her with a smile, but he wasn't smiling when he stood again and turned to Davy. "Here's how this will work. You will return that money to Wilhelmina, and I'll call her and explain that this will never happen again."

Davy shook his head. "Wilhelmina's pretty upset."

"Then I'll go see her," Lucky snapped.

Davy still shook his head. "She was really upset." In Davy's world *really* was clearly a step up from *pretty*.

"Then I'll go see Wilhelmina *now*," Lucky amended. He took hold of Davy's arm, leading him out the door. "Watch the girls," he added over his shoulder to no one in particular. He also took the time to fire off one last scowl to Mackenzie. "And watch Cassie." Again said to no one in particular.

Cassie wanted to tell him that she didn't need watching, but that would have required her to talk about the panic attack. No way did she want to discuss that.

"You need help?" Riley called out to his brother.

Lucky shook his head. "I'll be back as soon as I smooth things over with Wilhelmina."

Cassie figured that would require him to semipimp himself with some flirting and winking. Perhaps even a coffee date. She wasn't usually in favor of that sort of thing, but she couldn't see much benefit in Mackenzie being hauled off to jail. Although it would keep her from running away. Still, Mackenzie didn't need that kind of trauma in her life and neither did Mia.

Davy reached his cruiser, and he aimed his parting comment at Cassie. "If Lucky's silver tongue turns out to be brass, I'll be back. And none of you will stop me from making that arrest."

He drove off with Livvy's shout coming through even over the sound of the car engine. "Duckweed!"

LOGAN SIPPED HIS whiskey and stared out the bay window of his suite. Definitely not his usual view from his town loft. Or at least it hadn't been for a long time now. But since this had been his childhood room, it was a view he knew well.

The pastures, the barns and the white fences to contain it all. Since the place had been his father's design, everything was aligned just the way it should be. The pastures had even been leveled out so that the fences were in a perfectly straight line. No dips or peaks. His father hadn't been a fan of the rolling-hills effect.

There was something reassuring about that. Everything in its place. Too bad Logan couldn't do that with the family.

If his dad were alive, he would have said Logan had failed. And he had.

Riley was back now, and happy—to Logan that was equally important, though his dad would have been content with him just being back. Anna would soon return, once she'd finished her degree and her fiancé finished his military commitment. And Anna would get married and continue with the next generation of McCords. So would Riley. A generation to build on what their father had started thirty-five years ago.

That left Lucky.

Logan's biggest failure.

His twin brother was filled with anger, and Logan hadn't been able to do anything about it. The more Logan pushed, the more Lucky backed away, and when he didn't push, Lucky kept backing further away anyway.

Keep the family together.

That was one of the last things his father had said to him. Logan had been nineteen and had come home from college for reasons he couldn't remember. It had been an ordinary conversation, one he'd had with his dad countless times since he was more likely to listen than Lucky was. However, Logan hadn't known that it would be their last—that less than twelve hours later both his parents would be dead from a car accident. One that could have been prevented.

But that was an old scabbed wound that he didn't want to pick at tonight.

Still, he couldn't push it completely aside. His father had told him to keep the family together. Maybe because he'd had a premonition about his death, maybe because he was feeling down about Lucky and him going off to college. Either way, those words had become Logan's fuel.

And the source of plenty of sleepless nights.

Probably the source of the migraines he'd been having, too. That also was a different problem for a different day. As long as a migraine wasn't chasing him right now, he could put it out of his mind. But he couldn't do that with family. It was always there, always on the front burner, right where his father had put it.

If he couldn't draw Lucky back into the family with work, then he needed to find another angle, because losing his brother wasn't an option. That was the problem with a mandate from a father who was now dead. The mandate couldn't be changed, and Logan was as stuck with it as the rest of his siblings were.

"Are you ever coming to bed?" Helene asked.

Thanks to the moonlight spilling through the window, Logan had no trouble seeing his longtime girlfriend, Helene Langford.

Her long blond hair, spilling onto her creamy white shoulders. Her smile. The way she touched her tongue to her top lip when she looked at him.

She was naked, but she had the white sheet clutched to her midsection. Her long bare legs were on top of the cover. Her head was tilted to the side as she studied him. All in all, a beautiful sight.

Perfect.

Everything aligned as it should be, and he wasn't just talking about her face and body. Helene was the perfect woman for him, right down to her double degrees in business and interior design. She could make things pretty and organized, just the way he liked them.

They'd been together for eight years now. Since Logan's twenty-fifth birthday when Anna had set them up on a date. Soon, he'd propose, and they could start on their own next generation of McCords. First, though, Logan had to make sure everything was in place.

"I mean, are you coming to bed to sleep?" Helene clarified, smiling. Because he'd already been in bed with her but had gotten up after they'd had sex.

"Soon. I'm waiting on an email from the PI."

"Another one? You've been exchanging emails with him all night."

Yes, and he might have to exchange even more tomorrow and the day after. "The PI's still doing the background checks on this situation."

No need to explain what that situation was. Helene was well aware of this custody mess Dixie Mae had dumped on Lucky and Cassie.

"Any red flags yet?" Helene asked.

The whole thing was a red flag as far as Logan was concerned. Still, he knew what she meant. "Dixie Mae did have temporary guardianship of the girls prior to her death. The girls' grandmother had her lawyer do the paperwork, and it all looks legit to the PI."

"But?"

Logan had to shrug. "There might not be any buts. If this is some kind of scam, the PI isn't finding the angle."

"What about Cassie's father?" Helene asked. "Mason-Dixon could have orchestrated this."

He nodded. Definitely. "The PI hasn't found any connection between Mason-Dixon and the girls. No connection between him and their parents, either. Their dad died the same year the younger one was born. Accidental drowning. He was drunk and drove his truck off a bridge."

"So, not father-of-the-year material," Helene mumbled.

That was only the tip of the iceberg when it came to the man's father-of-the-year status. He'd had several other arrests, most involving alcohol or theft, and he'd never paid a dime of child support.

"And their mother?" Helene asked.

"Not mother-of-the-year material, either. Gracie Compton. She died of a drug overdose last year. That's how her mother ended up with custody."

Of course, that hadn't lasted long because the grandmother had then died from cancer. The girls had really been through hell in their short lives, and while Logan wasn't untouched by that, he also didn't want someone using this situation as a chance to scam them or his brother.

Helene patted the spot beside her. "Come to bed," she insisted. "And if you do, I'll make sure to work extra hours to finish the renovation on the loft so we can get back into our own bed by next week. I'll work some extra hours on the Founder's Day picnic, too."

She was already working extra hours. Because that's what Helene did. She worked as many hours as Logan did, maybe more, and her only downtime seemed to be the Friday and Saturday nights she spent with him—in their bed.

Well, a bed that she'd picked out anyway.

Actually, six years ago Helene had picked out everything in the loft when he'd first had it repurposed from guest rooms to his private suite. Since the company offices were on the ground and second floors of the Victorian house, it had made sense for him to have a place to sleep there, too. It wasn't home exactly, but it was better than being alone in the empty place.

Too many memories here. And those memories seemed to come tapping on his shoulder whenever he stayed the night.

But for now, Helene was doing the *tapping*. She patted the bed again and gave him a look he had no trouble interpreting—Did he want seconds?

He sure did, and Logan was headed in that direction when his phone dinged. It was the email from the PI, and hopefully this would be the last report on the matter of the guardianship issue. However, it wasn't the girls' name or even Dixie Mae's on the background check from the PI.

It was Cassie's.

Logan had asked for any and all information, and the PI must have thought that included Cassie. He thumbed through it, not expecting to see anything that would surprise him.

He was wrong.

Logan did see something.

Hell.

CHAPTER EIGHT

LUCKY WASN'T EVEN sure sleep would help. He thought he might be past the point of return on that. Every muscle in his body, especially his butt, was aching, but all that was a drop in the muscle-aching bucket when it came to his head.

Oh, man.

He needed a handful of aspirin and a faster solution to this whole temporary-custody situation.

Of course, sleeping in the hall on the floor hadn't helped, but it'd been necessary to make sure Mackenzie didn't try to go on the run again. Lucky had gotten especially suspicious that she might try that when she'd insisted on Mia and her sharing a room. And when Mackenzie had asked for an umbrella when it had started to rain. Lucky had made sure all the doors were locked up. And the umbrellas. But for insurance, he'd slept outside their room.

Outside Cassie's, too, since hers was right next to the girls'.

Cassie had agreed to stay at the window all night to make sure Mackenzie didn't try to slip out and shimmy down the gutter. Which meant Cassie, like Lucky, was getting little to no sleep.

This was not a situation of misery loving company, though. Lucky didn't want a repeat of Cassie's panic attack so he hoped she'd managed to get in at least a couple of catnaps. In case she had, he'd stayed right next to the girls' door so he could hear if there was any moving around in there.

He hadn't heard anything, thank goodness.

That was one thing off his list. Make that two. The day before, it'd taken Lucky hours of talking to fix the problem with Wilhelmina—and the promise to take her for a drink at Calhoun's Pub. Only then had she agreed to drop the charges against Mackenzie. However, dropping those charges was contingent on one more thing.

Mackenzie's apology.

Thankfully, Wilhelmina hadn't required that apology to be face-to-face. Probably because the woman was a little afraid of Mackenzie, but that meant Mackenzie would have to write it, and Lucky would have to deliver it personally to Wilhelmina. Lucky only hoped Mackenzie could write a convincing apology. Again, he was stereotyping here, but she didn't look like star-pupil material.

Lucky had given Mackenzie until morning to produce the apology. Whether she would do it was anyone's guess, and he was too tired to guess anyway. If she didn't do it, he might have to teach her a really bad lesson and let Davy arrest her. For a couple of minutes anyway.

He heard footsteps on the stairs. Smelled coffee. And even though it was Logan approaching him with a cup in each hand, Lucky didn't even mind an early-morning encounter with his brother if it meant one of those cups was for him.

Both were.

Logan handed him the two cups and sank down on the floor next to him. His brother was already dressed for work in his jeans, cowboy boots and dress coat. He probably wasn't taking any pictures for magazine covers today, but he looked ready for a photo op.

"Anything I can do to help you resolve this?" Logan asked.

Lucky didn't doubt it was a genuine offer. The coffee proved that it was. But Lucky was never sure what Logan's motives were. For Logan, it was all about the family business. That was his bottom line. And somewhere along the way, Logan had forgotten about the family part of family business.

Of course, Lucky was no better.

It was a cow-eat-cow world when it came to McCord Cattle Brokers and the McCord brothers.

But Lucky got the feeling that Logan's offer had more to do with avoiding bad publicity. It had to be all over town now about Mackenzie stealing that money, and the embellished amount was probably in the thousands—and might include diamond jewelry. Maybe even a black-market kidney.

People in Spring Hill had good imaginations when it came to gossip.

"If the girls are going to be here much longer, I'd look into getting a security system," Lucky grumbled. Though it was the first time he'd ever considered it. Unlike gossip, the crime rate in Spring Hill wasn't anything to worry about.

"I could arrange something temporary," Logan suggested.

Even something temporary would take time to install, and Lucky preferred the energy to be spent on finding the girls' next of kin. "Thanks, but no. What would help, though, is some aspirin for this headache," Lucky said. "Got any?"

Logan fished through his pocket and came up with a bottle of meds. Not aspirin, though. This was prescription stuff. Logan took out one of the pills and handed it to him. Lucky washed it down with the coffee.

"Should I ask why you have headache meds like this?" Lucky threw out there.

"No. And I won't ask you if you plan to keep your hands, and other parts of yourself, off Cassie."

Lucky made a face. "Why would you care what happens between Cassie and me?"

Logan didn't answer. He took out something else from his pocket. Not his meds this time but rather a folded piece of paper. "Last night I had background checks run on the girls so I could help look for any of their relatives. I also had checks run on Dixie Mae and Cassie, just to make sure there wasn't anything…out of place."

Uh-oh. Lucky had heard Logan use that term before. *Out of place*. It meant he was digging for dirt.

"And before you start lecturing me about their privacy and such," Logan continued, "I just wanted to make sure these girls weren't part of some kind of scam. That maybe there wasn't someone out there using them to get anyone's money. Yours, Cassie's or Dixie Mae's."

Since Lucky had already opened his mouth to lecture him, he closed it. Because Logan was right. It was something he should have already checked on. Dixie Mae had a good BS meter, but that didn't mean she couldn't have been duped and then unknowingly passed that duping onto Cassie and him.

"The girls are legit," Logan went on. "It was just as Bernie told you. Both their parents are dead. Grandparents, too, and that's why they'd been staying with Dixie Mae and then Scooter. But according to one of the late grandmother's neighbors, there's an aunt, the mother's half sister, who I'm trying to track down. The neighbor didn't know the half sister's full name, but her first name is Alice."

An aunt. That was definitely a close enough blood relative. Lucky had figured they might have to resort to looking for distant cousins.

"The girls never mentioned an aunt," Lucky said.

"Because I doubt they know about her. Neither did Dixie Mae. That's why the custody agreement reads as it does. She wanted the girls to go to a suitable relative, if one could be found. If not, they're to remain with Cassie and you. But this aunt could be the fix to all of this."

"Thanks." Lucky paused. He apparently wasn't the only one who hadn't gotten any sleep. Neither Logan nor the person he'd paid to do these checks had, either. "But what does all of this have to do with me staying away from Cassie?"

Logan tipped his head to the paper.

Lucky wasn't sure he wanted to know what was there, and he didn't get a chance to read it. That's because Cassie's door opened, and she came out into the hall with them. Logan immediately took one of the cups of coffee from Lucky and handed it to her. He also glanced at the paper that he'd given Lucky, and even though Logan didn't say a word about it, Lucky got a clear signal—don't let Cassie see that yet.

Cassie had a big sip of the coffee, as if it were the cure for everything, and it was only after she had several more sips that she mumbled a "Thank you."

"A reporter from LA called the local newspaper," Logan told her. "He talked to Marlene Holland and was asking questions about you."

Cassie didn't seem especially surprised about that. She just sighed. "What did he want?"

"I think he was sniffing for a story, that's all, but Marlene did say he wanted to know about the girls. She didn't have any facts to give him, but he wanted her to call him if she learned anything."

Cassie didn't ask how a reporter hundreds of miles away would have found out about their custody situation. Probably because she was aware of how fast and far gossip traveled. Added to the fact that Cassie was a celebrity of sorts, and it would make a juicy story if the LA press picked up on the fact that she was a temporary guardian to someone who looked and dressed like Mackenzie.

"I instructed Marlene to call me if the reporter contacts her again," Logan added. "I think this guy's running background checks on all of us. Someone is anyway, and I need to find out who." He glanced at his watch, stood. "I have to leave for work, but if I hear anything more about the girls' aunt, I'll let you know."

"Aunt?" Cassie said, looking at the paper. "Did Logan find something?"

Evidently, but Lucky didn't want to share what was on that paper until he'd had a chance to read it. "Logan's looking for their mother's half sister." And Lucky had no doubts that he'd find her.

As long as Mackenzie was in the house, there was potential for bad press, something that Logan would want to avoid. For once, though, Lucky was glad his and his brother's agendas meshed.

"Good." Cassie had more coffee, and since her attention kept going to the paper, Lucky stuffed it in his jeans pocket.

Out of sight, however, didn't mean out of mind, since Cassie's gaze just went in that direction. Which meant it went in the direction of his crotch. She quickly looked away, but not before it got Lucky to thinking.

Why would Logan warn him about getting involved with Cassie?

And why did that warning only make him want to get involved with her even more? Because he was stupid, that's why. Of course, he hadn't needed a warning to make him remember the attraction.

Not with the attraction sitting right next to him.

Even though Cassie probably hadn't slept, she still managed to look amazing. Hair done, makeup. But that was just surface stuff. Beneath that, she was beautiful, always had been. That wasn't only limited to her face. Her body was a sizzler, too. Not overly curvy but more than enough to catch and hold his attention.

Especially those legs.

She was wearing a skirt again today, a slim white one. It hit several inches above her knees, and with the way she was sitting, the skirt had ridden up even more. Not as much as the night before when she'd had the panic attack, but he could see plenty of her long legs and had no trouble imagining where those legs stopped.

"You're wondering about the shoes," she said.

Uh. No.

But he would take to the grave what he had been wondering about.

However, she was indeed wearing shoes. Heels about four inches high and pale pink, about the same color as her mouth.

"This isn't about what happened yesterday with Livvy," Cassie continued. "I really do wear shoes like this—often."

Lucky had no idea how to respond to that so he just nodded. That was enough of a cue to keep Cassie talking.

"I only wear those flat shoes when I'm traveling. Because I twisted my ankle once while running to catch a flight. And that gray outfit I had on yesterday? Again, just for traveling."

Of course, that only made him notice her legs again. And the fit of her top. Snug in just the right places.

"Anyway, I thought you should know," she added. Cassie drank more coffee, fast, as if trying to give her mouth something else to do other than talk.

"Wanna know something?" he asked.

She didn't jump to answer that. Cassie stayed quiet for a while, studying his face and no doubt trying to figure out what this was about. She finally nodded.

"You'd look good in anything," Lucky admitted.

"Oh," she said. Yeah, that was definitely a surprise. Because it threw the attraction right out there. And there was no doubt about it now—there was an attraction. If there hadn't been, she wouldn't have cared what he thought about her clothes and shoes.

"Oh," Cassie repeated, tearing her lingering gaze from his. "Well, thanks. Now, to what we really should be talking about. The girls," she clarified. Probably because he looked at her breasts, she clarified even more. "Mia and Mackenzie."

"What about them? Mia and Mackenzie?" he clarified, too.

"I don't have any experience counseling or dealing with troubled children, but I have a friend who does. Dr. Sarah Dressler. I called her last night and asked her to come. She might not make it here before it's time for the girls to leave, but just in case this lingers on..."

No need to finish that. If this lingered on, they'd need help and lots of it. Lucky wasn't about to turn down anything or anybody, especially when that anybody might know how to deal with Mackenzie.

"I suspect Mackenzie's acting out because she has abandonment issues," Cassie added. "It's fairly common with children who've lost their parents. They challenge authority, break rules, run away. They run because they fear abandonment again, and they believe running will fix the problem. If they don't stay in one place, they can't be abandoned."

Lucky replayed all of that. Word for word.

Well, hell.

Was Cassie analyzing him now, or Mackenzie?

"There's no quick, easy solution," Cassie went on. "She'll need lots of love, reassurance. She'll need to believe she can fit into a new life where someone will love her... What?"

"What?" Lucky repeated.

"You're looking at me funny," Cassie said.

Lucky quickly tried to fix that. "Just thinking, that's all." And comparing.

But he ditched the comparison. He was nothing like Mackenzie despite what Cassie had just said. Despite, too, what Riley had said the day before about Mackenzie reminding him of Lucky.

Cassie stared at him a while longer. "Anyway, I thought maybe you could talk to her about what it was like to lose your own parents."

This would have been a good time for him to nod and agree. He didn't. "I don't think it's a good idea to dredge up all of that."

More staring at him. "Okay." Lucky figured what she was doing was using a therapist's ploy: waiting for him to spill more.

He wouldn't.

"Why don't you check on the girls?" he asked. It was time to get to his feet and head out. "I'll see about getting us some more coffee and some breakfast." Lucky walked away, hoping that was the end of the subject for Cassie.

It'd never be the end of it for him, though.

Lucky had plenty of memories of that night he'd become an orphan, and he didn't intend to share them with Cassie or anyone else. He hadn't been able to save his mom and dad.

They had both died in a car crash that could have been prevented.

And it was all his fault.

CASSIE WATCHED AS Lucky walked away. She didn't need any psychology degrees to know something was bothering him. Maybe something on that piece of paper that he'd shoved into his pocket.

Something he clearly hadn't wanted her to see.

For just a second she had considered trying to talk him into showing it to her, but it was his own business and had nothing to do with her. And it wasn't as if she didn't have anything else to do. She had to deal with the girls, and that started with her knocking on the door of the guest room where they were staying.

No answer.

It wasn't exactly late, just after eight, but she couldn't imagine the girls—well, Mia anyway—ignoring a knock. Cassie knocked again. Still no answer, and she was about to test the knob when the door opened. Relief flooded through her when she saw Mia. Panic came just as fast, though, when she didn't see Mackenzie.

"I can't tie my shoes," Mia said. She tried to stick out one foot and nearly lost her balance. Cassie caught onto her to stop her from falling.

"I'll tie them for you. Uh, where's your sister?"

"Bathroom. It takes Kenzie a long time to do stuff in there."

Yes, it had to take time to spackle on that much makeup. The bathroom was en suite, but the door was closed and Cassie didn't hear anyone moving around. Since there was a window in there, it was possible Mackenzie had used it to get away. But Cassie rethought that. She wouldn't just abandon Mia. Well, she wouldn't if Cassie's theory was right.

Of course, that theory was just as likely to be wrong. It wasn't as if she had a stellar track record when it came to doling out diagnoses.

Cassie set Mia on the bed so she could tie her shoes. She hurried, too. All in all, the little girl had done a good job dressing herself in a pair a pink overalls with a white shirt beneath.

"I pulled up my own panties," Mia volunteered. "And I didn't get 'em bunched up."

Cassie wasn't sure if that was a big accomplishment or not for a four-year-old, but she said, "Good girl," and made her way to the bathroom door. She leaned in, pressed her ear against it and almost fell when Mackenzie threw it open.

"I'm still here, all right?" Mackenzie snarled. "And I wrote that stupid apology to the old woman at the ugly lawyer's office."

Since it had worked with Mia, Cassie went with another mumbled "Good girl," though it didn't have the same effect on Mackenzie. Mia had smiled at Cassie. Mackenzie was sporting her usual scowl and a fresh slathering of makeup. Sheez, considering the amount she used, her entire suitcase had to be filled with the stuff.

Mackenzie thrust a Post-it note at her. "Take it. It's the apology."

Cassie did take it and saw the two words scrawled there. "I'm sorry."

"I told Kenzie to say it like she means it, and that'll make the lawyer lady feel better," Mia said.

"I do mean it!" Mackenzie growled. "I mean it because I want to get everybody off my back."

It probably wasn't the heart-wrenching regret and promise that she'd never do it again that Wilhelmina would be looking for. Hopefully, it would be enough to keep the woman from going through with filing those charges, though. Cassie hated to think that Lucky might have to kiss Wilhelmina, or something more, just to get Mackenzie off the hook. There was also the added problem of Mackenzie not learning anything if Lucky paid for her crimes.

Of course, Lucky wouldn't want to have to pimp himself out to pay for those crimes, either. It wasn't as if Wilhelmina were a tasty morsel like Livvy.

"Cat!" Mia squealed.

Cassie whirled around, expecting to see Ethan's yellow cat, but this one was black. And it was one that Cassie recognized.

Oh, no. He hadn't.

Cassie hurried toward the stairs and encountered another cat. Yet another one she recognized. Both of them had belonged to Dixie Mae, which meant her father had dropped them off.

Or rather he was still dropping them off, she realized, when she spotted Mason-Dixon in the foyer.

He was in the process of letting a third one out of a kitty kennel. The moment the Siamese was free, she shot toward the hall. Her father stood there, smiling, the trio of kennels now at his feet. And he wasn't alone. Della was there.

"Mason-Dixon let himself in," Della said, sounding about as pleased with this visit as Cassie was. "I should have locked the door after I brought in the newspaper."

Her father offered no apology for that. "This'll teach Dixie Mae," he said. Which was a stupid thing to say.

"Gran's dead," Cassie reminded him. "You can't teach her

anything now. Besides, you gave me two days to find homes for the cats, and it hasn't even been twenty-four hours."

"What's going on here?" Lucky asked, coming into the foyer.

He was holding the folded piece of paper, the one he'd had in the hall earlier, and he stuffed it back into his pocket. Judging from his expression, whatever was on it was bad news. Or maybe the expression was simply for the bad news right in front of them.

Her father.

"I'm delivering the cats." Her father looked as if he wanted to add some profanity to that, but he must have changed his mind. Maybe because he spotted the kids who'd followed Cassie down the stairs, but it was more likely because Lucky was giving him a "make my day" kind of glare.

"You could have called me first," Cassie scolded. "Or at least knocked."

"I'm tired of being polite." Laughable since Mason-Dixon was rarely polite. "I was also tired of waiting for you to do something about this mess your idiot grandmother made."

"I've been busy," Cassie grumbled.

"Yeah, I can see that." Her father's attention landed on Mackenzie. "Dixie Mae left you a mess, too."

That was *not* the right thing to say. Lucky stepped forward as if he might slug him. Cassie wouldn't have minded that so much—Mason-Dixon deserved a good butt-whipping—but she didn't want that to happen in front of the girls.

"Just leave," Cassie told her father. But then she paused and glanced at the three kennels again. "Where are the other three cats?"

Her father smiled.

Oh, no. That couldn't be good.

"Here's how this will work," he said. "You get the rest of the cats, and I get half of whatever Dixie Mae leaves you. Up front. I don't want to wait weeks for her will to be read. Find out what she left you and write me a check for half. I'm giving you two days. If not, you'll never see the other three cats again."

Cassie glanced at Lucky and Della to make sure she'd heard her father correctly. Apparently, she had, because they looked just as bewildered as she felt. Well, Della did anyway. Lucky looked ready to start that butt-whipping.

"You're holding the cats for ransom?" Lucky asked.

"You're damn right I am. Dixie Mae didn't give me a choice. She's the one who started this by giving me those cats. Well, I'm the one finishing it. Pay up."

Cassie shook her head. "It's possible that Gran didn't leave me any money in the will."

"Oh, she left you plenty all right. And if she didn't leave it to you, she left it to him." Mason-Dixon shot Lucky a glare. "Either way, I want to get paid, and I want it to happen sooner than later."

Lucky stepped closer. "Or?"

Mason-Dixon smiled again. "That's the thing, Cassie won't know what the *or* will be. And I know she wouldn't want to see anything happen to her grandmother's precious cats."

"I'll call the sheriff," Della volunteered.

But that only caused her father to laugh. "Dixie Mae left those cats to me. They're mine now. The sheriff can't take my property without cause, and for now I'm not giving him any cause." He headed out the door and down the porch steps. "Pay up," her father added in a growl as he left.

Lucky started to go after him, but Cassie took hold of his arm. "Don't give him the fight he wants. I'll figure a way to work this out." Though at the moment she couldn't think of how to do that.

So much was hitting her at once, and all Cassie wanted to do was curl up somewhere and calm down before she had another panic attack.

Thankfully, Lucky didn't go after Mason-Dixon. They all just stood there and watched her father drive away while the cats darted around the room. Cassie shut the door to keep them from darting outside, and when she turned Mia was there, her hand outstretched. She had the gold star that Livvy had given her in her palm.

"I can use my wish to make you happy," Mia said.

It was such a touching gesture that it brought tears to her eyes. Of course, she'd been on the verge of crying all morning—heck, all night—so just about anything would have set her off. Still, it was an amazing thing from an amazing little girl.

"Thank you," Cassie told her. "But you keep it. Use it on something for yourself."

It probably wasn't a good thing for her to continue to let Mia believe the star was magic, but Cassie was too drained to change that now. Maybe Mia wouldn't be too disappointed when it didn't work.

"You want me to make some calls to see if anyone is willing to give at least one of these cats a good home?" Della asked.

Cassie nodded. Thanked her, too. Cassie would have loved to have kept the cats herself, but she couldn't. Not unless she moved. And changed her work schedule to stay home more. If she did that, she'd basically have to quit her job, which would mean she would have no income.

"So, you gonna pay him or what?" Mackenzie asked. She didn't seem especially concerned one way or another.

"No," Lucky answered before Cassie could say anything. "You're not paying that duckweed a dime. I'll find out where the other three cats are and…negotiate to get them back."

Since he paused before the word *negotiate*, Cassie was concerned. "What does that mean exactly?" she asked.

Lucky looked her straight in the eyes. "It means I steal them."

Cassie was about to give him several reasons why he couldn't do that. Well, one reason anyway. He'd be arrested. But the sound of the approaching car stopped her, and she hurried to the sidelight window to look out. Maybe, just maybe, her father had had a change of heart—or to be more accurate, acquired a heart—and had decided to give her the rest of the cats.

But it wasn't her father's yellow Cadillac. It was a taxi, and it came to a stop directly in front of the house.

"Are you expecting anyone?" Della asked.

Cassie nodded. But certainly not this early. She wasn't ready to deal with...

Too late.

The taxi door opened, and the woman stepped out. Marla Candor.

"Hey, I've seen her on TV," Della said. "She's on one of those reality shows. A skanky one."

Yes, she was. She was also Cassie's client.

Marla had followed in the paths of other reality stars to achieve fame. She'd done a sex tape, then made sure it was leaked to the press. When that hadn't given her the desired results, she'd made six more tapes. She also had a laundry list of mental issues that probably couldn't be addressed with a lifetime of therapy, much less the weekly session she scheduled with Cassie.

And her real name was Wendi Myrtle Stoddermeyer.

Marla wasn't alone on this particular visit. But then she never was. She had a cameraman with her who would film every minute of the session so that the best parts could be edited and included in the TV show. Of course, the "best parts" would be when Marla talked about her so-called sex addiction. Cassie wasn't convinced that sex was her addiction so much as her need for people to hear about her having sex.

"Della, would you please take the girls to the kitchen?" Cassie asked.

Thankfully, Della scurried them away.

"You should go, as well," Cassie said to Lucky.

But it was too late. Marla's attention had already landed on Lucky. Her eyes widened. She smiled, and while she didn't exactly lick her lips, it was close.

"Cassandra," Marla purred after she told the taxi driver to wait. But the purr was really for Lucky. So were the massive boobs she thrust in his direction. "I need to see you right away. It's been days since I had an orgasm, and I'm about to explode. And I see the very person who can help me with that."

"Play along," Cassie whispered to Lucky.

To save him from Marla's clutches, and the rest of the horny woman, Cassie leaned in and kissed him.

CHAPTER NINE

LUCKY HAD BEEN so focused on their guest—and he used that term loosely—that he hadn't seen the kiss coming. A first for him. He could usually spot the beginnings of a kiss at fifty paces, but here Cassie had been elbow-to-elbow with him and it had still taken him by surprise.

Not the surprise of the kiss itself.

He knew it was fake. No doubt meant to stop Marla from jumping him right there in the foyer so she wouldn't "explode." But the surprise came from the fact that for a fake kiss, it sure packed a wallop.

Oh, man.

This wasn't good. Fake kisses weren't supposed to taste like that. Or feel like that. He hadn't exactly had a barn full of fake kisses, but Lucky had some pretty realistic expectations in that area. This kiss had shot those expectations to smithereens.

"Oh," Marla said, making her way up the steps. "So that's how it is."

Cassie pulled away from Lucky, and he couldn't help but notice that she was breathing a little harder than she had been ten seconds ago. So maybe it had exceeded her expectations, too.

"Yes," Cassie insisted. "Marla, this is my *friend*, Lucky Mc-Cord."

That perked Marla right up. "A friend who shares his benefits?"

"No," Cassie said without hesitation. "His benefits are exclusively with me for the time being."

That didn't perk up Marla at all. "So, what about—"

"Come on," Cassie interrupted. "We should get started with the session. I'm sure you're anxious to get back to LA."

Marla looked far more anxious to examine his benefits, but Cassie hurried her out of the foyer and in the direction of the office she'd already scoped out.

"You gotta watch her hands," the cameraman whispered to Lucky as he trailed along behind them.

It was obvious Cassie was trying to keep Lucky well out of reach of Marla's hands. Also obvious that she hadn't wanted Marla to finish whatever she'd been about to say.

That might have something to do with the note Logan had given him.

Soon, he'd need to talk to Cassie about that, but for now he had a cat issue to deal with, and he also needed to call Bernie to see what progress had been made on finding the girls' aunt or some other next of kin.

Lucky made his way to the kitchen, dodging two of the cats along the way. Since he doubted Mason-Dixon had brought litter boxes, he moved that particular task to the top of his list. He called the grocery store and asked someone to bring over cat supplies and lots of them.

He didn't have the number of the one stripper that he did know at Mason-Dixon's club, but it didn't take him long to get it from a ranch hand. Lucky made the call to find out if she'd spotted the other three felines, but the call went to voice mail. Lucky left her a message.

He found the girls at the kitchen table eating breakfast. At least that's what Mia was doing. Mackenzie was poking her fork at a pancake as if testing it for signs of life.

"Miss Della made shapes," Mia announced, proudly showing

him the remains of what appeared to be a heart-shaped pancake. Mackenzie's had probably been a heart, too, but it was hard to tell with all the punctures.

Della smiled, dished up a pancake for him, but Lucky frowned when he looked at it. It definitely wasn't a heart even if he squinted. "No shape for me?" he asked, hoping he didn't sound too disappointed.

"Round is a shape," Della reminded him. She dropped a kiss on the top of his head and put a jar of peanut butter on the table. His favorite thing to eat with pancakes, so he thanked her.

"So, is the skank staying?" Mackenzie asked.

Lucky debated if he should correct her for saying *skank*, but it seemed a G-rated enough word, especially considering Mackenzie could have used something much, much worse.

"No. She'll leave after her therapy session." Lucky hoped. The taxi was waiting for her out front, so that was a good sign.

"And what about the cats? Are they staying?" Three questions in under a minute. A record for Mackenzie.

"I'm still working on that."

"I want 'em to stay," Mia declared before cramming more of the pancake in her mouth.

Since this might be his best chance at having a real talk with them, Lucky dived right in. He dived right into the pancake, too. "Tell me about your aunt Alice. Is she a nice person?"

He might as well have asked what it was like to walk on the moon because both girls gave him a blank stare. "We gotta an aunt Alice?" Mia asked.

Lucky tried not to groan. He'd hoped that since the woman was their mother's half sister they had at least met her. It would have even been better if they'd known her and been excited about the possibility of living with her. But no dice.

"Did your mom ever talk about her sister?" He aimed that one at Mackenzie since he wasn't even sure Mia would remember their mom.

Mackenzie continued to put fork holes in the pancake. "Is that who you're trying to pawn us off on?"

Honestly, yes. But he wouldn't dare say that to them. Besides, they wouldn't be going with the aunt unless he was sure she would give them a good home. And just because they didn't know her, it didn't mean she wouldn't be a good guardian.

"A lot of people are trying to find your next of kin," he explained. "Your aunt Alice is just one possibility."

"What's a poss-a-bilty mean?" Mia asked at the same moment her sister demanded, "Who else?"

Lucky glanced at Della to see if she could help, but she gave him a "you're on your own" shrug.

"A possibility is someone who might get the chance to take care of you and love you." That part was for Mia. Lucky turned to Mackenzie for the rest. "Right now, only your aunt Alice is on the list," he admitted. "But we're working on others. My brother Logan is making some calls. So is the lawyer. I'll also be making some myself."

He'd barely finished the explanation when he heard a sound. A moan of some kind. The sort a water buffalo might make when in heat. And it was coming from the office at the back of the house where Cassie was having her therapy session with Marla. When there was a second one, even louder than the first, Lucky hurried back to make sure someone wasn't having a seizure.

"Is everything okay?" he asked when he reached the door.

"Why don't you come in and see," Marla said, giggling. And moaning.

The door opened, just a fraction, and Cassie poked her nose in through the narrow opening. "She can have orgasms by just thinking about it. My advice, don't come in here. Oh, and watch out for her hands."

Lucky was so intrigued by the double hand warning that he almost wanted to go in there just to see what it was all about.

Almost. But he'd moved out of the curiosity-killing-the-cat stage about the time he'd sprouted his first chest hair.

"It won't be much longer now," Cassie assured him. "Once she's finished this orgasm, she'll be ready to go." And she shut the door.

This sure seemed like a long way to come for an orgasm, especially one Marla could have just by thinking about it. But maybe she needed Cassie coaxing her or something.

Which, of course, totally interested him.

Lucky blamed that on the fake kiss. It had heated up some things inside him.

He started back to the kitchen so he could keep an eye on the girls, but he'd hardly made it a few steps when the office door opened again, and Marla came waltzing out. She looked a lot happier than she had when she'd gone in even though there hadn't been much time for mental foreplay.

She smiled when she saw him, continued waltzing. Except she grabbed his balls when she went past him.

Well, hell.

It not only shocked him, it also hurt. That's what the warning was all about. The grab wouldn't hinder his chances of fathering children should he ever plan on doing that, but he might walk funny for a while.

"I did warn you," the cameraman said, and that's when Lucky noticed that the guy was keeping his distance. And walking funny.

Cassie followed the pair, but she stopped once they'd cleared the kitchen. Probably because she didn't want Marla around the girls. Lucky agreed with that.

"You want to talk about this?" he asked Cassie.

"No," she said without hesitation. She checked her watch. "I guess I can get started with some calls about the cats."

"Not just yet," Lucky said. Since the girls were still at the breakfast table, this might be the best chance he got to talk to

Cassie alone. He pulled her back into the hall and out of ear-shot of anyone in the kitchen.

"If this is about that kiss…" she started.

"It's not." Best to leave that subject alone. He had a lot of experience with lust clouding his judgment, and that kiss had fallen into the lust category for him.

"Then if it's about Marla grabbing you—"

"That's not it, either." Lucky took out the note. "It's about what's in this."

"That's the paper you had in the hall earlier. Is it about the girls' aunt?" But she froze. No doubt because of the expression on his face. "It's about me."

Cassie groaned and would have moved away from him if Lucky hadn't taken hold of her.

"Let me guess," she snapped. "Logan went digging into my life."

Since that about summed it up, Lucky nodded.

"He had no right," Cassie insisted.

"I agree with you, but it's just something Logan does. He wanted to make sure none of this was a scam. And yeah, his digging into your life probably started to make sure you weren't part of that theoretical scam. But no scam."

However, it was something much worse.

"Let me see the note," she demanded.

He handed it to her, but Lucky figured she wasn't going to like some of it. Mainly because it wasn't just a note. It was a one-page report from a private investigator Logan kept on retainer.

Lucky watched as her eyes skirted over the first part. Her bio and work history. No surprises there, but her eyes stopped skirting on the section that had caused him to pause, too.

Involuntary commitment to Sweet Meadows Meditation and Relaxation Facility in Oregon.

There weren't many other details, only her commitment date, which was a week ago. But Lucky figured that "involuntary commitment" phrase said it all. There was also the name of the person who'd had her committed, but that was all that the PI had apparently been able to get.

It was enough.

"The only reason I showed you that," he said, "was because I want to make sure you're okay."

"Yes, I'm okay!" she snapped. But then almost immediately she sagged against the wall. Just that short outburst seemed to have exhausted her, and Cassie gave a weary sigh. While still clutching the paper, she covered her face with her hands. "Obviously, I'm not okay. You saw what happened to me."

Lucky wasn't sure how to approach this, whether he should question her more about that or not. She certainly hadn't seemed eager to discuss the panic attack. However, while he was having a mental debate with himself, Cassie must have taken his silence as an opening to explain herself.

"The panic attacks started last month," she said. That seemed to make her angry. Maybe at herself. Maybe at him. Maybe at Logan for uncovering this. "I missed some of the signs with a patient. I screwed up big-time."

Lucky took her hands from her face so he could make eye contact. "You want to talk about it?"

She scowled, maybe because he sounded a little like a therapist. Not intentionally. He just wasn't sure where to go here. When women started crying, he usually found some excuse to get the heck out of there, but that was part of his old baggage. Cassie might need him to ditch that baggage for a while and listen to her.

Or not.

"I'll check on the girls," she said, and she would have darted right out of there if he hadn't stepped in front of her.

"The girls are fine." He hoped. But he wasn't so sure about Cassie. "Look, I can handle them and the cats. If you need to go back to that place in Oregon, then go."

Her eyes narrowed. "I'm not crazy."

Lucky held up his hands in defense. "I didn't say you were."

But this would have been a good time for him to say something else, something reassuring, instead of letting his gaze drift to the paper that she had wadded up.

Because he was right in her face, Lucky saw the exact moment that she got it. That he was concerned about those two words.

Involuntary commitment.

Cassie backed up, huffed. Then sighed again. "I had a bad attack and ended up in the ER. Someone convinced the staff that I needed help, and that's how I ended up at Sweet Meadows."

Lucky got the feeling that was the toned-down version of what had happened.

"Someone?" he repeated. And he knew the name of that someone because it was on Logan's report. "Who is this Dr. Andrew Knight who had you sent to that place?"

More huffing and sighing. "I meant to mention all of this earlier, but it slipped my mind. He's my boyfriend. More or less."

Well, that was a mouthful. This was the first he was hearing of a boyfriend, even one that she considered more or less.

Whatever the heck that meant.

"Andrew overreacted," she added. "He does that sometimes, and we're having a cooling-off period because of it."

Translation—she was pissed because he'd put her in that place. Lucky didn't blame her. He would have been pissed, too, and there would have been more than just a cooling-off period. He would have dumped the jerk.

And, no, that didn't have anything to do with the fake kiss Cassie and he had shared. It had more to do with the real moments they'd gone through in the past twenty-four hours.

"Andrew's a shrink?" Lucky asked.

She nodded. "But he knows he made a mistake sending me there, and he signed my release papers as soon as I told him I needed to come home to attend my grandmother's funeral."

"What a prince." Lucky didn't bother to take the stank off that, either.

Cassie didn't huff again, but she did fold her arms over her chest and stare at him. "I'll discuss Andrew with you if you'll explore in great detail why you haven't had sex in three months."

She probably thought there was no way he'd chat about something like that. Well, she was wrong.

"Dixie Mae's the reason I haven't had sex. She wasn't spending much time at work so I took over things she normally does."

That was close to the truth anyway. He wouldn't get into the fact that Dixie Mae's failing health hadn't exactly put him in a romantic frame of mind.

"I could feel her slipping away, and there was nothing I could do about it." Lucky hadn't intended to discuss all this. Too similar to another death.

His mother's.

"Oh," Cassie said. The tone of a woman who'd just been put in her place. Something that Lucky hadn't intended.

"You were there for her, and I wasn't," Cassie admitted.

Hell's flipping bells. The tears watered her eyes again. "You weren't there for her because that clown Andrew put you in a nuthouse."

She shook her head. Cried. Yep, no stopping those tears now. She was in a full boo-hoo mode. Lucky had no choice but to pull her into his arms.

"I swear, I didn't know Dixie Mae was that sick," Cassie added through the sobs.

"Because she didn't want you to know. She knew how busy you were, and she didn't want to disrupt your life."

"She disrupted yours," she pointed out just as quickly.

He would have used his shoulder to shrug if Cassie hadn't been crying on it. "I didn't mind. Dixie Mae got me through some hard times. She's kept me under her wing ever since my folks were killed."

"Yes," she whispered.

It was just one word, but it seemed to him to mean a whole

lot more. Lucky eased back so he could look at her. That look was enough of a prompt for her to continue.

"I remember when they died," she said.

Again, there was a whole lot more that went with those additional five words.

Of course she remembered. Everyone in town over the age of twenty-five probably did. It'd been talked about, gossiped about, for years. And Lucky was pretty sure that somewhere in all that gossip, there'd been talk about him. About what he'd done.

Or rather what he hadn't done.

"All right," Lucky said. "If we keep on this subject, you'll have to talk about Andrew."

As expected, that hushed her. Cassie gave the tears another wipe. "I'll just freshen up before I see the girls," she insisted, and she ducked into the powder room that was across the hall from the office.

Lucky didn't know all that'd gone on with this Andrew, but it had to be damn bad for her to back off the conversation like that. Especially since she probably wanted to know what'd actually happened the night his parents were killed. Yes, most folks over the age of twenty-five knew about the car wreck, and those same folks wanted the dirty little details. But Lucky figured that was something he might have to take to the grave.

Talking about it just wasn't an option.

He decided to wait for her before facing the kids again. Mainly because he needed a couple of seconds, too. He didn't want Mia picking up on his suddenly sour mood. As sweet as she was, she'd probably want to use her magic star to cheer him up. But even magic wouldn't work on this.

His phone rang, and he saw the name on the screen. Sugar Monroe. One of the calls he'd been waiting for. And nope, Sugar wasn't her stage name. It was the name her mother had given her at birth, and maybe it had been what had set her on her present career path.

As a stripper at the Slippery Pole.

"Lucky," Sugar said the moment he answered. "I got your voice mail, but I'm a little confused. Were you actually asking about cats or was that a G-rated way of asking about p—"

"Cats," he quickly supplied. No sense letting Sugar get the idea that this was a hookup call. He hadn't hooked up with her in years and had no plans to rehook. And Lucky hoped no single, unattached straight man ever knew he'd had a thought like that.

"You mean those cats that Mason-Dixon inherited from his mama?" Sugar asked.

"The very ones. There should be three of them, and I need to know where they are."

"Last time I saw them, they were in Mason-Dixon's bedroom. Well, it's really more of a dump, but he sleeps here sometimes if he can coax one of the girls into joining him."

Not a pretty picture. And especially not one that Lucky wanted in his head.

"Can you check and see if they're still there?" he asked.

"Sure. Anything for you, Lucky. I'm at the club to pick up some stuff and I'm walking over to Mason-Dixon's room now. Say, when are you coming back here? It's been a while since I've seen you."

"I've been kind of busy."

"Right. What with Dixie Mae dying and all. And what with inheriting those kids. Mason-Dixon said the older girl could work for him soon."

Over Lucky's dead body. Over Mason-Dixon's dead body, too. "She's only thirteen."

"You're sure? Because Mason-Dixon said she was—"

"Sugar, if you don't mind, I'd rather not hear what he has to say about her. Because I'd have to beat the shit out of him. Understand?"

"Yeah, I guess. Okay, I'm outside Mason-Dixon's room, but it's locked. Hold on a second, and I'll put my ear to the door and listen for anything or anybody moving around in there. Yeah," Sugar added several seconds later. "I hear cat sounds."

"Uh, you're sure it's cats and not Mason-Dixon?"

"It's cats all right," she verified. "Mason-Dixon's a moaner, not a meower."

Yet something else Lucky didn't want in his head. "Any sign of Mason-Dixon?"

"Not yet, but he'll be here any minute. He usually comes in around this time."

Not good. "How late will he stay?"

"Late," Sugar verified. "Again, it goes back to if he's able to coax one of the girls to his room. Won't be me, mind you. Don't shit where you eat. That's my motto."

Apparently, that was a motto that Mason-Dixon didn't embrace. "Is it possible he could end up staying there all night?"

"If he hooks up with Cherry, yes. She's an all-night kind of girl."

Hell, he'd need a shower after this conversation. Lucky suddenly felt as if he'd just had a bucket of scum poured over his head.

"So yeah, if he goes with Cherry," Sugar went on. "That's not her real name, by the way. It's Jennifer. Anyway, it'd be the wee hours of the morning before Mason-Dixon leaves."

Lucky hated to plan this around Mason-Dixon's *love life*, but he didn't have a choice. Cassie's father likely carried a gun, and even if he didn't, Lucky preferred not to get arrested.

"If you're wanting to come by when you know for sure Mason-Dixon's not here," Sugar added, "then I'd say stop in around nine in the morning."

"You think the cats will be okay until then?" Lucky asked.

"I can make sure they are."

Good. "Thanks. And I have another favor. Can you be at the club tomorrow morning to let me in?"

"Sure. But if I scratch your back, you can scratch mine. Deal?" He could almost see her smiling.

"Deal," he agreed.

Damn. First Wilhelmina and now Sugar. If he kept owing

women all these favors, he wasn't going to have time for anything else. Whatever Sugar wanted to do with him, it wouldn't lead to sex, he'd make sure of that, but it might mean hours and hours of keeping her at bay.

"I'll be there at nine in the morning," Lucky told her.

And after that, he'd be able to add "cat thief" and "bay-keeping gigolo" to his resume.

CHAPTER TEN

CASSIE HAD NEVER stolen anything in her life. Not even another girl's boyfriend, but she had no doubts that this theft had to happen. With the state of mind her father had been in, he could hurt the cats. Or else just lock them up somewhere and not bother to take care of them. No way did Cassie want that to happen.

A theft probably seemed extreme to some people, but the cats were her last living link to her grandmother. And no, she didn't count her father. It'd been a long, long time since Mason-Dixon had been a son to Dixie Mae, and he had such a mean streak that he might do something to the cats just to get back at his dead mother. And back at Cassie.

"I can still do this solo," Lucky offered. "You can wait in the car."

It wasn't his first time offering. Right from the start, he'd insisted she not go with him, but there was no way she was going to let him do her dirty work. Though she'd had a moment's hesitation when Lucky had reminded her that if they got caught they could be arrested.

And locked up by Deputy Davy.

Lucky had added that if he went in alone, at least she'd be there to take care of the girls for the half day or so it would take him to get out of jail. Cassie wasn't comfortable with the possibility of being arrested, but if they did get caught, she had already decided that she would take the fall so Lucky wouldn't land in jail. That way, he'd be the one there for the girls.

The only thing they had to do now was hurry. Della and Stella were watching the children, but Cassie didn't want Mackenzie using this as an opportunity to run away again. That's the reason Lucky had called in reinforcements.

In this case, Livvy.

Livvy had agreed to call Mackenzie with the promise that she'd bring by some of her shoes later for the girl to try on. Maybe the shoes would have high enough heels that if Mackenzie did decide to run, the heel height alone would slow her down.

Cassie reminded herself to give Livvy a huge thanks for this.

Lucky drove out of town and to the outskirts where it didn't take long, less than a mile, for her to spot the Slippery Pole. The exterior was just as tacky as the name. It was flesh pink, and it had a neon sign of a woman with massive breasts. Since it was daylight, the sign wasn't on, but Cassie knew that when it was, the woman's nipples blinked in invitation.

Her father probably thought that was classy.

There was only one vehicle in front of the place—an older-model red Mustang. It was pocked with dents and rust spots, but despite that the vanity plates were gleaming with one word.

Sugar.

Thank goodness the stripper was there to let them in.

Lucky pulled the car to the back of the building and parked out of sight. The car itself was another sneaky ploy since it wasn't a vehicle her father would recognize should he drive up. Lucky had left his truck at the ranch and used one of the vehicles from the family's garage instead.

The moment they got out, the back door opened, and a red-haired woman stuck out her head. According to Lucky, this was Sugar Monroe, one of her father's employees. The woman hurriedly motioned for them to come in, but the hurriedness didn't extend to the long look she gave Lucky.

Good grief.

This happened wherever they went, and the woman just kept giving him the look until they were inside. Then she kissed him. A loud smack right on the lips.

"Looking good as always," she purred.

Lucky stepped back, and since the overhead lights weren't on, it was hard to see his expression, but Cassie thought he might have blushed. Of course, it could also be a flush of arousal.

Not that she cared.

Okay, she did, but it was stupid because the kiss that Lucky and she had shared was a fake one. The one the stripper had given him was likely the most recent of many.

"Sugar, this is Cassie, Mason-Dixon's daughter," Lucky said, making introductions.

Until then Sugar hadn't noticed Cassie in any way. That happened a lot, too, whenever Cassie was around Lucky, but Sugar acknowledged her now. "Don't you breathe one word to your dad about this," Sugar warned her. No lovey-dovey look for Cassie. "I could lose my job."

Apparently, that was a big deal to Sugar, though Cassie couldn't imagine this being a job worth keeping. The place smelled like a urinal mixed with other bodily fluids that Cassie didn't want to identify. There were always rumors that her father was pimping out his girls, but to the best of her knowledge, he'd never been arrested for it.

"This way," Sugar said. "But you need to hurry. No telling who could come walking in here."

Sugar herself didn't exactly hurry. She fell into step alongside Lucky. "How much longer are you gonna be in town?" she asked.

"I'm not sure." Unlike Sugar, he seemed focused on the task. "Cassie and I have been busy with the girls."

Sugar glanced back at her, giving her a head-to-toe examination in the span of a couple of seconds. Apparently, she didn't approve, but Sugar's narrowed eyes relaxed when she turned back to Lucky.

Cassie had only been to the strip club once in her life, and that was when she'd been trying to mend fences between her father and grandmother, but she'd never been to this back hallway. Only to her father's office just off the front of the building. At the time, she'd thought his office had to be the worst part of the place, but she'd been wrong. This was.

It was a tangle of dressing rooms and rooms with unmade beds. Junk was strewn everywhere, including outside the door where they stopped. There was a pair of red thong panties on the floor and someone had used a black marker to scrawl Mason-Dick on the door.

"Mason-Dixon keeps this locked," Sugar explained, but she plucked a bobby pin from her hair and had the lock open in a snap.

The moment Sugar opened the door, Cassie heard the cats. And smelled them. She hadn't thought anything else could cut through the Slippery Pole smells, but she'd been wrong about that, too. Apparently, her father hadn't changed the litter box, though at least there were bowls of food and water. That still wouldn't earn him any favors in her eyes. He simply didn't want his "investments" to starve to death.

All three of the cats started meowing, and the Persian—her Gran's favorite—began to coil around Cassie's legs, looking for attention. Cassie gave all three a quick pet, but they had to hurry now. She and Lucky put the three into their kennels and started back out.

They didn't get far.

"Sugar?" her father called out. Judging from the sound of his voice and the footsteps, he was headed straight toward them.

"Oh, God," Cassie whispered, something that she was fairly sure was said often in this place. Not as a prayer, either.

"Sugar?" he repeated. "What the hell are you doing here so early?"

"Go," Sugar insisted, closing the door to her father's room and locking it. She started toward those footsteps. "Hurry."

It was really good advice, but it came a few seconds too late. Her father was right there, and Cassie braced herself for a confrontation, but thankfully he had his attention fixed on Sugar.

Lucky pulled Cassie into one of the junky rooms, but he didn't stop there. He yanked her to the floor on the other side of a bed, and he threw some clothes over the kennels. Probably so her father wouldn't be able to hear the cats should they start meowing.

The covers worked. Maybe it was the sudden darkness, but the cats stayed quiet. Cassie's breathing, not so much. That's because in the scurry to hide, she had ended up with Lucky on top of her. With her head right next to a box of condoms. If she believed in such a thing as fate, she might have thought it was trying to tell her something. But Cassie didn't believe in that kind of fate.

However, she did believe in basic animal attraction. Lucky was an animal. So was she, and she was attracted to him. Along with seemingly every other female in town.

For some stupid reason, she remembered the part about him not having had sex for three months. Maybe that made his body more attentive to hers. And vice versa. Maybe it was because he'd just risked jail to save the cats when he didn't even like them.

Maybe it was because she herself hadn't had sex in such a long time.

Whatever the reason, Cassie found herself thinking about kissing him. No. She thought about having sex with him, which, of course, would have included kissing.

She couldn't be sure, but Cassie thought maybe he was thinking about it, too. He shifted a little. The right kind of shift to align the parts of their bodies required for sex.

And yes, he was *interested*.

The alignment gave her proof of that because she could feel

the beginnings of his erection. It was stupid to be flattered by that. Even more stupid to make him harder, but that's what she did when she shifted her hips a little. Just enough so that if they'd been naked, they would have had accidental sex.

A hoarse sound rumbled in Lucky's throat, and when his eyes came to hers, he had a "what do you think you're doing?" expression. Or maybe "two can play this game" one. He shifted, this time moving his erection against the vee of her thighs. Then *into* that vee.

Cassie made her own hoarse sound.

And shifted again.

Good grief, this was what horny teenagers did to get off. Not that she'd ever done it, but she was fairly sure now that with some kisses it would work. Of course, just because it would work didn't mean it *should*.

She could hear Sugar and her father talking, figured what they were saying might be important for Lucky's and her escape. Still, Cassie couldn't get her mind completely off what was happening with Lucky's erection and her vee.

Then Lucky kissed her.

It wasn't really a kiss, though. He was breathing heavy now, and it was hitting against her mouth. Against her neck, too. Coupled with the shifting, Cassie thought she might be within seconds of having an orgasm. A rare event for her.

And then it all vanished.

The footsteps started again, coming closer to the door of the room where Lucky and she were shifting and veeing.

"You're sure you haven't seen them?" her father asked Sugar.

"Trust me, if I'd seen Lucky McCord, I would have remembered," Sugar answered. "Say, are Lucky and your daughter doing the nasty?"

"Not a chance," her father growled. "She's not his type."

Cassie's eyes narrowed because that was almost certainly an insult. Well, apparently she was Lucky's type because there were only a few millimeters of fabric stopping her from *doing the nasty* with him.

"Remember, if you see my daughter or Lucky anywhere near the place, I want you to call the cops," her father added to Sugar.

"Will do. Well, everything's locked up back here. I was just headed to the front door."

There were a few footsteps, but then they stopped. "What were you doing back here anyway?" Mason-Dixon asked.

Cassie felt her breath freeze, and this time it didn't have anything to do with Lucky's body pressing hard against hers. Almost anyway. She didn't want Sugar to get fired, and that's exactly what would happen if her father went into his room and realized the cats were missing.

"I was picking up some makeup I left—"

"Well, clear out," her father snapped, cutting off Sugar. "I've got some company with me."

Cassie's heart dropped even more when she heard a woman giggle, and she didn't think it was Sugar's giggle, either.

"Is that one of the Nederland sisters?" Sugar asked.

"Not that it's any of your business, but yeah. Now, clear out."

Cassie knew the Nederland sisters. They were all the size of tree trunks, and it wasn't a good idea for her father or any other man to play around with them.

That's because the Nederland sisters had brothers.

They were double the size of tree trunks, and they used their limb-size fists to pulverize any man they thought was disrespecting their sisters. Since men "disrespected" the sisters a lot, the brothers got to do a lot of pulverizing. She was surprised that her father would choose one of the sisters for a lover, but maybe he wanted to add some variety to his life. Could also be that all the strippers were just plain fed up with him and had turned him down.

"You're sure you want to take a woman into your room?" Sugar asked. "Even with the door closed, it smells really bad.

Can't imagine how bad it is in there. Why don't you use the costume room instead? There's a chaise in there and some fun toys."

"Fine," her father barked, though his bark couldn't hide that he thought the costume room was a good idea. "Now, leave."

She heard the sound of his footsteps again, headed to the front of the building this time. Sugar's ploy had worked.

"I owe Sugar big-time," Lucky mumbled, not sounding very happy about that. "This might require more than back-scratching."

Cassie wasn't sure she wanted to know what he meant by that, and there wasn't time to find out. Lucky threw the covers off the kennels and they hurried out of there. The moment they were in the car, he sped away.

"How much time do you think we have before my father figures out the cats are missing?" she asked.

"How long does it take to screw a Nederland?" he countered.

Cassie suspected not long, but it sounded like the start of a joke that she didn't want to hear.

"We can't take the cats to the house," Lucky continued. "That's the first place Mason-Dixon will look. We'll take them to my office instead."

Cassie had no idea what he meant by that until Lucky pulled to a stop in the parking lot of McCord Cattle Brokers. "Logan had offices done for Riley, Anna and me, and the cats can stay there for a while. I'll bring over food and a litter box for them later."

Lucky grabbed two of the kennels, Cassie took the third, and with the cats howling now, they raced inside. Of course, they'd have to tell Logan they were there so he didn't think strays had gotten inside the building. Logan's car wasn't in the lot, but there were two others plus a work truck loaded with paint and supplies. No doubt part of the redecorating effort.

There was evidence of that redecorating as soon as Lucky and she went inside. A man on a tall ladder was painting the high ceiling. There was also a tarp covering the floor.

Lucky led her to an office, one totally different from her father's. For one thing, it was clean and perfectly decorated with a high-end desk and bookcases. The windows all overlooked a rose garden. Even his name was on an etched copper plate on the door. Considering the way everything was placed and arranged, she doubted he'd even stepped foot in the place. And he didn't even step foot in it now. He turned the cats loose from the doorway and was in the process of closing it when someone called out his name.

Helene.

Looking more like a cover model than some cover models, Helene breezed toward them. Cassie didn't really know her. Helene's family had sent her to private schools in San Antonio, but of course, Cassie had seen her around town and shopped in her businesses. Helene owned both the antiques store and the clothing boutique, as well as an interior decorating business.

"Cats?" Helene asked, getting a glimpse of them just before Lucky shut the door.

"A temporary fix," he assured her. "I'll be back later with supplies."

"No need. I can do that for you. I understand you have your hands full with Mia and Mackenzie."

It wasn't a question, which meant Helene likely knew all about it. Of course she did. Cassie had heard Della buzzing about Helene staying the night before so certainly Logan would have discussed things with his girlfriend.

Oh, God.

Did that mean Helene also knew about the background check Logan had done on her? Or rather what he'd learned in that background check, about her being sent to Sweet Meadows? Cassie hoped not because she didn't want it getting all over town. If the press picked up on it... Well, Cassie didn't want to think about that.

But she thought about it anyway.

She definitely wouldn't be asked to be on any other talk

shows and she'd lose the few clients that she had. She wouldn't mind saying goodbye to Marla, but if she lost the others, she'd lose her source of income.

"I take it you'd like to keep this a secret?" Helene asked. She tipped her head to the office, but she also gave Cassie a lingering glance.

Yes, Helene knew. Things passed between them—woman to woman—and Cassie tried to plead her need for silence without actually saying anything. She didn't want to open this up for discussion.

"Definitely keep it secret," Lucky insisted. "And especially don't tell Mason-Dixon. If he comes here—"

"He won't get anywhere near your office," Helene assured them. "Anything else I can do to help?"

Lucky shook his head and turned to leave but then stopped. "Has Logan been having headaches?"

Cassie certainly hadn't expected the question and apparently neither had Helene, and Cassie didn't think the woman's surprise was because she didn't know the answer. "Have you asked Logan about it?" Helene responded.

"Is there something to ask?" Lucky fired right back.

Judging from Helene's sigh, this could go on for a while. "It's not my place to say anything." She tipped her head to the cats. "I'll see about getting them whatever they need." And with that, Helene glided up the stairs.

Lucky stood there a moment as if he might call her back, but his phone buzzed before he could say or do anything. He cursed the moment he looked at the text message that popped onto the screen.

"It's from Della," he said, holding it out so she could see.

But it was hard to read it since Lucky started running toward the exit. Cassie caught up with him, but she didn't get a chance to read it until they were in the car:

We got some problems. Two of them. Get home fast.

"DON'T SPECULATE," Lucky warned Cassie. "It could be just about the cats."

Though he doubted that would have prompted a text from Della. Heck, Lucky hadn't even known she could text. But he figured it had to be something urgent for the woman not to call him and give him some details. And that something urgent was likely to be that the girls had run away again.

That wasn't even the worst thing he could come up with, though.

After all, there was the possibility that Mackenzie was suicidal. Had she done something to hurt herself?

Lucky cursed, again. He shouldn't have left them. He should have had some friends deal with the cats at the Slippery Pole, or even paid the Nederlands to do it.

Cassie didn't speculate about the possibilities of what Della's text could mean, at least not out loud. But the moment the house came into view, they spotted two cars in the driveway, and one of them was a Spring Hill police cruiser. Maybe Della had already called out a search party. At least there wasn't an ambulance, but Lucky had a sickening thought—maybe the ambulance had already come and gone, and Mackenzie was at the hospital.

Two days.

That's all it had taken for him to have the "lying in a ditch" fear that he'd heard his mother and other parents go on about. Not that he was a parent, but he now had an inkling of what not knowing could do to a person responsible for a child.

Lucky was right behind Cassie when she bolted out of the car, and he raced into the house fully expecting Della to be standing there with the bad news. But it wasn't Della.

Mia and Mackenzie were in the foyer.

Mackenzie didn't appear to be hurt. Neither was Mia. And he was so relieved to see them that he hauled them into his arms. However, Lucky hadn't seen Cassie moving closer to do the same thing, making it a group hug. Mackenzie went stiff, but Mia hugged them right back.

"I thought you'd left," Lucky admitted. He wouldn't mention the other bad thought he'd had. "I'm glad you didn't. But when Della texted and said there was a problem—"

"Two problems," Mackenzie interrupted. "The deputy's here, and he's searching for the other cats."

Della came out from the living room to finish that explanation. "Apparently, Mason-Dixon called him about fifteen minutes ago, and Davy came rushing right over."

Well, it sure hadn't taken Mason-Dixon long with the Nederland sister.

"I'm gonna find those cats," Davy called down from the top of the stairs. "And when I do, I'm gonna have to arrest you, Lucky, because I know you're the one who took them."

Cassie huffed. "And how would you know that? I had more motive to take them than Lucky. They're my grandmother's cats."

"You're not a troublemaker like Lucky." Davy gave his head an indignant wobble and hooked his thumbs over his equipment belt. "Go ahead, ask him how many times he's been in jail."

This wasn't a subject he wanted to discuss in front of the girls, but since Davy had brought it up, Lucky went with it. "And how many times have I been in jail because I stole something?" He made a goose egg with his fingers.

That caused Davy to come back down the stairs. "That doesn't mean you didn't take 'em. Where have you been for the past half hour?"

"With me," Cassie jumped to answer. Which, of course, wasn't much of an answer at all.

Davy came into the foyer and stared at them, clearly waiting for more. And Cassie gave him more all right. She hooked her arm through Lucky's and got very close. Shoulder to shoulder. Hip to hip.

"Lucky and I wanted a little time alone," she added. Not exactly a lie, but Cassie probably didn't understand where this would lead.

To gossip and lots of it.

In an hour it would be all over town that Cassie and he were sleeping together, and it didn't help that this attraction was whirling all around them. No doubt leftover lust from that "cuddling" session on the floor of the Slippery Pole. Lucky was certainly still feeling the effects of that. It might take a week for him to go fully soft again.

Davy's gaze whipped back and forth between them as if trying to decide if Cassie was telling the truth. He must have decided that she was because the deputy headed for the door, already taking out his phone. "If those cats don't turn up soon, I'll be back," he warned them.

Davy would, and that was a reminder for Lucky to move the cats, maybe out of town.

"We could blackmail my father," Cassie suggested. "We know he was with one of the Nederland sisters, and we could threaten him with that if he doesn't back off."

Lucky had to nod. No way would Mason-Dixon want that to get around since then he'd have to deal with the Nederland brothers.

"Blackmail?" someone said. It wasn't a voice Lucky recognized. Nor did he recognize the dark-haired man who stepped out of the living room. The guy was tall, moved like a dancer. Sort of looked like one, too, in his blue suit. The wrong color blue to be from around Spring Hill. That suit had big city/expensive tailor written all over it.

"Remember I texted you that there were two problems," Della said. "Davy was one." She hitched her thumb to the visitor. "He's the other."

"Andrew." Cassie's voice was hardly louder than a whisper, but there was plenty of emotion in it. Mainly surprise. However, Lucky thought he detected some other things, too. Things he couldn't put his finger on.

It took Lucky a moment to make the connection. Dr. Andrew Knight was the person who'd committed Cassie to that "relaxation" place.

And he was her boyfriend.

More or less.

Andrew came closer, and without even acknowledging that Cassie still had her arm looped through Lucky's, he took hold of her and pulled her into his own arms. Cassie had a similar reaction to Mackenzie's, from when they'd shared that group hug earlier. She went a little stiff, but maybe that didn't have anything to do with an absence of attraction. Maybe she was just uncomfortable because her more-or-less boyfriend had caught her hugging up another man.

"Andrew," Cassie repeated when he finally let go of her. "Why are you here?"

"Blackmail?" he repeated. He spared the girls a glance. Finally, he spared Lucky one, too. "It sounds as if I got here just in time." He stepped away from Cassie, extended his hand for Lucky to shake. "I'm Dr. Andrew Knight."

"Lucky McCord."

"Interesting nickname," he said, managing to sound like a pompous ass with just those two words. Lucky's opinion of him didn't improve when Andrew opened his mouth again and continued with, "I understand you ride bulls for a living?"

Yeah, definitely pomp with plenty of ass thrown in.

"Among other things," Lucky answered.

It would have been so easy to get into a pissing contest with this ding-dong. After all, Lucky co-owned a rodeo promotion business. A successful one. Plus, he was a McCord. That came with trust funds and shit.

Especially the shit.

But even if Lucky hadn't had those things, it still didn't give Andrew the right to look down on him. Or the girls. Though that's what he appeared to be doing when he turned his attention in their direction.

"And you two must be Mia and Mackenzie," Andrew said.

"Must we?" Mackenzie fired back.

Lucky tried not to laugh. Failed a little. It earned him a nasty side glance from Dr. Dickhead, and the man certainly didn't laugh. He sighed. The kind of sigh a person might make when trying to convey, *I've got my work cut out for me.*

"I'm here to help you," Andrew said to the girls.

"Uh, I called Sarah," Cassie interrupted. "Child psychology is her area of expertise. Where is she?"

"She won't be coming. Sarah called me after she spoke to you and wanted me to take some of her clients while she was here. I told her that wasn't necessary—that I'd already cleared my schedule and was booking the flight as we spoke."

Cassie shook her head. "But why?"

His next sigh was more of an *Isn't it obvious?* "Blackmail?" he repeated as if it were some big deal. Maybe to him it was, but Andrew didn't know Mason-Dixon. At least Lucky didn't think he did. Come to think of it, Lucky had no idea just how involved Dr. Dickhead was in Cassie's life.

Hell, she could be in love with the guy.

That notion didn't settle well in his stomach.

"I think it's obvious you have other things you need to be doing," Andrew said, speaking to Cassie now. "I expected you to be back at Sweet Meadows by now."

She flinched as if he'd spit on her. Probably because she hadn't wanted him to air her dirty laundry, especially since he'd been the one who'd created the laundry by committing her to that place. Sweet Meadows didn't exactly sound like a loony bin, though, so perhaps Andrew didn't think he was doing her any harm.

"My grandmother died," Cassie reminded him. "And she made us guardians of the children."

"Yes, I heard all about that when I called your grandmother's lawyer. You were only supposed to take the children for a day or two at most. It's been two days."

That was true, but two days hadn't been nearly enough time to find their next of kin. Of course, in the back of Lucky's mind, he'd known it wouldn't be, but he'd still held out hope. Now he was just hoping that it'd be resolved in a week.

"Plus, you should know there's a reporter who's been asking about you," Andrew went on, still talking to Cassie. "Theo Kervin. But reporter is too generous of a job title for him. He's actually a paparazzi from LA."

This had to be the same guy who'd called Marlene at the newspaper. Thank God this Theo wasn't in town to get the latest scoop. What with the gossip about Mackenzie and now the cat thievery, Cassie's reputation could be hurt. Of course, if Theo had also gotten word about Cassie being committed to that place, he might be digging for dirt on that, too.

"There's no story here for a reporter," Cassie insisted, but Lucky knew that was wishful thinking on her part.

"You need to make sure it stays that way—no story. I can handle whatever else needs to be handled so it'll take some of the pressure off you," Andrew said. "I understand you're looking for their next of kin. Well, they can be sent to foster care until you find him or her."

Lucky had held his tongue. Until now. "No. They're not going to foster care."

Clearly that didn't please Dr. Dundernuts. "And what makes you qualified to raise these children?"

Before Lucky could answer, Mia tugged on his shirtsleeve. "What does quala-fried mean?"

Andrew jumped to answer that. "It means *Lucky* should know how to deal with and talk to children." The doc said his nickname as if it were a persistent toenail fungus. "He doesn't. I do."

Lucky wanted to ask him what qualified him to do that, but he was afraid this jerk would have a good answer—like a bunch of degrees and tons of experience.

"I happen to agree with Lucky about the girls not going to foster care," Cassie spoke up. Good thing she'd finally found her backbone. Sheez. Couldn't she see that Andrew was a bully just like her father?

Maybe Andrew saw some of that backbone because after he stared at her awhile, he finally nodded. Then he patted her arm. The next sigh he added had a "just keep calm and don't go nuts again" tone to it.

"All right, no foster care," Andrew agreed, "but I think it's ridiculous not to use a system that's already in place to handle situations exactly like this."

"They're not a situation," Lucky said, stepping in front of them. "And besides, we have a lead on their next of kin. We should hear back from her soon."

Lucky had no idea if that was the truth, but Logan was working on it. If this Aunt Alice was anywhere on the planet, Logan's PI would find her. And soon. Because Logan didn't like unfinished business, either.

Andrew looked at Cassie, silently asking if that was true, and she nodded.

The doc smiled. "Well, good. Then it's practically settled." He seemed plenty gleeful about something that was far from settled.

Andrew looked at the girls. "Since I'm here, I might as well go ahead and have a session with the children. Is there some place quiet where I can talk with them in private?"

That question elicited a variety of responses.

Cassie: "Uh…"

Mia: "What's a session?"

Della: "There's an office."

Mackenzie: "I don't want your stupid help."

Lucky was in Mackenzie's corner on this. Or at least that's what he wanted to be able to tell the doctor. But the truth was, the girls did need help.

Especially Mackenzie.

And having them see a counselor was something he should have already arranged. He'd gotten so caught up with the de-

tails that he'd forgotten the devil that was in them. And the
devil in this case was that Mackenzie could be suicidal, and
Andrew could help.

"A session is where you talk to somebody," Lucky explained
to Mia. "It's supposed to make you feel better."

"Like a magic gold star?" Mia was wearing it on her right
earlobe today. Lucky hoped the glue kept sticking so she didn't
lose it.

"Better than a magic gold star," Lucky assured her. Possibly
another lie. But it made Mia smile.

Now, to Mackenzie.

"It might be a good idea if you talked to him," Lucky said
to her. That required him to eat some crow since he'd spent the
past ten minutes mind-bashing Andrew.

Mia nodded, of course. Always eager to please. Maybe too
eager. Now it was Lucky who was sighing, and his had an "I'm
in over my head" tone to it.

Mackenzie just stared at him.

"Please," Cassie said, taking the word right out of Lucky's
mouth.

"If nothing else, consider it payment for the money you took,"
Lucky whispered to her. Yeah, it was another version of blackmail, but Mackenzie did deserve some consequences for the
theft.

Though it was a little like the pot calling the kettle black since
he'd just stolen some cats. Of course, Lucky figured he'd have
plenty of consequences to face for that. Mason-Dixon wasn't
just going to drop this, and Lucky would eventually have to
offer him enough money to get him to back down.

Mackenzie finally huffed, took hold of Mia's hand. "All
right." But before she followed in step behind the doctor and
Della, who was ready to lead them to the office, Mackenzie
stopped next to Lucky. "You want me to make this bad for that
idiot?" she whispered.

It was tempting. God, was it tempting. But Lucky couldn't

pass up the chance to do something that might actually help Mackenzie. Mia, too.

"Just talk to him," Lucky settled for saying. "Tell him whatever you want to tell him, and if he offers any advice, consider taking it."

If Andrew heard any part of that, he didn't acknowledge it. He was checking his watch, but he did glance back at Cassie as Della was leading the girls and him to the office.

"After the girls and I talk," Andrew said to Cassie, "then you and I need to have a chat, too. We can do that on the way to the San Antonio airport. I've booked us on a three-o'clock flight."

CHAPTER ELEVEN

CASSIE OPENED HER mouth to say something—*anything*—but Andrew had already walked away from her.

"You're leaving today?" Lucky asked.

She shook her head.

"Well, he thinks you are. Did he tell you he was booking that flight?" Lucky pressed.

Cassie had to shake her head again. Andrew was a take-charge kind of person. There were times when that could be a good thing. Like when she'd been falling apart. But it wasn't a good thing now.

"Don't worry," Cassie told Lucky. "I won't leave you holding the bag with the girls. I'll stay until we find their aunt."

"You're sure? Because Dr. Wonderful will likely try to bull-doze you into leaving on that afternoon flight."

Yes, he would. And worse, there was a time she would have let him. But not now. It was her fault for giving Andrew power over her. Power to make decisions when she'd been too troubled to make them for herself. However, she couldn't let Andrew put her or anything else ahead of the girls.

Lucky was staring at her, and Cassie could tell he thought significantly less about her than he had just an hour ago. He no doubt thought she'd already lost the little bit of spine she'd found when she'd confronted her father.

"I know it's hard to understand," Cassie said. She moved into the living room and sank down onto the sofa. "But Andrew was the only one there for me after... Well, after."

After her client, Hannah Carpenter, had committed suicide.

"I'm not sure exactly what you were going through, but he was the only one there for you only because you didn't tell anyone else," Lucky argued. "If you'd told Dixie Mae or me—"

Her look stopped him. A reminder that there was no way she would have told Lucky because he wasn't on her emotional radar at the time. And as for Dixie Mae, Cassie had called her shortly after it'd happened, but then her gran had gotten sick, and Cassie hadn't wanted to burden her any further with it.

Lucky glanced in the direction of the office. Then at her. "Will he be okay with the girls, or will he act like an asshole to them, too?"

"He'll be okay. Andrew is actually really good at what he does." At relationships, though, not so much. He used every conversation as an attempt to fix rather than listen.

Lucky made a sound of disagreement. "He committed you to that place."

She had to nod. "I could have fought it. I could have stopped him from doing it. But I didn't."

Cassie hadn't meant to tell him that. It was one of those things she wasn't exactly proud of, but Lucky had already seen her at her worst—in the throes of a panic attack, and her wimpiness when dealing with Andrew and her father.

"So why didn't you stop Andrew?" he asked. "Is it because you're in love with him?"

"No." Cassie blurted that out way too fast and much too loud. Which meant she had more explaining to do. And that explaining certainly wasn't going to paint her in a good light, either. "I loved him. Once. When we were in college together. But he's changed since he became a psychologist."

"Good. I'd hate to think he's always run roughshod over you like this."

Oh, he'd always done that, but Andrew had added a lot more honey in those days so that the *shod* hadn't felt so *rough*. Plus, she had tolerated more from him when they'd still been lovers.

"Andrew and I haven't been together like that in a while now." Over a year. "But he still feels responsible for me."

And now more explaining was required.

"Let me guess," Lucky said before she could continue. "He dumped you, and he's feeling guilty about that, so now he's watching out for you."

"Close," she admitted. Actually, it was spot-on. "He can be a jerk, but I'm not sure I would have made it through these last months without him." Cassie paused. "I had a client named Hannah Carpenter."

Lucky didn't say anything. He just sat down on the sofa next to her. Not even that close. And he didn't look at her as if waiting for her to continue.

"As you've probably guessed from Marla, my clients don't usually have serious problems. They're more like small mental glitches. And in some cases, there aren't any problems at all. The client just wants to be in therapy because all his or her friends are. I call it the lemming effect."

"Sheez," he mumbled.

Her sentiments exactly. "They're semicelebrities with semi-problems," Cassie added. "And I thought I wasn't doing any harm by seeing them and letting them talk through whatever issues they thought they had. But I missed the cues with Hannah. I knew she was depressed and was on meds that her doctor had prescribed. I thought she was making progress."

"She was your patient for a long time?" he asked.

"Just a couple of months. We met on one of those advice TV shows where we were both guests, and she asked to continue seeing me."

And she had. Eleven visits total, and Cassie could remember almost everything they'd talked about. Everything except for that last visit.

"I'd been in a hurry during that final session with Hannah," she continued. "I was distracted thinking about another TV appearance. My mind kept going back to the notes I'd made for that, and I... Well, I messed up. I clearly didn't see how much distress Hannah was in, and later that night she took an over-dose of sleeping pills."

Lucky stayed quiet, but he did ease his arm around her, and he inched closer. She figured this was the point where most people would have added a horror story of their own to try to make her feel better. Especially since rumor had it that Lucky did have a personal tragedy. Something he felt guilty about.

Something to do with his parents' car accident.

There wasn't a general consensus regarding Lucky's involve-ment, but some said his parents had been so upset about some-thing he'd done that it'd caused them not to be attentive enough to the other car. Others claimed Lucky had been in the other vehicle. So far, Lucky hadn't publically confirmed or denied anything, which only kept fueling the old gossip. However, he had told Dixie Mae, and that's how Cassie knew the rumors were wrong.

"And the panic attacks started after Hannah died?" he con-tinued.

Cassie nodded. "But they're getting better. I haven't come close to having one since night before last."

"You're sure?"

Only then did Cassie realize her breathing was off. Way too fast and shallow. The classic beginnings of a panic attack. "I should probably take my meds just in case."

"Or we could try this."

Cassie didn't even see the kiss coming, but she certainly felt it. *Wow.* That was her first thought anyway, and the *wow* just kept repeating in her head. Maybe because of all the heat his mouth was generating. Perhaps it had melted her brain.

If so, Cassie didn't care.

Suddenly, this seemed a lot more important that having a functioning brain.

Of course, she had shared a kiss with Lucky before. The fake kiss. But this wasn't fake. Or if it was, it felt a lot less fake than the other one, and the other one had packed a wallop. This one packed three wallops, and she had to mentally up it to eighty million wallops when Lucky deepened the kiss.

Ever since Cassie had first noticed Lucky and the effect he had on her gender, she'd wondered what it would be like to kiss him, to have him weave that testosterone spell around her. Well, now she knew. The spell was warm, golden and delicious. Just like Lucky, and in those couple of seconds she understood exactly why he'd managed to attract every girl in high school.

And every girl since.

How she'd ever resisted this, she didn't know, and worse, she didn't want to keep resisting it. Cassie wanted to continue this kiss until it led to something much more. Something that would relieve this ache that was suddenly in the southern regions of her body.

But that didn't happen.

Cassie heard a sound. One she didn't want to hear because it was someone clearing their throat. She pulled away from Lucky just as he pulled away from her, and their attention flew to the doorway.

Where Della and Wilhelmina were standing. And watching.

"I was having a panic attack," Cassie blurted out. Good grief. Where had that come from?

"Okay," Della said, sounding as skeptical as she should be. "Are you better now?"

"Yes." And it was true. There were no signs of the panic attack, though her body was obviously prepping itself for something it wasn't going to get.

It wasn't going to get lucky. Or get Lucky for that matter.

"What about you?" Della asked, turning to Lucky. "Were

you having a panic attack, too?" With the deserved chain-yank-ing, she smiled and lifted her hand to Wilhelmina. "We have company."

Wilhelmina definitely wasn't smiling. Nor was she batting her eyelashes at Lucky today. And Cassie knew why.

"I'm so sorry," Cassie told the woman right away. "I know we were supposed to bring over Mackenzie's apology, but things have been so crazy."

Wilhelmina gave her a flat stare. "No, *Lucky* was supposed to bring me the apology and take me out to lunch."

Lucky nodded, got to his feet. He glanced at Cassie, maybe to see if she really had escaped that panic attack. Or perhaps just because he couldn't believe he'd kissed her like that. Cassie was certainly having some trouble believing it herself.

"We'll still have that lunch," Lucky assured the woman. He took the Post-it note apology that Mackenzie had written and handed it to her.

That didn't help Wilhelmina's mood any. "No longer lunch. You have to take me to dinner instead."

Cassie huffed. "Do you really think Lucky should have to pay for this with his time? With dinner?"

"Yes," Wilhelmina readily answered, looking not at Cassie but rather Lucky. "You can pick me up Tuesday after work, and I want to go to someplace fancy."

Since there wasn't any place that qualified as fancy in Spring Hill, that meant Lucky would have to take her into San Anto-nio. Here he was pimping himself, and even though it was for a good cause—to keep Mackenzie out of lockup—it still didn't sit right with Cassie.

"And don't bring her on our date." Wilhelmina shot Cassie a glare before she walked out.

"You should have told Wilhelmina that you were impotent," Cassie grumbled.

Lucky shook his head. "Someone started a rumor about that

when I was in high school, and nearly every girl in the senior class wanted to cure me."

Della chuckled. "I remember that." She patted his cheek. "What you should do is let everyone know you're off the market." And her gaze drifted from Cassie, to him, back to Cassie again.

"Oh," Cassie said. "Because of the kiss? Well, Lucky's not off the market. That was just, well… That just was."

"Yeah," Lucky agreed, though it was obvious none of them, including him, had any idea what he was agreeing with.

"You're sure?" Della pressed. "Because that kiss looked like—"

"Don't you have something to do in the kitchen?" Lucky interrupted.

"No. I have something to do right here." Della handed Lucky a note. "It's from Logan," Della explained. "Next week, he wants either Riley or you to go out and check on the park and see how the booths are coming along for the Founder's Day picnic."

Lucky stared at the message as if debating what to do.

"Riley's tied up with ranching and wedding stuff," Della reminded him. She gave his arm another pat. "I know it'll be hard for you. It always is. But maybe if you see the place before the crowds get there, it'll be easier."

"I'll go," Lucky said, his response too fast, as if he wanted to cut off anything else Della had to say.

He handed her back the note, leaving Cassie to wonder what was going on in his head.

"Maybe you can go with him?" Della asked her. It sounded as if Lucky needed that so Cassie nodded.

"Good," Della went on. "If you want to take the girls, too, I can do up a picnic basket for you. Might do you all some good to get out of this house and away from…things." Her gaze drifted toward the office where Andrew was.

Cassie definitely wouldn't mind getting away and catching a moment to clear her head, but then she heard the loud knock on the door. It didn't really even qualify as a knock, more like a pounding. Followed by several jabs on the doorbell.

"We might as well just leave the door open what with everyone coming and going," Della grumbled, heading in that direction. Lucky and Cassie were right behind her, and Cassie hoped this wasn't the deputy returning to search for those cats.

But it was her father.

"Where are those goddamn cats?" he yelled.

Lucky stepped in front of both Della and her, and he blocked her father from actually entering the house.

"They're not here," Lucky insisted. But his attention wasn't exactly on her father's face. It was on Mason-Dixon's arm. "Is that a misspelled tattoo?"

Considering the sheer ire in her father's expression, the question seemed odd. But then she remembered Lucky's extreme reaction to Dixie Mae's misspelled tat.

Mason-Dixon looked down at his right bicep where there was indeed a tattoo, one that Cassie had never seen. Regret Nothing. Except it was inked as *Reget* Nothing.

She was betting her father regretted something—that misspelling.

"Did you go to the same inker as your mom?" Lucky wanted to know. "Because if you did, give me his address so I can send that moron a dictionary."

Her father pulled down his sleeve. "You're getting off the subject, trying to distract me. Well, it won't work." His voice got louder with each word. "Davy said he looked and couldn't find those fucking cats. That means you have them stashed somewhere, and I want to know where. Those are my property."

Lucky tore his attention from the now-covered tattoo. "Property you were using to blackmail Cassie. I know that wasn't what Dixie Mae had in mind when she arranged to have them dropped off at the strip club."

Cassie agreed, but she had to admit she still didn't know what Dixie Mae had in mind when it came to that. Heck, when it came to everything the woman had arranged. If this was some kind of matchmaking attempt on her part, Cassie would hunt her down in the hereafter and have a "chat" with her about it. But for now, she needed to finish dealing with her father.

"What kind of bottom line are you looking at here?" Cassie asked. "Give me a number of how much it'll take for you to back off, and then you'll have enough cash to fix that misspelled tattoo."

"What's going on here?" Andrew asked.

Maybe because her own voice level had been way too loud, Cassie hadn't heard Andrew come into the foyer. The girls were right behind him, and thankfully Della swooped in to lead them back into the kitchen. Cassie definitely didn't want them to be around for what would be a profanity-laced tirade on her father's part. Heck, maybe on her part, too.

"My father wants money for cats," Cassie said.

"Cats that she and Lucky stole!" her father added. He was still shouting, and the veins were bulging in his neck.

"Cassie." Andrew didn't shout. He sounded horrified, though. "Are you trying to shred what's left of your reputation?"

That was not the right thing to say, and it set her teeth on edge as much as the Regret Nothing had riled Lucky. "Actually, I was trying to save my grandmother's cats."

"Cats that Dixie Mae left me," her father said. His attention was on Andrew, and Andrew's attention was on him. "You know how Cassie is. She can get all wound up when it comes to this sort of thing. She let Lucky talk her into doing something stupid."

Because Cassie was seething over the "wound up" remark, it took her a few seconds to pick through what her father had just said and find a little nugget that didn't belong there.

You know how Cassie is...

Lucky obviously picked up on it, too. "You two have met?" he asked Andrew and her father.

Silence.

Not the kind of silence one would expect from two men who didn't know the answer, but rather that of two men who didn't want to share said answer with her and Lucky.

"We've met," Andrew finally said, and judging from the way his mouth tightened, he wasn't too happy about revealing that.

Welcome to the club. For her part, Cassie wasn't happy being left out of this particular information loop.

"I'm going to want an explanation to go along with that," she said. "Because you know how wound up I can get about such things."

Andrew reached out as if to take hold of her, but Cassie stepped away. "Tell me," she insisted.

"It's nothing, really," Andrew answered after several tortoise-crawling moments. "I was just looking out for you. I knew if it got out that this was your father, then it wouldn't be good for your reputation."

Mason-Dixon shrugged. "Hey, I never asked him for a dime. I just asked him if it'd be a good idea if I talked to those reporters and talk-show hosts who are always interviewing you."

Oh. My. God.

Lucky looked at her, silently asking her if she knew anything about this. But she didn't.

"You gave him money?" she asked Andrew.

"Yes." He seemed surprised that she was upset. "Some," he clarified when he seemed to realize that she was past the upset stage.

"I never asked for it," her father repeated.

"You blackmailed him," Cassie shouted. She snapped toward Andrew. "And you paid him without telling me. Don't you dare say it was for my own good."

Judging from the way Andrew suddenly got very quiet, that was exactly what he'd been about to say.

"How much?" Lucky asked.

Andrew shrugged, glanced around as if he expected to find the answer in the hardwood floor.

Lucky snapped to her father. "How much will it take for you to drop this whole cat issue? And don't you dare say you want part of whatever Cassie inherits. Give me a figure."

Cassie was so frustrated and flabbergasted that it took her a second to find her voice. "You aren't going to pay him off."

"It's the only way to get rid of him," Lucky answered. "Clearly, he's got a track record for this sort of thing."

"Hey, I have a lot of expenses from the club," Mason-Dixon snarled. "And here my own mother denied me a loan."

Lucky groaned. "Yeah, yeah. The great dildo feud. I know all about it."

Cassie was really confused now, but she wasn't sure she wanted to know the answers to some parts of this conversation. Especially the dildos.

"Then you know Dixie Mae owed me," her father insisted.

"In your warped fantasy world maybe. So, how much to give Cassie all six of the cats?"

Her father smiled, and it was that sick smile that she'd seen way too often. "Give me your half of the rodeo business."

Cassie actually gasped. It was like asking Lucky to give up his firstborn child or his penis. She wasn't waiting for Lucky to answer.

"No way," she told her father. "You're not getting the business that Lucky and Gran built. And you're not getting anything else from Andrew, either. Here's how this will work. You'll give me the cats and in exchange I won't tell the Nederland brothers that you're sleeping with their sister."

Mason-Dixon made a sound that was part gasp, part huff. "You don't have any proof of that."

She took out her phone. Not that there was anything on there to show him, but she was pissed enough to make an empty threat. "Oh, no? Well, if you believe I could sneak into the club and steal cats, then why would it be so hard to believe that I took a picture of you and Becky Nederland having sex in one of the dressing rooms at the club?"

Cassie wasn't even sure it was Becky. She couldn't tell the sisters apart. But it was highly likely her father couldn't, either.

Her father volleyed glances from the phone, to Andrew, to Lucky and back to her before starting the volleying loop all over again. He finally cursed and turned to walk away.

"This isn't over," he warned them. "When Davy finds those cats, he'll arrest both of you."

Cassie felt as if she'd survived a storm. Part of one anyway. The rest of the storm was there in the foyer with her.

"I don't want either of you paying off my father. Or my mother," she added in case that came up.

But it apparently already had. Cassie could tell from the way Andrew got interested in the flooring again that he'd given her mother money, too. Good grief.

"I know my parents are less than stellar," she said. Such a huge understatement, but Cassie was making a point here. "But I don't need to be protected from them."

However, she might require some bail money if her father managed to get the theft charge to stick. Still, she didn't want this kind of protection from Andrew, Lucky or anybody else.

"Want my advice?" Andrew said, but he didn't wait for her to answer. "I say we leave right now. We'll go to the airport, have some lunch, and with you out of sight, you'll soon be out of your father's mind, too."

That caused some veins to bulge in Lucky's neck.

"I can't leave," she told Andrew. "Did you forget that Lucky and I have guardianship of Mia and Mackenzie?"

"Of course not. I just counseled them, remember? But I also know you can't help them. Especially Mackenzie. She's beyond help if you ask my opinion."

"I didn't ask," Lucky snarled.

"Well, you're not exactly qualified to have an opinion about this. Plus, if Cassie stays here, her reputation could be ruined to the point that no one would ever hire her. She could lose everything. Is that what you want?"

Cassie couldn't stop herself. She screamed. At the top of her lungs. It felt surprisingly good.

"At the moment I don't care what either of you want for me," she snapped. "You're not paying off my father, and I'm not leaving Spring Hill until the girls' situation is resolved."

Lucky shrugged. Nodded.

Andrew didn't shrug, and he certainly didn't nod. He looked about as happy with her as her father had. "Fine. But if you're staying, so am I. I can work from here just as well as you can." He glanced at Lucky. "Why don't you have your housekeeper get a guest room ready for me?"

Lucky looked ready to tell him hell no. Or at least that's what Cassie hoped Lucky would say, but he didn't get a chance to say anything. That's because a loud female squeal suddenly sounded from the front porch.

"Lucky!" the woman called out. She was blonde, busty and clearly very excited to see him.

"Angel," Lucky mumbled, not sounding nearly as excited.

"A friend?" Cassie asked.

Lucky appeared to be on the verge of a shrug when the woman launched herself into his arms and tongue kissed him.

CHAPTER TWELVE

ANGEL HAD NOT been a welcome interruption. It had taken Lucky a half hour to convince her that this visit wasn't going to happen and to send her on her unmerry way. That half hour had involved six more attempted French kisses and a successful crotch groping that she'd managed to get past him.

Of course, Cassie and Della being there hadn't helped. And Andrew had thoroughly enjoyed the debacle happening on the front porch.

But Andrew had then gotten his own comeuppance.

Della had made it clear to Andrew that there were no available guest rooms in the house. She'd been fudging a bit on that, though. There was an extra guest room if they wanted to keep Mia and Mackenzie in the same suite, but Lucky had wanted them to have the option of their own space. Just in case the guardianship lingered on.

Which it seemed to be doing since they were now a week into it.

Of course, Della could have put Andrew in Riley's room since he was practically living at Claire's now. Heck, Riley had even taken the family pet, Crazy Dog, to live there. Or Della could have given Andrew Anna's old room. But that had seemed like a big-assed accommodation to make for someone who was being such a big ass himself.

So, Della's news of "no rooms available" had prevented Lucky from getting ugly with Andrew and telling the ass outright that he didn't want him under the McCord roof. With Lucky's mood raw and his nerves on edge, it might have done him some good to tell the man to go to hell instead of just telling him to go to the Bluebonnet Inn—which now had open rooms because the reunion was over. What would have really felt good was for Lucky to punch him.

To punch Mason-Dixon, too.

But starting a brawl didn't exactly seem like a life lesson he wanted to teach the girls. Instead, Lucky and Cassie had called a truce and had spent the rest of the day and the following one with Mackenzie and Mia. Well, they'd spent it with Mia anyway. Cassie and he had played games and watched movies with her and had even taken her out for a ride on one of the gentler horses.

Mackenzie had spent her time scowling. It was possible her scowl was now permanent.

Lucky was hoping some sunshine would help with the scowl. Or at least melt off some of Mackenzie's makeup. That was why he'd suggested they all go to the park, taking along the picnic basket Della had generously fixed. This was a "killing two birds with one stone" kind of thing because he could also tick off that errand for Logan—checking on how the setup for the Founder's Day picnic was progressing.

For Lucky that meant driving all four of them to a place he didn't want to go while having thoughts he didn't want to have. At least Andrew hadn't tagged along, though he'd been calling Cassie practically every fifteen minutes. Thankfully the man had some live-chat therapy sessions and would be tied up most of the day.

Lucky still wanted to punch something, still would have loved to have gotten out of this particular chore of checking on the Founder's Day picnic, and at this point the best he was hoping for was just to get it over with while the girls got a little time outdoors.

Heck, it might help Cassie, too, since her mood didn't seem any better than his. Of course, she'd learned her ex-boyfriend had paid off her parents. But—here was the part he didn't understand—she hadn't demanded that the extortion-obliging moron leave Spring Hill and never come back. Nope. In fact, she'd given him the number to the Bluebonnet Inn. Obviously, she wasn't ready to let go of the head doctor just yet.

Even after she and Lucky had shared that kissing session on the sofa.

He was accustomed to having women kiss him and having it not mean anything. Hell, that was how it'd gone most of his life. Most women just wanted to be with him to see if he matched up to the hype. He had no idea if he did, but for some stupid reason he'd thought that kiss with Cassie had meant something.

Live and learn.

"This sucks," Mackenzie said. "You know that, right?"

"Which part?" Cassie asked. She was leaning her head against the window, but she lifted it enough to look in the backseat where the girls were sitting.

"All of it. I don't do fresh air and sunshine."

Yep, it was the fear of her makeup melting. Or maybe it just seemed like the ornery thing to say.

Of course, with his equally ornery mood, Lucky agreed with her. It did suck. The alternative, though, would have been leaving the girls with Della and Stella again, and they'd already watched them during the cat robbery. And he hadn't wanted to pawn this duty off on Riley what with all the wedding plans still to be finished.

"Do we have to see that idiot doctor again?" Mackenzie asked. "Because that sucked, too."

Neither Lucky nor Cassie had asked about the sessions, and despite how he felt about Andrew, Lucky hadn't wanted it to suck. Especially since Cassie and he didn't seem to be making any progress with the girl.

"I don't like the man doctor," Mia piped up. "But I like brownies and Frisbees, and Miss Della put some in the basket."

Yes, she had. And even though Lucky hadn't checked the other things Della had put in there, it would no doubt be filled with goodies. Other than the sunshine, that might be the only bright spot of this entire outing.

"You don't have to see Andrew again," Cassie assured them. She didn't say the same for herself, though. "But if you think you'd like to talk to someone, I have another friend I can ask to come over."

"I don't want to talk to anybody," Mackenzie snapped.

"Why we gotta talk to somebody?" Mia asked.

"You don't have to," Cassie answered. "But sometimes it makes some people feel better to talk." She slipped Lucky a side glance with that.

Lucky slipped her one right back. Yeah, he had some demons chasing him, but at least he didn't have a more-or-less girlfriend. What he did have, though, were more-or-less dates with Sugar and Wilhelmina. Cassie might have considered that an even-steven kind of thing, but it wasn't.

Lucky pulled to a stop beneath one of the many shady oaks. They'd need every drop of that shade today because it was Texas hot. A well-hydrated camel with an AC unit would have had trouble in this heat, and he felt sorry for the workers who were putting up the booths.

It didn't look like much now, what with work trucks, equipment and supplies all around, but in a week and a half, it'd be ready for the stream of visitors who would come to eat, listen to music and celebrate. Lucky would be there, too.

But not to celebrate.

Hell, he had way too many memories of this place. It had been his mother's and his thing.

"The banner's already up," Cassie pointed out.

It was a new one. Logan's or Helene's doing probably. This one was shiny silver and copper and had McCord Founder's Day Picnic on it. It was stretched across the grounds above the booths being constructed. It should have read Betsy McCord Founder's Day Picnic.

"Why don't you suggest that?" Cassie asked.

At first Lucky wasn't sure what she meant, and then he figured out he'd said that last part aloud. Too bad. Because it put a new layer of trouble on her already troubled face.

He didn't want Cassie worrying about him. He didn't want anyone doing that. So, maybe it was time to do some "Lucky" stuff. Go out with a woman—not Wilhelmina or Sugar, either. But a woman he could take to Calhoun's Pub for some tequila shots and a long enough make-out session to create some gossip. He'd do that as soon as this situation with the girls was worked out. As soon as Cassie returned to wherever she would be heading with her more-or-less ex.

Yep, that's what he'd do.

"Do what?" Cassie asked.

Shit. Had he done it again? Had he blurted out what he was thinking? But this time it was a false alarm because Cassie was talking to Mackenzie while she was spreading out a blanket on the ground. Mia was helping her. Mackenzie wasn't. She was glaring and pouting.

"I said I don't want to hang around here and eat out of a basket," Mackenzie snapped. "I don't want to share my food with ants and sit in bug poop. I want to go for a walk."

Lucky was instantly suspicious, but his suspicions lessened a bit when Mackenzie strolled off and left Mia, who was still helping Cassie. If Mackenzie was planning on running, she wouldn't have left Mia behind.

"Stay where we can see you," Lucky called out to her just in case.

Whether Mackenzie would or not was yet to be determined, but with the road behind them, there weren't many places for her to go. Especially in those heels. They were clearly a gift from Livvy since they were higher than some stepladders.

"Della included this in the basket," Cassie said, handing him a note.

Curious but reluctant to read what was on the paper, Lucky hesitated. And then he unfolded the note. It read, "It's okay, Lucky. Your mom would be so proud of you. Della."

That was bullshit, and Lucky paused a moment to make sure he hadn't said that aloud. He hadn't, but Cassie was watching him while Mia started in on one of the sandwiches Della had packed.

"Bad memories here?" Cassie asked, sitting down next to him. They both kept their eyes on Mackenzie.

"Some." Plenty. Of course, there were bad memories all over town because everywhere reminded him of his mother, of her death. Every place but Calhoun's Pub. To the best of his knowledge, his mother had never gone in there. "All of this was my mom's idea."

"I remember hearing that. I remember her being here, too, every year. She loved it."

Yeah.

The silence settled between them. Before long, Lucky saw something that got his attention and changed his mood from sullen to suspicious. Mackenzie had stopped her strolling and was talking to Brody Tate, who was showing her the mechanical-bull-riding stations he was setting up. That got Lucky on his feet.

"You know that boy?" Cassie asked.

Lucky nodded. "He's Elgin Tate's son."

That got Cassie on her feet, as well. Elgin had been their year in high school but had dropped out when he knocked up his girlfriend. And his girlfriend's best friend. And the best friend's sister. Rumor had it that there were a couple more knock-ups in there, as well. If Brody was anything like his father—and rumor had it that he was—Lucky might have to kill him, or at least superglue his zipper.

"Come on." Cassie took hold of Mia's hand. "Let's go check on your sister."

"Is she in trouble?" Mia asked.

No, but her getting in this kind of trouble was exactly what Lucky intended to stop. It was time for some bud-nipping. Especially when Lucky saw that Brody was leaning in closer and closer to Mackenzie. Lucky recognized sweet talk when he saw it. Heck, Lucky was the Spring Hill king of sweet talk.

By the time they reached Mackenzie, Brody had escalated things to nudging the girl's arm with his. Crap. This was moving fast, and it didn't help Lucky's anxiety when he saw a truly horrifying sight.

Mackenzie smiled.

At Brody.

The girl hadn't come close to a real smile since Lucky had first laid eyes on her, and now she was smiling at a turd who no doubt wanted to lay something more than eyes on her.

"Mr. Lucky," Brody said when he spotted them. He wisely stepped away from Mackenzie. "We were just talking."

Maybe Brody had added that preemptive explanation because Lucky's eyelids were narrowed to slits. Of course, Mackenzie did her own eyelid-slitting when she looked at Cassie and him. She clearly wasn't pleased with the interruption.

"Talking about what?" Lucky asked, and yep, he sounded like a cop or a father or something.

It wasn't a tone he'd ever used, but he'd heard Logan dole it out often enough. Since Logan and he were identical in looks and that tone got him results all the time, Lucky figured it was his best shot at letting Brody know that any sweet-talk shit was about to stop.

"Bull," Brody and Mackenzie answered in unison.

At first Lucky thought they were sassing him, but then he realized the mechanical bull was only a few yards away in the booth behind Brody. It was already all set up with the bull in the center of a hay-strewn area that had been made to look like a barn. Beneath the hay was the padded mat to break the riders' falls.

"Where's his legs?" Mia asked, sounding alarmed.

Lucky could see why she sounded that way. This looked like a real white-faced Hereford with sloping horns—minus the legs. It was as if someone had chopped them all off.

Yet something else Lucky would do to Brody if the boy touched Mackenzie.

"He's not real," Mackenzie grumbled. She rolled her eyes. "It's a fake bull."

"Not like that one," Mia said, pointing to Lucky's belt buckle.

"That one's not real, either." Mackenzie again, complete with another eye roll.

"But Mr. Lucky does ride real ones," Brody explained. And he sounded, well, nice. Maybe he was doing that to get on Lucky's good side, but it was working on Mackenzie, too. She quit eye-rolling long enough perhaps to realize that Brody wasn't snapping or snarling at Mia's questions.

"The real ones got legs?" Mia clarified.

"They sure do, four of them," Brody jumped to answer. "In fact, I've watched Mr. Lucky ride, and he's real good at it."

More sweet talk, but Lucky had no intention of letting it sway him into trusting this son of a baby maker. Besides, he was only "real good" at it 30 percent of the time.

"I was thinking about bringing in a rodeo clown this year," Brody continued. "Thought it would be fun—"

Lucky swiped his finger across his throat in a nix-that sign. "Logan hates clowns. Not a phobia exactly, but close. Since he's the one actually paying for this, I'm thinking that's not a good idea."

"Right," Brody agreed, and there was even more eagerness in his tone.

"You gonna ride this bull?" Mia asked Lucky.

"Why don't you ride it?" Brody suggested to Mia before Lucky could answer.

Mia's eyes lit right up at the possibility, but then she looked at Big Sis, Cassie and Lucky to see if it was all right. Cassie turned to him, probably because she didn't have a clue if it was safe or not. It was, for the most part, but Lucky intended to add his own safety precautions.

"Put it on the greenhorn setting," he instructed Brody, and he helped Mia onto the bull. "To win, you need to stay on it for eight seconds." Lucky looked at Brody again, a silent warning that she would stay on that long or longer, and he wouldn't do any speeding up or joggling that would make her fall.

"Hold on to the rope," Lucky instructed, and since this wasn't a competition, he added, "with both hands."

Lucky stepped back only when he was sure Mia had a good grip, and he stayed close enough to catch her. Brody waited until Lucky gave him a signal before he hit the greenhorn setting. Mia probably would have gotten more movement from a wave in a kiddie swimming pool, but she laughed with each gentle rocking motion.

"One," Brody counted. And he just kept counting while Mia laughed.

Lucky couldn't help it—he laughed, too. So did Cassie, and she moved beside him, maybe to help in case of a fall, or perhaps just to get closer to that very happy kid. After all the crap they'd been through in the past couple of days, it wouldn't have mattered if Mia had lasted eight seconds or not. It felt as if they'd won. But she did last eight seconds, and at the end of it, she slid off as if she'd been born to do this.

She hadn't been, of course.

No way would Lucky ever let her get on the back of a real bull.

"Now it's your turn," Brody said, looking at Mackenzie.

It was hard to tell with the makeup, but Lucky thought she might have blushed. "Not me. Cassie."

Cassie didn't blush, but she looked intimidated. Then she looked down at her skirt. So maybe not intimidation after all, but concern that she was going to pull an "I see London, I see France."

"Here, use my hat," Brody said, tugging his off. "Hold it on your lap."

Lucky didn't know whether to thank the boy or slug him for even thinking about Cassie's underpants.

Hell.

He really did need to rein in some of this jealousy and fatherly twinges. Cassie wasn't his, and he had no right to be jealous. No right to feel fatherly about Mackenzie and Mia.

Cassie got on the bull, placing the hat strategically in front of her pantie region. It was somewhat of a balancing act, but she managed to hold on with both hands while still pinching the hat between her legs.

That lasted about a second.

The moment Brody turned on the bull, he realized his mistake. This wasn't the greenhorn setting. This was more the expert-on-steroids notch, and Cassie let out a shriek as she went flying. Thankfully, she landed on Lucky. Not in his arms, though.

On. Him.

They fell onto the padded mat in the exact position a couple might need to be in to have accidental sex. With the hat no longer in front of her pantie region, that particular part of her landed right against his dick. All in all, it was bittersweet. Bitter because it hurt like hell. Sweet because his dick thought it was about to get some action.

Cassie scrambled to get off him. Lucky scrambled to get his hands on Brody's soon-to-be-broken neck.

"Gosh, I'm real sorry, Mr. Lucky and Miss Cassie. The switch must be messed up or something."

Lucky stood, met him eye to eye and looked for any sign whatsoever that the faulty switch thing was bullshit. But Brody seemed genuinely shocked and sorry. Especially sorry. Now Brody was blushing. Mackenzie was still blushing, as well. Cassie was flushed, however, and the flush went up a notch when her gaze drifted to his zipper.

"Are you okay?" she asked.

"Other than perhaps losing any possibility of ever fathering children, I'm fine."

Brody laughed. Not a good idea. But he must have realized that because he shut up and backed away several inches. Then a few more.

"Why can't you father children?" Mia asked.

That caused some more snickering, and Lucky was on the verge of fighting his own snickers when Mia added some words that nearly stopped his heart.

"You could father us," Mia said. "And Miss Cassie could mother us. Y'all could do it together."

It suddenly got quiet. Too quiet. Lucky couldn't be sure, but he thought maybe even the summer breeze had stopped dead in its tracks. Cassie joined in on that quietness, though her mouth was slightly open, as if she were trying to come up with an answer.

"Bull riders like Lucky can't be daddies," Mackenzie finally told her sister. It was either the wisest assessment on earth or the biggest insult. Lucky wasn't sure which.

Thankfully, he didn't have to decide. Or try to add more to Mackenzie's explanation. That was because he saw Riley and Claire approaching them. Lucky was so glad for the interruption that he had to stop himself from hugging them.

"Bull-riding lessons?" Riley asked, but then his attention dropped to Cassie's pantie zone and Lucky's zipper.

Until then, Lucky hadn't realized he still had his hand on Cassie's hip, and Cassie probably hadn't realized that the side of her skirt was hiked up to her pantie leg. If the kids hadn't been around, it would have looked as if Cassie and he had just had a getting-dirty session.

"Lesson's over," Lucky explained, and he made the mistake of helping Cassie with her skirt. He just ended up groping her, and by the time she finally had it straight, he was aroused despite his "injury" on the bull mat.

"Ethan!" Mia squealed when she spotted the boy, and they took off chasing each other in circles.

Mackenzie and Brody seized the moment to step away from the adults, but Lucky gave them the eyes-on-you gesture.

"What brings you out here?" Riley asked.

Lucky had no trouble hearing the concern in his brother's voice. Or seeing the concern in Claire's eyes. Damn. Had everyone in his extended gene pool remembered that coming here would be tough for him? Even the bull looked as if it were in on this shit-filled old baggage.

"Doing a favor for Logan and having a picnic," Lucky answered. "What about you? Why are you out here?"

"Doing a favor for Logan."

At first Lucky thought that was code for checking on him, but then Riley handed him a piece of paper that he'd taken from his pocket. "Logan thought it best if I delivered the news in person."

What now? Because if it was good news, a phone call would have worked. Lucky hoped Cassie and he weren't about to be carted off to jail for those cats.

But it wasn't about the cats. Or jail.

"The PI located the girls' aunt," Logan had written. "Her name is Alice Murdock. She's out of the country on business but will come to Spring Hill next week. She said for us to have the girls' things ready to go, that they'll be leaving with her as soon as she gets here."

MACKENZIE STARED AT Brody from the back car window as Lucky drove away from the park. Brody waved, gave her the call-me sign, and she smiled.

She made sure no one saw it, though.

She'd also made sure no one saw when Brody had written

his number on her right hand. He'd done that when Lucky had been talking to Riley and Claire. At the time Mackenzie had thought it was a lucky break that they hadn't had their nosy eyeballs pinned to her. But Mackenzie should have known her luck sucked and that the only breaks she'd be getting were the ones she'd always had.

Bad ones.

Mackenzie looked at her hand again. At Brody's number. He'd drawn a heart around it. Her first heart. Her first boy's number. And no boy had ever given her the call-me sign. No one, boy or girl, had ever looked at her the way he had. Of course this would happen now, just when she wasn't going to have time to do anything about it.

"Will Aunt Alice be nice?" Mia asked.

Even though Mia used her mousy-whisper voice, Lucky and Cassie must have heard it because Cassie glanced back at them. Lucky glanced in the rearview mirror, his eyes meeting Mackenzie's.

Considering Cassie and he had just gotten the best news of their lives—no sucky luck for them—they weren't acting all happy and everything. Probably because they were still mad about the bull throwing Cassie and her landing real hard on Lucky's privates.

But that hadn't been Brody's fault.

At least Mackenzie didn't think so, but even if it had been, Lucky and Cassie didn't have a right to be mad. They just didn't want her to be happy, that's all. Nobody did.

Of course, maybe they were all mopey because they were going to have to keep playing mommy and daddy for another whole week. They'd made it clear right from the start that they'd wanted to ditch this job, and now they couldn't. Yeah, that had to be it. They weren't happy because they were stuck with Mia and her—her more than Mia—until their aunt showed up.

"Well?" Mia pressed, tugging on Mackenzie's arm. "Will Aunt Alice be nice?"

"How the heck should I know? Neither one of us has met her, have we?"

"No. But you think she'll be nice?"

"Sure."

Mackenzie didn't think that at all. If the woman was anything like their mom, then she might use stuff, get drunk and sleep around with men. Mia was too little to remember a lot of that, but Mackenzie had no trouble remembering. And her kid sister wasn't going through something like that again. Heck, *she* wasn't going through that again.

Brody was fifteen, two years older than she was, and he had a job. A summer one anyway. Maybe he could lend her some money so she could get Mia out of there. Of course, getting out of there would mean never seeing Brody again. Unless…

Maybe she could talk him into taking Mia and her somewhere?

After all, Brody said he had his learner's permit, so that meant he could probably drive. And he had given her his number. Had smiled at her and talked to her as if she was, well, special. Yeah, that was it.

Brody made her feel special.

So maybe he could keep on making her feel that way by helping her. And soon. Because Mackenzie had to make sure she had Mia far away from Spring Hill before "Aunt Alice" showed up.

CHAPTER THIRTEEN

IT WAS WRONG on so many levels to stare at Lucky's crotch, but that's what Cassie found herself doing. Why, she didn't know.

Yes, she did.

It was because of those leather chaps he was wearing. They just sort of framed his crotch and acted like a neon sign that said, *Look here, look here!*

So Cassie looked.

At least now her tongue was no longer on the ground, though that's where it'd landed when Lucky had first called out for her to come watch him ride. She had stepped out of the house, expecting to see him in his usual jeans, boots and shirt. But instead, she'd gotten this.

The chaps, leather vest, denim shirt, spurs, gloves and the bull rope he had looped over his shoulder.

Her eyes had instantly gone to his crotch, but her mind had taken an even dirtier side trip. He looked just as ready for some BDSM as he did a bull ride. Not that she was into BDSM, or bull rides, either, for that matter, but it was an interesting image to add to her fantasies.

She only got to enjoy the fantasy a whole couple of seconds, though, before her phone buzzed and Cassie saw Andrew's name on the screen. He'd no doubt finally listened to the voice mail she'd left him.

"Another week?" Andrew snapped, his disapproval coming through loud and clear from the other end of the line.

Even though Cassie couldn't see his face, she figured the disapproval was in his expression, too, and that was why she wouldn't mention that she'd put off telling him for two days that that was how long it would be before the custody issue was resolved. Thankfully, Andrew had been so busy with his therapy sessions that he was conducting online from the Bluebonnet Inn that he hadn't pressed Cassie on nailing down a specific time for them to leave.

Well, they had a specific time now.

A week, or rather only five more days, until Aunt Alice arrived. It was exactly what Lucky and she had been waiting for ever since they'd gotten the girls, but it somehow felt like a hollow victory. Mackenzie was still sullen. Still hurting. Still needed help that she might not get with her aunt. At least Mackenzie was talking to Brody, a lot, and that was better than her moping around the house and labeling everything and everyone as sucky and stupid.

"The aunt might get here sooner," Cassie continued. "The week was just a general estimate. She was out of the country on business, but when she gets back home, she'll be coming from Phoenix."

"Well, she must be infirmed or hobbling because it doesn't take that long to get from there to here."

"No, but I suspect she had some things to take care of first. Like maybe getting the girls' rooms ready and such."

At least Cassie hoped the woman was making those kinds of plans, and making them in blissful anticipation of getting Mia and Mackenzie.

Because the girls deserved that.

"Certainly *Lucky* can handle those *children* until the aunt arrives," Andrew insisted. He'd said *children* and Lucky's name as if they'd caused a rash on his tongue.

"Lucky's very busy. He's co-owner of a rodeo promotion business, remember? In fact, he's testing out a new pair of bulls that were delivered to the ranch earlier."

Something Cassie fully intended to watch.

Lucky probably didn't know that she had seen him ride once before when she'd been visiting her grandmother. He hadn't worn chaps and the vest that day, though. No bull rope, either. Cassie had watched him climb onto that bull and then had held her breath when it'd bucked.

That day, Lucky had won, not the bull.

And Cassie had been forced to admit that she saw in him what other women saw. A great butt. Great face, too. Now here she was watching him again from the barn as he was preparing to ride.

The ranch didn't have an actual setup for bull riding, but several of the hands had helped build a makeshift shoot and gate where the bull was being held back. Cassie didn't have a good view of the bull from where she was standing, but she could see Lucky straddle the top of the fence, looking down at the animal. He was talking to the bull as if getting acquainted with it. Strange, it was like chatting up someone who wanted to sling your internal organs out of your body.

"Are you listening?" Andrew said, snapping her back to reality.

She hadn't heard a word in the past fifteen seconds or so, but Cassie didn't let him know that. "I'm just a little distracted, that's all. I've got a lot on my mind." And on her eyes. She could feel the adrenaline start to pump through her and figured it was a drop in the bucket compared to what Lucky had to be feeling.

"I know," Andrew agreed. "It's those *kids*." That tongue rash sounded as if it had gotten worse. "They're too much for you to handle."

No, he didn't know. At the moment, it certainly wasn't the

kids distracting her. Lucky looked back at her, snaring her gaze, and gave her a smile that could have melted chrome.

This was so stupid. She shouldn't be getting warm in all the wrong places. She was watching him prepare to ride a bull. He wasn't stark naked and—

"I'm canceling my afternoon appointments and coming over there right now," Andrew insisted.

"No." Cassie couldn't say that fast enough. It always turned ugly whenever Andrew was around Lucky, and she didn't want to deal with ugly today. "I'm really busy. I wouldn't be able to spend any time with you, and besides, you can't let your clients down like that."

"Busy with the girls?" he asked, suspicion in his voice.

"Of course. What else?"

It was a lie. Mia was at Claire's having a playdate with Ethan, and Livvy had taken Mackenzie on a shopping trip into San Antonio. For the first time in days Cassie actually had a free afternoon, and here she wanted to spend part of it watching Lucky climb onto the back of an ornery two-thousand-pound Angus bull.

"You sound funny," Andrew added.

"Do I?" She quickly tried to sound unfunny. "Must be because I'm still distracted. I should go now, but I'll call you later."

She hung up before he could protest or make any more obvious observations about her sounding funny. Of course she sounded funny. She was lying and breathing hard. Watching Lucky get ready for the ride was better than foreplay.

Cassie groaned.

She'd let that "foreplay" distract her. Instead of agreeing to call Andrew, she should have insisted he leave town. Of course, Cassie had been doing that for two days with no results. Andrew would leave Spring Hill when he got good and ready, and arguing with him about that would only make him dig in his heels more. She owed him, she really did, but Cassie was too drained to deal with Andrew right now.

Not too drained to watch Lucky, though.

He slipped down off the railing, easing onto the bull. Even from where she was standing, she could see the muscles ripple beneath Lucky's shirtsleeve. Normally, Cassie wasn't into muscle rippling, but she apparently was now.

The ranch hand opened the gate, and the bull charged out. Snorting and bucking. Its massive head was down while the animal spun around, trying to hurl off the rider. But Lucky held on. He squeezed his legs around the bull's sides, the chaps reacting to that pressure.

Cassie reacted, too.

And she thought about how it would feel to be that bull right now. Oh, yes, she was worked up all right.

The bull bucked even harder, slinging Lucky around, but Lucky just adjusted, his long, lean body sliding into the bucking moves. His left arm stayed high, dipping and lifting only when his body did. It was like watching some kind of dance. With a guy wearing chaps and spurs.

Cassie completely lost track of time. Eight seconds or an hour could have passed for all she knew, but then Lucky threw his left leg over the bull's head, and he jumped off. Lucky landed on his feet and hurried to get out of the corral before the bull came back at him.

He laughed.

And that's when Cassie realized she was holding her breath. Possibly drooling, as well.

Lucky looked at her again, their gazes connecting and holding for a couple of seconds. Cassie didn't believe in ESP, but something passed between them. He said something to the hands who were still watching the bull, maneuvered off the railing and came toward her. She had another chance to assess that ESP thing, but this time she knew what it was.

A really hot look.

Lucky walked toward her, the spurs jangling and the chaps swaying to give her another *Look here! Look here!* moment.

Cassie tried to look unaffected by all of this and failed so badly that she just gave up.

"Yeah," Lucky said, his voice doused with testosterone. He bit down on the fingertip of his right glove to remove it. Then did the same to the second one. "It has the same effect on me."

This probably would have been a good time for her to play innocent and say *oh?* or maybe a *huh?* But after watching what he'd done to those gloves, her innocence was shot to Hades.

Lucky kept coming closer, and the moment he reached her, he slid his hand around the back of her neck, hauled her to him and kissed her.

Cassie said *huh* all right, but for a different reason. Because she hadn't been expecting to feel the slam of heat. It was as if that bull had just rammed into her.

Lucky didn't stop with just one bull-walloping kiss, though. He deepened it, pulling her closer and closer until she was plastered right against all that warm leather.

And his erection.

The chaps made it easier to feel that, too.

"Are you always like this after a ride?" she asked.

"Only when I see you afterward," he answered.

Mercy, that was probably a line he used all the time, but the problem was—it worked. All of it worked, and that's why Cassie melted right into the kiss.

Lucky didn't break the kiss when he pulled her to the side, maybe to get them out of the line of sight of the ranch hands, but it also landed them against the barn wall. She'd never considered barn walls before, but the hard wood had a wonderful effect when Lucky pressed her back against it. All that hardness at her front and back was creating some amazing pressure. Friction, too, when Lucky's body moved against hers.

"What about the ranch hands?" she asked.

"I told them I had to talk to you about the girls. They're so interested in the bulls they won't come in here."

Cassie tried to make herself remember that Lucky had done

this too many times with too many women. That should have put her off, but she was so hot now that she reasoned that all his experience would just make this better.

And worse, of course.

Because they shouldn't be doing this.

She was leaving town soon, and she didn't need to pack a broken heart to take back with her to LA. So the rationalization started. This was just a kissing session. A very good one. But it wouldn't lead to anything more.

That's when she realized she was moving.

Or rather Lucky was moving her. He dropped some kisses on her neck, at the base of her earlobe. Then her ear.

Good grief.

How had she not known before now how sensitive of a spot that was for her? And how had Lucky known that it was?

Soon, those questions and all logical thoughts flew right out of her head.

Lucky led her to a ladder, and Cassie wasn't sure how he managed it, but he continued to kiss her as they made their way up the steps. One rung at a time. With more of those body-melting ear kisses. By the time they reached the top, Cassie was so worked up that she didn't even notice where they were at first.

A hayloft.

That gave her just a moment of hesitation. It was one thing to kiss in the barn. No threat there of having full-blown dirty sex—because in her mind, it would be dirty with Lucky—but here they had privacy. And with privacy came the threat of sex, that broken heart and some serious complications added to her already complicated life.

"Do you take a lot of women up here?" she asked.

He was breathing through his mouth when he eased back and looked her straight in the eyes. "You're the first."

That was probably more bullshit than was in the bull pen.

Still, Cassie wanted to believe him even if she knew she shouldn't.

"Let's take it one step at a time," he said. Was his voice always like this? All low and husky. If so, she was surprised he hadn't seduced her whenever he'd said hello. "Just say yes or no. I'll stop at the first no."

The rules were easy enough. Cassie thought she could manage the breath to give a one-syllable answer. Of course, the rules were tested with Lucky's first move when he gave her another of those ear kisses.

"Yes," she eked out.

The next kiss landed on her throat. Or at least that's where it started. But with the dexterity of a magician, he opened the buttons on her shirt, and without breaking the next kiss, his mouth went lower, lower.

Until he had her right nipple in his mouth.

"Yes!" she said a little louder and more enthusiastically than she'd intended.

Lucky lingered there a moment, all the while easing her lower until they landed on some hay on the floor.

Heck, she said yes to that, too.

And Cassie kept saying yes when Lucky undid the rest of her buttons, pulled down her bra and kissed the living daylights out of her.

"If you want me to stop," he reminded her, "just say no."

No was the last thing she wanted to say, but Cassie had to hang on to what little sense she had left.

"You know we shouldn't have sex," she said.

He didn't even pause. Lucky just kept trailing kisses lower and lower until he circled her navel with his tongue. "What's your definition of sex?" he asked.

The question seemed like something that would require a lot more functioning brain cells than she had at the moment, but Cassie gave it a try. "The F-word."

He smiled as if charmed by her inability to say a word that she heard daily. After all, if she couldn't say the word, then she probably shouldn't be doing the act.

"Okay, no F-word," Lucky agreed. "But I can still kiss and touch you. Remember, just say no if you want me to stop."

There was that single brain cell that wanted her to stop, but the other cells were clamoring so hard for the kissing and touching that it got drowned out.

Lucky's mouth came back to hers for the kissing part, and he moved on top of her for the touching part.

Or so she thought.

But the touching part was a whole lot more than that. He unzipped her, all the way down, and he slid his hand into her panties. He didn't stop there. Lucky kept kissing her, kept moving his hand until it reached the most sensitive part of her body.

Oh, yes.

This was that lightning bolt of pleasure. The one she hadn't experienced in so long that Cassie had forgotten what it was like to have a man touch her like this. Lucky's fingers slid right through all that slickness and just kept on sliding. Over and over again. Until Cassie thought she might literally, truly explode.

But she didn't.

Just when she was nearing the climax of the one and only hand job she'd ever gotten, she heard something she didn't want to hear.

Her name.

And it wasn't Lucky saying it, either.

"Cassie?" Andrew called out. "Are you up there? The housekeeper said you were out here in the barn."

Judging from the sound of Andrew's voice, her more-or-less ex was heading up the hayloft steps.

CHAPTER FOURTEEN

HELL IN A HANDBASKET.

What was Dr. Dundernuts doing here?

Lucky wasn't opposed to Andrew learning that Cassie and he had the hots for each other, but he didn't want Andrew or any-body walking up that ladder while he had his hands in Cassie's pants.

"Oh, God," Cassie mumbled, and scrambled away from him. Scrambled to fix her clothes, too.

Lucky didn't have anything unbuttoned or unzipped so there was nothing to fix. Nothing but his hard-on, and scrambling around wasn't going to help that.

"Cassie?" Andrew called out again. The man sounded even closer than before.

"Lucky?" someone else said. Livvy. Heck, she was close, too, and that meant Mackenzie probably was, as well.

"They're around here somewhere," one of the ranch hands explained. It was Zeke Daniels, and he'd been the one who'd helped rig the riding arena for Lucky to test the Angus. "Maybe they went into the other corral to check out the second bull. Come on this way."

Lucky wanted to kiss Zeke for giving them a chance to get down the hayloft ladder without an audience. Lucky didn't mind

Andrew knowing what they'd been doing. Or even Livvy. But it was best that Mackenzie be kept out of this particular information loop.

Cassie scurried to the ladder and looked down. She craned her neck and body so much that she nearly fell right out of the loft. Lucky caught onto her, moved in front of her and went down first. At least if anyone was still in the barn, they might think he'd been up there alone. Considering he still had a partial hard-on, though, they might be wondering what he'd been doing.

Once he was down the ladder, he helped Cassie and then put his cowboy hat in front of his crotch. It wasn't a second too soon.

"There you are," Livvy said. At least it sounded like Livvy, but the woman walking toward them was dressed like Mackenzie. In fact, exactly like Mackenzie, right down to the black lipstick and black spiked hair.

Mackenzie was trailing along behind Livvy. Andrew, too. And Zeke.

"I wanted to try a different look," Livvy said, twirling around. She looked like a character in a Tim Burton movie. "And tomorrow I'll try a different look, one where people can see my actual hair color." She winked at Lucky.

Not a flirty wink but one that was perhaps meant to let him know that she was teaching Mackenzie a lesson—that it was okay to look normal every now and then. But the wink sort of got stuck in Livvy's eye when her gaze skirted over them.

"Hay in the hair," Livvy whispered almost frantically.

That sent Cassie and him into a frantic hair search, with them raking at their heads with their fingers. Livvy didn't help at all. In fact, she picked up a handful of hay and, giggling like a loon, tossed it at them.

Okay, maybe Livvy helped after all, because to the others it might have appeared they were in the middle of a hay fight. Of course, such a fight wouldn't make sense to a normal, sane person, but Livvy wasn't known for doing normal, sane things.

Andrew and Mackenzie stopped right in front of them.

Mackenzie was giving them her bored look while Andrew took notice of everything around him. Particularly of the placement of Lucky's Stetson. Lucky hoped the guy didn't ask to try it on.

"Chaps and spurs, huh?" Livvy asked, tossing up another handful of hay.

"Lucky was riding the bull," Cassie explained. Which sounded dirty because she'd hesitated slightly after the word *riding*.

Livvy picked up on it, of course, and threw more hay, causing Andrew to cough and fan his hand in front of his face. Maybe the sudden allergy attack would get him moving so Lucky could have a few more seconds before he attempted to walk.

"That's something I would have loved to watch," Livvy declared. "Any chance you can ride the bull again so we can get a look-see?"

"I don't think that's a good idea right now," he managed to say. "Maybe later."

However, if he did ride the second bull, he'd make sure Cassie wasn't around. Bull riding had always given Lucky the mother of all adrenaline highs, but this was a first for making him horny as hell. Naturally, Cassie was responsible for that. There had just been something about seeing her standing there while he'd been getting his brains scrambled, and he hadn't been able to resist her.

But then she hadn't resisted much, either.

At least she hadn't in the hayloft, but Cassie was definitely putting some distance between them now. That was partially thanks to Andrew. He'd slipped his arm around her waist and was trying to inch her away from the rest of them.

"Cassie and I need to talk," Andrew finally said. "It's important," he added. "It's about Hannah."

Until he tacked on that last part, Cassie had been holding her ground. But what he said caused her gaze to meet Andrew's. Lucky was betting there was no way she'd pass up any and all news about Hannah, her client who'd committed suicide, and he was right. Cassie nodded and stepped away with Andrew. Far away. They went out of the barn and headed toward the backyard.

Livvy glanced at Cassie and Andrew. Then she glanced at Lucky. Then the hayloft. Then Mackenzie—no doubt to see if she was picking up on any of this, but the only thing Mackenzie was picking at was some hay that'd landed on her black top. After all the glancing, Livvy looked at Lucky and raised her eyebrow.

Lucky understood the question. *What's going on?* But since Lucky didn't have an answer to that, he just shrugged. And changed the subject.

"How'd the shopping trip go?" he asked.

Mackenzie kept picking at the hay. Thankfully, Livvy was more accommodating, especially since Lucky needed a distraction. He kept looking at Cassie and Andrew, and every time he did, they were looking at him. He would have just moved this conversation into the house and out of their line of sight, but that would have meant walking right past them. If Cassie had wanted him to hear what Andrew and she were discussing, she would have asked him to join them. Or just stayed put.

"We bought drugs," he heard Livvy say.

That caused Lucky's and Mackenzie's attention to snap back to Livvy, who now had a gotcha look on her face. "Just checking to see if you were listening."

"Well, I am now. What'd you buy?" Though he didn't think for a second that it was drugs.

"The shopping bags are in the house," Livvy went on when Mackenzie didn't say anything. "Don't worry. We didn't max out the credit card you gave us, but we got some things for Mia. Some things for Mackenzie, too, of course. Tops, shoes and... other things."

Now Mackenzie looked at him.

"Other things?" Lucky pressed. He had to tear his eyes away from his latest glimpse of Cassie and Andrew so he could look at her.

"A dress," Mackenzie finally said. "To wear to Riley and Claire's wedding."

At first Lucky didn't see a problem with that. Then he did. The timing of Aunt Alice's arrival, and the woman's insistence that she wanted the girls to leave with her right away.

"Mackenzie and I were thinking that it would be fun for Mia and her to stay for the wedding," Livvy suggested. "Thinking along those same lines, we also got Mackenzie an outfit for the picnic."

The truth was that Lucky wanted the girls at both events. After all, Mia had gotten close to Ethan and Claire, and Mackenzie had apparently gotten close to Livvy. But Lucky had to shake his head. "I'm not sure it'll be up to me."

"Oh, you can sweet-talk Aunt Alice into letting them stay," Livvy insisted. "I mean, especially after Cassie and you stepped up to take custody of her nieces. Heck, the aunt could go to the picnic and wedding, too."

It was true about the sweet-talking part. He might be able to pull that off, but there was something fishy going on here, and Lucky was pretty sure what that fish's name was.

"I know Brody will be at the picnic," Lucky tossed out there, "but I'm guessing he'll now be at the wedding, too?"

Mackenzie nodded and had the decency to mix a little sheepishness in with her insolence. "I asked Claire to invite him, and she said she would. I'd also like to go on a date with him."

Lucky had hesitated about the wedding and picnic possibilities, but he didn't waste a second responding to this part. "No way. He's too old for you."

"Only by two years," Mackenzie protested after a loud huff.

That was more than enough. "Look, Mackenzie, Brody doesn't come from a good family."

"Neither do I!"

The jury was still out on that, depending on Aunt Alice, but Mackenzie had a point. Her mom and dad hadn't been stellar examples of the human race. Aliens looking for higher life-forms would have skipped right over those two. Still…

"No date," Lucky insisted, and he tried to make sure it sounded like his bottom line. Because it was. "You're too young. He's too old. And that's not a good combination."

There. Bottom line, finished, and Lucky punctuated it with a firm nod.

But Livvy shrugged and did some hemming and hawing. "What if I chaperoned the date?"

Clearly, Livvy hadn't picked up on the bottom line. "My answer's still no. I like you, Livvy, but if I looked for a picture in the dictionary next to 'responsible adult chaperone,' you're not going to be there."

That didn't seem to hurt her feelings. Livvy just shrugged again. "Then what if Claire and Riley chaperone? I've already asked," she quickly added, "and Claire said if it's all right with Cassie and you, then Riley and she would do it."

"And it would just be a date to the dance at the civic center," Mackenzie begged. "We could even put a time limit on it—like two hours. Miss Claire and Mr. Riley could drive us there, stay with us the whole time, and then drive us back."

Apparently, Livvy and she had already worked out their own version of a bottom line. And Lucky could feel himself wavering. Damn it. That's because Mackenzie actually looked happy for the first time since she'd arrived at the ranch. But he was still wavering.

"Here's a different scenario," he suggested. "I'll talk to Cassie about it, but if she agrees—and that's a big *if*—" he hoped she would "—then Cassie and I will chaperone. And there won't be any slow dancing."

Of course, with Brody's fifteen-year-old body fueling his every thought and move, just laying eyes on Mackenzie would work him up.

Some of Mackenzie's glee went south, but she finally nodded.

Now all Lucky had to do was convince Cassie. And if he managed to do that, it'd sort of be like a date for him and her, too.

Sort of.

Other than that, there was one other silver lining here. With Mackenzie leaving town soon, there wouldn't be much time for a romance to develop between Brody and her. That was something at least.

Lucky glanced at Cassie again, but she was no longer talking to Andrew. However, she was chasing him, and Andrew was storming right toward Lucky.

"Lucky McCord!" Andrew shouted. "What the hell did you do to Cassie in that barn?"

CASSIE HAD TO run to make it to Lucky before Andrew got to him. Not because she thought Andrew would punch Lucky or anything. But she didn't want Lucky to blurt out something before he understood what'd prompted Andrew's question.

"Lucky didn't have anything to do with that," Cassie insisted.

Andrew didn't pay any attention to her, and Lucky just looked confused. Because he thought Andrew was asking about what had gone on in the hayloft.

Her ex just kept charging like a bull toward Lucky, and she could see Lucky already posturing for a fight. A fight that wasn't going to happen.

"Lucky doesn't even know," Cassie tried again. She managed a burst of speed at the last moment and darted in between Lucky and Andrew.

"Of course he knows," Andrew argued.

Lucky was still looking perplexed, no doubt because he thought this had something to do with her near orgasm. Of course, Cassie knew Lucky would have had no trouble actually making that happen if they hadn't been interrupted. But it was best not to think about that right now.

Even though it was difficult with Lucky still wearing those crotch-framing leather chaps.

"Uh, what do I know?" Lucky asked.

"You somehow talked Cassie into wanting to quit her job," Andrew accused.

"No, I didn't," Lucky said at the same time that Cassie repeated, "Lucky didn't know."

Cassie huffed and continued while she looked at Andrew. "In fact, I didn't know I was thinking about quitting until just a few minutes ago when I was talking with you."

"You're quitting?" Lucky asked.

Andrew came with his own quick follow-up, not to Lucky's question but to Cassie's comment. "You can't quit. Being a therapist is who you are."

Lucky cleared his throat to get her attention. "Does this have anything to do with, well, anything?"

Since Mackenzie was standing there, Andrew perhaps thought Lucky was referring to the children, but Cassie suspected it had more to do with their near sex. Hopefully, Lucky didn't think she'd seen that as some kind of commitment.

"No. Nothing to do with…anything," Cassie assured him. "I just… Well, I think that maybe I'd like to try something different."

"Hogwash," Andrew spat out. The ranch setting must have rubbed off on him because to the best of her knowledge, he'd never said anything like that. "What would you do if you couldn't be a therapist?"

Cassie had to shrug. She wasn't sure, but she wouldn't mind having a job where people didn't die because she'd botched things. Or a job that didn't spur a panic attack just thinking about it.

And no, it didn't have anything to do with Lucky and the girls.

Andrew huffed and snorted, sounding like a smaller version of the bull Lucky had ridden. He opened his mouth a couple of times as if to dole out the perfect words to make her change her mind. But perfection must have escaped him because he turned to walk away.

"I'll talk to you tomorrow," Andrew said. "By then maybe you'll come to your senses and won't even be thinking about making the biggest mistake of your life."

"Is he right?" Lucky asked her. "Would this be a mistake?"

"Tell you what," Livvy interrupted before Cassie could answer. "Why don't Mackenzie and I go inside and try on those new clothes?" She slipped her arm around the girl's shoulder and led her toward the back porch.

Cassie thanked Livvy for picking up on the cues that this wasn't a conversation Cassie wanted to have in front of Mackenzie. In front of anyone, really. However, she couldn't help but notice that Mackenzie seemed less sullen than usual. The girl actually seemed happy.

"Yeah, she's smiling," Lucky verified. "You probably don't want to hear why since you're going through your own personal crisis right now."

Of course, that meant she had to hear. "Mackenzie's smiling because of a personal crisis?"

"No, I'm the one having the crisis. She's smiling because she's happy that I lost my mind and just agreed to let her go on a supervised dance date with Brody. Claire and Riley volunteered to chaperone."

"You agreed to that?"

She was about to tell him that nothing would have made her give consent for a date between those two. But then she remembered Mackenzie's smile. Yes, that's why he'd done it. And while Cassie wasn't exactly comfortable with it, she knew how persuasive teenage girls could be.

"I'm thinking it might be a good idea if we go to the dance, too," Lucky went on. "Maybe we can hang back near the wall. I could bring binoculars. Maybe a stun gun. A shovel in case we have to bury Brody's body."

Cassie couldn't help it. Despite her blue mood, she smiled, too.

"There it is," Lucky said, joining in on the smile. His was a lot better than hers, though.

She mentally caught hold of that smile for a couple of moments, bracing herself for the nonsmiling conversation to follow. Lucky didn't keep her waiting, but it wasn't exactly the subject she'd been dreading—the one where she'd been thinking about quitting her job.

"Mackenzie wants to stay for the wedding," Lucky went on. "For Brody, of course."

"Of course," Cassie repeated. "You think the aunt will agree to that?"

Lucky lifted his shoulder. "You think she'll agree to let us see the kids after she takes them? I don't mean right away or even that often. I'd just like to check on them every now and then."

"So would I."

But she wasn't even sure if the aunt would grant them any concessions. Or if legally Lucky and she could insist on visits. Cassie seriously doubted temporary custody would trump blood kin.

However, that led her to her next thought. She did want to keep tabs on the girls. Mackenzie likely had a tough road ahead of her, and Cassie wanted to give Mia and her at least the option of calling from time to time. And to think, a week ago Cassie would have been glad to get rid of them.

"Your wanting to quit your job is about Hannah," Lucky concluded. "How serious are you about it?"

"I'm toying with the idea." She was terrified about it, too. "And it doesn't have anything to do with the hayloft," Claire added. "And I'm not thinking about quitting all of it. Just the clients part. I could still do the TV and radio shows."

Lucky stayed quiet, staring at her. She stayed quiet as well, and tried not to stare at him. Mainly because her gaze kept drifting to those chaps. Talk about fueling a fantasy.

"All right, then," Lucky said. "I'm sure you'll figure out what you want to do." He paused. "And the hayloft?"

Cassie figured the right answer wasn't to say she wanted to go back there and have him finish what he'd started. No, definitely not the right answer. They had the girls for six more days at the most, and after that Cassie would leave. Lucky would leave, as well. And if they decided down the road that there should be other trips to the hayloft, then they could make their decision without so much hanging over their heads.

It was the adult thing to do.

Or...

She could offer Lucky a one-night stand. Or even a six-night stand.

Nothing bad could happen from that, *right?*

Plenty of good could come from it, though. Like a minimum of six orgasms.

But the other little voice in her head reminded Cassie that in her messy emotional state, she might not be able to deal with any more emotional mess. She wouldn't die from the broken heart she would get because of Lucky, but she might not recover from it, either.

Cassie wasn't sure she would have shared that info with Lucky anyway, but thankfully she didn't have to. Mia came running out the back door of the house, and she was waving a piece of paper in her hand.

"I got a letter!" she said as if someone had just handed her the leprechaun's pot of gold. "It's got my name on it."

Cassie smiled at first, but then realized it could be from the aunt. Maybe a letter to say she was coming even earlier than expected.

Lucky scooped Mia up in his arms when the little girl reached them. "Who's it from?" he asked.

"Miss Dixie Mae. Miss Livvy said it comed from the grave." Mia's forehead bunched up a little. "What's a grave?"

"A place where people don't send letters from," Lucky mumbled, looking at the envelope. "But that's Dixie Mae's handwriting."

"Course it is," Mia verified. "She wrote me a letter from the grave. She wrote one for all of us. Yours and Miss Cassie's letters are in the house."

CHAPTER FIFTEEN

LUCKY WASN'T SURE how he got from the corral to the house. His feet were working just fine, but his mind was solely on what Mia had just told him.

The last time he had gotten a letter from Dixie Mae, she'd left Cassie and him temporary custody of the girls. Lucky hated to think the worst of someone who was dead, but he wasn't exactly sure he wanted to read the letter that Della was holding up when he stepped into the house.

Cassie took her letter, not opening it but rather holding it to her chest. Lucky put his in his pocket. He'd read it, later, but he thought he first might like those Jameson shots that he'd been promising himself for days.

"Read mine! Read mine!" Mia insisted. She was bouncing up and down as if she were on a trampoline.

Mackenzie, however, was of a like mind as Lucky. She crammed hers in her pocket, too. Livvy had apparently already left, and there was a stash of bags in the entry. The cats were trying to get into them. Mackenzie gathered those up and went upstairs. Lucky would need to check on her soon, to make sure whatever was in that letter hadn't upset her even more. Mackenzie certainly wasn't smiling now.

Unlike Mia.

"Read mine!" she repeated. And Lucky hoped that joy would continue afterward. Of course, he couldn't imagine even Dixie Mae squashing the joy of a four-year-old.

Since Lucky's legs weren't feeling too steady—probably from the bull ride—he went into the living room and sat down, with Mia scooting into the space right beside him. Cassie sat on the other side of her. Mia had already opened the envelope so he took it out and hoped for the best.

He unfolded the letter and saw the date. Dixie Mae had written it a week before she died. So not from beyond the grave after all. And it meant she'd given the letters to someone so they could be mailed. Bernie, probably.

"'Dear Mia,'" Lucky read aloud. "'I know you're being a good girl for Lucky and Cassie, but they'll still like you even if you mess up every now and then.'"

"Will you?" Mia asked. A two-word question coupled with a worried look that squeezed his heart.

"Of course," Cassie said. Lucky echoed the same. It was something Lucky should have already figured out a way to tell Mia.

"'You're like Lucky's twin brother in some ways,'" Lucky continued to read from the letter. "'But being perfect all the time gets on people's nerves and takes just as much of a toll on the body as messing up all the time. Understand?'"

Mia shook her head. It was well beyond her four years. But Lucky got it all right. It was the story of his life. The story of Logan's, too.

"'Just live your life, sweet girl,'" Lucky read on, "'and keep making people smile. That's your gift. Love, Dixie Mae.'"

Mia stayed quiet a moment. "She loves me?"

Considering that short letter had been filled with things that must have been confusing to a young child, it surprised Lucky that Mia picked up on that one thing.

Love.

Talk about him feeling another heart squeezing. Too bad

Dixie Mae hadn't told him about the girls sooner because it would have been nice to have seen her with them. It was obvious from this letter that Mia had given her some happiness in those last days of her life.

"Dixie Mae loved you," Cassie assured her.

Mia smiled. "I loved her, too. She was sparkly."

Yeah, she was. But since Dixie Mae had gotten so truthful with Mia, Lucky had to wonder what was in his letter.

And Mackenzie's.

Hell, if Dixie Mae was going to hold up a mirror to Mackenzie's face, Lucky didn't want her alone when she read the letter. He stood to go to her room, but the front door opened before he even made it to the stairs.

Logan.

"Got a minute?" Logan asked, and he specifically looked at Lucky, which meant he had something that he wanted to discuss privately.

"I'll go up to Mackenzie," Cassie volunteered, and Mia and she went in that direction.

"Trouble?" Logan asked.

Lucky patted his pocket. "Dixie Mae sent the four of us letters."

That put some extra concern on Logan's face. "Trouble?" he repeated, no doubt remembering what'd happened the last time Dixie Mae had done something like this.

Lucky shook his head. "I think it's just her way of saying goodbye." Heck. He hoped so anyway.

"Do you think you're too good sometimes to compensate for me being too bad?" Lucky asked.

Logan gave him a blank stare, and Lucky decided it was a good question to wave off. "You said you wanted to talk," Lucky reminded him.

Logan nodded and seemed relieved about the wave-off. "The reporter Theo Kervin is in town."

Lucky was certain he also had some concern on his face now. "Where?"

"Staying at the Bluebonnet Inn in the room next to Andrew. The clerk said now that she's put a name to a face she's pretty sure she saw him hanging around not long after Cassie arrived."

Crap on a stick. Maybe Andrew wouldn't let anything slip about Sweet Meadows. Lucky wasn't at all convinced that Cassie would quit being a therapist, and having something like that on her "résumé" wouldn't be good. Of course, Andrew had protected her by paying off Mason-Dixon and her mother so maybe the doc would make sure to protect her now by not spilling anything.

"Theo will talk to people," Logan went on. "I can't stop him from doing that, but I've put out the word that he's looking to paint Cassie and maybe you in a bad light. That might cause folks to watch what they say."

Or else it could make them chatterboxes. This was some of the shit that went with being a McCord. The money and power made some people want to take them down a notch.

"I've also told the hands to keep an eye out for Theo in case he tries to come here to the ranch," Logan went on. "If Cassie wants to talk with him, it's probably best if she does that elsewhere so that the ranch and the business won't be brought into it."

That was Logan, always thinking about McCord Cattle Brokers, but in this case his concern might be warranted. Lucky was also betting there was no way that Cassie would want to speak to this reporter, especially if the guy had any info about her stay in Sweet Meadows.

Cassie appeared at the top of the stairs. "Mackenzie isn't going to read the letter so she and Mia are going to watch a movie in their room." She gave Logan an uneasy glance. "Is everything okay?"

"Fine," Lucky assured her. "I'll come up in a bit." And then he'd tell her about Theo, along with deciding what to do about reading his own letter.

"A couple more things," Logan said. "Helene wanted me to ask you if you wanted her to find homes for the cats."

"Not just yet. Though it might come to that if Cassie can't take them with her to LA." That was a reminder Lucky didn't want, but he had to be realistic here. Cassie would leave soon. Even if she did go for a different career, it wouldn't be here in Spring Hill.

Logan nodded. "Now to Riley's bachelor party. He wanted to keep it local so I booked Calhoun's Pub. It'll be two nights before the wedding. I thought maybe you could arrange the entertainment, though."

"Sure. But there'll be no strippers from the Slippery Pole." He'd had enough dealings with Mason-Dixon. Still, he'd have to find something bawdy and inappropriate—which Logan no doubt thought was Lucky's specialty.

"Whatever you decide is fine," Logan assured him. But his attention wasn't on Lucky or the conversation. It was on the back windows. Logan watched as the hands moved a bull from the corral area into the pasture.

"I heard about the bulls," Logan said. "A project of yours?"

"Just testing them before I buy them," Lucky said as he made his way to the door and headed out into the backyard.

"How much does one cost?"

"The buyer is asking thirty grand each."

"Are they worth it?" Logan said without hesitation.

"The Angus is worth more than that. He's been trained well and will draw a crowd. Not sure about the Brahma. A lot of riders steer clear of them."

Logan still didn't seem to be listening, and Lucky thought he knew why. Logan was seeing dollar signs, and it didn't take long to confirm that. "How much does it cost to buy an untrained bull and make him worth thirty grand?"

"Bulls are like relationships. Lots of factors to consider, but you could get a young bull from a good bloodline for about ten grand, maybe less. After you add in training and care, you're probably looking at an average profit of ten to fifteen thousand tops."

That was chump change considering what Logan made off his cattle brokering deals and what Riley made from the cutting horses, but his brother was no doubt thinking in bulk. Once, Lucky had as well, but somewhere along the way the rodeo promo business had eaten up his time.

"I'm not going to buy and train bulls for you," Lucky let Logan know right off. But then he frowned. Saying things like that to Logan was practically a knee-jerk reaction.

"Of course. I knew you wouldn't be interested, but I was thinking I could get someone else. Maybe even use the ranch for holding and training them. There's plenty of space and acres of pastures we don't use. A couple of the corrals could be converted into training areas."

It was a good idea, and instead of completely nixing it, Lucky just put it on the back burner. It was possible he wouldn't have any time to take on even a smaller version of a project like that now that Dixie Mae had passed and he didn't have any help with the rodeo promotion.

Logan stayed quiet a moment, and Lucky figured he was already working out profit margins and such, but that wasn't all that was on his mind.

"You asked Helene about my meds." A muscle flickered in Logan's otherwise unruffled jaw. "I have migraines, but I don't want it to get around."

Lucky couldn't imagine why someone would want to keep that a secret, but he wasn't in Logan's head. Maybe Logan thought it would make him appear weak.

"Mom had them," Lucky reminded him.

Lucky figured he was giving his brother old news. Apparently not, judging from the look of surprise. Maybe Logan had been too busy working the ranch with their dad to notice when their mother had taken to her bed for hours on end. But Lucky had sure noticed.

"That explains why Dad was worried," Logan commented.

Now, that was news to Lucky. "Worried?"

Logan nodded. "It wasn't anything he said specifically, just a gut feeling I got."

Lucky wished he'd had gut feelings about his parents' car accident. Hell, he wished he could go back in time and undo what'd happened to them.

Since that put a damper on his already dampered mood, Lucky was about to excuse himself and go back inside. But his phone buzzed, and when he saw the name on the screen, he stopped in his tracks.

Alice Murdock.

The girls' aunt.

Lucky took a moment, gathering his breath before he answered it, and since Logan had been responsible for finding her, Lucky put the call on speaker.

"Mr. McCord," she greeted. "How are Mia and Mackenzie?"

It was the right question to start with, but it still caused his chest to tighten.

"They're okay." Since he wasn't sure what Logan's PI had told her, Lucky decided to keep it at that.

"Good. Could you please give them my number so I can chat with them sometime?"

"Of course. Any idea when you'll be arriving?"

"I'm finishing up a project now so it shouldn't be much longer. I'm a field director for a nonprofit group that provides medical care in third-world countries, and once I have all of the staff back safe, I'll catch the first flight to Texas."

So, she had a job, one that sounded as if she hadn't followed in her drug-using sister's footsteps.

"Unless you think it's critical that I come now?" she added.

"No. Like I said, the girls are fine." Lucky paused, then proceeded to ask the question he'd had from the beginning. "Why don't they know you? Why didn't you come and get them when your mother died?"

Alice paused, too. "Because I didn't know. My sister and I had a parting of the ways years ago. I just couldn't be around her when she was using, and my mother enabled her. Not by buying her drugs or anything but by refusing to admit she was killing herself. I would check my sister into rehab, and before the day was up, my mother would get her out."

Lucky hated to think that the girls had been through all of that. This woman could have maybe stopped it. Maybe. Then again, he was betting her sister wouldn't have just handed over custody, even to someone who was more capable of caring for her daughters.

"My mother didn't even call me when my sister died," Alice went on. "Nor when she got sick, so I didn't know about their deaths until the private investigator contacted me. Trust me, if I'd known those girls needed me, I would have been there for them."

The jury was still out on that, but she was certainly saying all the right things.

"My brother's getting married in a week," Lucky explained, "and Mackenzie asked if she could stay for the wedding."

"Of course," Alice said without hesitation. "I can adjust my schedule for that." Then she paused again. "I'm sorry, but I have another call coming in from Colombia that I have to take. But just tell the girls that I'll see them in a couple of days. I can't wait to bring them to their new home in Phoenix."

When she ended the call, Lucky just stood there, staring at the phone.

"Are you okay?" Logan asked.

"Sure. This was exactly what we all wanted."

And he hoped if he repeated that enough, Lucky would start to believe it.

CHAPTER SIXTEEN

CASSIE SAT ON her bed, staring at the letter. It was silly not to just open it and see what her grandmother had written, but she wasn't sure she was ready to see those final words just yet. She wasn't anywhere close to a panic attack, hadn't been close in several days now, but this might push her back over the edge.

After all, she'd had a lot of edge-pushing things happen to her today.

That kissing session in the hayloft. The run-in with Andrew. The tornado of confusion going on in her head when it came to the girls, and the rest of her life. Now, this.

She was still staring at the letter when there was a knock at the door, and Cassie knew who it was before she even opened it. Lucky. He was there, no doubt to figure out if he had a reason to be concerned.

"You want me to stay with you when you read it?" he asked, tipping his head to the letter.

What he didn't do was come in, even though she stepped back so he could do that. Maybe because he was giving her some space. Too bad Cassie wasn't sure if space was the way to go.

"No. I'll be okay. I'm a little worried about Mackenzie, though," she said.

Lucky nodded. "I'm checking on her next."

And that was yet another reason why he probably wasn't coming in. Lucky was like chocolate—she wasn't to be trusted around it. Or him.

"Alice Murdock just called," he added a heartbeat later.

Mercy, was that the reason for his concerned expression? "And?"

He took a deep breath as if he needed it badly, and Cassie tried to steel herself for bad news. "She seems, well, great. It's hard to gauge someone from a phone conversation, but she seems to want the girls, seems to be have their best interest at heart."

"Seems?"

Lucky lifted his shoulder. "Seems is as good as I can get from what she said. She didn't seem anything like her half sister, though."

Cassie was going to take what he was saying as a red flag. Exactly what kind of red flag, she didn't know yet, but she wasn't just going to hand over the girls until she was certain this was the right guardian for them.

Except she might not have a choice.

The woman was blood kin so it was possible neither Lucky nor she would have any say in this. If Alice Murdock *seemed* suitable, then the courts would side with her. Not that it would come down to courts and such.

Her phone buzzed, and Lucky was still close enough to see Andrew's name pop up on the screen. "I'll go check on Mackenzie," he said, getting out of there fast. Probably because he thought she needed privacy for this talk.

But no privacy was needed. Not for the talk anyway. She shut the door after Lucky walked away, let the call go to voice mail and opened the letter. It was handwritten and dated the same as Mia's.

"Dear Cassie," it read. "I figure you're ass-kicking mad at me right about now. I knew it'd be a lot to ask, but I knew you'd do right by the girls. Right by Lucky, too."

That brought Cassie to a dead stop and she scowled. She turned that scowl to the heavens just in case Dixie Mae was watching her. Of course, no matter where Dixie Mae was in the hereafter, she probably wasn't watching. Her grandmother hadn't exactly been a sit-around-and-watch kind of person.

"No, I'm not matchmaking," Cassie continued to read. "I just think it'll help Lucky if he's got bigger problems than the ones festering in his own mind. Plus, he's easy on the eyes. Don't shake your head."

Cassie stopped shaking her head.

"You know he is," Dixie Mae had added. "Just don't let the problems festering in your own mind stop you from seeing that. Anyway, I love you to Pluto and back 'cause if you remember, to the moon and back was never far enough for us."

Cassie smiled. Yes, she remembered. And the feeling of that love came flooding back. In addition to being a nonwatcher, Dixie Mae hadn't exactly been sweet and cuddly, but she had loved Cassie, and Cassie had never doubted that love for a moment.

Well, maybe a moment when she'd first found out Dixie Mae had left Lucky and her with guardianship of the girls.

Dixie Mae had scrawled "Love, Gran," but that wasn't the end of the letter. "PS. Try to make Lucky understand that his parents' deaths weren't his fault."

LUCKY KNOCKED ON Mackenzie's door and was surprised when she answered right away. Not with a scowl or a smart-mouthed response, either. She still looked plenty happy. At first, he thought that had something to do with Dixie Mae's letter, but she was clutching it unopened in her hand.

So this was no doubt some leftover happiness from his agreeing to that dance date. Something that Lucky hoped he didn't regret. However, for now he'd take that happiness. And even add some more.

"Your aunt Alice called, and she thinks it won't be a problem for you and Mia to stay for the wedding."

"Really?" Mackenzie didn't sound like goth moody girl now. She was fully smiling again, and she launched herself into his arms for a very unexpected hug.

And Lucky got an unexpected jolt from the warmth that went through him. Of course, none of this would last, but he decided to hang on to it for a while. But Mackenzie didn't hang on.

"I have to call Brody," she insisted, and practically shut the door in his face.

He had to smile, though. Apparently, she was a normal girl beneath all that anger and makeup. In fact, Mackenzie might just thrive with someone like Aunt Alice. That caused his smile to fade a little. Not because he didn't want her to be happy—he did. But it would have been nice to see both girls come into their own.

Lucky went back downstairs to check on Mia, but Della and she were tied up with a cookie-baking lesson, which meant he didn't have any excuses not to read the letter. He went to his room for that, though. He preferred not to have an audience for what could turn out to be gut-wrenching. Or just plain frustrating. Heaven knew Dixie Mae could be both in the span of two seconds.

"Dear Lucky," he read "I'll try to spell all the words right so you won't scowl. I suspect you're cussing me right now, but that's okay. It makes up for the times you wanted to cuss at me but were too much of a son to do it. Yes, I called you a son, because you were like that to me. That's why I wanted you to have the girls until something *permenent* could be worked out. I knew you'd do what was best for them because it would be like doing what was best for me."

Lucky had to admit she was right. And that part about his being like a son to her? That watered his eyes a little. But it would have watered them significantly more if she hadn't misspelled *permanent*.

"I didn't tell you about the girls sooner," Lucky continued reading, "because you were so busy with the rodeo stuff. I thought I'd have more time. More time to find their kin and get them settled before I passed. It was never my plan to keep them, even for a month, because let's face it, those girls deserve better than me."

Lucky wanted to disagree, but he couldn't. Dixie Mae wasn't the conventional mothering sort, and the girls needed someone normal and stable in their lives.

"Anyway, be good to yourself and Cassie," he read on. "And remember what I told you about rusting up your zipper a bit. Love, Dixie Mae."

He hadn't exactly planned on taking the zipper-rusting advice to heart, but it had worked out that way. Thanks to Andrew's interruption in the barn. If he hadn't shown up, there might not have been enough rust in a junkyard to stop Lucky from finishing what he'd started with Cassie.

Lucky was about to refold the letter, but then he saw the PS at the bottom. "Make Cassie understand that that woman's death wasn't her fault."

And those were Dixie Mae's last words to him. They were good last words, too. Not like the bull remark she'd made on her deathbed. This was solid advice that he should start working on.

Like now.

He hurried upstairs, knocked on Cassie's door, and the moment she opened it, Lucky hooked his arm around her, hauled her to him and kissed her. Of course, Dixie Mae hadn't specifically told him to kiss Cassie. In fact, she hadn't said anything about a lip-lock, but Lucky figured it might help them both.

It was stupid logic, but that brainless part of him behind his zipper thought this was the cure to any and all world problems. Personal ones, too.

Cassie made a soft sound of surprise, a sound that got trapped in the kiss. A lot of things got trapped. Her hand. Her breasts.

Basically the entire front part of her body ended up squished against his while he took the kiss to the next level.

It was the only way to make sure that Cassie knew this was a real kiss and not some peck of reassurance about their situation and those letters. And since it was a real kiss, Lucky made sure it went on for a while. That it involved some touching, as well. He kept kissing, kept touching, until air became a serious issue. He either had to break away from her or suffocate.

It took him several seconds to decide.

He finally pulled back, his eyeballs meeting hers. Cassie looked dazed. Aroused. And a whole bunch of other things that his hard-on wanted him to explore. But it wasn't the time or the place.

"Sometimes the bull doesn't win," he said.

Lucky didn't have a clue what that meant in this context. Didn't care. He walked away, smiling, and he was certain he'd just given Cassie something to think about.

MACKENZIE HATED TO leave a message for Brody. She wanted to tell him the news now, but the call went straight to voice mail. She mumbled a "call me" and hoped it wouldn't take him too long to get back to her.

She waited a minute. Then two. And since she didn't have anything better to do, she opened the letter from Dixie Mae and started reading.

Dear Mackenzie,

I hope you're behaving yourself and have found a good makeup remover. Clear skin really is one of the keys to a woman's happiness, though I'm sure you'll hear that love is. It can be, but you know firsthand that love can also be shitty. Yes, I know I shouldn't cuss around you, but it's hard to come up with another word for shitty, especially one that I can spell right off the top of my head. Probably should have taken that dictionary that Lucky was always trying to give me.

Anyway, just keep putting one foot ahead of the other. Never really did understand that since I'm not sure how you'd put two feet ahead without busting your ass, but again I'm drifting off point and cussing. Keep growing. Keep living. Keep loving. One final thing: help Mia understand that life is more than the bucket of puke you two have had so far.

Love, Dixie Mae.

Mackenzie couldn't help it. She smiled. Dixie Mae was crazy, but crazy in a good way. Not like Mackenzie's mother. Probably not like Aunt Alice, either, but at least her aunt had agreed to let her stay for the wedding.

Her phone rang, finally, and she nearly dropped it trying to answer it.

"Kenzie," Brody said.

God, she loved it when he called her that. Of course, that's what Mia called her, but it sounded so grown-up when Brody said it.

"I got your message," he continued. "Good news, huh? But I got some more good news. Guess where I am right now?" Brody didn't wait for her to guess. "I'm in the barn behind the McCord house. There's nobody out here but me, so why don't you come out? We can hang out together."

"Okay," she heard herself say, though she knew Lucky and Cassie wouldn't allow this. That's why she had no intention of telling them. "I'll be down in a couple of minutes."

The instant Mackenzie ended the call, she wished she'd told him a half hour so she could pull herself together. Her heart was pounding like a gorilla on the inside of her chest, and she could have used that time to steady herself. She didn't want to go out there looking like an idiot kid who'd never done anything like this before.

Even though she hadn't.

Sure, she'd done some sneaking out in the past, but it'd never been to meet a boy. A boy who liked her! It had usually been to get Mia away from their mom when she was high and acting stupid.

Mackenzie hurried to the bathroom to fix her makeup. That alone took a minute of that couple she'd given herself. On top of that, she couldn't just run down the stairs. She had to sneak, to make sure she didn't draw anyone's attention. Thankfully, there was no one in the front part of the house so she crept her way to the back door and slipped out.

Until she made it to the backyard, Mackenzie hadn't realized that the sun had already set. That was probably why Brody had picked this time to come. There were no ranch hands around, and it was already dark enough that she hoped no one would spot her. Wearing all black would finally work in her favor. And besides, Brody seemed to like it.

"Over here," Brody whispered when she got closer to the barn.

Good thing, too, because Mackenzie hadn't seen him at all. He was also wearing all black—maybe her taste in clothes had rubbed off on him—and he was standing in the shadows inside the barn.

"Hi," she said.

Brody took hold of her arm and yanked her into the barn, right into those shadows. "I don't want your watchdogs to see us," he said. "Because Lucky might not like me doing this."

And what he did was kiss her.

Brody smashed his lips against hers. It was rough, and Mackenzie nearly pulled away before she came to her senses. This was her first kiss, so how was she to know if this was rough or not?

"You taste like a birthday present," Brody whispered to her.

Mackenzie had never had a good birthday, certainly didn't know how one tasted, but Brody seemed to like it. He made a grunting sound and kissed her again. Mackenzie felt the warmth trickle through her, but she also felt something else.

His hand going up her top.

Again, it was rough. He had calluses, and they raked across her skin. He shoved down the right cup of her bra before she even realized what he was doing.

Mackenzie stepped back, her breath gusting.

"You're not quitting, are you?" Brody asked. "Because you don't look like a girl who'd quit to me."

"I don't quit," she said. In the past that was her answer to anyone who wanted to fight, but Brody must have figured out that she didn't want to fight with him. So what did not quitting mean to him?

Certainly not *that*.

"But maybe we can just kiss," she whispered.

Mackenzie couldn't see a lot of his face because it was so dark, but Brody still had his hand on her arm, and she felt his muscles tense. Then relax.

"All right. For now, we kiss," he agreed.

The relief flooded through her, along with a new trickle of heat when his mouth came back to hers. Not so rough this time. It was gentle, and strange. Strange because it made the heat trickle even more than it had when he was being rough. She wasn't sure why that would make a difference. Mackenzie wasn't sure of anything except that she wanted Brody to keep on kissing her.

And he did.

Until there was a bright flash of light. Not from overhead but from outside the barn. At first, she thought Lucky or Cassie had found them, but this wasn't anyone she recognized. It was some bald guy with a camera.

The flash went off again.

This jerk was taking their picture. But why?

"Hey!" Brody warned him. "You stop that now."

Well, the guy did stop taking their picture. But he didn't

stop moving altogether. He took off running, taking the proof of the kiss with him.

Mackenzie held her breath, waiting to see if someone was going to come running out of the house. When that didn't happen, she figured that she'd pushed her luck enough for one night. If Lucky or Cassie caught her out here, they might not let her go to the dance.

On a date, she corrected.

Her first date. And there was no way she wanted to ruin that.

"Gotta go," she said.

Before he could say something to stop her, Mackenzie brushed a quick kiss on Brody's mouth and slunk back toward the house.

CHAPTER SEVENTEEN

CASSIE CAME DOWN the stairs and immediately had to dodge a cat that zipped past her. The dodging caused her to sidestep, and in turn she tripped over a basket of toy cars. Ethan's "flower boy" offerings no doubt. She hadn't needed another reminder that Claire and Riley's wedding was only three days away, but the stubbed toe now served as notice that the clock was ticking.

Too fast.

Business had made that time jet by even faster. First business on her part—Marla had made a return visit, this time to lament over whether or not her kneecaps were too saggy. A lover—Cassie didn't bother to ask which one—had mentioned it, and it'd sent Marla into a tailspin. Or rather straight to the airport. Cassie had calmed the woman down but then had suggested she might want another therapist. Marla had balked about that for hours until Cassie had suggested Andrew.

Success.

Marla was no longer on Cassie's client list. In fact, her client list was down to just a handful now, even though she did have two television appearances still scheduled for the end of the month. By then, the wedding would be over, the girls would be with Aunt Alice and Lucky's kisses would be a memory.

It was getting harder and harder for Cassie to hang on to

those memories. Mainly because Lucky hadn't exactly been around much to remind her.

Or kiss her again.

In fact, it'd been three days since he'd done that.

The business bug had bitten him, too, and he'd been forced to spend time in his San Antonio office to put out whatever kind of fires a rodeo promoter had to put out. Thankfully, Mackenzie had behaved herself even if she'd pretty much stayed in her room. And besides, the time spent not kissing Lucky had given Cassie a chance to hang out with Mia.

Which was both fun and exhausting.

She wasn't sure how parents did that day in and day out, but at least now Cassie knew if she ever had children of her own, she'd be able to handle it without going into panic mode.

That left the letter. Cassie wasn't sure how to deal with her grandmother's letter. Well, one specific part of that letter anyway.

PS. Try to make Lucky understand that his parents' deaths weren't his fault.

Cassie wasn't sure how Dixie Mae had expected her to fix that since Lucky wouldn't even talk about it. Worse, Cassie wasn't sure she wanted him to talk about it. That was how she'd gotten into trouble with Hannah. She'd encouraged the woman to open some old wounds that had apparently been so deep they'd caused her to kill herself.

Still rubbing her toe, Cassie made her way to the kitchen in the hopes of finding a second cup of coffee. Maybe finding Lucky, too, or the girls. But what she found was Andrew sitting at the table, drinking what appeared to be the last cup of coffee. The pot was empty, and Della was at the counter prepping lunch.

Since Andrew had been making daily appearances at the ranch to counsel the girls, it wasn't much of a surprise to see him. However, the fact that he had an open bottle of whiskey next to his cup gave Cassie a moment's pause.

"Uh, is something wrong?" Cassie asked.

Della glanced at her, giving her what Cassie could only describe as a sympathetic look. "I sent Mia to the sunroom to play with the cats," Della said. "Mackenzie's with her. I thought it was for the best." Then she excused herself and left the kitchen. Definitely not a good sign since she'd been in the middle of chopping an onion.

"Sit down," Andrew said, and it sounded like an order.

For that reason alone Cassie stood, and she huffed. "Look, Andrew, I'm grateful you were there after Hannah died. You kept me from falling apart—"

"You did fall apart," he argued.

"No. I had panic attacks, and plenty of people have them without having to stay in Sweet Meadows." It had taken her a while, too long, but now that she'd distanced herself from that place, she knew it hadn't been a good idea. "Being there made me feel as if I needed to be there."

That probably didn't make sense to him, but she wasn't sure she cared. What she did care about right now was a cup of coffee. The caffeine hit would help her headache so Cassie went to the counter and started a fresh pot. While she was waiting, she decided to wash her hands and finish chopping the onion for Della.

"Is there a reason for all this hostility I'm sensing coming from you?" Andrew asked. This time he sounded like a therapist. *Her* therapist. "Maybe there's something you'd like to tell me? You know, before I find out on my own."

That didn't sound like a fishing-expedition sort of comment. Of course, Cassie had been chilly to him so maybe he was picking up on the fact that she wanted him to leave Spring Hill.

"I know you're thinking about throwing your career away," he continued. "But I didn't think you'd trash mine in the process."

Cassie stopped, turned, and she was certain there was confusion and alarm on her face. On Andrew's face, too, but then she realized her eyes had watered from the onion and she was holding up the knife as if she were the star of a slasher movie. Cassie eased the knife back onto the counter.

"What are you talking about?" she asked.

"Don't play games with me."

She shook her head, causing him to huff. Apparently, he wasn't going to take her head shake as proof that she didn't have a clue what was going on. Then she rubbed her eyes and made the stinging and burning significantly worse.

"Use your words, Andrew," she snapped. Cassie also snapped a paper towel from the roll, dampened it and pressed it to her eyes.

"I don't need words because these pictures are worth a thousand of them." And Andrew slapped something on the table. Perhaps something he'd taken from his pocket, but with her having to blink ten times per second, it was hard to tell.

Hard to see what'd gotten him so riled up, too.

Hard to see, period.

Cassie went closer, blinking even more to get her eyes to focus, and she finally saw the photo clearly. At first she wasn't sure what she was actually looking at, and it took her a moment to realize it was Mackenzie and Brody. Kissing in the barn.

Sheez, Louise.

The photo was indeed worth a thousand words, and the word at the top of that list was *grounded*.

Since it was obviously dark in the picture, this meant Mackenzie had no doubt sneaked out to meet Brody. Cassie wasn't sure when the girl had done that, but she hadn't had eyes on her 24/7, mainly because Mackenzie had been so happy lately. Well, if happiness was graded on the Mackenzie scale anyway.

But that was only part of the problem Cassie had with the unauthorized smooching. It was the fact that there was a picture of it. A picture that Mackenzie and Brody clearly hadn't taken because they'd been too busy exploring each other's tonsils.

"Who took that picture?" Cassie demanded.

"The same person who took this one." Andrew reached into his jacket pocket and extracted another photo.

Not of Mackenzie and Brody this time. Of Lucky and that sleazy woman, Angel, who'd French-kissed him on the porch. Even though Cassie knew nothing had come of it, that Lucky had quickly gotten rid of her, the photo made it look as if they were making out in public.

"Who took these?" she repeated.

Andrew didn't answer that time, either, but he did pull out a third picture. Another one that had been taken in the barn. It was a shot of Lucky and her. Snapped on the day that she was now referring to as the great chaps lapse.

Oh, mercy.

Lucky and she were doing some smooching, too. And he had his hand on her butt while leading her up the ladder to the hayloft.

Cassie groaned, but what she wanted to do was scream her head off. She hadn't caught even a glimpse of anyone taking their picture. Of course, that had been the last thing on her mind. What she'd been focused on was getting that orgasm from Lucky. Besides, the photo of Lucky and her appeared to have been taken with a long-range lens. Ditto for the one of Lucky and Angel. So it was possible that the photographer hadn't even come onto the ranch.

She couldn't say the same for the one of Brody and Mackenzie, though. That one had been taken up close and at night. There was no way they wouldn't have known about it.

Cassie's stomach knotted into a giant ball, and it was churning as if a basketball point guard were dribbling it. That didn't help her breathing, either, and her heart was thudding in her ears.

Breathe.

She refused to have a panic attack. Cassie tried to put this in perspective. No one was dead or even hurt. Yes, she'd screwed up again, but the damage wasn't anything like it'd been with Hannah.

She hoped.

"What's going on?" Mackenzie asked.

Cassie hadn't heard her, but the girl was right there in the kitchen, and her attention landed on the photos.

"Oh, God." Mackenzie's hand went flying to her mouth. She shook her head. "Who took that picture?"

That was a really good question, but it wasn't nearly as good as the one Cassie had for her. "What were you doing kissing Brody in the barn?"

And apparently Andrew thought he had the best question of all. "What were you doing kissing Lucky in the barn?" he asked Cassie.

Since Cassie didn't have anything near a good answer, she repeated Mackenzie's question. "Who took those pictures?"

"Theo Kervin, the reporter who's been sniffing around town for a story," Andrew said, but his huff and glare let her know that his question was still on the table—literally. That was where the picture of Lucky and her kissing still rested.

"Why would some stupid reporter take a picture of me?" Mackenzie asked.

Maybe it was that her eyes were still burning, or because she still had that headache, but it took Cassie several seconds to piece it together. "This Theo Kervin wants to paint me in a bad light because it'll hurt my reputation as a celebrity therapist. It'll be *news*."

"Bingo," Andrew confirmed. "I don't know all the details of what will be in the article in the Friday paper, but I know he's mentioning me as your spurned lover. It'll make me look like a fool."

"Ex-lover," Cassie corrected, though that was splitting hairs. She knew how tabloid journalism worked, and "ex-lover" wouldn't be nearly as tawdry as having her step out on a distinguished psychologist so she could make out with a cowboy.

All the while she was supposed to be parenting two children in her custody.

All the while one of those girls was making out with a wannabe cowboy.

If Theo had found out about Sweet Meadows, then he could seal the career-ruining deal by just mentioning it. And yes, that would hurt Andrew, too, because it would make it seem as if his lover was a sex-crazed lunatic with no regard whatsoever for the children.

Breathe.

The reminder wasn't working so Cassie put her head between her knees again. And that's how Lucky found her when he walked into the kitchen.

LUCKY HURRIED OVER to Cassie, lifting her head so he could see what was wrong. He saw her red eyes and whirled around to beat the shit out of Andrew for whatever he'd done to make her cry.

But then his attention landed on the photos.

Oh, man.

It felt as if someone had sucker punched him, and he instantly knew. Andrew wasn't the reason for Cassie's tears. He was.

"Theo Kervin took those?" Lucky asked Andrew. "Or did you?" While he was in the Q & A mode, his gaze shot to Mackenzie. "And what the hell were you doing kissing Brody?"

"Uh, kissing him," Mackenzie answered.

No smart-assery in her tone this time. She gave him a truthful answer that in no way answered his question. But Lucky would deal with her later. For now, he needed to stop Cassie from having a panic attack. However, when Cassie lifted her head again, she didn't seem to be in panic mode but rather anger mode.

"I'm going to sue Theo Kervin," she insisted.

"They'll be in the morning papers," Andrew added. "Including the local one here. I tried to stop it, tried to pay off the idiot, but he wouldn't take it."

Maybe because someone had already paid him—like Mason-

Dixon. Of course, Cassie's father was more the type to extort money than to pay it, but if he'd wanted to burn Cassie and Lucky for the cats, then this would have been the way to do it. It wouldn't hurt Lucky's reputation. In fact, it would confirm what most people thought about him anyway, but it would hurt Cassie. Would hurt Mackenzie, too.

First things first, though.

"You're grounded," Lucky told Mackenzie. "I let the money thing slide with just an apology, but this isn't sliding."

"Grounded?" she howled as if she'd just been sentenced to be pecked to death by rabid ducks. "This isn't fair."

"Probably not, but you're not allowed to sneak out of the house and make out with boys. I'm just funny that way."

Mackenzie flung her hand toward the other pictures. "You made out with Cassie and that skank."

"Not to the skank. To Angel," he corrected. "Yeah, to Cassie. But Cassie and I are adults." Though it hadn't felt like it that day. Lucky could have sworn he'd felt a few raging teenage hormones himself when he'd been with Cassie.

Mackenzie huffed and puffed a few seconds while she stared at Cassie, apparently waiting for a second opinion on the grounding verdict. But Cassie just shook her head. "You're grounded. We'll talk later."

After more huffing and puffing, Mackenzie spun around to leave. Lucky followed her a few steps to make sure she was actually going upstairs rather than heading out the front door. She not only went upstairs, he heard her slam her bedroom door.

Good.

Slamming was preferable to running. Heck, he might slam a door or two himself before this day was over.

"What can I do to fix this?" Lucky asked Cassie.

But she didn't give him a good answer. She only shook her head.

"You can't fix this," Andrew insisted. Not a good answer, either. "If you're the one who talked Cassie into giving up being a celebrity therapist, then the timing couldn't have been worse. There's no way she'll be able to build a new client base once this story gets out. Plus, how do you think the girls' aunt will react?"

Probably not well. Heck, Alice might get on the next plane to whisk the girls away. Of course, Alice's whisking was only days away anyway, but Lucky didn't want things to end like this. And speaking of whisking things away, that's what Andrew did to the photos. He stuffed them in his jacket pocket and looked at Cassie. "I'll be leaving for the airport in a few hours. If you have anything to say to me, then I suggest you say it now."

Lucky wasn't sure exactly what Andrew wanted to hear Cassie say. Did he want her to beg him to forgive her and stay? Did he want a goodbye? Cassie didn't give him either of those, though. She just sat there staring at the now empty spot on the table where the photos had been.

"Fine," Andrew snapped, and he hurried to the door.

And yep, he slammed it on his way out.

LUCKY STOOD IN the shower and let the scalding-hot water do its job. Not with the cleaning part. He could have accomplished that with a much cooler temperature. What he needed was some of the muscles unknotted in his back and shoulders.

The house was essentially on lockdown. Lucky wasn't sure if that was the right thing to do or not, especially since he'd have to leave in a couple of hours for Riley's bachelor party. He'd considered skipping it, but Della, Stella and Cassie had all assured him they'd keep an eye on Mackenzie.

That might not be enough, though.

But Lucky kept going back to bull logic. Some bulls were just harder to fence than others, and a few were downright impossible. They'd break fences no matter how strong. It was a bad analogy, but there might not be a fence tall or strong enough to keep Mackenzie from sneaking back out again.

Lucky gave up on getting relief from the shower. He toweled off, pulled on his boxers and jeans and headed back into his bedroom to get a clean shirt. And he stopped in his tracks.

Because Cassie was sitting on his bed.

Her eyes weren't red as they'd been in the kitchen, but she wasn't exactly sporting a sunshiny smile, either.

"Is Mackenzie all right?" he asked.

"She's still in her room. Mia's with Della, and the ranch hands are watching to make sure Mackenzie doesn't sneak out again."

Since that was about as good as they could expect right now, it didn't explain Cassie's "somebody died" expression.

Hell, unless somebody *had* died.

After all, that lunatic client had flown in the day before for another session. Had Marla done something? Or had Andrew? Lucky figured the guy was far too egotistical to end his life, but maybe he'd said or done something to hurt Cassie. Or to get back together with her. She hadn't gone running out of the house after Andrew, but that didn't mean she hadn't called him afterward.

"Are *you* all right?" Lucky asked, sitting down on the bed next to her.

Cassie gave a little laugh, definitely not from humor. "I'm fine. I'm worried about you, though."

"Me?" Lucky wasn't sure where she was going with this. "I'm not the one who'll lose clients or have my reputation ruined. Heck, I'll probably get some calls for dates after the story runs and they see me with both Angel and you."

He'd meant that as a joke, but Cassie must have thought he was serious because it put that troubled look back on her face. Then he noticed what she had in her left hand.

The letter.

She unfolded it for him to see. Lucky glanced through it, the PS snagging his attention right off, and he groaned.

PS. Try to make Lucky understand that his parents' deaths weren't his fault.

"Dixie Mae had no right," he snarled.

Cassie nodded. "And I suspect she had no right to give you a PS about me. Let me guess—she told you to make sure I understood that Hannah's death wasn't my fault?"

Since that was almost verbatim, Lucky just nodded. He was about to say Dixie Mae had no right to say that about Cassie, either, that it wasn't Dixie Mae's place. But hell, it sure felt like it was his place to try to help Cassie.

Without her trying to help him, of course.

Lucky frowned. He didn't want to be fixed. Didn't deserve it.

"I'll show you mine if you show me yours," Cassie said.

His mind, and body, immediately started to fill in the blanks, but he didn't think his dick was a blank in this. No, this wasn't something nearly as much fun.

"I'll start," she said, though he'd given her no encouragement whatsoever to do that. "I can't forgive myself for what happened to Hannah because I don't feel as if I deserve forgiveness."

Well, now. Since that, too, was almost verbatim what Lucky had been thinking, he had to wonder if Dixie Mae was somewhere in the spiritual realm making all of this happen. It didn't matter. Lucky still didn't want to play this game.

"I figure I deserve the panic attacks, too. Deserve my inability to commit because I haven't gotten past the baggage my parents left me." She paused. "And I have trouble having orgasms."

Lucky had tried to anticipate what she was going to say. That last one hadn't been anywhere on his list, and it didn't fit with the other things. Or maybe it did. Did she truly feel she didn't deserve orgasms?

"Really? Because you seemed to be doing okay with that up in the hayloft," he reminded her.

"I know. But that was a fluke. At least, I think it was."

And then Cassie did something else that would have knocked his socks off, had he been wearing any.

She kissed him.

Cassie took hold of him, dragged him to her and kissed him. Again, it didn't go with the first part of the conversation, but it certainly went with the second because it seemed as if Cassie was in search of that orgasm—right here, right now.

Lucky felt the kiss all right. Not just in the usual places, either. This was a head-to-toenails sort of sensation as if every bit of him had managed to toss back some shots of hundred-proof. It was an especially good feeling since he was already half-naked, and Cassie and he were on the bed.

So Lucky kissed her right back.

He kept on kissing her until she did something else surprising. Cassie moved away from him and stood.

"I just wanted to give you something to think about," she said as if that explained everything.

And Cassie walked out, leaving him there with that warm head-to-toe feeling and a raging hard-on.

CHAPTER EIGHTEEN

CASSIE WENT TO the window and checked again. No sign of Lucky. Of course, it was barely 10:00 p.m., and it was possible Riley's bachelor party would go into the wee hours of the morning. Still, she was hoping he would get home early just so she could explain herself.

Kissing him like that had been a bold move. Sort of throwing down the F-word gauntlet. And he would have known that, too. She wasn't a tease, and there was only one reason for her to kiss a man like that.

Because she wanted to F-word him.

Now that the fire in her body had cooled just a bit, she was feeling all the nerves beneath her skin. That was why she wanted to talk to him. Or preferably have sex with him. Sex wouldn't help with the PS from Dixie Mae's letter, but Cassie was reasonably sure it wouldn't hurt.

The knock at her door sent her racing to open it, and she tried not to look disappointed to see Mackenzie standing there. Because Cassie really wasn't disappointed. She'd tried to talk to Mackenzie several times since Andrew's photo bombshell, and the girl had clammed up. However, Mackenzie certainly looked ready to talk now.

"Mia's asleep," she said right off. "Can I come in for a minute?"

"Of course." Cassie ushered her in and shut the door.

"I'm sorry," Mackenzie said before she even sat down on the bed. It not only sounded genuine, it looked as if she'd been crying. There were some visible streaks in her makeup. "I didn't mean to mess up anything for you and your job. I just wanted to see Brody."

Considering Cassie was fighting her own hormonal impulses, she totally understood.

"I'm really sorry," Mackenzie added, and yes, there were tears now. Unlike her apology to Wilhelmina, it sounded as if the girl meant it.

Sighing, Cassie sat down beside her and slipped an arm around her. This time, Mackenzie didn't go stiff as she usually did when Cassie touched her. She actually leaned against Cassie.

"I just thought Brody wouldn't like me if I said no," she went on. "That's why I went to the barn. I didn't know he was going to kiss me, honest."

Cassie got that, as well. Of course, from the moment she'd seen Lucky walking toward her in the barn that day, she'd pretty much figured a kiss or something more would happen between them. But she was an adult, and she'd known the consequences of her actions. Her limits, too. Maybe Mackenzie didn't.

"You shouldn't say yes to a guy just so he'll like you," Cassie told her. "Because it might not stop at a kiss. He might want *more* to keep on liking you. Understand?"

Apparently, she did because Mackenzie's gaze darted away. "Brody wouldn't do that. He just wanted to kiss me."

"Maybe. Guys can be...complicated." But then Cassie shook her head. "Actually, that's not true. Many of them just want sex. I'm not saying that's true for Brody, but it's their hormones." Something she completely understood since her own hormones were in a tizzy over Lucky. "Plus, you have to consider that you might not be here at the ranch much longer. I know it doesn't seem that way right now, but it might be only a short while before you forget all about Brody because you've met someone else."

Mackenzie sucked in her breath as if horrified by that thought. Cassie was about to start drilling home that it was just the way these things worked, but that might not be true, either. After all, Cassie had had a thing for Lucky all these years, and that thing was stronger than ever. It might happen to Mackenzie—thirty years from now.

Mackenzie looked up at her. "I get what you're saying, but I just want to be with Brody. Even if it's only for a day or two. I know you don't owe me any favors, but I really want to go to that dance with him tomorrow night."

There it was. The megaproblem that Mackenzie had just dumped into her lap. If Cassie held firm and said no, it would break Mackenzie's heart. Temporarily. But to a thirteen-year-old girl, it would feel as if it were a permanent scar. On the other hand, if she said yes, then it could make her look like a wimp.

Mackenzie put her own hand into play. She opened her palm, and Cassie saw the gold star that Livvy had given her the day she'd arrived at the ranch. It had a little less gold on it now, and there was no way Mackenzie really believed it was magic. Still, it had sort of a magical effect on Cassie when Mackenzie gave it to her.

Cassie decided to go with being the wimp. It would be far easier for Cassie to mend her own ego than it would for Mackenzie to mend her teenage heart.

"Yes, but with rules," Cassie quickly added when Mackenzie started to squeal—yes, squeal—with enough excitement that you would have thought she'd just been granted every wish she'd ever wanted.

"Any rules are fine as long as I can go."

"Hear the rules first," Cassie warned her. "And I have to clear all of this with Lucky, understand?"

Even that didn't seem to diminish a drop of her happiness.

Mackenzie nodded. Too bad she didn't have a second gold star for Lucky.

"We'll drive you there and bring you home," Cassie continued. "At no point will you slip off to be alone with Brody. We'll make sure of that because we'll be watching you."

Still nodding, she seemed surprised when Cassie didn't add any other conditions. "I don't have to, like, dress like you or anything?"

"No. You can wear what you want as long as it covers all parts of your body from here to here." Cassie pointed to her neck, then to her midthigh. "Now get some sleep."

"I will. Thank you, Cassie. Thank you." She hugged Cassie again and practically skipped out of the room.

After being given such a huge concession, she doubted Mackenzie would skip out of the house, but just in case she watched Mackenzie go into her room and shut the door. Cassie was about to do the same thing when she heard the footsteps on the stairs.

Lucky.

"You're home early," she said, and it was a good thing she said it fast, too, because it was all Cassie managed to get out before he reached her.

Lucky hooked his arm around her waist, snapped her to him and kissed her. All in all, it was a lot better than him saying hello or responding to her comment. And he didn't stop there. It was like the loft ladder all over again. Kissing her, he pushed her deeper into the room and kicked the door shut.

Mercy, he smelled good. Tasted good, too. Cassie had expected him to smell like strippers and taste like tequila, but the only thing she was getting here was the heady scent of cowboy and testosterone. Lucky should bottle it.

But for now, no bottle required. He was giving her a full dose of not just the kiss but of body contact. His chest against her breasts. His left leg wedged between hers. He was working that leg, too, giving her just the right kind of pressure to go along with the kiss.

Lucky broke the contact only to reach back and lock the door. He came back to her, his mouth already finding hers. And then he said the exact thing Cassie wanted to hear.

"I thought about that kiss," he said, "and now I'm thinking it's time we did a hell of a lot more."

LUCKY WAS TIRED of debating with himself over whether this was a good idea or not. It wasn't. But some of the things that had turned out good in his life had started with not-so-good ideas.

Or at least that was the logic he'd used on the drive home from the bachelor party.

It wasn't necessarily good logic, but then who cared. Cassie certainly seemed willing to jump into this, and even if this was their one and only time together, that just meant Lucky had to make the most of it.

She reached behind him, groping. Not for his back, he realized, but for the light switch. Lucky maneuvered her away from that right off. He wanted to see her, along with tasting lots and lots of her body.

"You're used to being with hot women," she mumbled. "I'm not hot."

There weren't many things that could have made him break the kiss, but that did it. "You're hot."

And since Cassie screwed up her mouth and didn't look sure of that at all, Lucky went down on his knees, pushed up her skirt, yanked down her panties and put her knee on his shoulder so he could give her a kiss to make her body feel as hot as she looked.

It worked.

Not just for Cassie—she made a gasping sound of pleasure—but for him, too. Of course, he had been sporting a hard-on for days so he didn't need anything additional, but the taste of her gave him a nice buzz.

"I wasn't expecting that," she said, gasping again.

Good. It was nice to keep her a little off balance so that

maybe those orgasms she said she had trouble with would sort of sneak up on her. Lucky helped with that. He added a little nip—the kind that would hurt so good—and deepened the kiss. Lucky took her to the brink.

Before he pulled her back.

She cursed him and called him a bad name when he stopped.

"Foreplay," he explained but since she'd brought up the subject of ass with her name-calling, he got to his feet, turned her and put her against the door.

Normally, this was the part where he would want her stark naked, but if that happened, the *fore* would leave the foreplay, and he'd fuck her brains out. He preferred a more controlled fucking right now, to test to see just how sweet the part of her he'd just kissed was.

He shoved up her skirt again, though it was already practically around her waist. The panties went. He pushed them to her knees, caught onto them with his boot and pushed them the rest of the way down. He raked them aside when she stepped out of them, and Cassie put herself against the door again.

Holding her in place, he managed to put on a condom, and he moved her legs apart so he could enter her from behind. Not deep. Just enough to let him know what he was up against. Kissing Cassie there was one thing, but his dick was a lot more sensitive than his tongue.

Oh, man.

He was in trouble. He shouldn't have waited this long to be with her because Cassie was tight, wet and yeah, hot. All the things that would end this much too fast. Good thing they weren't face-to-face because he would've been a goner if she'd kissed him. Or if he had been looking into her eyes.

She made that moan again and went still a second as if trying to steady herself. Lucky knew exactly how she felt—literally. He wasn't too steady, either, and he got even less steady when Cassie pushed herself against him, taking him deeper inside her.

Hell in a hurricane.

When he was a teenager he'd used a trick so he could last long enough to do things the right way, with both him and his partner getting off. He mentally quoted the recipe for his dad's barbecue sauce. Ketchup, brown sugar, vinegar and mustard. Yeah, it was stupid, but it always worked. Though when Cassie kept moving, kept pushing herself so that all that slick heat was sliding right against his hard-on, Lucky was forced to repeat the recipe three times.

"Vinegar?" she asked.

Crap. He hadn't meant to say it aloud, and that meant it was clearly time to take this to the next level. He pulled out of her, causing her to call him a name again. The woman did like variations with the root word of *ass* in them. She turned so that they were face-to-face, and she would have taken him back inside her if Lucky hadn't scooped her up and carried her to the bed. He put her on the mattress, her legs still spread, and he damn near lost his breath. Damn near came, too.

Maybe he should have turned out those lights after all.

Too late.

Things were moving very fast now, and despite the fact he still had on his jeans, Cassie pulled him down on top of her. It was as if his dick had a homing device on it instead of a condom because he went right inside her, pushing through all that tight heat until he was exactly where he wanted to be.

Cassie didn't groan this time. She stopped breathing, and for a moment he thought she'd fainted or something. But no. Lucky looked in her eyes and saw exactly what he wanted to see—a beautiful woman on the verge of a beautiful orgasm. And she wouldn't have to work for this one.

Lucky did it for her.

As a teenager he'd had a very good teacher, a girl two years older than him who'd made him take exams of sorts on locating what she'd called her love button. Hours and hours of practice had made him particularly aware of how important it was to find any and all love buttons of his sexual partners. Cassie's was pretty easy to find, and he knew he'd hit pay dirt when her eyes practically rolled back in her head.

Lucky didn't have a choice about moving then. She caught onto his hips and helped him with that. Not that he actually needed help, but it was obvious that Cassie was on a mission to make the best possible use of his hard-on.

She moved.

He moved.

Faster.

Deeper.

Until recipe-quoting time was over. It was time to finish, and he made sure that's exactly what Cassie did. That was the nice thing about a woman's climax—all those muscles squeezing him until he wasn't sure of his own name, much less barbecue ingredients. Lucky let her love button do the rest of the work for him, and he let himself go.

Lucky collapsed on top of her, trying not to crush her, and as soon as he could get his body working, he flopped down on his back beside her like a landed trout. Cassie's breath was gusting, and she was making little sounds. Mumbling something.

And then she laughed.

He lifted his head to see what the heck was going on. Usually he didn't leave a woman laughing after an orgasm.

"You know it was great," she said, clamping her teeth over her bottom lip for a second. "Don't look so pleased with yourself."

Did he look pleased? Probably. He'd just had sex with a woman who'd been causing his body to burn for years.

Cassie laughed again, turned her head and kissed him. Not the long, lingering kiss, though, of a woman who might want seconds. Seconds done the right way, with them both naked as jaybirds.

"I don't think I've been this relaxed in years," Cassie said. "All the muscles in my body are slack. You're a great stress reliever, you know that?"

He smiled.

Then he didn't smile.

A stress reliever? Was that what this had been for her? Yeah, he'd been a player most of his life, but for the first time, that was starting to wear thin. Maybe he was looking for more than being just a bull rider/player/screwup after all.

Well, fuck.

When had that happened?

CHAPTER NINETEEN

THAT WONDERFUL SLACK feeling hadn't lasted for Cassie. It had vanished shortly after Lucky had kissed her good-night and headed off to his room. And the vanishing act had happened only minutes after he'd given her that equally wonderful orgasm.

Cassie knew she'd blown it.

For someone who had been trained to deal with people's emotions, she'd sure missed the mark when it came to Lucky. Clearly, she'd hurt his feelings with her stress-reliever remark. Strange. She hadn't thought he would be sensitive about something like that, especially since they had known the sex was just that—sex.

Wasn't it?

Cassie had to shake her head. She wasn't sure about anything anymore, but she knew she had to talk this out with Lucky now that it was morning, and she wanted to do that before any of the wedding crew showed up. They weren't setting up for the actual wedding just yet since it was still two days away, but they needed to start clearing out the furniture so there'd be room for the chairs and flowers.

She checked on the girls first by putting her ear to their bedroom door. No stirring around in there so Cassie headed downstairs. Before she could make it to Lucky's room, though, she heard the voices in the living room. One was Lucky's, but the other Cassie didn't recognize. However, she immediately knew who the woman was when Cassie spotted her.

Alice Murdock.

She was tall, blonde and, well, stunning. She was wearing sensible traveling clothes that managed to look fashionable on her model-thin body. Alice stood the moment Cassie stepped into the living room, and with a smile on her face, she approached and shook Cassie's hand.

"I apologize for being here two days early," Alice said, her voice a whisper. "I rescheduled some work and took an earlier flight because I was so anxious to finally get here. I hope you don't mind. I was going to wait outside in my rental car for a while, but then Lucky saw me and invited me in."

Of course, they'd been expecting Alice but not until later that week. Cassie had wanted those extra hours to ready herself for this. Then again, readying apparently wasn't necessary. Alice certainly didn't appear to be a drug-addicted lowlife like her half sister.

"Alice and I were just talking about her job," Lucky said.

And they were drinking coffee. Judging from the fact that both their cups were nearly empty, they'd been chatting for a while.

"Oh?" Cassie settled for saying.

She hated to sound even remotely catty. Hated to feel it even more, but there was something about this that put her off. Maybe it was just jealousy. Not just because this woman would soon whisk the girls away but because of this cozy time she was having with the man who'd given Cassie an orgasm about ten hours earlier.

"You remember me mentioning that Alice heads up a nonprofit. It arranges for medical and dental care in third-world countries," Lucky explained.

"And Lucky told me all about his bull riding," Alice quickly added. "He even showed me the bulls he just bought. No way would I climb on one of those things." She chuckled. Then she looked at Cassie. "Of course, I've seen you on television, so I know what you do. It must feel good to be able to touch so many people like that."

It did, sometimes, and it was the perfect thing for this woman to say. Cassie settled for a nod.

"So, you live in Phoenix?" Cassie asked, sitting on the sofa. Not too close to Lucky, but it was close enough that another woman might notice she was marking her territory.

Sad, very sad, that Cassie felt the need to do that, especially since Lucky wasn't doing any territory marking of his own.

"I moved there about five years ago, after my divorce." Alice dismissed that with a wave of her hand. "The job was just too tempting to pass up. Our organization helps several thousand people each year."

"It sounds as if you work a lot of hours." Cassie tried to sound like she was making casual conversation rather than appearing as if she was fishing for anything negative.

"I do, but I know that'll have to change now. I'll need a new place, too. And a nanny, of course. Any idea how the girls do in school?"

"Mia hasn't started yet," Cassie answered. "She'll be going into pre-K at the end of the month. Mackenzie will be in eighth grade. Her grades took a hit when her mother died."

"But she's good in English," Lucky added.

Cassie hadn't even known that Lucky had checked on her school records, but it didn't surprise her. They'd both gotten more involved in the girls' lives than Cassie had originally planned. That's what made this meeting all the more difficult.

"So, you want children?" Cassie didn't even attempt the casual, conversational tone that time.

Alice nodded without hesitation. "I can't have children of my own." Had her bottom lip trembled? Heck, it had. "That's the reason my ex divorced me. I'd given up on the idea of being a mom, and when I got the call about Gracie's death, I was naturally upset, but I was glad to finally be able to do something to help her."

Before the woman had even finished, Cassie heard a familiar sound—Mia talking to the cats. It didn't take the little girl long to make it to the living room, holding one of the cats in her arms.

Alice got to her feet again. "Hi. You must be Mia. I'm your aunt Alice."

Mia looked at both Lucky and Cassie, maybe asking for some kind of signal that it was okay to go closer. Cassie nodded, and Mia took more steps toward Alice.

"This is Sassy," she said, introducing the cat. "Are you a nice lady?"

Alice chuckled again, apparently thoroughly enchanted. "I like to think I am. Do I look nice?"

Mia studied her a moment. "I guess so."

More footsteps, and Cassie knew Mackenzie was on the way. Cassie would have bet her favorite jeans that Alice's enchantment would diminish considerably when she saw Mackenzie.

But she was wrong.

Alice gave Mackenzie an equally warm smile and then pressed her hand to her heart. "You look so much like Gracie."

Mackenzie flinched as if someone had struck her. "Then I must not have put on enough makeup."

It was inches deep as usual, and it broke Cassie's heart a little not to have seen why Mackenzie put on this mask each day. She probably didn't want to be reminded of her mother whenever she looked in the mirror. Some therapist she was not to have picked up on that.

"Is it still okay for us to go to the wedding even though she's here early? I mean, we don't have to leave right away with her, do we?" Mackenzie said to Cassie. She tipped her head to Alice. Then she did a second head tip to Lucky. "And did you ask him about that other thing we talked about?"

"Of course, you can still go to the wedding," Alice assured

Mackenzie before Cassie could speak. "I've reserved a room at the Bluebonnet Inn, and I figured we could all fly out on Sunday night. Or maybe Monday if that works better with everyone's schedule."

Cassie figured she couldn't ask the flight to be changed to next year.

"What are you supposed to ask me?" Lucky pressed.

Cassie had wanted to have this chat in private, but she really should include Alice in this anyway. "I didn't know her aunt would get here this soon so I told Mackenzie that if it was okay with you that she could go to the dance tonight." She didn't mention the part about Mackenzie being grounded. If Mackenzie wanted her aunt to know, then she could tell her. But Lucky would perhaps think that the grounding extended to the dance.

Judging from his expression, that's exactly what he thought.

A flatter look would have required Lucky getting his eyelids steamrollered.

"Of course, I'll chaperone," Cassie added.

"Please," Mackenzie begged, not sounding at all hostile or surly. She was the normal thirteen-year-old again, standing on the brink of what she no doubt considered to be a life-and-death matter.

"A dance?" Alice questioned.

Oh, no. If both Lucky and Alice were on team no, then Cassie wouldn't stand a chance of convincing them.

"It's at the town's civic center," Cassie explained. "All the local kids used to go to dances there when they were Mackenzie's age." Or at least she was sure Lucky had. Cassie had always had her nose in a book from the time she'd been able to turn pages.

"Brody still has plans to be there," Lucky practically growled, and it certainly wasn't a growl of approval. Alice followed up with a "Who's Brody?"

"Brody Tate," Cassie said.

"A friend," Mackenzie said.

"A boy," Mia said.

Alice looked at Lucky, apparently wanting his take on the situation. Lucky glanced at both Mackenzie and her aunt. Scowled. "Brody is someone who thinks he's Mackenzie's boyfriend, but he's not. He can't be because Mackenzie's too young for a boyfriend."

While his tone wasn't exactly friendly, Lucky hadn't mentioned the shovel or stun gun. That was something at least.

"I'll be late for chaperoning duties," Lucky said. "I thought the plans for the dance were out…because of the other thing."

He meant the grounding over the photograph. So obviously Lucky had mentally nixed the dance. Which was reasonable, but Cassie had just had such a hard time saying no after her talk with Mackenzie.

"Because I thought I'd be free, I've got that dinner thing tonight with Sugar and Wilhelmina," Lucky added.

Yes, payment for keeping quiet. The "date" had been postponed so many times that Cassie had forgotten about it. Apparently, Lucky had decided to kill two birds with one stone and wine and dine the women together. She was betting that wouldn't be a pleasant evening.

"I don't think both of us would need to be at the dance anyway," Cassie explained.

"I could do it," Alice volunteered.

"Uh—" Mackenzie said at the same time Cassie said "Huh?"

It wasn't that Cassie didn't want Alice there— All right, she didn't. Cassie also wasn't sure how Alice would take it when she learned Brody was older than Mackenzie. And that he had somewhat of a reputation. No way would Alice be able to get out of that civic center without hearing a boatload of gossip.

Including gossip about those photos that would be in the paper. Since Spring Hill wasn't that big, the local newspaper only came out three times a week, but the latest edition came out this morning, which meant people were probably looking at them right now.

Of course, Alice would hear about that soon enough any-way, but Cassie hoped she could put off explaining it until after the dance. If she told her now, Cassie doubted even the perfect Alice would agree.

"So I can go?" Mackenzie asked.

"If it's okay with Lucky," Alice assured her.

Now all eyes turned to Lucky. Even the cat in Mia's little arms was staring at him.

And he finally nodded.

Mackenzie squealed again, and she rushed to hug all of them. Including Alice and the cat. "I want to go try on my dress," she said, and she bolted for the stairs.

"I remember those years," Alice said, smiling. She touched her finger to Mia's nose. "Your years not so much. So will this kitty be coming with us to Phoenix?"

That got eyes back on Cassie. And like Lucky, Cassie nod-ded. Mia squealed.

Squealing aside, everything was falling into place.

Alice picked up her purse. "Let me see if I can get checked in to the inn. I'll be staying in the garden room. And then if it's okay, I'll come back and spend some time with the girls."

"Of course," Cassie mumbled. Lucky mumbled it, as well. Mia was still squealing and running around the room with the cat.

Lucky and Cassie followed the woman to the door. "I'm so sorry about losing my sister," Alice whispered to them. "But you can't imagine how much joy the girls have already given me."

There were tears in her eyes, and Cassie guessed they were of the happy variety. Alice gave a little wave goodbye before she headed out.

Lucky and Cassie stood there in the doorway, waving back. Smiling. Until Alice had gotten in her rental car and driven away.

"Shit," Lucky mumbled. "She's perfect."

CASSIE HAD BEEN right about the gossip and those pictures. No one at the civic center was actually saying anything to her face—not to Mackenzie's or Brody's faces, either—but a lot of hands were being used in the dance hall to cover whispers. Cassie suspected that the whispering would increase significantly when Lucky finally arrived.

He'd gone on the payback date after all but had promised to get to the dance as soon as possible. He had also somehow talked Alice into not coming. Cassie wasn't sure exactly how he'd accomplished that, but she was glad he had. The wedding chaos would start again first thing in the morning since the furniture had been cleared and the decorating would begin. So these were likely her last few hours to spend with Mackenzie.

And fifty other teenagers.

The civic center was jammed, and even though Cassie had never attended a dance here, it was how she'd imagined it would be. Crepe-paper decorations. Toilet-paper roses. Dim lights. Really loud music. But Mackenzie didn't seem to notice any of that. She had her eyes locked on Brody as they danced.

Cassie's phone buzzed, and she took it from her pocket long enough to check the screen. It was her agent, who'd no doubt gotten word of the photos. He was probably calling to tell her that her reputation had been as sullied as Andrew had claimed it would be. Or heck, maybe this had put her even more in demand, sort of like those pseudocelebrities who did sex tapes.

Either way, Cassie didn't intend to find out what was going on until after the wedding. It wasn't very healthy to take the head-in-the-sand approach with something as big as this, but it beat having a panic attack.

She let the call from her agent go to voice mail. The very thing she'd done with Andrew's calls. And the one from her mother. The four from her father, too. She decided the only non-McCord/Compton call she might answer would be from a Girl Scout who wanted to personally deliver a case of Thin Mints. Everybody else could leave a voice mail.

"Enjoying yourself?" someone asked from behind her.

Deputy Davy.

He was in uniform, his thumbs hooked over his equipment belt, his legs apart as if he was ready to pounce on any situation that might require pouncing.

"So, did Lucky dump you already?" Davy asked.

There were so many things wrong with that question, and any way she tried to answer it Cassie would say more than she wanted to. So she didn't answer at all. "Why are you here?"

He gave his thumbs an adjustment. "To stop underage drinking. You can't trust these kids, and I figure somebody will try to sneak in some liquor."

Maybe, but since there were just as many adults there as children, it wouldn't be easy.

"It's all over town, you know," Davy went on. "Not just those kissing pictures, but about the cats. Folks know that Lucky and you took 'em."

She grunted again. And considered a pretend gag. If Davy thought she was about to barf, he might move away from her and pester someone else.

"I went to the McCord building," he continued, "to search for those cats."

This time she grunted because her stomach got a sudden knot in it. Certainly Helene or Logan would have called if Davy had found the cats, though.

"Helene wouldn't let me in," Davy added. "Said I had to get a search warrant. I'm working on it, and once I have it, I'll go back and search that place from top to bottom."

She seriously doubted any judge would sign a search warrant for a building that Logan owned, but just in case, Cassie made a mental note to arrange to have the cats moved. Where exactly she didn't know, but she might have to fly them to California with her and kennel them for a while until she could find permanent homes for all of them. But that still wouldn't get her father off her back.

Or off Lucky's.

Heaven knew how long her father would hound Lucky.

And Cassie decided to try to fix that. "The next time you talk to Mason-Dixon," she said to Davy, "tell him I'll offer him fifty grand for the cats."

Davy looked at her as if her functioning brain cells had been killed with the loud music, but he finally nodded. Finally, he moved away from her, taking out his phone as he walked. No doubt to call her father.

With the deputy finally out of her hair, Cassie turned her attention back to Mackenzie. And she immediately frowned. Yes, the light was dim, but she had no trouble seeing that Brody had taken hold of both of Mackenzie's wrists, and it didn't look like a dance move. He appeared to be "coaxing" her toward the corner, and he didn't look especially happy that she was putting up some resistance.

Cassie made her way to the dance floor, hurrying but trying not to look as if she were. On the outside chance she was misinterpreting Mackenzie's expression, Cassie didn't want to embarrass all of them. But the moment she reached Mackenzie, Brody let go of her as if she were an electric fence gone live, and he marched toward the drinks table.

"Everything okay?" Cassie asked her. Of course, she had to shout it. And of course, that was when there was a dip in the music volume, so Cassie hadn't managed to do this without drawing attention after all.

"Everything's fine," Mackenzie snapped, but then she huffed and led Cassie off the dance floor, toward Brody and the drinks table—though she stopped a good distance away from him.

"He's the only boy who's ever noticed me, all right?" Mackenzie threw out there.

There were as many things wrong with that comment as there had been with Davy's question about Lucky dumping her.

"You're thirteen," Cassie reminded her. "There'll be plenty of years for boys to notice you."

"Mom said she lost her virginity when she was thirteen."

Good grief. "There'll be plenty of time for that, too," Cassie assured her.

Mackenzie made a sound that might or might not have been of agreement. "Brody likes me, okay?"

"Okay. But that doesn't mean you have to give him your virginity. Or anything else for that matter." Cassie paused. "Did Brody force you to kiss him that night in the barn?"

"No. I wanted to kiss him," Mackenzie insisted. "Anyway, it doesn't matter. This is the last night I'll be with Brody like this, and I don't want to spend it standing here, talking to you." Her tone was sharp, but Mackenzie brushed her hand on Cassie's arm before she stepped away and joined Brody.

Even with the music still going, Cassie became aware of the hush that had come over the room. For a moment she thought it was because all eyes had been on Mackenzie and her, but then she noticed Lucky. He came in through the door, looking exactly like the hot cowboy fantasy that he was.

And she'd had sex with him.

Something that made her all tingly. And then it made Cassie frown. Because apparently everyone in town was aware of that and then had made the assumption—based on what, she didn't know—that Lucky had dumped her. Of course, maybe they thought that because Lucky didn't spend too much time with any one woman.

Cassie saw him glance around. Their gazes met, and he started to weave his way through the crowd to get to her. He was a different fantasy tonight. Not chapped and spurred but rather suited. He had on a dark-colored jacket paired with his jeans. Clothes for a "date."

"Everything okay?" he asked the moment he reached her. But then Lucky glanced around the room. "Hell, what's everybody saying about us now?"

"That you dumped me."

He repeated that "hell," huffed and then kissed her. Not a

friendly peck, either. He kissed her so long and with so much body contact that Davy called out for them to break it up. Probably not the best behavior for chaperones at a teenage dance where hormones were zinging, but it did start a new ripple of behind-the-hand whispers.

"Something for me to think about?" she asked.

"Something for them to talk about," he corrected.

Oh. So it hadn't been an invitation to go back to his bed. Cassie really did need to apologize for that stress-reliever comment.

"Is Mackenzie all right?" he asked.

Cassie nearly blurted out her concerns right there, but since everyone had their ears and eyes still turned in their direction, she motioned for Lucky to follow her to the side double doors. They were wide-open, mainly because the AC wasn't cooling off the room nearly enough and also because there was a steady trail of older teens coming and going.

Something Mackenzie definitely wouldn't be doing.

Of course, everyone inside probably thought Cassie was hauling Lucky off to make out with him, but she wasn't. Even if her body thought that might be a fun idea. Nope. She just needed to tell him that she thought Brody was pressuring Mackenzie and then hope Lucky didn't find a stun gun and shovel to use on the boy.

Since Gladys Ellsley, the minister's wife, was in their path, Cassie stopped a moment and asked Gladys to keep an eye on Mackenzie. It really wasn't necessary. If Mackenzie did anything, or even if she did nothing, Cassie figured she'd have a full report from at least a dozen people.

Lucky and Cassie stepped just outside the door and definitely weren't alone. There was a couple kissing, but they either didn't notice or didn't care that they had an audience because they didn't stop. On the other side of the doors were five teenage boys. They were huddled in a circle, their backs to Lucky and her, but a sudden breeze sent a familiar scent right at Cassie.

Booze.

No, Mackenzie definitely wouldn't be coming out here.

Cassie turned to Lucky to start the conversation she didn't want to have, but he was already moving away from her. He broke through the circle of boys like a bowling ball, scattering them and sending a bottle of cheap whiskey splatting to the ground.

"What the hell do you think you're doing?" Lucky shouted at the same moment one of the boys shouted something similar.

The boy was clearly drunk, and he threw a punch at Lucky. Lucky ducked, and in the same motion he put the boy against the wall.

"I said what the hell do you think you're doing?" Lucky's voice was even louder this time.

"Drinking," the kid snapped, sounding pretty cocky for someone who was being restrained.

Cassie hurried to help, not that the other boys were in fight mode. They were all backing away, and they backed away even farther when Deputy Davy came waltzing out. Davy repeated a version of Lucky's original question, and he nearly tripped on his own feet trying to get to Lucky and the boy.

"He was drinking," Cassie volunteered.

Though Davy no doubt saw the bottle on the ground. The other boys took off running, and Davy went in pursuit.

Cassie went to Lucky and, because his grip on the boy seemed a little too tight, she took hold of his hand to get him to let go of the kid. That's when she realized Lucky was shaking.

"Come on," Cassie insisted. "Let go of him, and we'll get out of here."

"No. Mackenzie—"

"Gladys is watching her, and we won't be long. We can go back in as soon as we've talked." And as soon as Lucky had had a chance to settle his nerves.

Lucky finally backed away, and even though the kid took off running as well, Lucky picked up the bottle and threw it against the brick wall. It shattered and sent what was left of the whiskey and the glass scattering around them.

She led him away from the kissing couple, who still hadn't stopped to draw breath despite the disturbance, and took him to a large oak. Not very private, but it was the best she could do. Suddenly, his head and back went against the tree, and his breath started gusting.

"Are you having a panic attack?" she asked.

Lucky shook his head. But didn't say anything else. Cassie decided just to wait him out because whatever was going on had gotten to him.

"I didn't stop him," Lucky finally mumbled.

"But you did. The boy was drinking, and…"

This wasn't about that boy. This wasn't about tonight. This was about his parents.

"The teenager who killed your mom and dad had been drinking," she said.

Well, according to the rumors he had been anyway. Cassie seemed to remember reading in the paper that he had a blood alcohol level that had exceeded the legal limit. Added to that, he hadn't even been old enough to drink.

"Brian Ducal," he said.

Yes, that was the boy's name. He'd been alone in his car and had swerved and hit Lucky's parents' vehicle in a fatal head-on collision. The only survivor had been Claire, who had been riding in the backseat because Lucky's parents had given her a ride home from a ball game. Cassie was away at college at the time, but she'd heard plenty about it from Dixie Mae.

"I saw Brian that night," Lucky continued a moment later. "He was drinking, and I was too busy making out with a girl to take the time to stop him."

Oh, God.

"I didn't stop him," Lucky repeated. He jerked away from the tree. Away from her, too. "I have to go. Please stay here with Mackenzie and make sure she gets home all right."

Lucky didn't give her a chance to say anything. Not that there was anything she could say that would help him right now.

Cassie just stood there and watched as Lucky walked away.

THE BULL RIDE hadn't worked for him. Not that Lucky had expected a good crap-slinging to erase his bad mood, but a ride usually jacked up his adrenaline enough for him to nudge the old memories into the back of his head.

Not tonight, though.

Even the Angus had seemed confused as to why Lucky was leading him into a gate this time of night. Hell, so had the ranch hand. Hank Granger hadn't complained, not out loud anyway, but then the man had worked for the McCords for nearly twenty years. He knew plenty of the things Lucky had done didn't make sense. After all, Lucky hadn't gotten the label of screwup by doing nothing.

Well, except for the nothing he'd done the night of his parents' death.

No nighttime bull ride was going to erase that.

Lucky heard the footsteps and knew it was Cassie before he even looked over his shoulder. He got that funny feeling in his stomach again, the one he always got when he saw her, but tonight neither the funny feeling nor Cassie herself were going to help.

Hank mumbled a good-night and said something else that Lucky didn't catch before he ambled off toward the guest cottage that he'd called home for the past decade.

"Did the ride help?" Cassie asked. She joined him at the fence where he was still watching the bull. The bull was watching him, too, and even though Lucky knew he was projecting, he thought the Angus was calling him an asshole.

Lucky didn't answer her question but instead went with one of his own. "Did Mackenzie have fun?"

"I think so. I think she floated up the stairs to her bedroom."

Yeah, he'd seen the light come on in her room, so he figured she was back safe and sound. Safe and sound for two more nights anyway. After the wedding the day after tomorrow, the girls would be heading to Phoenix.

"I'm sorry about ditching you at the civic center," he said.

But Cassie waved him off. "Davy arrested a couple of the boys. Personally, I was surprised he was able to catch up with them, but he did."

Good. Maybe that would teach them a lesson about underage drinking. Of course, Lucky had gotten arrested for it once, and it hadn't stopped him, but what he'd never done was drink and drive. Brian Ducal had taught him that lesson quite well.

Cassie's phone buzzed, but she didn't even take it from her pocket to look at the screen. "It'll be from my agent, Andrew or someone else I don't want to talk to."

"Your agent?"

"He'll want to tell me that my career is over."

Hell. This wasn't making things better. "Is it?"

She shrugged. "Probably. At least my old career is finished. I doubt anyone will be calling me for TV appearances, but I guess I'll just do something else. Like you will when you get tired of having your vertebrae snapped and popped by a two-thousand-pound bull." Cassie paused. "Is that bull looking at us?"

"Yep. I think he's mad because I've kept him up past his bedtime."

She smiled. It was short-lived, though, because her phone buzzed again.

"Maybe you should at least see who it is," he suggested.

"Nope. The only person I want to talk to tonight is you."

It was going to be a short conversation, then, because Lucky didn't have a clue what to say. Or do. "I don't know if I'll ever get past this," he admitted.

Cassie made a sound of understanding. "I don't think you do. Sorry. I believe the scab just stays over the wound until something or somebody picks at it. Like tonight. That kid picked at it, and you bled all over again."

"Bled all over *you*," Lucky corrected. "I shouldn't have dumped that on you."

"I dumped my panic attacks on you. I poured my heart out to you about Hannah. Think of this as a tit for tat."

Ever since he'd been a horny teenager, the expression had always made him smile. Lowbrow humor usually did. But even that wasn't working tonight.

"So, how are you getting past Hannah?" he asked. And it wasn't just Dixie Mae's letter that had prompted him to ask. Lucky was hoping Cassie had a magic pill for this, or had at least figured out a way to stop her panic attacks.

"By trying to remember the good parts. Not that there were a lot of good parts with Hannah, but I had them with other clients. I think I helped some people. I just didn't help her. I don't believe I can ever completely forgive myself for what happened, but I'm finding some peace with it. I'm accepting that it wasn't totally my fault."

Peace. That was a good thing to have. Lucky was still searching for it in a couple areas of his life. Especially when it came to his parents. But like Cassie, he was getting there. Some of that soul-crushing guilt was easing up. Finally.

"And the panic attacks?" he asked.

"I haven't had one in weeks. If they return, I'll deal with them. Deal with my father, too. I would like for things to be different between us, but there's no fixing it."

No. Assholes weren't fixable, and Mason-Dixon was the king of assholes.

"So in the grand scheme of things," Cassie continued, "I failed with Hannah. I can never undo it, but I have some little dots of success surrounding it."

"I've failed at a lot more than saving my parents," he confessed.

"You mean your long string of lovers? Or maybe trying to push Logan out of your life?" she asked, causing him to frown.

He'd at least expected her to sugarcoat some bullshit. Apparently not. He was just going to get the shit tonight. And he deserved it.

Cassie patted his arm. "Lucky, you're not a screwup. You helped Dixie Mae build a successful business. You've won more rodeo buckles than you can wear in a lifetime."

Lucky dismissed both of those. "I didn't stay around here after my folks were killed. I left and allowed Logan to put everything on his shoulders."

"Logan wanted it on his shoulders. And besides, you're entitled to the life you want to lead. You didn't call Riley a screwup when he left to go into the Air Force. You don't call your sister a screwup, and she's off in Florida going to law school."

"They don't get drunk and sleep around," he pointed out.

Another sound of agreement from her. "It's because you're hotter than they are. Though Riley is pretty hot. I'd probably think Anna was hot, too, if I were a guy."

That got him to smile. A little. "Logan and I are identical twins," he pointed out.

"Yes, he's hot, too," she admitted. "It's just a burden you McCord brothers have to bear. But you got the looks *and* the charisma. It makes it easier to sleep around when women are throwing themselves at you."

Lucky wished he could be flattered by her description of him. "I could have dodged them. I didn't." Not many of them anyway. He looked at her. "You dodged me, though."

Cassie nodded. "Because I thought you'd break my heart."

She leaned in, kissed him. Not the hungry "I want you now" kind of kiss that led to sex. This was, well, sweet. And it sent up red flares in his head. Because it was exactly the kind of kiss that Lucky had spent his adult years avoiding.

The kind of kiss that meant something.

Lucky didn't move into the kiss. Definitely didn't deepen it because it already felt way too deep as it was.

"And now?" he asked when she pulled back and met his gaze. "Do you still think I'll break your heart?"

"No." Cassie smiled. The deep kind of smile that meant something, too. "I *know* you will. And I'm going to let you do it."

CHAPTER TWENTY

THERE WAS EXCITED chatter downstairs. People were working hard to pull everything together for Riley and Claire's wedding, which would happen in less than twenty-four hours. Everyone was thrilled.

Including Cassie.

Thrilled for Claire and Riley anyway, but that's where her joy ended.

The heart-to-heart she'd had with Lucky the night before had left her raw—and wanting more. She'd nearly stayed there by the corral. A few more kisses and it would have led them straight to bed.

Or rather to the hayloft since it was closer.

But Cassie hadn't stayed. She'd shielded her heart for one more night. It wouldn't help, of course, because the broken heart was inevitable. Even if she stayed in Spring Hill and ditched her entire life in LA, that didn't mean she would get Lucky. He wasn't exactly the type of man to settle down with one woman. And she wasn't exactly the marrying sort, either. Not after living through the disastrous relationship that her parents had called a marriage. And not after seeing the failed marriages of 90 percent of her clients. No, marriage was messy and painful and not for her.

She'd just have to deal with a broken heart, that's all.

Of course, the broken heart wouldn't just be because of Lucky. Losing Mia and Mackenzie would add to it. Thankfully, the girls hadn't seemed that sad about leaving. Of course, with the excitement of the wedding, maybe they hadn't had time to consider it. And wouldn't for a while. When Cassie had seen them last, they'd been in the sunroom with Livvy, helping her decorate.

There was a knock at her bedroom door, and like all the phone calls she'd been getting, Cassie nearly didn't answer it. Not until she realized it could be one of the girls. But it wasn't. It was Claire. Or least she thought it was. It was a woman holding a plastic garment bag.

"Can I put my wedding dress in your room?" she asked. Definitely Claire.

"Of course." Cassie stepped back so that Claire could squeeze the dress inside.

"Thanks. Livvy's taken over Anna's room with the rest of the decorations, and I don't have anyplace else to stash this dress where Riley won't see it. He'll peek if he gets the chance."

"Can I peek?" Lucky asked.

Cassie hadn't even seen him behind Claire, but then it was hard to see much of anything because of the dress.

"No peeking for you, either," Claire insisted, and she dropped a kiss on Lucky's cheek. Dropped one on Cassie's, too, surprising her. "Livvy got carried away with the whole idea of a fairy-tale wedding."

Yes, but Cassie was pretty sure Claire was loving every second of it. Claire draped the dress over a reading chair in the corner of the room and turned back around to face them. Cassie wasn't sure exactly what Claire saw in their expressions, but it had her frowning.

"Is, uh, everything okay between you two?" she asked.

Cassie glanced at Lucky to see how he was going to answer that. He didn't.

"I mean, what with the girls leaving soon," Claire added.

Cassie thought the quick breath that Lucky took was one of relief. "It's tough," Cassie settled for saying.

"Yeah." And that's all Lucky said for several moments. "I hadn't expected to feel this ache in my heart."

Claire nodded, took a quick breath of her own. "It'll be a bittersweet day. Hopefully more sweet than bitter, but I think we'll all be remembering the people who aren't here. My grandmother, for instance."

Cassie knew that it'd been less than a year since Claire had lost the grandmother who'd raised her, and from all accounts they'd been very close. Bittersweet indeed.

"I was hoping you'd give me away," Claire said, and when she looked at Lucky, there were tears watering her eyes. "I know I'm late asking. And that the wedding's so informal what with there not even being an aisle—"

"Of course I'll do it."

Claire's eyes watered more, and heck, now Cassie was feeling all teary and sentimental.

"I figured you'd want Logan," Lucky added.

Claire managed a smile. "I've always been a lot closer to you than Logan. And when you look at me, I've never seen any blame in your eyes. Not ever."

Lucky shook his head. Cassie also didn't understand.

"Because of your parents," Claire said.

Lucky just gave her a blank look.

"See?" Claire said as if that proved her point. "You didn't even think to be mad. But sometimes when Logan looks at me, I believe he blames me for what happened."

"What?" Cassie blurted out, though this was too personal a conversation for her to be a part of. She should just step out of the room and let them finish. But she didn't. Her feet seemed glued in place.

"Claire." Lucky put his arm around her, pulled her to him and kissed the top of her head. "That wasn't your fault."

She shook her head. "Your folks offered me the ride home from the game because it was raining, but I forgot my clarinet in the band hall and had to go back for it. If I'd left with them right away, or if they'd never waited to give me a ride, then they wouldn't have been on that part of the road at the exact second of the crash."

Lucky kissed her hair again. "That wasn't your fault," he repeated.

Claire nodded, pulled back and wiped the tears from her eyes. "See? You never blamed me. Riley, neither. But he blamed himself. He thinks if he hadn't been making out with Misty—" she paused, rolled her eyes at the mention of Riley's old flame "—then he might have stopped it somehow."

Cassie hoped all of this was sinking in. In a town the size of Spring Hill, every single person had probably thought they could have done something to stop them from dying in the accident. Not just his parents but the other driver, too.

"Sorry about that." Claire wiped away more tears. "Talk about bringing up the worst subject possible. Anyway, thanks for agreeing to give me away." She brushed another kiss on his cheek and walked out.

Lucky didn't say anything, and Cassie wanted to give him some time to absorb all that. And hopefully connect the dots. But her darn phone buzzed again, and when she saw her father's name on the screen, she figured she should take it.

"I'll take this in the hall," she said, moving to do just that. Not that she wanted to talk to him, but it would give Lucky some privacy to think about what Claire had said.

"What do you want?" Cassie greeted when she answered.

"Well, good morning to you, daughter of mine." Mason-Dixon's tone was just as "friendly" as hers. "I thought you'd like to know that I accepted the offer you made to Davy. I'll take fifty grand for the cats. Transfer the money to me today, and Bernie will give you the ownership papers. They've already been drawn up."

Fifty grand probably seemed like a lot to most people for three cats, but at least this would put an end to something that had been very important to Dixie Mae. "You'll have your money as soon as I can arrange it. I'll have the funds sent to Bernie's office."

She hung up so she could call her investment manager and have him do a wire transfer ASAP.

"I can pay for the cats," Lucky offered when she finished the call.

He'd obviously heard her conversation, which meant he hadn't been using the time to think. Or maybe he had. He looked a lot more relaxed than he had in days.

Lucky reached for her, easing her to him, and Cassie readied herself for a kiss. One of those scalding-hot ones that he was so good at giving. But the raised voices downstairs stopped him.

"Alice?" Lucky questioned.

Cassie turned her ear toward the voices and realized it was indeed Alice. And that the woman's voice was indeed raised.

"Cassie! Lucky!" Alice shouted. "I need to talk to both of you right now."

Even without that demand tacked on, Cassie knew something was terribly wrong. They hurried down the stairs and found the woman in the foyer. Della was there, too, along with the florist and two other people who were moving furniture out of the living room.

"What happened?" Lucky asked the woman.

"I just saw this." Alice lifted the newspaper for them to see. The two kissing photos on the front page.

Cassie hadn't thought the pictures could look any more tawdry than when Andrew had brought them over, but she'd been wrong. Whoever had arranged them in the paper had adjusted the lighting so that it appeared Cassie's breasts were actually heaving. And the adjustment made Lucky appear to be past the well-endowed stage when it came to male genitalia.

Mackenzie and Brody hadn't fared much better in the other

picture. Their kiss looked more like a zombie attack with Mackenzie playing the role of the zombie.

"Are these pictures real?" Alice demanded. She wasn't the cool, composed woman that'd visited the day before. In fact, she hadn't brushed her hair and had clearly thrown on her clothes in a hurry. Her breasts were heaving, too, but Cassie was betting it wasn't from lust. It was because she was breathing so hard she might hyperventilate.

"They're real-ish," Cassie admitted. "Obviously the reporter took a few liberties with the shots."

But that *obviously* wasn't obvious to Alice at all. Her mouth dropped open and she grabbed the entry table so she wouldn't pitch right over.

"My niece is thirteen," Alice said, stating the obvious. "And I'm assuming this is the same boy you let her take to the dance last night. Since the newspaper came out yesterday that means you knew about the photo before you let her go."

There was no way around that; both Cassie and Lucky nodded. "But Cassie chaperoned the dance," Lucky added.

"She shouldn't have been allowed to go at all!" Alice was shouting again now. Well, as much as she could shout considering her breath was vanishing fast. "And I won't even address the other picture." But she did address it. "You're both adults. What kind of an example does this set for impressionable young girls? Girls who have had their lives turned upside down?"

Cassie wanted to give Alice a really good explanation for all of this, but she didn't have one. Lucky and she hadn't made out in front of the girls, but it didn't matter. They could see the photograph. Heck, anyone could.

And that wasn't even the worst of it.

Lucky and she had done all of that when they should have had their focus on Mia and Mackenzie.

Alice shook her head. "I can't believe neither of you told me about this before now."

Neither could Cassie. "I'm sorry. I meant to tell you, but it slipped my mind." It shouldn't have, and Cassie wanted to kick herself. "There are a lot of gossips in this town, and I figured even if you didn't actually see the newspaper, then someone would let you know."

"The maid at the inn did. She gave me a copy and said the photographer, Theo Kervin, even sold the pictures of Lucky and you to one of the big LA tabloids."

Great. Cassie groaned. Now all of her friends, business associates and clients had seen it, as well.

"The maid told me about you, too," Alice went on, her attention on Lucky now. "Apparently, you do this sort of thing all the time." She stabbed her finger at the picture but probably wasn't aware it was on Lucky's photographed crotch. "You are not the kind of man who should be around my nieces."

Since Lucky wasn't defending himself, Cassie decided to step up. "Lucky's a business owner. And a McCord. They're a prominent family around here."

"He's also been arrested several times. And he went on a date last night with two women. One of them was a stripper. Did you know about that?" Alice didn't give Cassie a chance to answer. "Of course you did, because the stripper works for your father."

Obviously, the gossip had made its way to the garden room of the Bluebonnet Inn.

Cassie wanted to tell Alice that she had no connection to her father and the Slippery Pole, but that wasn't exactly true. She had been there to steal the cats, and she'd just had a phone conversation with him that some could have construed as bribery. Hardly good bargaining examples to use to profess her innocence.

"And then there's your job," Alice went on. "I thought you were a real therapist. But you just appear on those terrible TV shows where people air their dirty laundry. How can that be good for the girls?"

"Cassie's an excellent therapist," Lucky spoke up.

Cassie appreciated him coming to her defense, but she doubted anything could change Alice's opinion of either of them.

"I want you to get the girls ready," Alice insisted. "Because I'm taking them away from this house—and away from the two of you—*right now*."

LUCKY OPENED HIS mouth to say whatever it would take to keep Alice from taking the girls. But then he realized he was on the losing side of this. Everything Alice had said was true. Except for the part about Cassie. Though if he was being honest, even that had some truth to it.

Cassie must have come to the same realization because he heard the sigh leave her mouth. It was the sound of surrender.

"Now!" Alice repeated. "I don't want them here a minute longer."

Cassie nodded, and Lucky and she started toward the sunroom. Of course, Mackenzie and Mia were going to be upset about missing the wedding. Ditto for Mackenzie not being able to see Brody, but Lucky had known right from the start that this was temporary.

Well, temporary had come to an end.

Alice didn't follow them to the sunroom. Maybe because she didn't want to step another inch inside the house, but Lucky was glad for the small reprieve. This way, they would get a chance to break the news and have time for a short goodbye.

Or not.

When they got to the sunroom, they found Mia wearing a tiara and dancing around like a fairy princess while Livvy strung twinkling lights around the windows.

"Here to help?" Livvy asked. She was grinning, but the grinning came to a quick end when she saw their expressions.

"Their aunt is here to pick up the girls now," Cassie told her.

Mia stopped in mid–dance step. "We gotta go?"

Lucky nodded, not trusting his voice.

Livvy nodded, too, and she hiked her thumb to the door. "Mackenzie went out to see the bulls."

"I'll find her," Lucky volunteered, and he turned to Cassie. "You can help Mia start packing."

"We gotta go?" Mia repeated, and Lucky nearly lost it when he saw her big eyes get all shiny with tears. Her bottom lip started to tremble.

He went to her, going down on his knees so he could pull her into his arms. Lucky wanted to assure Mia that this wasn't a real goodbye, that he'd see her again, but after the way Alice had just reacted, he'd be surprised if the woman didn't try to file restraining orders against Cassie and him. Not that she had actual cause to do that, but their behavior might not sit well with a custody lawyer.

"Everything will be okay," Lucky told her, and he prayed that wasn't a lie. Mia deserved the best. Mackenzie, too.

Lucky stood, meeting Cassie's gaze. The sadness he saw in her eyes matched his own. He brushed a kiss on her cheek and headed out to find Mackenzie for what would no doubt be an even more emotional encounter than the one he'd just had with Mia.

Mackenzie wasn't by the corral, and he didn't see her in the pastures. However, Lucky did hear something in the barn. It sounded as if some kind of struggle was going on. Lucky ran toward the noise and rage filled him the moment he reached the barn.

Brody had Mackenzie pinned to the wall. From what Lucky could see, Brody was trying to kiss her. And Mackenzie was resisting. She had her hands on his chest and was trying to push him away, but Brody was shoving right back.

After that, all Lucky saw was red.

He charged toward them and caught onto the back of Brody's shirt, and Lucky slammed him against the barn door so hard that it rattled. Lucky figured Mackenzie would jump to defend this dickhead.

She didn't.

Mackenzie stood there, shaking, with tears in her eyes. The red that Lucky had seen before was a drop in the bucket compared to what went through him now. It didn't get better.

"She wanted me to kiss her," Brody snarled. "She wanted a lot more than that."

Obviously not. Lucky gave Brody another slam and had to rein in his rage to keep himself from ripping off the guy's arm and beating him to death with it.

Lucky's teeth were clenched so tight his jaw was throbbing. His fist, too, but that was just because he'd never wanted to punch someone as much as he wanted to punch this kid. And he forced himself to remember that Brody was indeed a kid.

"You have two options," Lucky managed to say. "You can go to the police, turn yourself in and admit to attempted assault, or I beat the shit out of you. Your choice."

Lucky was really hoping Brody picked option two.

"Assault?" Brody howled. "I barely touched her."

"Barely is enough, asshole. When a girl says no, she means no. Even if she doesn't say it, if she's trying to get away from you, the answer's still no." Lucky hadn't even realized he was yelling until Hank came running into the barn.

"You need some help, Lucky?" Hank asked.

"I think I might. Brody's either going to need to go to the hospital or the cops. And I'll need someone to escort him."

Brody's glare turned to a stare. Then he looked away from Lucky. "The cops."

Lucky forced himself to back away, and Hank took over from there. He waited until Hank had Brody out of earshot before Lucky looked at Mackenzie.

"Are you going to tell me that I overstepped my boundaries—" he started. But he didn't get to finish.

Mackenzie hurried right into his arms. "I was so scared," she whispered through the broken sobs.

That did two things to Lucky. It made him want to give

Brody that shit-kicking he deserved, but it also crushed him to think of Mackenzie afraid while a bully groped her. Part of him knew he should lecture her about never risking anything like that again, but Lucky could tell from her tears that it was a lesson she'd already learned.

"I wish I could promise you that you'll never run into another guy like Brody," he said, brushing a kiss against her temple. "I can't. But if it ever happens again, just call me. Or better yet, just knee the idiot in the balls."

She nodded and kept crying. So Lucky just stood there, feeling like shit because he hadn't been able to protect her from this. However, he also felt something else. He felt what it was like to be a father.

Hell.

This wasn't any fun at all, but the fact that Mackenzie was here, crying on his shoulder—literally—also made him feel, well, loved. Too bad the feeling wasn't going to last. Also too bad he still had to tell Mackenzie about what else had gone on.

"Your aunt saw the pictures in the paper," he explained. "She's upset about the one with Cassie and me. And she should be. We didn't set a very good example for Mia and you."

Mackenzie pulled back and looked at him. "You're wrong. You and Cassie did okay."

Coming from her that was high praise, and Lucky felt that L-word again along with another round of getting his heart crushed.

"Your aunt's insisting you and Mia leave with her right away," Lucky added.

The tears hadn't stopped yet, but that put a fresh batch of them in her eyes, and Mackenzie took off running toward the house. Lucky wasn't sure if that meant she was ready to get out of there—a strong possibility after what'd just happened to her—or if she was upset about having to leave so soon.

He hurried after her, but she didn't go through the sunroom. She went in the back door and headed straight for the foyer.

Cassie and Mia were there, and Mia's suitcase was beside her. She had her little hand outstretched, and Lucky could see the gold star that she was offering to her aunt.

"You let her believe it was magic," Alice said, shaking her head. Clearly, the woman had something else to be pissed about now. "Put that away, Mia. And Mackenzie, get your things. We're leaving now."

"Please, no," Mackenzie begged. "Just let us stay for the wedding. Please."

Alice huffed. "This is about that boy, isn't it? The one in the picture—"

"No, that's over," Mackenzie assured her. She exchanged a glance with Lucky. A glance that Cassie noticed. He'd tell her all about Brody soon, but he had no intention of mentioning what had just happened in front of Alice. If the woman heard anything about it, it would come from Mackenzie.

"Well, good," Alice answered. "But there's no reason for you to stay here. Not with these people."

"But I gonna be a star girl," Mia said. "I'm gonna throw gold stars and wear a princess crown."

"And Claire wanted me to be an usher," Mackenzie added. "Please. The McCords have treated us good. Like family. We want to stay for the wedding. After that, we'll leave with you." She added another please. Mia chipped in a couple, as well.

Lucky could see the debate going on in Alice's head. Could also see her displeasure anytime her attention landed on Cassie and him. Thankfully that displeasure wasn't for the kids, though.

"All right," Alice finally said. "We can stay one more day for the wedding. But not here. Get your things and you can stay at the Bluebonnet Inn tonight. I'll bring you back for the wedding, and we'll leave right afterward."

All four of them mumbled a version of "thank you." Mia even hugged Alice. Then Lucky and Cassie. It wasn't goodbye, yet, but Lucky knew he had less than twenty-four hours before he'd have to say a real one.

Mackenzie and Cassie went upstairs to get her suitcase, and Lucky was about to assure Mia that everything was going to be okay, but his phone buzzed and he saw Bernie's name on the screen. It was instant hope.

Stupid hope, too.

Because for just a couple of seconds, Lucky thought the lawyer might be calling with some kind of info that would stall Alice from taking the girls.

"I know you're probably in the middle of wedding stuff, but I need Cassie, you, Mia and Mackenzie to come to my office first thing tomorrow morning," Bernie said the moment Lucky answered. "I don't normally go into the office on Sundays, but it's important." That sure didn't sound like the kind of news that would give Cassie and him some extra time with the girls.

"What's this about?" Lucky asked.

Bernie cleared his throat. "Dixie Mae's will. Per her specific instructions, it's to be read at eight in the morning. Brace yourself, Lucky. There are some surprises."

CHAPTER TWENTY-ONE

CASSIE WAS SO not in the mood for a girls' night, but this was for Claire. A last-minute bachelorette party. Claire more than deserved something like this the night before her big day, but Cassie just wasn't up to a celebration.

The only redeeming thing about it was that it was small—just Claire, Livvy, Helene and her—and it was in the sunroom at the ranch. It meant Cassie could put in an appearance and then excuse herself.

So she could go to her room and cry.

And pack.

Which would only result in more tears. But by tomorrow, she'd be ready to cry again. She always cried at weddings, and this one would be a tearjerker because shortly afterward Lucky and she would have to say goodbye to the girls.

The house already seemed way too quiet without them. And that was saying something since Livvy was doing the "Boot Scootin' Boogie" to the popular Brooks & Dunn song.

"This would have been so much better with strippers," Livvy insisted, tossing back another glass of wine.

"No, it wouldn't have," Claire replied. Both Helene and Cassie agreed. Helene probably for a totally different reason than Cassie, though. Helene didn't appear to be the stripper-watching type.

Claire had apparently had very specific instructions. No male strippers or anyone else that Livvy might try to sneak in to liven things up. Claire had instead wanted wine, cheese and girl talk. Other than the dancing and the Brooks & Dunn, Livvy had abided by that.

"I understand you're the owner of three more cats," Claire said to Cassie.

She nodded. "I bought them from my father. Had Bernie draw up ownership papers that I signed this afternoon. It's all official now—I'm the owner of six cats." Of course, on the way to the lawyer's office, Cassie had parked in front of the Bluebonnet Inn hoping to get a glimpse of the girls. She hadn't, though.

"And I'm happy to say that after the wedding, the cats will be brought here," Helene explained. "Not that we weren't happy to have them at the office, but some of the clients are allergic."

Cassie thanked Helene again for taking care of them and assured her she was already working out something more permanent. With a single phone call, she'd put her LA condo up for sale and had asked her Realtor to look for a place that allowed more than two pets. However, the idea of taking six cats still seemed a little daunting.

"Cats?" Livvy huffed. "That's what we're going to talk about tonight?"

"No subject is off-limits," Helene said.

"Except for the kids. Sorry," Livvy immediately added.

"That's okay," Cassie assured her. "They're on my mind whether we talk about them or not."

Which was a serious mood killer.

This time Livvy groaned. "Can we at least talk about sex, then?" Livvy asked. "Dirty sex," she qualified. "The nastiest sex you can think of. How about I start? Blow jobs—yea or nay?"

Cassie laughed, causing the other three to look at her.

"Something you want to tell us about Lucky?" Claire said.

That stopped her laughing. "No."

Clearly they wanted more, but Cassie didn't have more to give them. Lucky and she had had sex, but it hadn't involved a blow job.

"Then Helene can tell us," Livvy insisted. "Since Lucky and Logan are identical twins, it'd be pretty much the same account anyway."

Helene smiled and sipped her wine. "A lady doesn't talk about such things."

Too bad because Cassie wanted to hear. It was silly to want details, but it felt deliciously naughty doing this. And it got her mind off the girls for a few seconds. Too bad her mind kept going back to them, though.

"I've got a sort-of BJ sex story," Claire volunteered. "Not about Riley, though. About Logan and Lucky."

That got their attention, and even Livvy stopped dancing so she could rejoin them on the sofa.

"Logan might have told Helene about this and, Cassie, you might remember," Claire went on, "but when Lucky and Logan were seniors in high school, Lucky was seeing Darla Jean Nederland. *Briefly* seeing her."

Cassie had to shake her head. Helene shook her head, too. By her senior year, the only thing on Cassie's mind had been getting a high score on the SATs, and she had especially shut her ears whenever there was talk about Lucky.

"Well, anyway, Lucky wanted to break up with Darla Jean, but every time he'd try, she'd cry and carry on," Claire continued. "So Logan lost some bet to Lucky, can't remember what about, and the payoff was that Logan would pretend to be Lucky and do the breakup. Logan was a lot better at that sort of thing anyway."

All of them made a sound of agreement about that. Logan

wouldn't have had any trouble ending a relationship, even with a Nederland.

"So Logan dressed up like Lucky and went to Darla Jean's house to tell her it was over. But when he opened the door, she was standing there stark naked, and she tackled him. Even after she kissed him, she still didn't know it wasn't Lucky and tried to give him a BJ." Claire patted Helene's hand. "Don't worry, Helene. It didn't work."

Helene dismissed that, too. Clearly she wasn't worried about her man. And shouldn't be. Logan and she had been together a long time and seemed perfect for each other.

"Then what happened?" Livvy pressed.

"Darla Jean was, is, quite aggressive. And strong. She managed to get Logan unzipped, but Logan was finally able to get away from her. The next day at school, Darla Jean told everyone that Lucky was impotent."

Livvy laughed like a loon. "As if." But then she blushed. "Sorry, Cassie."

Cassie waved her off. "I know Lucky's had a lot of lovers. And besides, it's not serious or anything between us."

There was no mistaking the look all three of them gave her. Skepticism. A big dose of it, too.

"Uh, Cassie," Claire said. "I'm pretty sure Lucky's in love with you."

Cassie choked, not on the wine but the huge gulp of air she sucked in. She wasn't sure what surprised her more—that Claire had said that or that Livvy and Helene made sounds of agreement.

Good grief. They had all lost their minds. Lucky wasn't in love with her. And vice versa. And this wasn't a conversation she wanted to have. Nope. She was already on the path to a good heart-stomping, and if she added even a smidge of the notion that the no-rings-attached Lucky had real feelings for her, then she might give him too much of herself.

Her heart might never recover.

It was time for a subject change. "I can't believe Darla Jean couldn't tell the difference between Lucky and Logan," Cassie said.

"I know," Helene agreed. "They're nothing alike. She should have been able to tell the second she opened the door."

Definitely, and that gave Cassie something to think about. For a second or two. But her stupid brain kept going back to Claire's L-word remark. And to the skeptical look the others had given Cassie.

"You know, Lucky's in his room," Livvy whispered to her.

Mercy, was she that obvious? Apparently so. Because Claire and Helene nodded. "We won't talk about you behind your back if you want to sneak out and see him," Claire offered.

"Oh, yes we will." Livvy laughed again. "But your choices are us, sex talk, wine and cheese—or Lucky. I'm thinking that's not really a choice."

Livvy was right. It was sort of embarrassing to duck out when the women obviously knew the reason for the ducking. And when one of those women had been Lucky's previous lover. Still, that didn't stop her.

Cassie finished off her wine, gave her best wishes to Claire and walked to the other side of the house to Lucky's room. She knocked once, then opened the door before she could change her mind. Not that she had time to change it anyway because Lucky was right there.

"What the heck took you so long?" he asked and pulled her to him and kissed her.

She'd intended to bring up Claire's comment in a round-about way, but that kiss stopped Cassie from saying anything, and after a few seconds of being in Lucky's arms, she wasn't sure she could think, much less speak. In fact, she didn't want to speak. Cassie wanted to be swept away, and sweeping away was Lucky's specialty.

However, the sweeping stopped almost as fast as it had started.

"Are you okay?" Lucky asked her.

Cassie knew he wasn't talking about that kiss. This was about the girls. "I miss them already," she admitted.

"Yeah." That's all he said for several long moments, though he did push her hair from her face and kiss her again. Not like the knee-weakening kiss from before, but it was still a kiss.

"Stay with me tonight?" he asked.

"What the heck took you so long to ask?" she countered.

He smiled. It was that "I'll make you melt" smile. Of course, he'd already seduced her so it wasn't necessary to bring out the big guns, but a dimple flashed in his cheek.

Despite the smile, there was a sadness around them. One that Cassie felt bone deep. So maybe their being together right now didn't have as much to do with the scalding attraction as it did with needing to be with someone who understood.

Of course, the attraction was a big part of it.

No use trying to fool herself about that.

Cassie stepped back into his arms and right into another kiss, and she tried to prepare herself for the onslaught. For the fierce intensity that'd happened the other time she had been with him.

But no fierceness.

Lucky kissed her as if he had all the time in the world. Slow. And easy. He didn't even press her to him. He kept an inch or so of space between their bodies, just enough room for her breasts to occasionally brush against his chest. Cassie hadn't expected this from Lucky. Wasn't even sure she wanted it. Fast and frantic didn't give her time to think. It only gave her time to feel, and that kind of swept-away feeling was exactly what she needed now.

Or maybe not.

The long, dreamy kiss continued. No pressure. He definitely didn't take it up to the French stage. And then something happened to her. Cassie started to relax. She started to move into the kiss without actually moving into him. It reminded her of those long-lost innocent days when she'd first been kissed. A time when there were no other expectations but to feel, to be in the moment.

So that's what she did.

She took a mental trip back to high school, and even though she'd never kissed Lucky then, she knew this was how it would have been. Cassie wasn't sure how long it went on. The time just slipped away. But not the need. Lucky was building the fire slowly inside her, making her want him even more.

"Where next?" he asked her. He must have doused himself with pheromones or something because that two-word question sounded sexy as hell.

She glanced at the saddle. Lifted her eyebrow.

"Well, I've never used it as a sex toy," he said, "but if it's what you want…"

Cassie considered it. Dismissed it. For now. "My neck," she settled for saying.

Of course, it wasn't really where she wanted him to kiss her. She wouldn't have minded him getting on his knees again and giving her another of those special kisses, but Lucky was creating a mood here. Best not to spoil it with a blatant request for oral sex.

He didn't kiss her neck, though. He stared at her, his right eyebrow lifted. "You can do better than that," he challenged.

So maybe blatant was okay here after all. And maybe she could create her own mood. Cassie pinned him against the door, unzipped him and went to her knees. Lucky managed a hoarse sound of surprise before she took him in her mouth.

There.

Challenge accepted.

Cassie was pretty sure he had not expected this, but since the next sound he made was one of pleasure, she thought maybe she'd hit the right chord. She took and tasted until the pleasure was hers, too.

She never would have done this in high school.

Cassie continued for several more seconds before Lucky gutted out some profanity, caught onto her shoulders and hauled her back up to him.

"I'm not getting off with my clothes on this time," he insisted. "And you're not getting off unless you're bare-assed naked."

Cassie wanted to tell him not to expect too much, that her body in no way qualified as hot. Especially compared to the kinds of bodies Lucky was no doubt used to seeing. But then he pulled off her top and her bra and went after her breasts with his tongue, and she no longer cared if she looked hot. Because she was hot. Her body was burning.

Mercy, the man was good.

For once, she was seriously glad he'd had all that experience because Cassie wanted to benefit from it.

Since he was kissing her and ridding her of her jeans, Cassie got to work on making him naked. That gave her a moment's pause, though, and she suddenly wanted to slow things down again. She'd fantasized about seeing Lucky naked for a long time, and she wanted to appreciate every moment of this, every inch of him.

Even though she was standing there, topless and with her jeans and panties pooled around her knees, Cassie stopped him, then had to stop him again when he tried to kiss her. The kiss would be amazing. But it would nix the peep show she had planned.

Cassie started with his shirt, opening it button by button and slipping it off his shoulders. Of course, he had a six-pack. Of course, he was perfect.

"You're amazing," he said, his gaze shifting over her body.

She thought maybe she said, *Thank you but that's BS*. Or maybe she just said it in her head. That's because her mouth was occupied with kissing his chest. He tasted as good as he looked, and she would have made her way back to his erection if Lucky hadn't stopped her.

All this stopping and starting made her want to scream. Or

just screw him. Cassie was leaning heavily toward the latter option.

But Lucky was no longer in fast-screw mode. He went gentle on her again, sliding her jeans and panties the rest of the way off. She did the same to his pants and underwear and got that peep show.

It was really easy to have an orgasm with a man who looked like that. Of course, he didn't have to rely on his looks for it. For a mouthwatering man, he had certainly taken the time to learn the ins and outs of a woman's body.

He kissed her again. Used his tongue. And then nipped her lip with his teeth. Cassie thought she was floating, but Lucky was actually moving her. Slowly again, but not wasting a second for a chance to kiss her.

Lucky wasn't just a pretty face—he was limber, too, and could kiss her breasts and back her up to the bed at the same time. They landed on the mattress, him on top of her. Between her legs. They nearly had accidental sex, but he moved out of the way, fished through his nightstand drawer for a condom and put it on.

The seconds it took him to do that felt like an eternity.

Followed by the pleasure of Lucky pushing into her. He wasn't gentle. Which she didn't want anyway. Cassie wanted a full dose of Lucky McCord. And that's exactly what she got.

Every inch of him.

Inside her.

Oh, mercy. For a woman who had a hard time achieving an orgasm, the one Lucky gave her happened way too fast. Just a few strokes. And while the pleasure racked through her, wave after wave, Cassie couldn't help but want him all over again.

Immediately.

How could that be? How could she want him this much? How could she feel this much?

How could she have been so stupid as to play with such fire?

She gathered him close, lifted her hips and helped him reach his own release. She felt the climax rack through him, too. Felt his body relax, then tense.

"What the fuck did you just do to me?" Lucky asked.

Cassie had no idea because minus the F-word, it was exactly what she'd wanted to ask him.

LUCKY WAS CERTAIN he could have handled their latest round of mind-blowing sex better. Clearly, he hadn't made it end on a romantic note.

What the fuck did you just do to me?

She didn't answer, but with the way he'd growled that out, he was surprised she didn't state the obvious.

That she'd F-worded him.

And that he'd F-worded her right back.

Instead, Cassie got all quiet, maybe regretting the amazing thing that'd happened.

The shitty thing that'd happened, too.

He wasn't supposed to feel this way. A good fuck was supposed to make him relax, make him quit thinking. Sex was his drug of choice. But it hadn't worked this time. Instead of numbing his mind and body, it was as if Cassie had flipped a switch in his head, and everything had come flooding into him.

Losing his parents. Losing Dixie Mae. Losing the girls. Now losing his mind.

It wasn't as if he was opposed to having feelings like this. Especially feelings for Cassie, but the problem was, Lucky didn't know exactly what he was feeling. And even if it was the thing that normal, unbroken men felt, what the hell was he supposed to do about it? He sucked at commitments, sucked at staying in place.

Sucked, period.

Still naked, still rosy and glowing from the orgasm, Cassie leaned over and kissed him. Then she got up, and while he watched her, she dressed. Slowly, like those kisses he'd given her earlier. It was like a striptease in reverse.

If he'd been a teenager, watching her would have given him an instant hard-on, but he needed at least ten minutes to recover.

Five, Lucky silently amended when she bent down to pick up her panties.

Two, he amended again when she shimmied into those panties.

But Cassie probably wasn't ready for another round so soon. He figured this was the part where they were going to have the talk. *Where is this going? How do you feel about me?*

But Cassie didn't say anything close to either of those things. When she'd finished dressing, she came back to the bed, kissed him.

"I love you," she said.

And then she walked out, closing the door quietly behind her.

CHAPTER TWENTY-TWO

LUCKY WASN'T SURE what he was supposed to say. Or how to act. So he decided to stay quiet and let Cassie take the lead. The problem with that?

No lead.

She didn't mention a word about her bombshell as they drove to Bernie's for the reading of Dixie Mae's will the next morning. And Lucky wasn't sure he should even push it. Not with Bernie's warning flashing in his head.

Brace yourself, Lucky. There are some surprises.

As if he hadn't had enough surprises already. There were a few good ones, though. The hug from Mackenzie in the barn. Sex with Cassie. But Lucky was afraid any surprises Dixie Mae had in store for them now would not be of the good variety.

Nor was Cassie's *I love you.*

Hell, he hadn't meant for that to happen. He sucked at relationships, and the last thing he'd wanted was for her to fall in love with him. Or for him to feel this way about her.

Which he still wasn't exactly sure about.

This was new territory for him, and Lucky thought if his life would just settle down for a couple of minutes, he'd be able to figure it out. Unfortunately, a settled life wasn't going to happen until at least after the will reading and the wedding. Then he'd have to say goodbye to the girls—he didn't want to know how long it would take him to get past that.

Maybe never.

Lucky parked in front of Bernie's office, a reminder of the last time he was there. No doubt a reminder for Cassie, too, judging from the heavy sigh that left her mouth.

"I don't want to cry in front of the girls," she insisted, as if saying it would prevent it from happening. Heck, maybe it would, but Lucky knew Cassie was hurting just as much as he was.

Cassie reached for the door but didn't open it. "Della said Brody confessed to assault and that he's going to have to do community service. Anything you want to tell me about that?"

Lucky hadn't intentionally withheld the incident from her. They just hadn't had a chance to talk, with the exception of the conversation they'd had pre- and postsex.

I love you.

Yeah, that and Cassie's quick departure from his room had pretty much put an end to open communication.

"Brody was trying to kiss Mackenzie in the barn." Maybe trying to do more, but since it made his blood boil to think of that, Lucky went with the sanitized version. "Mackenzie resisted, I stopped Brody, and I told him to turn himself in to the police or else. He opted against the *or else*."

Judging from the way Cassie put her hand on her chest, Lucky's explanation had gotten her heart pumping. "Is Mackenzie all right?"

He nodded. "She hugged me afterward."

The corner of her mouth lifted. "Good. She needs to know the world isn't filled with assholes."

She did. But there were other assholes out there. Too many of them, and Lucky wouldn't be around to protect her from them. Nor would Cassie. Since that made the knot in his stomach even tighter, Lucky got out of the truck. Cassie, too, but they hadn't even reached the front door to Bernie's office when someone called out her name. It was a sweaty-faced, middle-aged man getting out of a car parked just up the street.

Cassie groaned. "That's Simon Salvetti, my agent. What the heck are you doing here?" she asked as the man approached them.

He took her phone from her hand, made a show of pointing to it. "This is an amazing talking device, but when it makes a ringing sound, dings or plays a song, that means you should answer it because someone likely wants to communicate with you."

"I didn't want to *communicate* with you. Or anybody else from LA. I knew the newspaper photos would get around. I knew what that would do to my career, and I didn't want to hear a lecture from you."

"No lecture. What I was calling to tell you is that my talking device has been ringing nonstop with TV and radio shows who want to book you. Those pictures are freakin' gold, Cassie. You've got work lined up for the next two years." His attention finally landed on Lucky. "And this is the cowboy who made that possible."

Lucky sure hadn't kissed her to help her career. It had been for a more basic reason than that—lust. But he was glad it hadn't *hurt* her career, though work lined up for the next two years no doubt meant he wouldn't be seeing that much of Cassie after today.

That knot in his stomach was tightening like a vise.

"Anyway, since I wasn't able to talk to you," the man went on, "I hurried through one of the contracts and brought it with me for you to sign." He handed her a folder. And a pen.

Cassie glanced at the folder, Simon, then Lucky. She frowned. "Look, uh, Simon, there's a lot going on today—"

"Yes, the wedding and the reading of your aunt's will. I was out at the McCord Ranch, and the housekeeper told me about it, told me you'd be here. It won't take long for you to sign them, and then I can be on the next flight out."

She made another glance at the folder. Another glance at

Lucky. As if she were trying to make up her mind about something. Was she thinking about turning down the jobs? Because Lucky certainly couldn't offer her anything better.

"Simon, I can't do this now," she finally said. "I'll take a look at the contract after I'm finished here."

Her agent opened his mouth as if to argue, but Cassie gave him a stern look, and with the folder clutched to her chest, she went inside the office.

"You're not trying to convince her to stay here, are you?" the guy asked Lucky.

"No." It was the truth. A truth that made Lucky want to do something really unmanly, like puke.

Simon tried to tell Lucky why it would be a bad idea for Cassie to stay, but Lucky tuned him out and went into the office. Thankfully, Simon didn't follow.

Wilhelmina was there behind her desk, and her feathers were no longer ruffled. She was back to batting her eyelashes at Lucky.

The puking feeling eased up a little when he saw Mia in the waiting room. She was hugging Cassie. Even though the wedding was still hours away, Mia was wearing a pale pink fairy-princess dress, complete with tiara, and she had a huge basket of gold stars clutched in her hand.

"Livvy's doing," Cassie said to him.

Lucky nodded in approval and made a mental note to thank Livvy. He'd thank Alice again, too, for letting the girls stay for the wedding. And speaking of Alice, she was right there next to Mia, and she wasn't in much of a festive mood. Her mouth was still tight. Her body, too. And she didn't soften even a little when Mia rushed to hug Lucky.

"I'm a star girl," Mia proudly announced.

"I can see that, and you look beautiful." He kissed the top of her head and turned to Mackenzie to tell her the same thing, but Lucky nearly tripped over his tongue.

Not his goth girl today, but rather a wedding girl. She was

wearing a pink dress. Probably still too short. Of course, part of him wanted her to cover up from head to toe like a nun. And her hair wasn't spiked and black. It was pink to match the dress. She looked thirteen instead of twenty. Something he'd take to the grave because he doubted any thirteen-year-old girl actually wanted to look her age.

"I wanted to try something new," Mackenzie mumbled, looking uncomfortable. Did she think she was selling out? Not a chance.

"You look amazing," Lucky told her, and he also gave her a kiss on the head. "But then, you looked amazing before, too." Before, however, it'd just taken him a little longer to see through the makeup.

"I understand the wedding is at two o'clock," Alice said, standing. She had her purse in front of her like a shield. "The girls and I will be leaving immediately afterward so if you could please bring them outside to the car then, I'd appreciate it."

Talk about killing the mood. Or rather what little mood they had. Even Mia's shoulders dropped. Too bad. Because seeing the joy on her face might be exactly what Lucky needed to get through the next few hours.

"You can come to the wedding, too," Lucky offered Alice.

"No, thank you," she jumped to say. "The girls and I are already packed to go."

Yes, she'd made that abundantly clear.

"I told her we wanted to stay with you," Mackenzie said, springing to their defense.

"And I told Aunt Alice I'd give her my cat if we could stay," Mia piped in.

Those two sentences warmed Lucky's heart. And crushed him. Because Alice wasn't going to take those things into consideration. She had already made up her mind.

But Lucky had been a master of mind swaying for years.

Lucky looked at Wilhelmina. "Could you go ahead and take

the girls back to Bernie's office? I'd like to have a word with Alice."

Wilhelmina nodded, then ushered Mia and Mackenzie away, and Lucky made sure they were out of hearing range before he continued.

"I'm either going to insult you," he said to Alice, "or make your day. But I'm offering you a million bucks to sign over custody of the girls to Cassie and me."

Alice rolled her eyes. Obviously, his offer insulted her. "Cassie already offered me money." She huffed. "Do you really think my nieces are for sale?"

"Of course not," Cassie and he answered in unison. It was Lucky who continued. "But you heard what they said. They want to stay here. I believe they're happy at the ranch, and I think Spring Hill would be a good place for them to be raised."

"With Cassie, you and your family." Alice made them sound like fungi.

He wasn't sure Cassie would be in that equation, but he hoped she knew she was welcome, too. Well, welcome as long as he didn't have to deal with her hit-and-run *I love you.*

"My family would be a good support system for the girls," Lucky explained. "There'd be no need for a nanny since we have Della and Stella. My brother Riley and his soon-to-be wife live just minutes away—"

"Cassie brought up all of this when she called me this morning," Alice snapped. "But what both of you seem to be forgetting is that you're not fit to be parents."

"Bullshit." Lucky hadn't meant to curse, but he didn't take it back. "Cassie and I love the girls. We're not lowlifes like their parents. And we want them. That makes us fit."

He was clearly losing this argument since Alice was making sounds like a riled rodeo bull. "This discussion is over."

Maybe, but Lucky wasn't giving up. "Do you love the girls? And I don't mean the kind of love that happens just because they're blood kin. Do you love them?"

The bull sounds turned to more glaring and staring. "I'm sure I will once I get to know them."

Yeah, she would. But Lucky doubted she'd ever love them as much as he did.

"Uh, Lucky and Cassie?" Wilhelmina said from the hall. "Bernie says you two should go on back for the reading."

Alice didn't even ask to go with them, and while Lucky wouldn't have refused her, he was glad to have a few more minutes with the girls away from her. Yeah, Alice was perfect all right, except for being pigheaded. Of course, Lucky wasn't even sure it was right to blame her. He hated to admit it, but if their situations had been reversed, he'd be pigheaded, too, if doing so would protect Mia and Mackenzie.

"Thanks for trying," Cassie said, giving him a pat on the back.

"Thanks for trying, too. How much did you offer Alice?"

"Everything in my savings account. Not as much as you, though. You really have a million dollars?"

He shrugged. "I think I do. I haven't touched my trust fund. And yeah, I have a trust fund," Lucky added almost defensively. "Never felt I deserved it so I didn't touch it, but using it for this seemed the right thing to do."

She nodded, paused outside Bernie's door. "I don't suppose Alice would budge if we pooled our money?"

Lucky had to shake his head. "I don't think money will do it. Nor a pound of flesh."

But what would exactly?

Obviously, Alice seemed to have the girls' best interest at heart, so what would make her believe that Cassie and he would be the best thing for her nieces? A few ideas came to mind—contributing to her charity, vowing chastity, joining the priesthood.

"We could get married," Lucky threw out there. He wouldn't dare tell Cassie that the notion had come in fourth—after chastity and the priesthood. "Then we could make our own petition for custody."

Cassie didn't exactly jump at the offer—his first marriage proposal ever. And it wasn't as if they were strangers. They'd had sex twice. Great sex, too. Then there was that part about her saying *I love you.*

"Marry you?" she questioned.

Since she had sort of a sneaky look in her eyes, Lucky just settled for a nod.

She nodded back. It was sort of sneaky, as well. "If you want me to even consider marrying you, you have to do one thing." And she reached for the doorknob to Bernie's office.

"Wait a minute. What one thing?"

The sneaky look intensified. "When you figure it out, you can ask me again."

Well, hell. It was one of those riddles, and he hated riddles. When she reached for the door again, Lucky stopped her.

"You want me to say I love you?" he tried. It was the only answer on his list of possible answers.

But Cassie shook her head. "When you figure it out, just let me know," she said and then opened the door despite his still trying to stop her.

"Are you two getting married?" Mackenzie immediately asked.

"Thin door," Wilhelmina grumbled, and she walked past them as she headed back to reception.

"And yes, your trust fund is worth more than a million," Bernie said to Lucky. "If you want to know the exact amount, I can look it up for you."

Lucky shook his head.

"Did you pay enough money for us?" Mia asked. "What one thing do you haveta do to marry Cassie?"

"No, we're not getting married," Cassie answered Mackenzie.

Lucky had to give the same no answer to Mia coupled with a "heck if I know" to her second question. And Lucky was glad everybody had read his thoughts in addition to hearing every word he'd uttered in the past five minutes. Hell, he was already flustered and frustrated, and the meeting hadn't even started.

And the meeting got even worse when he spotted Mason-Dixon.

The man was sitting in the corner, literally as far away from the rest of them as he could get. Of course, it was his right to be there since Dixie Mae was his mother, but if Dixie Mae did come back as a ghost she might try to kick her son's butt right out of the room.

Cassie and Lucky took a seat next to the girls when they went into the office. Bernie was wearing jeans and a Beatles T-shirt today. Probably because he was planning to head to the Founder's Day picnic later. Lucky would still have to make an appearance at that as well, something else that would no doubt be flustering and frustrating. Painful, too, because it would push his memory buttons about his mother.

Well, maybe.

After Claire had said how she felt guilty about the accident, Lucky was starting to see things in a slightly different light. Yeah, he was still responsible, but it had still been an accident.

"You said there were surprises," Lucky prompted Bernie when he just stood there, will in hand, and stared at them.

Bernie took a deep breath. "For the record, I tried to talk Dixie Mae out of this."

Shit.

This was going to be *bad*. Bernie began to read.

> "I, Dixie Mae Weatherall, revoke all previous wills made by me and declare this my last will. And we're not even going to get into that monkey crap about me being of sound mind because all that's somebody's opinion. Just in case it's brought up, though, especially by my so-called son, I've given Bernie a copy of a psych eval to prove I'm not crazy, just mean and opinionated."

Lucky concurred on all points. Sane, mean, opinionated.

Bernie paused, looked at them. "I'm omitting some of the curse words, but they're here in writing if anyone wants to see them for themselves." He glanced at Mason-Dixon. "She called you a few choice names."

"I'll bet," he snarled. "Just tell me what the old bat left me."

Bernie took another deep breath and continued.

"To Mia and Mackenzie Compton and my granddaughter, Cassandra Weatherall, I leave my half of Weatherall-McCord Stock Show and Rodeo Promotions, which will be divided into thirds among them. My partner, Austin McCord, will maintain majority percentage in the company and act as the trustee until the Compton minor children are each twenty-one. Also in accordance with my wishes, Cassandra, Mia and Mackenzie will remain in the state so they can better deal with the operation."

Judging from the way Cassie, Mia and Mackenzie stared at the lawyer, that was one of those surprises. But not to Lucky. This was exactly the sort of thing Dixie Mae would pull, and he wished that it was the magic bullet to keep them all here. But a will couldn't force something like that, and he was betting Alice wouldn't care a rat about Dixie Mae's will or wishes.

"What does it mean?" Mia asked, tugging on her sister's arm.

"It means we own part of a rodeo."

Mia grinned. "Do I get to own a bull?"

"About 17 percent of each bull," Bernie provided.

Mia's grin widened. "Cool. I want to own his leg. And Scooter's clown nose."

Mackenzie gave an irritated shake of her head and an eye roll that only a big sister could have managed.

"'In addition to the part ownership of the business,'" Bernie read on, "'I leave Mia and Mackenzie Compton the sum of two hundred thousand dollars each to be placed in a trust fund and used for their college educations.'"

Lucky was glad Dixie Mae had obviously gotten so close to the girls and had provided something for them. Plus, the rodeo business would give them some solid income, too.

"Keep reading," Mason-Dixon snapped.

Bernie smiled. The look on his face was too accommodating. It was sneaky like Cassie's earlier one. "'As for my residuary estate, all my money and personal items will go to the person who has ownership of my six cats.'"

Yeah, it was a sneaky smile all right. Lucky didn't just smile, he laughed, and Cassie giggled right along with him.

"What?" Mason-Dixon howled. "She left those cats to me."

"And you signed over ownership to Cassie." Bernie held up a copy of the document. "Her ownership means she inherits the remainder of Dixie Mae's estate, and it's valued at…" Bernie paused, fighting back a new smile. "Nearly twenty million dollars."

Cassie stopped laughing. Perhaps because she was in shock at her grandmother being worth that much. But no. Her eyes watered, and Lucky knew that she would trade every penny to have Dixie Mae back.

"What does that mean?" Mia asked.

"It means Cassie's rich," Mackenzie explained.

"It means you're rich, too," Cassie told Mia, "because I gave you one of the cats."

Mia thought about that a second. "Do I still get the bull leg, though? And the clown nose?"

Mackenzie rolled her eyes again.

"That hellhound can't just write me out of her will!" Mason-Dixon yelled.

"There's more," Bernie said, and he continued to read. "'For my son, Mason-Dixon Weatherall, I bequeath him a truckload of merchandise that will be delivered to his place of business today.'"

Bernie stopped and motioned for the three adults to join him at the desk so they could read the last line of the will for themselves. Mason-Dixon made it there ahead of them and tried to push Cassie aside. She held her ground. Then, she broke down in hysterical laughter when she read the last line.

Lucky had to laugh again, too, and he blew a kiss up to Dixie Mae.

"The merchandise consists of one thousand jumbo-size dildos," Dixie Mae had written. "Which my son can then use to go fuck himself."

CHAPTER TWENTY-THREE

"Uh, I'm NOT sure I can fit through the door," Claire said, studying herself in the large mirror.

Cassie wasn't sure of that, either. The wedding dress was as wide as Claire was tall. It was beautiful, though, with yards and yards of pearl-white organza and netting, but Cassie wasn't sure even the aisle of a cathedral would have been wide enough to accommodate it.

"It'll fit just fine," Livvy insisted. She wiped away another tear as she looked at Claire.

Cassie blinked back some tears, too. It had been an emotional morning what with Dixie Mae's will and Lucky's half-assed marriage proposal, and it was only going to get more emotional between attending the wedding and then saying good-bye to the girls.

"Riley'll be gaga when he sees you," Livvy said. She was fussing with the veil some more when there was a knock at the door.

"No one with a dick can come in," Livvy called out.

The woman opened the door and stuck her head in. "Good thing, then, I left my dick in Florida."

Anna.

She'd made it despite what had apparently been a couple of flight delays. It had been years since Cassie had seen her, and it was obvious that Lucky's little sister was all grown up. Cassie could see bits of all three of her brothers in that beautiful face, but that was hands down a genetic copy of Lucky's smile.

Anna eased into the room, shutting the door behind her before she hurried to Claire for a hug. Or at least she tried. "Air kisses and hugs only," Livvy insisted. "You'll ruin her hair and makeup."

Anna obliged, making a show of the air kisses and hugs. And of the real ones she gave to Livvy. Then Anna turned to Cassie. Cassie wasn't even sure she'd remember her, but she obviously did because Anna pulled her into a hug.

"I understand Lucky proposed to you," Anna said.

Cassie froze, but since Claire and Livvy didn't, she could only guess that this wasn't the first they were hearing of it. Cassie dismissed it with a wave of her hand.

"Lucky only did that because he thought it would help get custody of the girls."

Anna nodded as if that were old news, too. Livvy nodded, as well. Claire shrugged. Cassie dismissed the shrug. Because after all, Claire had been the one to say that Lucky was in love with her, and clearly he wasn't. If he had been, he would have done more than just give her a blank stare when Cassie had told him that she loved him.

"Is it true you said you'd marry Lucky if he'd do just one thing?" Anna asked. "But then you wouldn't tell him what that one thing was?"

Sheez. Wilhelmina had blabbed everything. Thin doors and a blabbermouth were a bad combination.

Anna, Claire and Livvy all stared at her, obviously waiting for an answer. An answer she didn't have to give because there was another knock at the door.

"If you got balls, you can't come in," Livvy said this time.

"I own a bull's leg," someone answered. "And a clown nose." Mia.

"Oh, God. Sorry about that," Livvy added.

Horrified that Mia might have heard what Livvy said, Cassie hurried to open it, and there they were. Mia and Mackenzie. Thankfully, they didn't seem as appalled as Cassie was over the balls comment. The girls looked perfect. Of course, she'd already seen them in their wedding clothes, but it was just as special to see them a second time. Cassie gathered them into her arms and kissed them.

"You two ready for this?" Livvy asked them.

Mia nodded. "Kenzie's been putting people in the seats." She lifted her basket filled with gold stars. "And I'm going to throw these at people." However, the moment Mia said the words, she glanced down at the stars. "There's a lotta magic wishes in here."

Claire smiled. "And everybody will get at least one today. Especially me. Can we just get downstairs and do this before Riley changes his mind?"

There was zero chance of Riley doing that, but Mia took off as if to make sure that didn't happen. Mackenzie looped her arm through Cassie's. "Come on. I'll take you to your seat."

They stepped into the hall, and Cassie nearly smacked right into Lucky. He, too, gave Mackenzie a hug and kiss. And Cassie got a look from him. A long, appreciative one as his attention slid from Cassie's head to her toes.

"There you are," Livvy said, catching onto Lucky's arm and pulling him into the room. "Now, here are some things you need to remember when you walk Claire down the aisle…"

That was Cassie's cue to get moving. Mackenzie and she went downstairs where there were guests milling around, making their way into the living room for the ceremony.

"What's Mia doing?" Mackenzie asked.

The little girl wasn't hard to spot with her sparkly tiara, but

Mia was racing out the front door. Alarmed, Cassie went after her with Mackenzie right behind her. Cassie doubted Mia was running away, and she wasn't. Mia hurried to a silver car where Aunt Alice was waiting.

Mia took out one handful of stars, as many would fit into her tiny hand, and gave the basket to Alice. "Magic wishes," Mia told her. "I want to use them so Kenzie and me can stay here with Miss Cassie and Mr. Lucky."

Alice's gaze flew to Cassie, maybe because the woman thought Cassie had put Mia up to it, but there must have been something in Cassie's expression that let Alice know otherwise.

Mia looked at her hand. "I gotta save these to throw at people." Then she gave the basket another look, picked several more stars from her hand and added them to the hundreds that were already in there. "And I can give you my bull's leg and clown's nose." She pulled off her tiara, added it to the basket.

"I can give you the money Dixie Mae left me," Mackenzie said.

Her aunt shook her head. "I don't want your money. Or the stars." She handed the basket back to Mia. "I just want my sister's children to live with me."

There it was. Alice's bottom line—again.

"But what if we really, really, really wanna live here?" Mia asked. "What if being here makes us really, really happy?"

Another head shake from Alice, but it also looked as if she'd swallowed hard. "I can make you happy, too."

"Yeah, but you can't do it really, really, really." Mia looked ready to cry, but she took several of the stars and put them in Alice's hand. "I'll give you magic stars anyway."

Great. Now Cassie was crying again. This time in front of the girls, something she'd sworn she wouldn't do.

"Hurry up," Livvy called out from the front door. "We're about to start, and we need the star girl."

Mia took off running, jiggling the basket and leaving a trail of magic gold stars behind her.

LUCKY WAS PRETTY sure he'd never seen Riley happier. Claire, either. And there had only been one mishap during the ceremony, when Ethan had tossed one of the toy cars a little too hard and it'd smacked Livvy on the forehead. Other than a few drops of blood, the wedding had been perfect.

But now perfect was over.

The thirty or so guests were already filing out of the house, all heading to the picnic grounds for the reception. Lucky and Cassie would soon follow, but first they had to say goodbye to the girls. Something they'd do as soon as the photographer finished taking pictures.

Della walked over to him, watching as the photographer posed Mia and Ethan in front of Claire and Riley. It was slow going because Riley and Claire kept kissing. Ethan kept trying to play with the cars he'd retrieved from the floor. Mia was darting out to retrieve gold stars, too. Cassie and Mackenzie weren't in the shot, but were helping Livvy arrange the flowers around the couple.

"An engagement ring," Della said to him.

"Huh?" Lucky figured he had spaced out and had missed whatever she'd said before that.

"An engagement ring," she repeated.

So he hadn't missed it after all. "Am I supposed to know what that means?"

"It's the one thing you've got to do before Cassie will marry you," Della clarified.

Oh, that. Lucky should have known. Clearly the gossip mill had worked overtime getting out the news of what Cassie and he had discussed outside Bernie's door.

If you want me to even consider marrying you, you have to do one thing.

Maybe he needed to build a room with concrete walls for his next chat. If there was a next chat, that is. After all, Cassie's agent had brought her all of those offers.

"A bunch of people already suggested that," he let Della know. "In fact, it was the second-most suggested answer."

"What was the first?" Della asked.

"Saying I love you."

"I just assumed you'd done that."

He had, but Cassie had let him know that was wrong. He'd been doing a lot of wrong things lately and hadn't done much of anything except fail to fix any of this. He was losing all of them.

"Getting down on one knee?" Della went on. "I heard that talked about a lot as a possibility."

So had he. Lucky wasn't opposed to that, but not for a marriage proposal. He'd rather spend time on his knees kissing Cassie in all the right places. Or rather one special place anyway.

Cassie turned, smiled at him, and he could have sworn that she had ESP or something because enough heat zinged between them that he almost forgot about having to say goodbye.

Almost.

Cassie finished whatever she was doing and made her way to Lucky. "They're a beautiful couple," she remarked, and the silence—and the heat—settled between them for several moments. "Everyone knows what we talked about at Bernie's office."

He nodded.

"And for the record, the right answer is *not* for you to wear chaps and spurs," she added.

Lucky frowned. "Who suggested that?"

"Livvy. She said it could be the tipping point, that it always gets women hot."

"Does it?" Automatic question. He would have been kicked out of the male club if he hadn't asked it.

"It worked for me," she admitted, smiling. Then, frowning, added, "But it's not the right answer."

Of course. It was just another bad suggestion, but it beat Hank's. The ranch hand had told Lucky that the thing he had to do was to knock Cassie up. All in all, Lucky had gotten some of the absolute worst advice of his life from people who were family and friends.

"Can I talk to you?" someone asked from behind them.

Alice.

Lucky had no idea how long she'd been standing there, but he hoped she'd missed out on the getting-hot-over-chaps chat. "Of course." Both Cassie and he turned toward her.

Alice looked at the girls, smiled, but it wasn't the smile of a victorious woman who had just gotten exactly what she wanted. She opened her hand to show him the gold stars.

Lucky wasn't surprised to see them. What with the way Mia was flinging the stars around, every inch of the living room floor seemed to be covered with them. They were in people's hair, on their clothes. He figured some of the little glittered bits had worked their way into places he didn't want to know about.

"I suppose you'll be leaving town soon?" Alice asked, and it took Lucky a moment to realize she was talking to him. "Gossip," she added in a mumble. "The consensus is you don't stay here much."

"Not usually, but I'll be around for a while."

Another nod. "Because of those bulls you're buying. The clerk at the inn said you'd want to work with the bulls yourself, that you're picky about that sort of thing."

Now it was his turn to nod. If Alice knew that, then she probably also knew about the rift that had formed long ago between Lucky and his twin brother. Except it no longer felt like much of a rift. Logan had his business to run. Lucky had his. There was no reason they couldn't run those businesses in the same town.

"And what about you?" Alice asked Cassie. "You'll be going back to LA?"

"No. I'm selling my condo, though, so eventually I'll have to go back for the closing. But not for work. I've, uh, decided to pass on some recent business offers so I'll be staying around here. I might open an office here in Spring Hill since there's not another therapist in town."

Finally, there was something the gossips hadn't gotten hold of yet. Probably because Alice and he were the first people she'd told. But that meant there was a silver lining in all of this. Cassie would be around so they could continue having sex.

And whatever the heck else was going on between them.

Alice's gaze drifted to the girls again, and she motioned for them to come closer. She didn't say anything until she had an arm around each of them. "I didn't reach this decision easily, and I'm still not sure it's the right thing to do. But if Cassie and Lucky are here, together, then I'll consider allowing you to stay with them. As long as it's what you girls *really, really* want."

Lucky was so lost in the thought of sex with Cassie that the words didn't sink in at first. Even when they did, he was certain he'd misheard the woman. Until he saw the tears in Alice's eyes.

"It's what we want. Really, really, really, really." But Mia didn't just say it. She said it while jumping around, squealing and eventually adding more *reallys*.

No squeals of delight or jumping from Mackenzie, but she did bob her head in agreement.

"They were willing to give up everything they have to stay here," Alice went on, speaking to Cassie and him now. "If that isn't love, I don't know what is. I love them, but they obviously love the two of you a lot more."

"We do love them," Mia volunteered. "But we love you, too," she added.

Another head bob from Mackenzie.

Alice tried to blink back tears. "Just promise that you'll visit me often. Every summer. School breaks. And promise me that I can come and see you whenever I want."

"Promise," Mia said, using her free hand to cross her heart. She left a trail of gold stars there as well, stuck to her fairy-princess dress.

"I promise," Mackenzie agreed. Heck, she also crossed her heart.

Lucky wasn't sure he could breathe yet—the air was caught

in his lungs and throat—much less speak, so he nodded. Cassie nodded, too. And yes, she was crying. Hell, he was crying. He was really going to get kicked out of the man universe now.

"The magic stars worked," Mia whispered to Lucky.

As a responsible adult, Lucky should have probably tried to dispel the notion of magic, but shit, maybe it was magic. He scooped Mia up, kissed her and passed her to Cassie so she could do the same. Then he pulled Mackenzie into her arms so they could share a group hug. Mackenzie didn't even give a protesting grunt.

Mia caught onto Cassie's face. Kissed her. "We gonna get to stay and run seventy-teen percent of the bulls. And the clowns."

"Yes, we are. Personally, I think we'll do a great job. What do you think?" Cassie asked her.

Mia giggled behind her hand. "I think we should give Kenzie all the bulls' bootees. She can own them."

"No bull bootees," Mackenzie grumbled, but she smiled a little.

When Cassie put Mia down, Alice gave both girls hugs. "I'll get your suitcases from the car," she added, then looked at Lucky and Cassie. "If they need anything, call me, and I'll stay in touch with them daily through calls and emails. Just make sure I'm a part of their lives."

Lucky nodded, and because it looked as if Alice needed it, he hugged her. "Of course. You're part of their lives. Ours, too. You're family now, and you're welcome here anytime."

That put some fresh tears back in Alice's eyes, and after another set of long hugs, more muttered goodbyes, she pulled away from the girls, her clothes and face sparkling from the stars.

Mackenzie folded her arms over her chest as Alice slipped out. "So, I guess you're, like, stuck with us now," she said to Cassie and him. The attitude was goth girl, and Lucky was a little surprised to realize he'd missed it.

"Seems like it." Man, his heart was about to burst, but it

would probably scare the hell out of them if he started jumping up and down and whooping like an idiot. A happy idiot, though.

"Of course, that means we're stuck with you, too," Mackenzie said. "Am I still grounded for all that mess that happened with Brody?"

"Absolutely," Cassie said, and at the same time Lucky added, "You bet. And you can't talk to any boys at the picnic today unless they're your age or younger. Preferably younger. In fact, Ethan will make perfect company for you."

Mackenzie lifted her shoulder, obviously expecting that.

From the corner of his eye, he saw Alice set down the suitcases just outside the door. Lucky mouthed a thank-you, but it didn't seem like nearly enough. Of course, nothing would ever be enough to thank her.

"So, are you and Miss Cassie getting married?" Mia asked him after Alice left. "Because Miss Cassie said you had to do one thing." She paused. "What's the one thing?"

To hell if he knew.

But Lucky went with his gut. "I love you," he told Cassie.

After all, those were magic words. Or so he'd been told. However, they didn't seem to do the trick here.

Cassie gave him a flat look. Mackenzie huffed. Mia tugged on his sleeve again.

"You gotta say it like you mean it. Like this. I love you." Mia stretched out the words, smiled and then hugged his leg.

Since Mackenzie didn't huff this time and Cassie's look didn't go flat, Mia might be onto something.

"Mia and I will get changed for the picnic," Mackenzie said. "Don't mess this up," she whispered to Lucky. "Say it like you mean it."

Was that it? Was it really that simple? Well, heck. Then he'd been close all along—even though he'd just realized it.

He pulled Cassie to him. Kissed her. A kiss that was too long and deep considering the minister and his wife were walking by them.

"I love you," Lucky said, and he didn't just sound like he meant it because he did mean it.

When the world didn't collapse and a lightning bolt didn't hit him, he said it again. And again.

Cassie gave it right back to him. "I love you, too."

Lucky smiled. "So, that was it, huh? I just had to say it like I mean it?"

She shook her head. Put her mouth right against his ear. He felt some tongue. "You have to say it tonight while wearing those chaps and spurs."

Oh, man.

This love shit was going to be fun.

* * * * *